# A PARABLE OF LIES

## LAWRENCE SPANN

Elizabeth Ann Robinson

If life is a river, you make the river flow.

"These novels will give way, by and by, to diaries or autobiographies—captivating books, if only a man knew how to choose among what he calls his experiences and how to record truth truly."

Ralph Waldo Emerson (1803-1882)

"I have a wonderful mind: Inventive. It is for you to find. Read me. Read my mind."

May Swenson (1913-1989)

# INTRODUCTION

"Don't let a day pass without recording it,
whether anything interesting has happened or not.
Something interesting happens every day."

Virginia Woolf (1882-1941)

T HE STORY STARTS HERE WITH me. My mother lay dying.
A trooper through surgery, chemotherapy, and radiation, she
had soldiered forward but now, her bones were too brittle
for her to walk. A hospital bed and walker displaced the floral
couch. She faced a draped picture window in the living room.

She'd always approached her life with the can-do attitude of a
nurse, and I remember that best from when we were children. My
brother, Bates, and the kid next door were throwing rocks and dry
chunks of mud over the back fence. The kid kept yelling, "Master
Bates, Master Bates. Why don't you go inside and Master Bates?"
Bates, flushed and in a rage, threw everything he could get his
hands on, including a garbage can cover he was using as a shield.
It happened so fast, then in slow motion, when Bates caught a
jagged stone above his left eye and it opened a huge gash. There
was blood everywhere. I thought his eye had popped out. My
mother, cool as a cucumber, grabbed a towel and told me, a gawky
preteen who sickened at the sight of blood, to hold it in place, and

then she drove us to the emergency room. There she knew the triage nurse, and Bates got stitched up by an intern lickety-split. I was hysterical, in tears, as was my brother. My mother remained unruffled and composed. She always had answers and knew what to do. So, it was no surprise when she got her cancer diagnosis that she became her own patient. Breast cancer was another task to tick off her list. But by the time I got home, she'd surrendered.

My father, or who I thought was my father, met me at the door. Bates and I, by his preference, always called him by his first name, Jason. With an uncomfortable A-frame hug, Jason greeted me and said, "Marla begged me not to let her"—he struggled with the word—'croak' in the hospital." He looked pale and worn but mustered a comforting half-smile and said, "She whines but never complains." It had been seven grueling months. He stood up straight, pulled back his shoulders, and asked, "How are things in Cincinnati?"

I shrugged, not wanting to talk about my life having been in turmoil the last couple months after my divorce. I said, "I didn't know things had gone so far. I wish I'd come sooner."

Bates and his wife and kids had already settled in for the vigil. That night, it was my watch and the first time I'd been alone with Marla since she'd taken a turn for the worse.

I daubed her cracked lips with a lemon/glycerin swab.

She signaled, "Come closer."

I turned my ear toward her lips and shivered when I smelled a peculiar dry metallic scent on her breath.

She whispered, "Your father kept a journal. He wrote every day. It was like a religion to him."

Startled, I thought she was hallucinating. I'd never seen her vulnerable and helpless like this before. I said, "Jason's in the kitchen with Bates, doing the dishes. He never wrote in a journal."

She signaled with a limp left wrist, saying, "Over there." She pointed to a wicker bin. "Your father isn't your father. Open the trunk."

And that's where I found the book you're about to read.

I said, "Shit, what are you telling me?"

She cracked a wrinkled smile. "You are my prize child."

We embraced and shook with tears.

I'd never met Neal Motherwell and, as I found out, my mother's encounter with him had been brief, though enough to get pregnant. At first, she explained this to me in a tired, matter-of-fact voice, and said, "It was a one-time thing."

I frowned and did a double-take.

Her face brightened, and her eyes rolled back. "Well, it was more than once."

I scrunched up my face, and we giggled.

She lowered her washed out face and blushed. "Well, to be honest, we never slept and that's all we did for three days."

They'd met for the first and only time at an American Heart Association national conference twenty-nine years ago, the year before I was born.

I wanted to know so much more but, shell-shocked, asked silly questions. "What did he look like?"

She said, "He was tall and had dark, straight hair and warm, brown eyes."

After she dozed off, I rushed to the mirror and looked at my eyes—brown, not blue like Bates's and Jason's. I smoothed back my eyebrows. *Who do these features belong to, my mother or my biological father?* People had always remarked that I looked different. I felt different. I stared into my doe-like, dark eyes and pulled back my dark brown hair. *Do these belong to him? Why did she choose to betray my father and never tell anyone until now?* And, as you'll find out in these pages, Neal also deceived his wife. *What drew them together? Was it the pure, raw energy and sex of*

3

*it, or something more?* I reverted to magical thinking. *Was it me? Did my unborn spirit drive such a reckless act?*

Neal had been thirty-three and Marla twenty-eight. My brother had only been five months old, the first time separated from his mother. And then she'd had me, another child to raise.

She swore me to secrecy. "Your father can never know, Cordelia. He simply *cannot* know. The manuscript belongs to you now. Say nothing about it."

In that moment, I realized our relationship had changed to something different. I'd become Marla's confident, no longer her daughter.

Life with Jason, a dull, overweight corporate psychologist, was routine and, even for me, boring at best. He was a dispassionate and conservative man with indifferent eyes who spoke in a monotonous and intellectual tone. Short on excitement and surprises but trustworthy and steady, the type women call "a good provider." Much like the one I'd married and divorced.

It pissed me off that Neal had impregnated her and never raised me. I wanted a father like Neal, especially after reading this book. In my heart, I knew something was wrong, that a lie festered beneath the surface. Something I couldn't justify, a dark secret. In a lover, I craved passion—a pirate, a gypsy, a madman who would ravish me. I never once heard my parents make love. Never noticed the suggestion of a furtive glance across the room. And Marla never lost her figure or good looks. I had a high school boyfriend, Cole, who checked her out when she bent over. He denied it, but I could tell. Our relationship didn't last long. For men, it's so easy, the romance, the excitement, the fun. But it was the wearisome man in the kitchen doing the dishes, not Neal, who had borne the responsibility of childrearing. He'd taken me ice-skating and dropped me off at school.

As far as I could tell, Marla hadn't had any other flings. Her parents were gone and other than a few nurse colleagues, she had no close friends, so her secret stayed concealed.

*What was it like to live with a lie burning a hole in your heart?* Neal wrote. My mother didn't. And she never went to therapy, did yoga, studied astrology, meditated, or sought clarity. Like most, she'd lived with it and suppressed her deepest needs. There was no outlet for her inner life. She'd parlayed her days between the hospital, homemaking, and raising children. As a cardiac rehab nurse, she was a gift to others' broken hearts. And she'd worked every day until she was too weak to function. At home, she'd shopped, cooked, and cleaned. She'd gone to church, sung in the Sunday choir. She and Jason had paid the mortgage, tuition, taxes, and taken us on family vacations in the Ozarks. My brother and I went to Ivy League schools. I'd graduated from Princeton. When I finished law school, I'd married and divorced, all by twenty-eight—the same age as Marla when she'd had her fling.

Neal's manuscript opened a secret life. I'd found it beneath some gift boxes and wrapping paper where it had been hiding in plain sight. The cleaning lady could have picked it up and read it. But my sense was, no one other than Marla had. It was covert and underground, a dalliance my mother had had into another life she'd never lived. And it was the most important thing she left behind. I understood her desires—she hadn't wasted her shot regardless of how constrained and narrow.

Neal had adhered to a fundamental principle in his writing practice—write the truth. But the truth is multilayered, and the purpose of writing is to dig. Marla said he wrote thousands of words every day. She said she'd found him writing in his notebook one of the mornings they were together, and he'd called himself a scribbler. Although they'd never seen one another again, he'd sent this manuscript—a thick stack of letter-size pages in a soft leather binding with a strap. It is hard to tell the date, and nothing gives it away within. The single-sided pages are yellowed and dog-eared, crudely transcribed on a manual typewriter with whiteouts, corrections, and annotations. Entries cascaded like a waterfall, spilling out his torment after his brother's death. She'd never acknowledged to him that she received it. But the worn and battered pages confirmed she'd pored over it and read it many times, an extension of the animated conversation they'd started in Milwaukee. For me, it demonstrated that my beginnings were more than a one-night stand. It was his letter to her written in blood.

I asked, and she told me that he never knew about me. That first night, she turned the pages and directed me to read the section about their love affair out loud. As she drifted in and out of sleep, I circled back and started from the beginning and never put it down. For three days before she died, I sat with her. My father and brother were glad for the relief and paid no attention. My brother asked what I was reading. I said it was a law brief, and he bought it. All I knew was that I needed to consume every word as if it would somehow resolve the millions of questions swimming in my head. There was no plot other than rough chronology, but the stream kept me engaged. It all made sense. Entries announced the time of day, day of the week, and place. In these pages, you'll find the past mixed with the present like in a dream. Thoughts are far-ranging, like in a journal—unfiltered and written in a fluent river of memory, many vaulted from the deep abyss of childhood to the present. Neal used fiction techniques like dialogue and metaphor to enhance the effect. But the real purpose of Neal's writing is to probe, excavate, and explore the inner workings of the unconscious mind, to ferret out hidden emotions in the pursuit of underlying truths, to make sense of the world around him in a conversation with himself.

As a reader, I allowed the analytical part of my brain to unclench. Neal used quotes at the beginning of each section to prime the pump. Handwritten in the margin of the first page, he wrote, "…the saddest lies are the ones we tell ourselves," from Lucille Clifton. The same quote is repeated at the beginning of the

January 3 entry. Later, I found out Lucille Clifton came from his hometown, Buffalo, which figured dramatically into the narrative.

As I sat with Marla, I started my own journal, a few pages every day. It's not as elaborate as Neal's, and I'm no writer. And I'm not possessed to put my innermost feelings on paper except in times of crisis. But knowing Neal "The Scribbler" was my father, I found particular strength in the connection.

People don't like to talk about it, but one in twenty-five children are like me. Their father never knew them. We are the lost babes, sired outside the legal mandates of marriage. Love children of electricians, UPS carriers, handymen, repairmen, poets, artists, and paramours. We, who never speak the truth as we live the parable of the lie. As humans, our genotype moves around. My mother's rendezvous with Neal could have happened to anyone. Neal remains a stranger, and I'll never know him other than through his words. He has no clue that I'm his child.

We stray and wander the earth, both inside and outside our sphere, searching for our true north. It was through Neal's writing that I came to know him. His semen fertilized my mother's ovum, so half of me is him. As it stands, I know much more about Neal than Jason, who raised me. I've found that his ancestors boil in my veins, and some crawl. DNA rushes out of my pen like a fountain. We comingle in blood.

Neal wrote about Buffalo, a city he moved away from but never left. In the nineteenth century, immigrants and adventurers poured through his hometown en route to the Great Lakes to pursue America, the promise of the beyond, the mid and far west. The father who raised me in Indiana has roots in Holland and Scandinavia. My DNA profile looks different. I'm a rebel, and I'm hungry, greedy, and determined, like Neal. I want more.

Publishing Neal's fictive healing is an act of purification. I wanted to set the record straight, which is my birthright. I waited until Jason died, six years after Marla, because I knew he'd feel betrayed. As Marla told me on her death bed, "Your father never needs to know." And he never heard it from me. Medical meetings convene each year and season. What goes on behind closed doors never makes it to the evening news. There's a lot history doesn't tell us. Their love affair brought Neal's journal to me unfiltered and gave me a father I know only through his words.

Am I angry I never met Neal? A little. I can relate to Neal's alienation in high school, and I wanted to be loved like Neal loved Mick. But how could he step forward? He made an effort to reach out, and my mother didn't tell him about me? I have no answers. The lesson? I'll never lie if I have kids, even if it hurts.

Neal wrote every day, and I wanted more. Where did the other writings go? This manuscript only represents twenty-four days. Where's the rest? I followed his peripatetic path laid out in this book and searched every juncture. Buffalo City Hall had no record, nor did Duke or the clinics in Santa Barbara. I came up short every time. Is Motherwell a pseudo name? Did any of this happen at all? In this day of easy access to data, how does he remain undetected? I've made the decision, for now, to be free of it, publish what I have and move forward.

My mother endured a sexless marriage, never again seduced and ravished like she'd been in Milwaukee. I had a father, and he thought he was my biological father. I grew up in a two-parent, middle-class home. There was no mention of Neal until the final days before my mother died. Now I have his words, avuncular, a script to read over and over again. That's enough. Like Neal's adopted father, I'll adapt and cross the Peace Bridge at Fort Erie to Buffalo, the sperm swimming west, bestowing lifeblood, moving me through the wilderness. Like Neal and his father, I've chosen to swim.

Cordelia Howell
August 15, 2021

# PART I

# 22 DECEMBER, 2:43 A.M.

## (SANTA BARBARA, CA)

"Am I my brother's keeper?"
Genesis 4:9

AWAKE. I JACKKNIFE STRAIGHT UP in bed. Mick is in the hospital again. Squeezed like a fist, I need to write. It's the only cure. He's ripping Victoria and me apart. He drinks and dials and wakes us up in the middle of the night, apologizes and forgets, and does it again. She says, "You're married and live three time zones away." I say, "I can't say no to Mick." She scowls. We're at loggerheads. I've failed at two marriages already, not this one too. And not for Mick and this nutty family that I escaped long ago. Why screw it up? Writing is the only way out.

And here I am again in the middle of the night, alone in the living room. A single light illuminates my fountain pen as it spits black ink on white, ruled paper, filling yet another composition notebook. In search of myself, I meditated, stretched, massaged, ate vegetarian, and lived in a confused soup until I found writing relieved the ache. Writing always makes me feel better. The pen squeaks as it scratches the page, and I follow its intent. I keep the hand moving, unconscious of what I write. To my surprise, there's always something more, a new thread. A decade ago, when I embarked on this practice, Victoria said, "I lost you when you started." She knew it was more than a passing phase or an exercise in self-improvement, because writing began for me with the first word, E-G-G. I scribbled it for my mother with a tiny, unsure hand. When I handed her the crumpled scrap, she smiled and her eyes shimmered. She provided me with steaming nourishment, rich and buttery, bright yellow scrambled eggs. I fell in love with words. Sometimes I eat them.

Yesterday was the most luscious of days. By lunch, it was seventy-two degrees, the heavens a feast of blue, not a hint of cloud. Palm trees rattled in a soothing breeze. Meanwhile, the rest of the country was paralyzed, ambushed by a polar vortex. As usual, I spent the day underground, where the waiting room overflowed into the hallway, and we dragged in extra chairs. The fluorescent lights flickered off the cement block walls. My province at Duke also subsumed in the basement. With this gig, geography doesn't matter.

Is it my destiny to toil in the bunker forever?

Esperanza, the new medical assistant (there's always someone new), directed patients without chairs to sit in wheelchairs down the hall, a clever innovation. It looked like a field hospital.

Katie's voice pierced the adjoining wall. "How are you, and how is he?"

In the lobby, I overheard Esperanza telling a patient, "She's a nurse practitioner, kind of a nurse and a doctor too." Midsentence, she skipped into Spanish, and I caught the gist. The guy (me) in the other exam room is a PA, a physician's assistant. Back to English, "One of them will see you next." I know it won't be long before Esperanza leaves us and transfers upstairs like the rest. She'll come to loathe this sunken crypt as much as I do.

Katie's voice grew louder. In a sing-song befitting Dr. Seuss, she said, "Shucker doodles. I don't know. I just don't know."

I couldn't hear myself think. Katie and I scurried like white mice between exam rooms, a conveyer belt of patients processed into cubbyholes. We couldn't keep up.

An hour before lunch, Esperanza rapped on my door. "Dr. Cornelius, you've got three in the lobby, you're fifty minutes behind, and Dr. Nasig is on the phone."

I adjusted my stethoscope's chest piece, ignored the intrusion, and placed the buds in my ears. As I leaned in to listen to Phil Zelinski's chest, the knock came again.

Esperanza stuck her head around the door and, in a harsh whisper, said, "Nasig's on line one."

"I'll call him back."

"He wants to talk to you now." She motioned with her fist against her ear and grimaced.

I stood and said, "Sorry for the interruption."

Phil flashed a toothy smile. "I've got time. Just don't leave me hanging."

When I walked out the door, Esperanza pointed at the phone and said, "There's also a voicemail from somebody named Gypsy. I didn't get the number."

When I picked up the blinking line at the nurse's station, Nasig said, "You busy?"

I sighed. "Wanna hear about it?"

"I'm sending over a student with a clot in her right leg and pulmonary embolism. She needs Lovenox."

"Now?"

"It's got to be today."

"Can't someone over there do it?"

"I'm on call." He paused for effect. "You'll like her…a college kid."

He knew I'd say yes. I always say yes. We hung up.

Katie caught my eye in passing and said, "This is a cluster." She implied the F with her upper teeth on her lower lip and added, "Poopers!"

I felt guilty having added one more patient to the shitstorm.

When I re-entered the room, Phil grinned and looked up from his perch on the exam table, feet dangling. He wore his uniform— baggy shorts, flip-flops, unbuttoned Hawaiian shirt, with scruffy, white chest hairs pushing out the worn collar. A threadbare, tan sweater rested on the chair. It was hard not to chuckle.

I pulled the door behind me and listened for it to latch.

He asked, "Tough day?"

I nodded and turned with my back to him to wash my hands in the tiny sink.

Phil said, "*Illegitimi non carborundum.*"

I turned my head and over my shoulder said, "Easy for you to say."

"Neal, don't let the bastards grind you down."

I took off my glasses, placed them on the metal shelf, cupped my hands, and threw water in my face. As I dried with paper towels, I turned and shrugged.

He said, "Neal, it could be a hell of a lot worse. On the way in, I saw some poor bastards grading and sloping asphalt on the freeway. They're working their asses off."

The eight-by-ten exam room shrank. I pivoted and changed the subject. "When did you retire?"

He counted with his fingers. "After my surgery, thirteen years. I've been coming to you for ten. What's up with your medical assistant? What's her name? I had to remind her to take my blood pressure."

"Esperanza. She's new, her first day with us, and her mother-in-law is in town from Guadalajara."

"I've never seen this place so gnarly," Phil said.

"Except when you worked here."

"Everybody's on edge, and I learned the hard way. It's not worth it."

I asked, "Don't you ever get cold? There's frost on the ground today."

He reached and picked up the sweater. "That's why I brought this."

"I've never seen you wear it."

"Once the sun's up, I don't need it. No more ties or white coats for me. I'm paddling this afternoon."

"Where?"

"Padaro Lane."

I stepped back in astonishment. "Somebody spotted a great white there last week."

"That's the point. You only live twice."

"What is this, James Bond stuff?"

He snorted and contorted his angular jaw. "It's a kick. You oughta try it."

I sat down on the squat, gray stool, wheeled toward the computer, and started typing. Suddenly lightheaded, my vision blurred, and I feared a migraine. I thought, *Shit, I'm booked every fifteen minutes through 4:45.*

I collected myself and said to Phil, "Your blood work looks great. Let's have a listen." I placed the diaphragm of the stethoscope on his thick, bare, hairy chest and closed my eyes.

His mechanical aortic valve clicked in rhythm like a clock, with a whoosh and a clatter. The titanium-coated carbon valve snapped open and shut like a carp's mouth feeding at the water's edge.

I supported his left shoulder with my right hand and moved the chest piece to his back. "Take a deep breath and blow it out." I inhaled with him, heard the rush, felt my breath expand my belly, exhaled with him, and my anxiety came down a notch.

It has forever amazed me that I can enter the dark cavity of someone's chest with my ears. A cardiologist at Duke told us, "Heart sounds are the last to go." They're low-frequency and remain accessible to clinicians with age-related hearing loss. When I was thirty, the significance of that pearl escaped me. Now I appreciate it more than ever. I want to remain useful as my cochleae fail. Another erudite guest lecturer at Duke told us about Laennec, the Frenchman who invented the stethoscope in 1816. It was the first instrument to explore the internal anatomy, and we still use it much as he did today. Before Laennec, clinicians put an ear on the chest. It's one of the facts PA school cemented into my brain that's never asked on the six-hour board exam I'm forced to endure every six years.

During the office visit, checking the heart and lungs is the only time I touch the patient. Over the years, I've come to believe it's the essential part. If I forget to do it, even a retired physician like Phil reminds me, "You didn't listen to my heart." The patient is saying, "You didn't touch me." Phil's blood pressure is better than mine, and he knows it. His concern is that Esperanza forgot to do it. She didn't complete the cycle, the fluency of the ritual.

I said to Phil, "Let's recheck your blood in a month. Otherwise, I'll see you on the beach."

He clapped his hands. "Great."

I handed him a calendar that showed how many milligrams of warfarin to take each day.

He nodded. "Same, same. No changes. Hang loose, and he shot me the *shaka* sign."

When we stood, he reached out, shook my hand, and said, "When you gonna get out of here?" He looked at the ceiling and sucked his teeth. "To live on California's central coast and work underground is a severe error in judgment."

I said, "I thought you said I was lucky not to be shoveling asphalt."

He grimaced. "Those bastards are outside all day."

I said, "It's not up to me. Blood clinics are always in the basement near the lab."

"How many hours you here each shift?"

"I'm booked for ten, but we stay until the work's done."

He shook his head. His stubbled beard glistened like hot sand in the sun. "Don't regret this. Better make a decision before your body does." He turned and lumbered out the door, toward the desk.

I followed. In the waiting room, a confluence of eyes was upon me. Like an ape in the zoo, I was a prime attraction. They scrutinized my every move, over-curious—bright and hopeful, youthful faces mingled with worn and wrinkled ones. Octogenarians and nonagenarians attended by a family member or caretaker. The trip to the clinic was the focal point of their day. It was an outing, the reason they showered, dressed, and left the house.

The conversation with Phil hit a chord. That very morning with rancor, I'd counted each of the twenty-five narrow steps that lead down the long, dimly-lit stairway into the basement—a slow, steep decline into a netherworld guarded by four two-inch-thick wooden doors. Biohazard signs mark each one, "LABORATORY PERSONNEL ONLY. DO NOT ENTER." I arrived soon after sunrise and with heavy heart, acknowledged it would be dark before I emerged.

After Phil, I stole a moment, ducked into an empty cubicle, sat down, and called Pixie. Everybody thinks her name sounds like Gypsy, and her nasal Buffalo accent doesn't help. While the phone rang, I thought, *How long has it been? She quit her job as a baker at Top's Supermarket two and a half years ago to take care of Mick full-time. They've been living together for seven and a half years. She got the worst of Mick. Why does she stay?*

In a rapid burst, she said, "They took his foot."

"What? Slow down. What's happening?"

"I had to sign a paper. The doctors said Mick would die if I didn't. I can't remember the word."

"Dismemberment?"

She said, "Amp-pooh-tate."

"Which foot?"

"Not sure. The left, I think." I heard her rustling, then she said, "Yeah, it's his left."

We both started to whimper.

I sat down. "How is Mick otherwise?"

"He hasn't woken up yet. He doesn't know, and I don't know how to tell him."

"I can't believe it."

"I'll call you later. I know you're busy." She hung up.

Stunned, I couldn't mutter a word. I felt like a boxer splayed on the canvas, crumbled by a blow I didn't see. Everything slowed down—Esperanza, all the waiting patients, and Ditzig Nasig's consult. There was only Mick.

A few months ago, he was in a coma, intubated at Strong Memorial Hospital in Rochester and waiting for a liver. Years of drinking, cocaine, all-nighters, and back to work the next day had taken their toll. For seven grueling months, we couldn't speak. He'd left the world, and Pixie and I talked every day. I consulted nurses, caseworkers, doctors, residents, interns…anyone who'd listen. I'll never forget that moment when Mick surfaced. The phone buzzed at 5 a.m., and in a raspy voice, he said, "It's Mick the mother, well, well, well, your fucking cooking brother. No white man, no woman, no monkey motherfucker can cook as good as me." His exuberant bravado was unaltered.

It was Mick! Where had he gone? He didn't remember. It was like he'd been asleep without memory or dreams. He'd returned, and by some act of fate, resurrected himself. Now, his foot.

Fans of *Good Morning Buffalo* knew Mick as "Mmm," Michael Morgan Motherwell, an eccentric local chef who appeared on random Wednesday mornings at 7:23 a.m. His supporters tuned in to see what he'd do next, and they were never disappointed. Even his detractors said, "Mick always makes me laugh." He'd invented a language all his own, a mouth-watering clash of consonants, vowels, and onomatopoeia. He rhymed words in odd and unusual ways and had sound effects for poultry, pork, and beef. He gobbled, grunted, squealed, and mooed. For seafood, he puckered his cheeks, pushed out his lips like a goldfish, and said, "Oww." The generous addition of wine to every sauce he accompanied with a shrill yelp, "Fwee, fwee," a word of childhood invention. He emphasized every sibilant and flattened every diphthong. And, like a jazz trumpeter, he spun off on an incredible improvisational journey. He shape-shifted, omnipresent, tethered only by food and its many enchantments. Off-stage his motto remained, "Fuck like a cook, cook like a motherfucker."

At Christmas, there were Mick's patented Mother's Booze Balls, known for their potency. At Halloween, he took to the stage, appearing as an alter ego, Count Spatula. And Mick was a magician, performing freewheeling sleight of hand as part of his act. On Valentine's Day, he appeared in full drag. His Julia Child impersonation spouted quarts of blood across the stage. His antics shocked the TV hosts, but they loved the ratings. Once, he fired up a gas-powered chain saw on a live set and carved a swan out of a massive ice block. Blue smoke spewed in puffs across the television screen, and the TV hosts had panic in their eyes but at the same time suppressed laughter. He'd do anything for a gag, and only his popularity with a devout, eclectic following kept him coming back.

The problem was his drinking. And he was always drinking, even in the hospital, except when he was in the coma.

"Dr. Cornelius. Dr. Cornelius," Esperanza slapped her palm on the office partition wall.

Startled as if from sleep, I stood up and adjusted my white coat and tie.

She scowled.

Bewildered, I started to take off my coat and said, "Can Katie take the consult? I've got some personal iss—"

She flashed her teeth and tossed her thick, black hair. "She's over two hours behind, and there are a dozen phone calls to answer."

"Why two hours?"

"Jill called in sick. The phones are ringing off the hook. Katie's seeing patients too."

"OK, so who's next?"

She took a white card out of her pocket. "We're too busy to see a consult."

"What am I supposed to do, send her to the hospital?"

She smirked. "I've heard about you. Everybody's friend, you never say no. You think you're nice, but you're running yourself and the rest of us ragged."

I changed the subject. "Why are you calling me Dr. Cornelius?"

"It's proper. You've got a lot of education, which demands respect."

"I'm not a medical doctor. I'm a physician assistant. The patients call me Neal."

She stepped forward, so close I could smell the coffee on her breath. "You've got a doctorate, don't you?"

"Yes, in creative writing. Nothing to do with medicine. I don't want patients to get the wrong idea."

"There you go, you don't recognize how privileged you are. If I had a doctorate, I'd demand that everyone call me Doctor." She wrinkled her upper lip. "Doctor, doctor, doctor. I'll send in Mr. Juarez and his daughter."

I looked her in the eye and said, "I'll see the consult during lunch. And please don't interrupt me when I'm in the middle of an exam."

The morning bled into the afternoon, four patients on the hour. Folmer Nielsen came in from Solvang with his daughter. He'd had a stroke since I saw him. His wife is debilitated, and he is her caretaker, both in their nineties. He gave me a half-smile of recognition and warmed up when I sat down. I was grateful because it got my mind off Mick.

I asked, "What are you doing for fun?"

In a thick Danish accent, he replied, "No fun."

Then I said, "No joy?"

And he repeated, "No joy," as if it were a foreign word.

I said, "Why go on living?"

He replied, "Apple pie," and a tear ran down his cheek, and all three of us roared with laughter.

The visit took longer than anticipated, and a restless mob was clamoring in the lobby. But I've learned to meet each person where they are and give them as much time as they need. It's better if they limit the visit rather than me, and most people are considerate of others. Folmer and his daughter knew the waiting room was full. Pushing people in and out is less efficient. Counterintuitive but true, visits go faster when I relax and listen. Getting uptight and imposing my will makes it worse and creates bad feelings. And it costs time.

When he left, Folmer patted my shoulder and offered a clumsy hug, then almost toppled over as he walked out with his daughter holding his arm.

At noon, while Esperanza registered the consult, I slipped upstairs to the break room where a pharmaceutical company had catered breakfast. A couple sad pastries and a plastic bottle of water had been left behind. I scarfed down a stale banana muffin and snatched the bottle of water. As I was tramping down the stairs, I spilled the water on my shirt and tie. When I dipped into the staff bathroom, I noticed oily splotches from the muffin on my shirt. I washed my hands and dabbed at the stains with a wet paper towel before heading down the hall to meet the consult.

When I entered the exam room, I met the gaze of an attractive young woman and did a double-take. Her eyes were different colors.

She said, "Yes, you've got it, congenital heterochromia. They didn't notice in the emergency room."

I said, "Maybe it was the light."

"How long is this going to take?"

I said, "Not long. I'll ask some questions, examine your heart and lungs, and write a couple prescriptions."

She broke into tears. "I'm sorry. I didn't expect this."

I sat down on the stool beside her, noticing she was wearing the hospital gown backward and clasping it closed with her left hand at her chest. Her blouse and bra were on the chair.

She brushed back her long, reddish-brown hair with her right hand. "What do you want me to do?"

"Did Esperanza explain how to put the gown on?"

"She was in a hurry and left it on the exam table. Why is everybody so rushed?"

"It's the holidays. It's lunchtime. It's always like this. Take your pick. The tie goes in back. I'll leave the room. Knock when you're ready." I stood to leave and asked, "They gave you the first injection in the emergency room?"

She nodded. "Ghastly! I was there all morning. They did all kinds of blood tests and filled a dozen tubes. A hyper-something workup."

"Hypercoagulable."

"I don't have any blood left. The doctor ordered X-rays and a CT. I don't understand why I have to go through this again."

"We'll go over everything and connect the dots when I get

back. You go ahead and get better situated in the gown, and I'll return." I slipped through the door and closed it behind me.

A few minutes later, she knocked, and I entered the room. Sitting tall, perched on the edge of the exam table with her gown properly situated, a frightened young woman looked up and gave a reluctant smile.

I said, "Ms. Wright, I've been looking at your chart—"

She said, "Call me PJ," and extended the long slim fingers of her right hand.

I shook them tentatively and said, "Please call me Neal."

Her right wrist clinked as it shook, covered in gold bangles. I noticed small red lacerations below her hand. Her left wrist was taped and bandaged.

I asked, "What happened to your wrists?"

"Oh, that happened before I left Boston. Nothing to do with this. How long do I need to be here?"

I said, "You're taking cephalexin and fluoxetine. Both can interact with warfarin."

She nodded. "That's part of the thing in Boston before I left."

"Let's take a few minutes. I want to hear your story."

"There's not much to tell. I flew the red-eye from Boston to Phoenix. That was OK. A long flight, but no problem. During the connecting flight to Santa Barbara, I got short of breath. I felt a pain in my side, like a catch." She pointed to her left side. "I thought it was nothing. The lady sitting next to me made me promise to go to the emergency room when we landed. The doctor said a blood clot in my leg had moved up to my lung."

"Where are your parents?"

"My mother is in LA and on her way back. She's sitting in traffic somewhere between here and Carpinteria. My father is on the east coast on business. He'll be back for Christmas."

"Do they know?"

"Of course. I spoke to my mother while I was in the ER. I'll be fine."

"How did you get to the emergency room, then over here?"

"Uber, and that's how I'll get to my folks' home on the Mesa. The doctor told me you'd give me a prescription for more shots and warfarin pills. Right?"

"It's more complicated than that. You'll have to watch your alcohol intake and the greens in your diet. They interact with warfarin. You can't get pregnant as the drug will affect the fetus."

"There's no chance of that. I broke up with my boyfriend. Also, I'm fixed."

"Fixed?"

"They asked me about birth control pills in the ER. I have an IUD."

I stopped and looked into her eyes, still wet with tears but sharp and fierce. The brown and blue eye gave her face depth, and I couldn't stop staring. Her nose seemed longer than average, like in a medieval painting.

"Also, you'll need to get regular blood tests to determine the correct dose."

She said, "I can handle that."

There was no swelling in her ankles or legs. She complained of left-sided chest discomfort when she took a deep breath, but her lungs were remarkably clear. Covering her back was an elaborate anatomical tattoo of the lungs. Below, on her sacrum, read, "Cosmic Love."

I said, "Thanks for the map. It's all here, so I know exactly where to put my stethoscope."

She brightened. "That's the idea. You like Florence and the Machine?"

"Is that what this is?"

"You know the album?"

I said, "*Lungs!*"

She said, "Like Florence Welch, I'm a Pre-Raphaelite."

I said, "Too bad they were all guys, a brotherhood."

"Don't you agree they need some feminine energy?"

I said, "That's for sure. I'll come back after you get dressed, and we'll go over everything."

When I returned, PJ was a quick study. After a single explanation, she demonstrated how to give herself injections. She understood which foods contain vitamin K and said she'd eat them consistently in moderation.

I laughed. "You're making this easy for me."

She gave me a warm, confused smile, then looked at the floor. "I knew I shouldn't fly."

"You can't predict or avoid these things. It's not your fault."

"That's not what I mean. A round-trip flight sucks the life out of the atmosphere. It's equal to one-fifth of the greenhouse gases per passenger a car produces in a year. We're eviscerating the conditions that make life for our species possible."

I said, "Believing one thing and doing another is how most of us live."

She wrinkled her lip, and I wondered why I said it.

She said, "Can I pick my prescriptions up today?"

"Yes, they're in the system. Come back Monday at 10 a.m. and get another blood test. You'll see Katie, and she'll adjust your warfarin."

She asked, "Where are you going?"

"I'm off for the holidays."

She offered a perfunctory hug and said, "Who can I call if I need something?"

"The clinic number is in the packet."

"What if they're closed?"

I wrote down my cell phone number in her folder.

She said, "Thank you, that makes me feel better."

I resumed the grind, and throughout the afternoon, I chewed

on PJ's word, "eviscerate." I'd heard they disembowel white fish on the Great Lakes to preserve freshness. Then, a flashback, my days on the ambulance, a slashed abdomen. Me scooping protruding bowels back into a screaming, shimmering pocket. But what does evisceration mean for the planet?

Patients kept coming. During a brief lull, I looked up "eviscerate" on Google. It also means to deprive of vital content or force. It rhymes with asphyxiate, assassinate, eradicate, exfoliate, exterminate, incinerate, hydrogenate, self-immolate, and vituperate. PJ used the word well. I couldn't get it out of my head, like a hook in a popular song.

Esperanza left at 4:30 without saying goodbye, and my last patient departed just before 6:00. I turned off the fluorescent lights and walked down the long hallway into the back office. The place felt like a morgue, a deep underground vault that could double as a bomb shelter. Every living being had departed except for Katie and me.

When I walked into the office, Katie jumped like a cat leaping for the ceiling. The small fan on her desk was blowing wildly against her coiffed, silver hair.

"Oh, Neal, sorry, let's shut down and skoodle doo."

"Are we done?"

She drew her fingers through her hair, "We've done enough for today. Let's blow this hotdog stand."

I said, "Thanks for getting all the calls done."

She turned her head. "I hope I'm good for something."

I said, "You know, I'm off tomorrow, and outta here day after tomorrow."

"Great and groovy. Just wish it wasn't getting cold. Should be OK in the desert. Who was that young woman you saw at lunch?"

"A student, Payton Jessica Wright."

"I thought so. I went to Santa Barbara High with her mom. I

remember PJ as a little girl, and she's in Boston now at MIT. What a hoot."

"I found that out. She corrected me when I wrote 'meteorology student' in her chart. She said, 'Meteorology is an antiquated term. My area of study is atmospheres, oceans, and climate.'"

"Sounds like her. Good kid. Smart too. She's had a few problems, an only child. Her mom's a movie producer. Her dad's a big-time entertainment lawyer. I hope she's OK."

"She's had a significant PE and doing well. It's good to be young."

"Yes, sounds like she was lucky."

"Check this out, PJ just texted me. 'Expect frost. Tomorrow is going to be the coldest day of the year. An unpredictable spinning pocket of instability blowing over the Channel Islands. Temperatures will dive hard. Wear a jacket.'"

"Neal, you gave her your cell number?" You'll get hammered with calls. You need the time off to be free of this place."

"She's a kid and needs reassurance."

"Don't give out your cell number. I'll take care of PJ while you're gone. We've talked about this before."

"I wanted her to have someone she could ask a question to. Also, there's other psychological stuff going on. She's scared."

"She can call us during office hours or go to Urgent Care or the ER."

"If it were me, I'd like to call someone immediately and avoid the red tape."

"That's not how it works, Neal. You and Victoria get out of here and have a good time. Leave this behind. Trust me. We can handle it. PJ will be fine."

I sat down at my desk, knowing she was right but still not liking it. I tossed her a beleaguered smile and concentrated on my charts. I heard her collecting her things to leave.

I said, "Want me to walk you to your car? It's dark."

"No, Wyatt just called, he's picking me up at the back door."

"You guys going out?"

"No, my car is in the shop, and he insisted. Such a dear."

"Have a good night."

"Toodle doo."

I stared at the screen and saw there were seven unfinished charts.

It was 7:30 before I tied up loose ends. My legs were wobbly when I climbed the stairs and pushed open the heavy metal door. A nippy chill gripped my chest, the temperature having dropped twenty degrees when the sun went down. The sky was black as a squirt of squid's ink, and there was no moon. The absence of warmth settled into my bones with a bite. The Santa Ynez peaks felt close and imposing. I zipped my jacket.

Thank goodness I didn't drive. The twenty-eight-minute walk home allowed me an opportunity to decompress. I thought about PJ. At least a third of people with an untreated pulmonary embolism die. Luckily, she was sitting next to a retired nurse who read her the riot act and urged her to go to the emergency room.

When I walked up the steps to the cottage, Victoria opened the screen door. "You're late. I thought you said you were going to mop the floor before we leave." She flashed a mischievous smile.

When I hugged her, I felt a light layer of sweat on her cheek and upper lip. "Did you get to yoga?"

"Yeah, Kat's class at 5:15. It was awesome."

She smelled clean, like Tide mixed with the comforting aroma of homemade bread.

She said, "I heard about Mick. Cassie called me."

She pulled me close and gave me a softball kiss on the lips that made me shiver. "Be easy with yourself, Neal. You can't help anyone else until you're grounded yourself."

I said, "I need to call Pixie."

As I hurried to the bedroom, she called after me, "I made a big garden salad, and there's chili you can heat in the fridge."

"Thanks, but I need to call Pixie first. It won't take long."

She shouted, "Neal, it won't take much, a wet mop to get up the floor dust and a broom to sweep away the spider webs. Fred and Cindy are passing through on their way back to San Francisco next week."

I left my pants, shirt, and tie on the bed and changed into my uniform—a T-shirt, cut off sweatpants, and flip-flops. I threw on a brown leather jacket and walked out the door. I dialed Pixie while standing next to the newspaper rack in front of the bodega, shivering in the cold.

Pixie burst out with, "What do they do with the foot?"

I said, "It's biowaste. It's incinerated."

"What else?"

"Some donate to medical schools. I saw a Jehovah's Witness at Duke. He had a ceremony and buried it."

There was no response and a long uncomfortable silence.

"Are you still there?"

I heard Pixie breathing. After an extended pause, she exclaimed, "What about the tattoo?" She started crying.

"I don't know. How high was the amputation?"

"It was his foot, at the ankle."

I said, "Ask the nurse to show you."

Silence.

"Are you still there?"

"I don't want to see it."

"It might be OK. I'll talk to the nurse."

She said, "What kind of ceremony? No way it's going to a medical school."

I said, "Most incinerate."

"He's going to be so upset."

"It didn't do much for the guy at Duke. He said it was like having one foot in the grave."

We chuckled.

I said, "Get some sleep."

"I'm going back to Buffalo General. What if he wakes up? I need to be there."

I said, "I'll look into the tattoo tomorrow."

"Promise?"

"I'll talk to the nurse. She'll know."

"He's going to be so upset." Pixie hung up.

I heated the chili in the microwave and ate the hearty salad. The warm tomato-based gallimaufry of ground turkey, turmeric, beans, celery, and carrots hit the spot. After dinner, I mopped the floor and whisked the spider webs from the corners of the ceilings.

# 23 DECEMBER, 4:25 A.M.

## (SANTA BARBARA, CA)

*"One day the house smells of fresh bread,*
*the next of smoke and blood."*
Arthur Miller (1915-2005)

ICTORIA TURNED OVER AND STABBED me with her elbow. She snapped, "It's your goddamn sister again. Why didn't you turn your phone off?"

I bolted upright. "This is about Mick." I fumbled to find my phone under the bed. The bright face blinded me. I winced. It was 3:37 a.m. I whacked the side of my head when I put the phone to my ear and stumbled out of the bedroom, pulling the door closed behind me. "Hello."

"Sweetheart, how are you? How's my baby brother?"

I said, "Do you know what time it is?"

"I always forget. The sun's up here."

I paced the living room floor and said, "Pixie told me about Mick's foot."

Cassie cackled, "Yes, you mean Mr. Stumpy?"

"Fuck," I replied, stifling an irrepressible laugh.

I slumped onto the floor with my bare butt on the Persian

rug, my back against the couch. We giggled uncontrollably, like children. I wrapped a throw blanket around my shoulders. Tears rolled down my cheeks.

I said, "You must be out of your mind. This is bad. Very bad."

"Darling, I'm worried too, but let me tell you what my girl did. You know Sylvie, she cleans, cooks, shops, takes care of things around here. She also throws bones. She saw a man with one leg, which indicates that Mick will be OK."

"She doesn't even know Mick."

"That doesn't matter. Her people have been practicing divination for thousands of years. The bones predict the future."

I shouted, "How's that going to help Mick get to the bathroom in the middle of the night?"

"We'll work that out. He'll get physical therapy, crutches, a walker, a wheelchair, a prosthesis. I don't know. Don't worry. God is good. Why do you have to be such a downer? We'll figure it out."

Her parrot squawked, and I pulled my ear away from the phone. My eardrum throbbed. I heard the receiver thump on a table, then a rattle as Cassie lurched across the room using her walker.

I heard her open the metal cage latch and say, "There, there, Chauncey. I told you it's my baby brother, Neal. You know Neal."

I heard the bird flapping its wings.

As I sat in darkness, my eyelids fell. I heard Victoria's heavy rhythmic breathing in the next room and thought, *Thank God, she's asleep.*

Cassie, like me, fled Buffalo as soon as she could. I remember a letter she wrote to my father that said, "We all love each other as a family but need our own space." It was then I knew that she had no intention of returning. She was twenty-one and I was twelve, and the separation cut like a knife. Our time living under the same roof was over. Extreme geographic separation left us to long phone calls and rare visits. Although, these last few years, we've talked almost every day about Mick.

"Darling, darling, are you there? Chauncey was making such a fuss. I don't know what got into him."

I asked, "Should we go to Buffalo?"

"Oh, no, sweetheart. Everything's under control. Pixie is there and will keep me informed, and in turn, I'll let you know if there's any change. It's snowing. You don't want to be there now. I talked to a nice young doctor named Sally Jones who told me Mick's heart is strong and that he should recover fine."

I said, "What about the tattoo?"

"Sweetheart, why are you bringing that up? Pixie asked me too."

I said, "What about it?"

"My guess is they got most of it. The amputation was at the ankle. I don't know what this tattoo thing is all about."

"It was important to Mick."

"I know it was, but they had to take the foot. It was gangrenous. You know his diabetes."

I said, "I would never have suspected this for Mick. I hope I die with both my feet."

She said, "At least it's his left. He'll still be able to drive. FDR drove without the use of his legs at all. He did all the shifting with his hands. Remember, he had a girlfriend too. And Mick will increase his disability check now that he's an amputee."

The bird shrieked.

I said, "Have you talked to any of the other doctors or surgeons?"

"No, darling. Pixie is there and taking good care of Mick. You know she is. She's uncommonly devoted. I talk with her every day, sometimes on the hour."

"This seems much worse than last time."

"Pardon me, sweetheart, Chauncey is having such a fit. We'll talk again soon." *Click.* She left me hollow in the emptiness of long distance, talking to air.

I sat dazed, neither awake nor asleep. Somewhere in limbo, shivering in the cold. The prickly Persian rug irritated my butt, so I climbed onto the couch, huddled under three throw blankets, and fell asleep.

Fifteen minutes later, Cassie called again.

"So sorry I had to go. Chauncy wouldn't let up, and I couldn't hear a word you were saying. I am worried, dear. But there's nothing we can do but pray. I know the bones are right. How are *you* doing?"

I yawned and sat up on the couch. "Good. We're leaving town for a few days around Christmas. Going to Palm Springs."

"That will be nice for Victoria. You should get away more. Anything new with her family?"

"No, she hasn't spoken to her brothers since Esme died."

"How long is that?"

"Thanksgiving, five years ago."

"That's odd. None of them have reached out?"

"Not since the dip shit younger brother changed the will, squirreled all the money away, and took the ranch. Her three brothers went along with it. One of Vic's friends thinks the scheming bastard poisoned her mother."

"Is that possible?"

"I don't think she's too far off. Some pretty shady shit went down."

"Do they all still get together for the holidays?"

"As far as I know. All but Victoria. Before Esme and Walter died, she got sad during the holidays, and now it's worse. It starts at Halloween and lasts through her birthday in January."

"All the more reason to get away. God is good."

"Yeah, and I hated every minute of those obligatory ranch gatherings."

"It will work out. Do you know anything about the 21-Day Digestive Health Detox?"

"Never heard of it."

"You won't believe it. I can eat as much as I want as long as I stick to the program."

"Sounds too good to be true. I've never seen anybody lose weight without cutting or burning calories."

"It really works. I've already lost five pounds. You eat yogurt and sauerkraut to fatten up the healthy bacteria in your gut, so you don't need to cut calories."

"This sounds like a fad diet."

"You should try it. I found this delicious yogurt I love, although they don't always have it at the SuperMax in San Juan. The sauerkraut isn't bad either."

I said, "I remember the sauerkraut Mom used to serve with boiled hotdogs."

She said, "The Polacks in Cheektowaga served it with pierogi. Delicious."

I changed the subject. "What's Mick doing for cash?"

"Oh, don't worry about that. You know, we put in new vinyl storm windows this fall. The heating bill is down. We also put in a new furnace. That thing was ancient from when Mother and Dad lived there."

I said, "Does he have any income? And what about all these hospital bills?"

"He's doing OK. Don't worry about that."

"Are you sending him money?"

"No, no, nothing like that, dear, although I'm available to help out when needed. Don't worry about it. Everything's fine. When I know more about Mick's condition, I'll call." Her voice drifted and she said, "Talk to you tomorrow," and hung up.

Cassie's obfuscation is chronic, habitual, and ever-familiar to me. She wields the technique with impunity regardless of whether it's about her diet, her weight, or Mick's finances. With any topic, she brokers a fine line with the truth, and often it ends badly.

When I was five, I adored Cassie. Nine years older, she was my best friend and companion, always available. She took me to the zoo, and we watched movies on TV like *The Wizard and Oz* and *West Side Story*. Any questions or concerns, I went to Cassie first. We were allies. She was my confidant. Constantly battling obesity, she was chunky and carried the shame in her deportment. She did her best to hide her rotund figure under baggy sweatshirts and loose-fitting clothes. She wore flesh-colored, cat-eye glasses that rested on her attractive, small, upturned nose. She told me they were "thinning" and made her face look elegant, chic, and stylish like Elizabeth Taylor. She had a pretty face, and I thought she was beautiful. My first memory is of sitting on the back of her bike, wind rushing through my hair, and me shouting in glee, "Faster, faster, go faster." I bounced a few inches with each inevitable bump. We whipped through corner lots, a neighborhood domed by massive elm trees, where dappled daylight flickered through thick branches and leaves. My parents frowned on this practice. They felt it was dangerous and someone would get hurt. It was the first time I experienced fear and exhilaration at the same time. I was small enough to fit through a twelve-by-sixteen-inch milk chute. When a neighbor forgot his house key, he would lift me, and I'd squirm through and open his front door. Cassie and I defied our parents and rode around the block where they couldn't see us. Cassie loved that bike, a pink Schwinn Women's Majestic three-speed with a glossy cargo rack atop the back fender. I held tight to her thick waist, and she pushed her full weight into every stroke. We almost fell one day, and I was reluctant to get back on next time, a few days later.

She'd insisted, "So, you're chicken?"

With trepidation, I'd climbed on and held tight. Though it felt a little shaky, she regained her cadence and pumped hard and fast.

I laughed and told her to peddle harder. I shrieked, "Wee," and as I got used to the speed, I touched the spokes with my right toe. I liked the *thump, thump* sound. The summer wind rushed into my face. It felt like we were flying as we approached two slabs of ruptured cement beneath an enormous maple tree. I probed my sneaker a little too deep, and the spokes swallowed my entire foot as we hit the crack in the sidewalk, flipped, and tumbled.

I don't remember how I got to the hospital. Cassie had scraped her knees and gotten a bump on her forehead. I'd broke my leg in two places. My father was furious. Although I was hurt and scared, most of all, I didn't want my father to punish or hurt Cassie, so I'd pleaded through a stream of tears, "Don't hurt Cassie. Don't hurt Cassie." With big crocodile tears, I'd said to the doctor in the emergency room, "Don't hurt Cassie. Don't hurt Cassie." The doctor said, "No one is going to hurt Cassie," and looked at my father, who nodded.

For me, wearing a full-length cast was a novelty. I enjoyed the attention and overnight celebrity status. I can't summon up the suffering or inconvenience or even remember which leg I broke. I wore a cast that people signed and made a big fuss over. A waitress at the Buffalo Athletic Club wrote her name, Lucy, in red lipstick that smeared. People teased me that I had a girlfriend. I enjoyed being the center of attention, and to this day can't remember the pain. As far as I know, my father didn't unleash his violent temper on Cassie, and I never rode on the back of Cassie's bike again.

My mind drifts. It's too late to go back to bed. I'm half asleep with pen in hand. When vacation comes, I'll sleep until noon, give up this nonsense of alarms that jar my sleep. Sleep. Sleep. Feet. Feet. Baby's feet. Wet feet. Cold feet. Perfect feet. Chubby feet. Obese feet that hold up mountains of flesh. Flat feet that get you out of the army. Black feet. Feet that cushion. Feet that smell. Feet that hurt. Feet that hold. Feet that touch. Feet that give hand jobs. Fetish feet. Tender feet. Feet that massage. Homeric feet that don't rhyme. Feet that bounce. Feet that lust for other feet. Broken feet. Stubby feet. Feet. The need for feet.

The smell of fresh red snapper on the grill. The eye-boggling smorgasbord of papaya, mango, pineapple, coconut, rice, and plantain. Clear blue lines on Condado Beach exploding in red and magenta reaching toward a tropical sunset. Bright turquoise pools, gentle waves and, most of all, the sensuality and natural movement of the people. Swaying hips and breasts, generous buttocks, the flash of white teeth. The grand colonial architecture of Old San Juan and Cathedral de San Juan Bautista.

Cassie, like me, had escaped Buffalo for warmer climes. And unlike me, she'd stayed put. When I left Duke, my boss had said, "You're an itinerant!" He was incredulous that I'd leave a stable job, benefits, a lovely home, colleagues, and lifestyle. I was fifty, no prospects, my career at Duke behind me, and on the move again. I looked up "itinerant" and realized it wasn't an insult. It was accurate. Three marriages, several careers, various jobs and locales—my life was a road map. Western New York, Ontario, Florida, North and South Carolina, and California. Like a chuppah, my life, four poles and a canopy, something mobile and movable. Like a tortoise, my home goes with me.

Cassie put down roots and taught Caribbean history to sixth graders for thirty years. Now she lives on her pension. How many hurricanes—Hugo, Marilyn, Georges, Irene—has she weathered? And those are the ones I remember. Prolonged power outages never brought her back to Buffalo. She's had an arrangement with an island man for as long as I can remember, a couple living separately. Together but alone. Her one-bedroom condo stuffed with unicorn figures, tiny chairs, and talking clocks is cluttered, out-of-control, and unmanageable. Most of the kitsch was purchased on television through QVC. How does she navigate that jumble with a walker?

She maintains a prodigious torso supported by sandpiper legs. Her lifestyle is simple, starting with what she wears—batik print muumuus with flip-flops. Nothing else is necessary for the Islands. She looks and behaves like my father—her skin, like his, is snow white, susceptible to burn. The rest of us are sallow, often mistaken for Lebanese. We have dark eyes, deep, hurtful, and probing. There is nothing of the Caribbean's turquoise reflected in us like in Cassie's baby blues. As a kid, I was mesmerized by a port-wine stain birthmark on her left arm below the elbow that looked like a wispy cirrus cloud. I imagined it to be a Scotty dog, and at other times a dragon. Cassie also functions like my father, with all her hurt and anger wrapped inside that wide girth, waiting to explode.

Then there's Saundra, my other sister, the black sheep. She's the living image of my mother, four years older than Cassie and thirteen years older than me. A couple days before I got the news about Mick's amputation, my cell phone had vibrated while shopping at Trader Joe's. Area code 716 flashed across the screen, so I thought twice before answering. Creditors are always after Saundra, and she often changes her phone number.

When I answered, she blurted, "Mick's in the hospital again."

"I know. I heard from Pixie."

I trolled the frozen food case.

She exclaimed, "He's done," and a cold chill ran up my spine.

I left my cart by the door and walked outside. "What do you mean?"

"He'll never work again."

I said, "He hasn't worked in five years."

She said, "Cassie's sending him money."

"Why do you say that? He never asked me for any."

"That's because he's got his sugar momma."

"I thought he gets a disability check."

"How do you think he's paying for replacement windows and a new furnace? They're not cheap, and he's not getting just any windows or furnace. This stuff is top of the line."

I said, "He told me he put fifty grand away while he was working."

"Believe that, and you're more of a sucker than I thought. And Cassie isn't doing well. Have you talked to her? She's on a binge."

"She told me she's on a new diet. Something about eating yogurt and sauerkraut."

"Well, she's eating everything else too. She's *always* on a whacky diet. She can hardly move since she had the second knee replaced. All she does is hang around and talk to that damn bird and send her girl, that Sylvie, out shopping. It must be nice, and she has a pension. While she was here, she was stashing popcorn, muffins, and candy in every drawer. She's so fat, someday she'll blow up and go kablooey."

I said, "She didn't sound any different when I spoke to her."

"You didn't see her in June. I took her to my doctor here in Buffalo, and she was tipping the scales at over three hundred pounds. He said her diabetes is out of control, but you can't talk to her about food. She gets quiet and moody. If you push too hard, she'll tear your eyes out. Well, for your information, Mr. Big Shot, she's not OK. She's obese and has diabetes, and something terrible is going to happen."

I'd heard Saundra's unrelenting monologue about Cassie's ill health for decades. I knew once she got rolling, like a train or an elephant, she'd be hard to stop. So, I redirected and said, "How are *you* doing?"

"I told you that I put you in my will. I've accounted for that five grand you sent me for taxes. You'll get your money. I don't see how I can do anything before then."

I said, "Why do you always bring that up? I gave up on ever seeing that money again."

She said, "I want you to know I haven't forgotten."

I said, "OK, fair enough."

She faded out and said, "I'm losing my connection."

Then there was air, and no need to call her back.

My parents' first child, born on the cusp of WW II, was a product of rations and hard times. It's irksome for me to remember how Saundra fits in because I try so hard to forget her. Coarse and direct, there are no amenities. How different from Cassie, who addresses everyone as "sweetheart," "darling," and "dear." Saundra minces no words. She is the scourge of the family, a manipulator, a thief, and a liar, always broke and robbing Peter to pay Paul. She is amoral, unethical, useless unless in a panic. The less exposure, the better. Even my parents agreed, especially my father, who had recommended, "Distance. Keep your distance." She marches through people like the blitzkrieg through Poland. Her occupation is selling low-end real estate, her avocation the flea market. She peddles chachkas at inflated prices on weekends. Despite her ambition, she's always broke and jonesing for a loan. After a meal out, she never offers to pay. She has little tricks like disappearing into the bathroom when others are settling the bill. Saundra buffaloes people. She bullies, harasses, and baffles, skilled in misdirection and discreet lies.

My father said she's a natural salesman. Unattached, relentless, she goes for the jugular. Never question her killer instinct. And, if that doesn't work, she'll bludgeon and beat you down. That's why keeping one's distance is crucial.

The etymology of our hometown is murky. There are several theories. I ascribe to the legend that it comes from the verb "to buffalo," which means to dupe or to string along. In this sense, Saundra is its standard-bearer. It implies a sleight of hand and royal bamboozlement—a con game executed by a pro with no conscience. Cities of the world, even big ones like New York, Rome, and Delhi, started as crude encampments. In Buffalo's frontier days, the story goes, a group of soldiers camped on a nearby creek. They sent out a detachment to procure game that came back empty-handed. Famished and overcome by hunger, the enterprising consort slaughtered a horse and told their compatriots it was buffalo meat. The creek, after that, became known as Buffalo Creek to commemorate the act of beguilement. No other word better describes the feeling of being a victim of a bald-faced lie.

Like everything American, the name "Buffalo" is a mongrel, an amalgamation. At one time, the woolly beast might have roamed the rivers and plains of the Niagara Escarpment. The American bison is well endowed to thrive through western New York's godawful winters. But that was too long ago for anyone to remember. There are no fossils, artifacts, or proof.

Yet the mighty image of the American bison resides as the primary symbol of the city. Jerseys, helmets, public documents, and building pediments double down on the icon. The city's animal image is representational and unique. It's inherent in its name. I still hold the conviction that it is a verb in origin, not a noun. Saundra has been buffaloing me all my life.

# 24 DECEMBER, 3:24 A.M.
## (SANTA BARBARA, CA)

*"If you can't get rid of the skeleton
in your closet, you'd best teach it to dance."*
George Bernard Shaw (1856-1950)

PREDAWN. COLD AND DARK. A single light bulb gives off a ghoulish yellow glow. I'm sitting in the living room in the big, blue leather recliner, my legs covered by a fleece blanket. I hear metal scraping on bare wood in the next building. It's Theodosius. There's a growl, a bloody shriek, some thumping, a hoot, a scream, and a moan. It happens every day about this time, in the pitch black before daybreak. When we moved in, Victoria asked, "Is he dying?" That was two years ago. We both wonder how much longer this can go on. Our next-door neighbor rises as if in chains and drags his walking aids like irons across a creaky, wooden floor. The floorboards rumble and squeak. He makes like he's dying. He bawls, yells, and howls—all in concert with hauling metal across bare timber. We've never seen him and know him only through his distressing cries. The suffering, at times, sounds like passion, a grunt a man makes when he enters a woman, when he becomes a locomotive, all piston and cock, all with a driving purpose. The irony, with all this commotion each day, is that we only know Theodosius through his pain.

Earlier, I woke in a panic, my heart racing. I sat up straight.

Vic was wide awake, her eyes open, staring at me.

"You OK? You were thrashing, mumbling in your sleep."

I said, "It was so vivid. I remember everything."

She said, "Who's Brandy?"

"A boxer."

"Like Muhammad Ali?"

"No, a dog, a mean dog, on my paper route when I was a kid."

She said, "Boxers are lovers, sweet dogs."

"Not this one. Brandy almost ripped my leg off and went for my throat. He scared the shit out of me whenever I came close to the door."

"Sounds like a nightmare."

"Do you ever feel like you're lucky when it's over?"

"What do you mean?"

"That it's a dream. It's over and done. You don't need to deal with it."

She crooked her elbow, put her left hand behind her head, and exposed her bare armpit. "All the time." She bent forward and stroked my forehead. "Can you sleep?"

"No way."

When I got out of bed, I noticed my T-shirt was soaked.

In the dream, I was fourteen, standing in my family's driveway in North Buffalo. A wicked gale was driving wet snow that stuck to my face like molasses, then melted. I tasted crisp, fresh, frigid snowmelt on my lips. My mother opened the storm door wearing a flimsy housedress with short sleeves and called out, "Mick, Mick." A blast of wind slammed the door shut, and she strong-armed it open, holding it in place with her hip. She turned her head slowly, looked around, and fixed her gaze on me. Her glare curdled my blood.

"Where the hell is Mick?"

I said, "It's too cold. He's upstairs watching TV."

She shrieked, "You're taking him with you. Goddammit. You knuckleheads never give me a minute's peace. Get in here now and get him ready."

I stepped into the vestibule and entered a narrow foyer lined with winter coats and scarves. A double-door refrigerator jerked and hummed at the other end. My face was so cold it felt like it was burning. Water dripped on the yellow linoleum floor. A low cabinet with sliding doors jammed with gloves, shawls, and sports gear cramped the restricted space. It was a safe harbor where we could stash things with impunity from our snoopy mother. The acrid smell of boiled hotdogs wafted from the kitchen. I heard little Mick raising a ruckus upstairs.

"I don't want to go. I don't want to go."

Five minutes later, he appeared in the hallway and said, "I'm going with you, Neal."

I gave him a bear hug and said, "Let's do it."

He said, "Mom's a Nazi."

"What? Where did you hear that?"

"Dad. He said, 'Bernice, you're a goddamn Nazi.' What's a Nazi, Neal?"

"Don't worry about it. Let's get out of here."

I helped him step into a tiny, brown snowsuit and flattened a short, knit scarf around his shoulders and chest. He pulled a wool beanie over his head, and golden sprockets of hair poked out beneath it. I zipped the snowsuit and tugged the hood strings tight, then wrapped another, longer scarf around his neck and covered his face. Only his eyes were exposed. One by one, I buckled his black rubber boots. When I tried to put on his tundra mittens, he pulled away and said, "Fingers."

I said, "Mick, it's freezing."

He insisted, "Fingers." I stuffed the mittens in my back pocket and helped him put on a tiny pair of brown wool gloves with leather palms.

He reached and grabbed a miniature Buffalo Bills' football from the cabinet.

I closed and latched the wooden door.

A gust of wind slammed the aluminum storm door shut.

My mother yelled from the kitchen, "Haven't you gone yet?"

He climbed into my navy-blue *Buffalo Evening News* wagon. I'd removed the wheels and rigged it with steel sled runners, so it slid with ease over ice and snow. I fretted about whether I'd dressed him warmly enough. Dark, sunless winter days in western New York were the norm, and gray light swiftly changed into black shadows while delivering my papers. I knew we'd be out past dark.

He yelled, "Go. Go."

I dug in with my boots and started running, slipping and sliding, pulling the wagon down the driveway. It almost flipped as we turned into the street.

Mick giggled uncontrollably and demanded, "Go faster. Go faster, Neal."

I responded by kicking snow and ice blocks and making a snorting sound like a horse.

My paper route was three blocks away, near St. Aloysius, where I went to school. The Angelus bells that rang at 6 p.m. signaled time to be home for dinner. Darkness was begging to settle in, and I folded newspapers and tossed them on frozen doorsteps.

As I bent to grab another paper, Mick said, "Catch," and threw the football. It hit me smack between the eyes and dislodged my glasses. I saw stars, and my eyes watered. I raised my hand and said, "Shit. What the fuck did you do that for?"

He said, "Let's play."

"No, not now, Mick. We've gotta get this done. We're late. You're my wingman. Do you know what that means?"

He replied, "Wingman. I'm Wingman." He moved his arms up and down like an eagle and blew out a frosty breath. Then he cooperated and folded papers for me and we zigzagged up and down frostbitten streets.

As fingers of natural light faded with a flip from an unseen switch, dozens of streetlamps illuminated the polar night. Cast iron urban beacons, as far as I could see, luminaria. I imagined roman centurions holding torches.

Tossing papers at front porches and inserting others inside storm doors, I pulled Mick behind me up and down the frozen streets. When I opened the final customer's door, a ferocious boxer named Brandy barked and growled. He scratched at the thick wooden door inches away and slammed against the wood with a thud.

Mick shivered in fright.

I said, "Hey, Mick, don't be afraid. Watch this." I rapped on the door and clicked the brass mail slot. When Brandy jumped to meet it, I thrust the newspaper at his face.

The big, muscular beast whimpered in pain.

I ran like hell, pulling Mick behind. My heart was jumping out of my chest. The Angelus bells were ringing. That's when I sensed something behind me. When I turned, Brandy leaped through the air, tackling me like a scared and sickly antelope on the Serengeti plains. The news wagon and Mick toppled over. I slipped and slid on the ice and grit and struggled to my feet. Brandy ripped my pants, and blood spurted from my leg. I swatted his muzzle with a rolled newspaper, which only made him angry. He vaulted for my neck, dug in with his fanged teeth, and wrestled me to the ground with his relentless jaws. His mouth foamed white, and drool spattered on my chest. I kicked and struggled with all my might. No matter how hard I fought, I couldn't pull him off. I feared for Mick. I'd failed to protect him.

That's when I woke up.

I can hear Theodosius rustling about. The disturbance now is muffled and not as unsettling. His pain seems less acute.

Yesterday, I bumped into the property manager, a tall, aging blonde named Stacy with a long, thin, stretched face, wrinkle-free from cosmetic surgery. Not a hair out of place. She was standing in front of Theodosius's place. It was a rare appearance. I can never get her on the phone.

She said, "The artist upfront has been here forever, for eons."

I looked at her and said, "Theodosius?"

With a twinkle in her eye, she slipped through the gate. And I forgot to tell her about the clogged bathroom sink, or about the windows that won't open, our back door that won't lock, and the toilet that won't stop running.

I'd never thought of Theodosius as an artist, but his wife had approached me when we moved in. Now she slips in and out of shadows and never says a word. On that occasion, she was outgoing and said, "My name is Carmen. I'm a bookkeeper. You may also see Theodosius. My husband is housebound and an invalid. He stays in the back, but sometimes he'll sit at the screen door. Likely you won't see him."

And she was right—Theodosius's blood-curdling outcries in the morning are the only thing that makes his existence known. While speaking with the building manager yesterday, I noticed a broken wooden anatomy manikin on the porch railing, evidence of Theodosius's avocation.

During that first encounter with Carmen, we'd exchanged names and phone numbers. I asked her to spell her last name, crossing it out twice before recording it as "Stikers."

She said, "It's pronounced Stickers. Like potstickers or what you get for doing well in school." And she never mentioned Theodosius again.

Five tenants share these dilapidated dwellings, flanked by an auto repair shop. The Stikers and a young, single, gay Asian man, Zhang, co-exist in the paint-distressed, single-story duplex upfront and share a common wall. Letters and packages are often lost. Even the postman gets confused. Victoria and I dwell in the century-old cottage outback. We call it the "Love Shack." We mounted a painted wooden sign above the door that says, "One Love." Visited by hummingbirds, populated by elephant palms, olive trees, and jade trees, most evenings, the secret garden is licked with the scent of night jasmine. There are other tenants, too, nocturnal ones, like opossums, rats, skunks, and raccoons. The exterminator calls it a "downtown habitat." All these buildings have stood the test of time.

Zhang asked Victoria and me over last night. It was our first time inside his place. We entered through a tiny kitchen that led to three block-like cubbies. Through a thin trail of worn rooms, we met a man he said was his cousin. A petite, pale man smiled at us, wearing a towel around his waist, still wet after getting out of the shower.

Zhang said, "I had to move my bed into the front room. It's supposed to function as a living room. I can't sleep with the man next door. He drags his walker and screams in the middle of the night as if he's dying. Have you heard him?"

We both nodded.

Victoria said, "Do you mean like Jacob Marley's ghost?"

I laughed.

Zhang glowered. "It's not funny. My mother told me to call the police, but I can't do it. I don't know how much longer I can live here."

Victoria and I looked at each other, then back to Zhang. We nodded and acknowledged his plight.

His cousin added, "I hear the toilet seat slam, no flush, and then the sound of scraping metal and heavy feet on wood."

Ten minutes after we left, Vic and I exclaimed at the same time, "Aren't you glad we don't live there."

As I'm writing, I keep looking down at my feet and ankles. I arch my toes, extend the Achilles tendons, lock and rock my feet, then move them from side to side. I looked it up. There are seven thousand nerve endings in each foot, thirty-three joints, a hundred tendons, and twenty-six bones. One quarter of all the bones in the human body are in the feet. We are the body. What a strange conglomeration of systems: bones, joints, tendons, hormones, organs, cilia, and spouts. So complex, and we never think about it. There are two hundred and fifty thousand sweat glands in the feet, and they produce four to six ounces of sweat a day. It makes sense why my feet stank up my dorm room in Miami. Walking down State St., I watch people eat, consume ice cream cones, burritos, Chinese fried rice, Pad Thai, and chips. Our species is one long snaking tract from mouth to anus, hungry and masticating at one end, needing relief at the other. We are the body. Pancreas, gall bladder, liver, spleen, stomach, small intestine, large intestine, anus combusting and releasing. We need the body, every part of the body.

While I was packing yesterday, Saundra called, and without as much as a hello, she said, "How much does it cost?"

Like a cold bucket of water in my face, I responded, "What the fuck are you talking about?"

"The pegleg. You know, the prosthesis."

"It'll be thousands. Insurance pays for it. And it's not a one-time expense. They only last three to five years."

"What's a phantom limb?" she said.

"A lot of amputees, in fact most, have sensation and get pain in the amputated limb. It feels to them like it's still there."

"That sounds like Mick. Always making a problem out of something that isn't there."

I paused, rubbed my face, took off my glasses, and said, "I would never have predicted this for Mick."

"What did you expect? This is God's punishment for all his

drinking and drugs. I lit some candles for him earlier today at the Carmelite convent."

"Do you think his punishment includes dismemberment?"

"It could. Cassie said he'll get more from disability, and he needs the cash."

"I'm sure he'd rather have his—"

She interrupted with, "We all have a contract with God. The small print includes stuff like this."

I said, "Let's hope neither one of us signed up for dismemberment."

"You never know, Neal."

"I hope I die with my feet, both of them."

The conversation went on, and she softened. It felt good to talk to a sibling, someone who knew Mick. We laughed about Mick putting a huge cardboard tub on his head while bathing in the kitchen sink with soap on his nose. Even then, he made everybody laugh. Her tough veneer melted, and for a moment, so did mine.

It's time to put down my pen, make coffee for Vic, and shower. We leave for Palm Springs in a couple hours.

# 25 DECEMBER, 4:28 A.M.

## (PALM SPRINGS)

*"Love is not a victory march.*
*It's a cold and it's a broken Hallelujah."*
Leonard Cohen (1934-2016)

VIC'S ASLEEP. I'M SITTING OUTDOORS on the steps of the motel, scribbling in my notebook. It's chilly. My fingertips are numb.

Yesterday before breakfast, both of us packed our bags, showered, and slipped out the door in silence. No delays. No excursions back because we forgot something. No petty arguments or complaints.

When Vic pressed the push button ignition switch, it was 7:06 a.m. The Honda S2000 purred. She said, "Not bad. We said seven."

I said, "I don't remember any such agreement."

Thirty-nine degrees outside, a thin layer of frost crusting the windows. Our teeth chattered before the 2000's robust heater kicked in. Vic was dressed in tight blue jeans and sandals and wore a red, ribbed turtleneck and a fringed leather vest. Her chest swelled, and her wavy blond hair sparkled. I noticed her fingernails had been groomed and polished and matched with cherry lipstick. Her hands moved with a deft grace as she gripped the steering wheel. A nurse's hands that never shy from disimpacting a patient, inserting a catheter, or starting an IV, yet delicate, ever-feminine, compassionate hands like Mary's in Michelangelo's *Pieta*.

We beat the commuter traffic through Carpinteria and rambled down Pacific Coast Highway. At Rincon, it settled in. *There's no family, no obligations this holiday break.* Surfers bobbed like seals against the horizon while others rode long, well-formed curls.

I had a playlist ready and queued. First up, Otis Day and the Knights, "Shama Lama Ding Dong," our favorite from the 1978 film, *National Lampoon's Animal House*. It starts with an iconic spoken introduction, "It feels so good to be back here at the Dexter Lake Club. We'd like to do for you now a tune entitled, 'Shama Lama Ding Dong.' So hit-t-it."

Vic pressed her arm across my chest and said, "Wait, stop. Play it again."

I pressed replay.

She tilted her head and, with a pert smile, pretended to hold a microphone with her free hand and said, "Hit-t-it!" On came the big, growling sax, plucking guitar, and lyrics.

We sang every word we could remember and mouthed what we forgot, tossing our heads and shoulders in circles like Stevie Wonder. We hopped up and down, rocking the car, and laughed so hard it hurt. Vic pulled the vest down over her shoulder and dipped into it like she was doing a striptease. She pulled up her shirt and flashed her breasts. A trucker in an eighteen-wheeler pulled up beside us and blew his horn.

I said, "Remember how you got down on the floor and did 'the Alligator' at Griff's wedding in South Carolina?"

She said, "It was four days after 9/11."

The music kept coming—Gladys Knight and the Pips; Crosby,

Stills and Nash; and Joni Mitchell. We rolled on to I-10 and into the desert.

I said, "What do you think's happening at the ranch this year?"

"Same old shit. Nothing much changes. Grandma always made shrimp curry with lots of condiments, a holdover from her days in Los Angeles."

"Don't you mean Los Angoolis?"

"That's how she said it. She's gone too. Most likely, they're eating pre-packaged shrimp from Costco."

I rolled my shoulders forward, folded my chin against my neck, pushed out my belly, and started to snore.

Vic laughed.

I said, "Do you think Cousin Charmaigne made it this year?"

She said, "Where else does she have to go?"

"She could stay in Arroyo Grande."

"Nah, she's there, and the best part is that we're not."

I said, "When I was with Scarlett, we didn't even notice Christmas. It came and went."

Vic said, "What about that black family in Johnson City?"

"The Raineys? Ah, they'd been Bible-thumping Southern Baptists before converting to Bahá'í. For them, Christmas came with all the trimmings: a big family gathering, turkey, ham, cornbread, collards, and yams. They decorated a tree and exchanged presents. It always felt a little weird. Scarlett said that was common in the south. Bahá'ís celebrate any religious holiday they want. They believe all the prophets are related. But most of the community thought the Raineys took it too far. Other Bahá'ís didn't do much for Christmas. Scarlett liked to check out their tree. She said they were her people because some had light skin and red hair. Until I met you, Christmas wasn't a big deal."

She said, "I'm done with it. I didn't even feel like getting the Christmas stuff out of the boxes this year."

I said, "After fourteen years as a Bahá'í, I don't miss it."

She said, "It was fun, but I showed up at the ranch out of loyalty. I could only be ten percent of myself. Nobody in that family wants the whole package."

"I remember you always got stuck in the mud on the ranch road. You're the best driver I know. You never get stuck."

She said, "I don't hide things very well. I knew what would go down after my parents died. It came sooner than I thought."

"Death always does."

"Let's not talk about that now. Tell me about your crazy family Christmases in Buffalo."

"My mother pushed herself to the brink of insanity. She went into a frenzy that went on for months. She dragged decorations accumulated by her children and ancestors out of the attic. It was extreme. She made everyone miserable. She saved a set of beat-up, gold-sprayed cardboard organ pipes my sisters made in grade school. They were falling apart and covered in gold glitter that got into your hair, nose, and mouth. She placed each pipe in a certain way on the mantle. I must admit the finished product looked pretty good. But she refused help. We all dreaded it. She had to do it her way and then complain that nobody supported her. I didn't get the sense that she liked Christmas, and her obsessions got worse every year. She cried a lot, especially after her sister died."

"I've heard all this sad stuff about your mother before. Tell me about Stinky and his crazy brothers."

"Dinky. And you know the story."

"Oh yeah, Dinky. It's funny. Let's hear it."

"That was the last family Christmas, my second year at the University of Miami. I'd hung out with friends in the dorm over Thanksgiving and loved it, and I didn't want to go home. My father summoned me under threat. A typed letter arrived that said he'd cut me off if I didn't show."

"Neal, I've heard all this before. I want a laugh."

"I remember his words: 'Neal, the whole family is going to be together this Christmas. Your mother and I will no longer support your education if you do not attend.' My father must have known it was the last Motherwell Yuletide extravaganza. As it turned out, I'm glad I didn't miss it."

Vic said, "Tell me about your cousins, 'The Boys.' I can't remember their names."

"Terry, Jerry, and Dinky."

She snickered. "That's rich. I love it."

"That Christmas, they drove nonstop across the western prairies like a blizzard. Three days with no sleepovers. Their visitations were always spontaneous and unpredictable. Terry, the oldest, was the instigator. He'd phone my mother, whom he addressed as "Aunt Boonie," and talk for hours. She'd sidle up to the kitchen table and howl. The three-hour time difference never hampered their connection. It could be ten in the morning or at midnight. He was desperate to be with someone and my mother, his dead mother's sister, waited in Buffalo with open arms. He needed my mother like an orphaned child, and she didn't disappoint.

"The Boys hauled a full-sized wooden bar in their pick-up truck that year. It had matching stools. Upon arrival in a snow squall, they dragged it into the house, leaving mud stains on the white carpet. It found a permanent home in the dining room. Terry, who'd been in jail for robbery, packed a pistol hidden in a slick holster across his chest. He'd gone straight and become a landscape foreman in the San Fernando Valley. Terry couldn't get it through his head why lawns in western New York didn't have irrigation systems. I'd explain that Buffalo receives plenty of precipitation. Too much. He never got it. Jerry also spent time in prison. He threw a police officer through a plate glass window during a bar fight. He was so drunk he didn't remember it. Jerry was tall, dark-haired, and handsome with a cleft chin. He had movie-star good looks. Terry stressed that Jerry never looked better than when he was serving time. He was svelte and working out with weights. Jerry was soft-spoken, with a quiet, combustible rage. His eyes were glassy, like a reptile with a nictitating membrane. I was never sure he heard a word anybody said. He simmered rather than surfaced unless he was drunk. Dinky, my contemporary, as a youngster living in Buffalo, was trouble. He was a pyromaniac and smuggled cherry bombs from Canada. He'd flush them down school toilets and blow out the pipes. He spent time in a juvenile correction facility and came back no better for it. The three together were incendiary and got meaner and louder the more they drank."

Vic asked, "How old were they?"

"Terry was in his early thirties, a half-brother from a previous marriage. Jerry and Dinky were a little older than me, in their early twenties."

"Didn't one of them feed the piranha Christmas dinner?"

"Jerry dumped turkey and dressing into my father's fish tanks. And that was only part of it. They took liberties nobody else could. They knocked over the Christmas tree, broke dining room chairs, and busted heirlooms. They pinched my female cousins on the ass. They insulted everybody. They slept wherever they fell. They barfed in toilets and pissed in the back yard, yet my mother always invited them back. My father was on high alert, anxious, never knowing what they'd do next. Yet my friends to this day ask me, 'What about your cousins from California? What about Dinky and the other guy?' "

"What happened to them?"

"Terry retired early, in his fifties, with big plans. He sold his condo in Canoga Park, moved to Idaho, and bought a place with his old lady on the River of No Return. He always called her his 'old lady.' He rode her hard and hung her up wet. He'd drink and dial pissed and pissed off, full of stories of how he was going to settle some scores. After my mother died, he called me instead of her. Then, one day the phone rang—this is years ago when I was at Duke—and he was gentle as a lamb. He'd had surgery for colon cancer that required a colostomy. With a tiny voice, he squeaked, 'I ain't shitting in no bag.' He died within the year, and Dinky shipped his ashes to Mick in Buffalo. I never heard a word from his girlfriend. Jerry got killed in a motorcycle accident on the 101. His ashes also were delivered to Mick in Buffalo."

She said, "And Dinky?"

I paused and looked out the window. "I like to think he's still alive. Last I heard, he was in a half-way house in Reno. He did some time for armed robbery. I haven't made contact."

Vic turned to me. "Have you tried?"

"I've searched for him on the internet. I found a name that matched, including his middle name, Irving. There was no further information, address, email, or phone number, only the location. My guess, he's on the streets of the Biggest Little City in the World, and I'd need to go there to find him. It's a mixed blessing."

"How's that?"

"The last few times I talked to him, he asked me for money and was only interested in when I could send him cash. His brain was mush. He had no interest in anything else."

She said, "Nothing like my boring family where nobody ever acts out."

I said, "A mixed blessing, and there's another story. The Boys played a crazy game during that last visit. Terry sent Jerry upstairs to fetch the bathroom scale, and he set it on the living room floor. Each got on and weighed. Terry announced, '222 pounds, 240 pounds, 275 pounds.' Dinky yelled, 'You Porker! You can't see your dick anymore. Man, have you let yourself go.' Then Jerry scrambled over to my mother and asked, 'How much will you give me for this one?' He lifted her, kicking and screaming. She resisted playfully, and no one interfered. Although, when she got close to the scale, she fought tooth and nail not to expose her weight. Jerry announced, '148 pounds. I'll take a hundred bucks for this heifer, nothing less.' He tried to get others to submit to the scale but found no takers. Then Terry and Dinky joined him and carried my mother above their heads around the living room. She struggled, laughing but awkward, her skirt raised, overpowered. As they lowered her, she kicked and caught Dinky in the groin. He fell to his knees. Hysterical, mean laughter followed as Dinky squirmed and writhed on the floor. Then he started laughing too. Two feet of fresh snow on the ground, icicles dripping from the roof. A polar-infused inferno. A liquor-fueled, three-bedroom, one-bathroom house. Outside, a polar vortex. Inside, an inferno about to explode."

Vic said, "I thought there was another bathroom."

I said, "My father's throne is in the basement. It's a Pittsburgh potty, a toilet on a cement slab with four crude, gray plywood panels. There's no sink. My father couldn't sit down without the door open."

She said, "You can pee there."

"What I'm saying is the place was small, and these guys were bouncing off the walls."

She turned her head and grimaced. "How did your father put up with it?"

"It wasn't easy. He drank and did his best to get everybody else drunk. He poured very generous high balls. But he didn't like it, especially the thing with the piranha. They overran his domain. He slunk around and stayed in the background."

"I thought you said he beat the shit out of you and your sisters if you looked at him cross-eyed."

"He bullied us but cowered to my mother. One time when I was eight, he came home drunk. When loaded, my father took on a different personality. He got mean, his wrists went limp, and he looked like an effeminate dancing bear. My mother saw him from the kitchen window, stumbling to get out of his car in the driveway. When he walked in the door, she pushed herself up against his chest and lambasted him, 'Don't lie to me, Cornelius. You sonofabitch. You're light as a daisy. Look at your wrists. You fairy. What kind of man are you?' He exploded, shook her shoulders, and pushed. She fell straight back like a cut tree and bounced on her butt on the linoleum floor. Sprawled in her house dress, legs akimbo, a look on her face I'll never forget. At once shocked, as if to say, what the fuck did he just do? On the other hand, a ferocious scowl with the will and intent to kill. She rose and cold-cocked him with a roundhouse right. He clutched his jaw like she'd rattled a tooth loose and retreated upstairs. After that, there was never a doubt in my mind about who was in charge. Drunk or sober, he never got physical with her again. They had knock-down, drag-out arguments. There was lots of screaming, yelling, and saber-rattling, but never fisticuffs. He'd retreat beleaguered and rumble down the basement stairs to his lair."

Vic said, "I've never heard that story before, but I believe it. I'm always finding out something new. Nothing like that ever happened in my house. I never heard my parents raise their voices. They told me that was their intent, never to show any discord in front of the kids. Did The Boys like your dad?"

I said, "They loved and respected him and went out of their way not to piss him off. It was a detente. My father knew how important it was for my mother to have them there. He blew up in bursts but never lost control. It was clear he wanted them out and never to come back, but he always maintained his cool. There were no incidents.

"I'm not sure I ever told you about this. The weirdest thing happened when my father took The Boys to the Buffalo Athletic Club. In an instant, their bravado paled. They draped towels around their waists to conceal themselves. When they dressed, they pulled the underwear up under the towel. It was ridiculous. They acted as if they'd never seen bare-assed men before. They giggled like children when they saw men in the buff in the swimming pool and hanging out in the steam room. My father's girth being too expansive for a single towel, he carried it over his right arm like a waiter, his stubby, thick cock and scrotal sack fully exposed."

She giggled, "What did they think of that?"

"They were shocked and embarrassed. They looked at the floor in silence. For me, being naked with my father and other men was commonplace and natural. For them, it was a source of awkwardness, bashfulness, and mortification."

She said, "Nothing like this ever happened in Madera. We're Methodists. You Catholics are wild."

"It got more primitive after dinner. My father skulked away and watched television upstairs in the bedroom. There was always dancing, and it got raunchier as the night went on. My mother and The Boys turned up the stereo, and the music got more risqué. The laughter became less restrained. My father would bellow from the landing like a wounded elephant, 'Bernice, when are you coming to bed?' She'd ignore him. The house shook with foot-stomping and heavy bass from a maxed-out woofer. People flooded in from the neighborhood, and relatives dropped in after their family Christmas get-togethers. Condensation dribbled down the windows. People opened the doors despite the freezing temperatures. The jokes got juicier. Terry and my mother pranced like Mick Jagger, jutting out their jaws and asses, and hopped along the floor. The rest of us stopped and watched. My mother grabbed a large, decorative wooden fork she'd received as a present and gripped it with both hands like a paddle. She waved it above her head and below her waist and started digging with it like a shovel. Terry grabbed it away and mimicked her every move. His wet, blue paisley cowboy shirt popped at the snaps. He thrust his thick thighs forward, exposing his bloated, white belly. He shimmied his ass in tight blue jeans. Dinky screamed, 'This ain't dancing. They're doing it.' "

Vic said, "Wow! Nothing in my family ever got close."

I shrugged and said, "That's why you married me."

She looked at me and shook her hair. "Yeah, maybe that's it."

As we drove on, the landscape shifted, and we entered an arid, uninhabited landscape with cacti and tumbleweeds scattered across a broken hip of hills and valleys.

I said, "What do they produce out here?"

Victoria said, "Sand and gravel."

"It looks like the Holy Land."

"Welcome to the Sonoran Desert, also called the Colorado Desert, take your pick."

I said, "What are those thorny plants with yellow flowers?"

"Mexican poppies."

"They're beautiful."

She said, "The ranchers don't feel that way. Livestock won't eat them because of the thorns. They take over and become a nuisance."

"Is it illegal to pick them?"

"If they're not on your land. It's more a weed than a plant, and it's poisonous to cattle."

"They're gorgeous."

"Native people make medicine out of them. The seeds are a laxative, and they make a tea out of the flowers. It's antimalarial. They're a little different on the ranch. More orange than yellow, and back home, they're called California poppies."

As we approached a vast expanse of white angular wind turbines, my phone vibrated. It was an 805 number I didn't recognize. I put it on speaker.

"Neal, I'm sorry to bother you. It's PJ. I know you're off on vacation, but there's nowhere else to turn."

I said, "That's OK. How can I help?"

She said, "I can't get the Lovenox. The insurance will only pay for generic. I called your office, and it's closed. I don't have an injection for tonight."

"The generic is fine. What's your pharmacy?"

"CVS at Five Points."

I turned to Vic. "Is CVS open on Christmas Eve?"

She nodded.

I said, "I'll call it in."

I dialed the pharmacy, and they took a verbal order. Then I rang PJ back.

"You can pick it up tonight. They're open till eight."

She said, "Thank you, Neal. Thank you so much. I can't tell you how much I appreciate this."

"No problem. How is everything else? Any bruising where you're giving yourself the shots? Any shortness of breath or swelling in your leg?"

"No, it's going well. My mother is helping me with the shots. I'm due back at the clinic day after tomorrow for a retest."

"Good."

She said, "It's still pretty cold in Santa Barbara. We had frost on the Mesa this morning. Thanks again, Neal."

As soon as PJ hung up, Vic said, "Who's on call? Couldn't somebody else have taken care of it?"

"They could if the clinic was open, but they're closed."

She said, "Neal, I've given up trying to change you. In fact, I like it, you care about folks who need your expertise. But I wouldn't take a call from a patient on Christmas Eve unless I was getting paid overtime. I've thought a lot about this, and I'd welcome it if you were my practitioner. It used to piss me off, but you'll never change."

I said, "I gave her my cell as a last resort. Shit like this always happens."

Then there was silence. The momentum shifted. For Victoria,

two plus two always equals four. There is no separation between fact and fancy, no bullshit, which is the antidote to my family. She doesn't tolerate ambiguity. In the blink of an eye, we were back to Mick.

She said, "You know, Mick will probably die this time and fuck up our entire vacation."

I went blank. Silence followed us to the motel. It hurt, but I knew Victoria was right and was telling me something I needed to hear. I'm glad she didn't hold back.

# 26 DECEMBER, 4:00 A.M.

## (PALM SPRINGS, CA)

*"A constriction in the chest, tears, a scream that*
*feels as if it would be endless if I let it out."*
Susan Sontag (1933-2004)

LAST NIGHT, THE PHONE RANG at 9:23 p.m. Vic and I were in bed. I fumbled in the dark and caught it before the second ring.

"Mick's dead. He had a heart attack," Pixie said.

I took a deep breath and sighed.

She said, "He just couldn't go on."

Then, she broke down and sobbed. I produced no words. Instead, I listened more intently to my brother's fiancée than I ever listened to anyone in my entire life. She raised her voice, bawled, and screamed—no words at first. I waited. She took little, energetic breaths like a choo-choo train climbing a hill. Eventually, she spat out, "Mick woke up. The fucking nurse told him. She asked if he wanted the stump dressing changed," she blubbered. "It would've been better if he didn't wake up at all."

I said, "How did he take it?"

"How would you take it? He was groggy and confused. It sucked."

"I'm sorry."

"It was awful. I was in the room. Why didn't that goddamned nurse let me tell him?"

"Sometimes health professionals are insensitive."

She blurted, "I didn't want him to know."

I said, "It was good you were there. Mick knows that."

I held my breath, and she continued to cry.

"Why didn't Cassie call me?"

"She asked me to do it."

I asked, "What time did Mick die?"

"Sometime this morning. I'll call you later."

"What are the plans?"

She'd already hung up.

Victoria sat up with sad eyes and faced me. "We'll buy winter jackets at Target and leave the car at LAX."

I said, "Shit, you knew this was going to happen. Why didn't I listen? I wanted something better to happen."

She nodded. "Something better happened."

"That he died?"

"You know it was getting harder for him. Mick lost his foot. He couldn't go on."

"I didn't want him to die."

She said, "I don't believe anything happens after death. There's no heaven or hell, no angels, no reunion with family and friends. We're gone. That's it. Something better. That's the place we all come to when our bodies wear out and it's time to let go. Everybody reaches it—a place where it's better to die than go on with the struggle."

I said, "But, but…I thought he'd stop drinking, get healthy, and make a triumphant return to *Good Morning Buffalo*."

"It didn't turn out that way. Sometimes nothing goes as planned."

"I miss him so much."

"What about him? Did you want him to go on suffering?"

We held each other in the darkness, Vic in her body and me in mine. We are the body, need the body, live through the body. What's it like on the other side?

My dear, sweet, and fucked up brother is dead. I hope he wasn't alone and scared. I can't help him anymore. When does it become better to choose death than life?

Our chests rose and fell. I felt angry. Why wouldn't Mick stop drinking? There were no words. A pain so deep and sharp settled in my chest.

Vic placed her right palm on my sternum and said, "I can feel your heartbeat. It's steady and strong."

She drifted off, and I got up and laid a bathroom towel on the carpet. From memory, I went through my yoga sequence—sun salutations, backward and forward bends, twists, a shoulder stand, a headstand. I saw a flashing light in the back of my right eye. Then I agonized the rest of the night and into the morning that I'd detached my retina.

My brother is dead, Christmas morning. And he expired a full half day before anyone let me know. Why didn't Cassie call?

# 27 DECEMBER, 3:07 A.M.

## (PALM SPRINGS, CA)

*"Somehow, this morning,*
*Things don't seem so bad—*
*I trim my nails."*
Takuboku Ishikawa (1886-1912)

S OMETHING CATAPULTED ME OUT OF bed this morning, a surge of energy protesting my grief. At first, it felt like nothing cataclysmic had happened. The room was hot and stale, and Vic lay on her back naked, kitty-corner across the bed without a bedsheet. I pulled on sweats and slipped out the door. Like stepping into a refrigerator, the bite assaulted my nostrils and made me sneeze. The desert sky was clear as rainwater and displayed a panoply of stars. Each concrete step resounded with a heavy *thud* as I descended from the second floor. I held the railing and calculated every move, not to wake up a sleeping baby or arouse a barking dog. My other hand muffling my sniffles with a handkerchief. The lobby, a rectangular room with blinding fluorescent lights, was vacant. Floor to ceiling windows made it feel like I was inside an aquarium. Now, I'm sitting in a corner in a puffy orange Naugahyde chair, my notebook on my knee. The cushion pops and groans like a fart every time I shift. I have lots of time to write. The continental breakfast doesn't start until seven.

Yesterday, we ate dinner at a German place downtown, Schnitzelhaus. I overheard an English couple say as we walked in, "This place looks like it's put together with spit." Vic took a chance on the cheese spaetzle with sausage, and for some reason, I did too. It's the first time I can remember that we ordered the same meal at a restaurant. Even in Tahiti and Thailand, we plunged in and ordered something exotic and sampled each other's meals. Beyond indigestion, it didn't feel right. We returned to the hotel, sat in a milky hot tub, and watched the sunset. Children ran and screamed and fought and fell on wet concrete and slipped on the tile. A couple bickered about who would sit in the hot tub while the other watched the kids. A middle-aged platinum blonde in a red bikini slipped in beside us and said, "Don't mind me." She lowered her chin, closed her eyes, and let out a sigh. Her husband slithered away to a lounge chair, sipping a beer.

We returned to the room while there was still a thin layer of crimson sun on Mount San Jacinto. We made love, red bodies, streaming heat and sweat, and fell asleep in a puddle without a blanket.

That's when Pixie called.

My last communication with Mick troubles me. It was a couple days before he went into the hospital. By then, he was calling me three or four times a day, often at odd hours. He'd prolong his monologue as long as I let him. It could go on for hours. I'd go about my business shopping, cooking, washing dishes, and doing laundry. And I hardly ever spoke. I could put the phone on the counter, wash my hands, and return, never missing a beat, and he wasn't aware I'd gone. He needed someone to listen. Sometimes when he called, I'd let it go to voicemail. When I didn't call him back, Cassie would leave urgent messages like, "Darling, Mick needs to talk to you right away. I can't tell you how much it helps when you call."

Yet the history of our relationship is far more complicated. For ten years, we didn't talk to each other at all. The hate between us during that decade was fierce and far exceeded any chance of reconciliation. He seethed when I opposed him staying in the family home after our mother died. My parents stipulated their estate distribution to be equal in four parts. Mick wanted the house free and clear. He argued that because he lived there, he should get it outright. It made no sense. I pleaded, "Let's sell it, and we all move on with our lives." During the dispute, he hunkered down, unwilling to leave. Bills piled up, paid for by the estate. Much of the inheritance was squandered in legal fees. After several years of this, Mick bought the house with a big mortgage he resented and cut me off. Out of the blue, ten years later, he called. It was after my second wife, Scarlett, and I split. Thrilled to hear from him, we talked for over two hours, and from then on, his phone calls kept coming. The feud had ended without apology or conscious acknowledgment. There was no admission of wrongdoing on either side. These past few years, Mick needed me more and more, and I responded. And it's wreaked havoc on my relationship with Victoria. My life was much more manageable before the armistice.

At Cassie's suggestion, I attended Adult Children of Alcoholic meetings. They preached tough love, which never worked because I couldn't cut Mick off. Their recommendation was to ignore his phone calls. When I did, I couldn't get Mick out of my mind and Cassie pestered me to call him. I thought about Mick all the time.

But it's that final conversation with Mick that haunts me. I was standing in line at the bank when the phone rang. The hair on the back of my neck stood up when I heard his voice. He was hallucinating, frightened, and agitated. Every word was a chore, his delivery slow and deliberate, like he'd developed a thick Southern accent with a slur. There were no jokes, pauses, or laughter. No patter. I left the bank and sat in my car.

He said, "Saundra's here. She's ripping me off."

I said, "Where?"

"She's on the floor of the bedroom. You gotta help me, Neal."

As if I could do anything from three thousand miles away. I heard Pixie shuffling in the background.

Mick said, "Kill her. Get that bitch the fuck out of my house."

Pixie screeched, "Saundra isn't here. Stop it." Her voice was shrill and contemptible.

He said, "My brother is on the phone."

She said, "He already hung up. Saundra isn't here."

I heard Mick fumbling in the sheets, trying to reach the receiver before Pixie slammed it down.

Mick sounded helpless and confused, a mixture of delusion, fear, and prophesy. I called back several times, but the line was busy. Later, I felt sick and vomited. I attributed it to the chicken salad I had for lunch. Nausea lingered. There was nothing I could do. I didn't want my little brother to die scared and alone.

We leave from LAX this afternoon. A blizzard delayed our departure yesterday. After breakfast, in the shower, I rehearsed for a fight with the hotel attendant. We'd booked and paid for seven nights, and the motel policy stated no refunds. Then, without a blink, the man at the desk refunded the remaining nights and threw in a discount.

He said, "We're very sorry for your loss. Let us know if there's anything else we can do." He was so kind I took note of his face and hoped I could find that Samaritan outlook in myself someday.

Here in the lobby, the fluorescent lights flicker. A low, cantilever roof obstructs part of my view. Even so, it's impossible not to sense the vastness of the winter desert sky. A new moon is ascending the eastern wall of Mount San Jacinto. The edge of the mountain forms a contour that looks like a sleeping brontosaurus.

One of my tasks yesterday was to call Conrad Loveday. He's the primary reason we came to the desert. We're both scheduled for archetypical astrology readings next week. He's impossible to book and very expensive. He's scheduled a year in advance and rumored to read for Sting. I left him a voice message: "My brother died on Christmas. Victoria and I need to cancel our readings next week." The message seemed so brief and harsh. I wanted to call him back and re-record it. I ran it over in my mind and asked Vic, "How does this sound? 'I have some terrible news. My brother died. We're leaving for Buffalo and won't be able to meet with you as planned.' "

She said, "Neal, the first message is fine. He'll understand. We've got lots of stuff to do. Let's not talk about it anymore."

Hard to believe it's been thirty years. I met Conrad at Duke Medical Center when I was a slave to buttoned-down shirts, striped ties, and twelve-hour workdays. My hair short, I relegated my spiritual life to organized religion. My second wife, Scarlett, thought astrology was a bunch of bull. For me, it was an escape from the superficial life I was leading. No store-bought religion ever settled my spiritual longings. At best, it served in the short term as a Band-Aid. Scarlett was a third-generation Bahá'í. When we first met, she'd handed me a book, *The Earth Is But One Country*, and said, "This is what I believe." Everything was tidy, in a singular package. I read John Huddleston's plea for world unity in one sitting. At the time, it made sense.

When it came to Conrad, Scarlett would say, "Neal, why are you wasting your time on that hoodoo? The truth is staring you in the face." It was the party line for any spiritual orientation outside the Bahá'í faith. I was defiant. Even after Scarlett and I left North Carolina, I made appointments with Conrad whenever I visited. I sought out his counsel and always found it reliable. What a surprise when I heard he'd moved to the California desert. I thought he'd never leave Chapel Hill.

It was Tate Joseph who introduced me to Conrad. At Duke, Tate was the thalamus who made all the connections. And for unknown reasons, she reappeared in my life again and again. We were like two trains on the same track, both graduates of the Duke PA school. A couple years ahead, she left her PA cardiology position to go to medical school, which opened a job for me. Once she said, "Neal, there's something to this, why we keep meeting up. I like you." She put her hand on my shoulder, and I discretely moved it away.

Years later, she joined the Duke Psychiatry faculty, and I ran into her on campus. She said, "Archetypical astrology should be part of our psychiatric armamentarium." I thought she was joking and gave her a dubious look. She said, "I'm doing a pilot study. You interested? It's free, and you're bound to learn something about yourself." She added, "You need to meet this guy. You won't believe what he'll come up with." She asked for my birthday, time of birth, and birthplace, and set up a date.

We were all very young. Conrad was lean, with a wolf-like face, long, wild, unkempt hair, and piercing eyes. He had exceptional confidence and looked straight through me. His first question was, "Are you happy in your marriage?"

I said, "I think I'm happy."

He said, "You'll have to be careful. In your chart, Uranus and Pluto are in conjunction. Normally, half the house has to come down. It's almost like you'll become a different person. Tate tells me you're part of a religious group. Aquarians aren't joiners. It's an inherent conflict for you."

He filled me with uncomfortable insights that otherwise would have remained hidden.

At the end of the session, Tate asked, "Do you see any compatibilities between my chart and Neal's?"

Conrad said, "No, although I guess you could press it that you are both dreamers and idealists. But at the core, you're unsuitable.

Aquarius and Pisces are a bad match. You have nothing in the houses that make me think you could sustain a romantic relationship. You're good as colleagues, not lovers."

Tate swallowed hard, shook her head, sat up straight, and turned her gaze toward me. "So, what do you think? Isn't Conrad amazing?"

When I was in Durham a couple years ago, I got sad news. I ran into Roger Wrightwood at the PA recertification conference. Roger never changes. He'll forever lurk in the long, dark, hallowed hallways of institutions like Duke.

I said, "Where's Tate's office? I'd love to drop in and see her."

He said, "You haven't heard? She's no longer with us."

"Did she go to NIH?"

His wrinkled face turned gray as ash and he said it again. "She's no longer with us."

It landed like a refrigerator dropped from the fourteenth floor. I said, "What do you mean?"

"You haven't heard?"

I shrugged.

Peeking above the rims of his glasses, he whispered, "It's not confirmed, but most think she took her own life. She was inclined that way."

I said, "When?"

"Four or five years ago. It might be longer."

At that moment, I felt severed. Tate's death had been a local scandal. How would I have heard? Tate and I didn't stay in touch, not even Christmas cards, or have mutual friends. It would take a trip back, like this one, to hear about it. I'd been away from Durham for seven years. The pain of leaving grieved me for a time. I longed for the chapel and the quad, the medieval library and its book-scented stacks. I yearned for the pace of North Carolina—hot, humid nights, a swim in the frigid quarry, long walks in the pine-scented woods. African American co-workers invited me to their church where I felt a belonging, a white face in a sea of black and blue. The fever pitch of Duke basketball. The insatiable hunger of Duke Medical Center to be world-class.

Is it the place or the person for which we grieve? Does the landscape remember us?

Now I knew Duke had forgotten me. Like a conveyer belt in a slaughterhouse, our time on the rack is short. The bone, blood, and marrow are sucked out, parts discarded, savory elements eaten. The blue-eyed boys and girls, all enthusiasm and smiles, slide toward death. Only memory could resurrect. I summoned to mind Tate, who seduced me and apologized. Tate, the mother of an abandoned son. Tate, the mystic who wanted to conjoin archetypal psychology and medical care. Tate, who went to PA school, parlayed it into medical school and an appointment to Duke faculty. Tate departed, never again a chance encounter with her in a hallway or on the Duke track.

Yesterday, Victoria and I had lunch at Sherman's Deli. The ambience oozes of pastrami. I ordered a chopped liver sandwich in memory of my mother, took one bite, and left the rest behind. At that moment, Conrad rang back.

He coughed and said, "Neal, I'm sorry to hear that. I mean about your brother." Then, without hesitation, he blurted, "You are experiencing a Saturn return on steroids. I've never seen anything like it."

I said, "How do you like California?"

"Ursula and I are splitting up. She's fucking someone else. Let's talk about your chart."

"Can we reschedule?"

"That will take some time. I'm traveling to Bali, then Japan. Can you talk now? I've already worked up your chart. I'll charge you the same as your usual visit, and this is the short version. I'll email the full audio."

I said, "Let me check with Victoria. We're at a restaurant." I motioned to Victoria.

She mouthed, "Conrad?"

I nodded.

She returned the gesture with a nod of approval and said, "I'll pay and meet you back at the motel."

A cute young waitress wearing red stripes and a black sash around her tiny waist bumped into me as I stood. She was carrying the house specialty, a massive slice of San Jacinto cake. People "oohed" and "aahed" as she passed. She said to the lucky recipient, "It's a combination of cheesecake and chocolate mousse, all dripping in ganache."

I nodded to Victoria. "I'll walk."

Stifling another cough, Conrad said, "This is an extraordinary Saturn return. You need to get this right."

I asked, "You feeling OK?"

"The cough hangs on. I had a sore throat last week. I'm about over it. Unfortunately, it continues to affect my voice."

When I got outside, I encountered an incessant riot of sound. Crows and ravens amassed on power lines and flew in a fever overhead.

Conrad said, "Neal, what's all the noise? Can you hear me?"

"It's a flock of black birds, all different sizes. I'm walking, give me a minute to get clear."

He said, "You mean a murder, an unkindness, or a conspiracy?"

"What are you talking about?"

"A flock of crows is a murder. Haven't you read Edgar Allen Poe? A gathering of ravens is an unkindness or a conspiracy."

I said, "I can never tell the difference."

"Ravens are larger, shaggier, with a beard. They have a thicker bill. The smaller ones are crows, and they're anxiety-prone and squawk when they fly."

"What are they doing here?"

"They abandon the fields and orchards in winter and converge on urban areas. How long have you lived in California? Everybody knows that."

I said, "One more question before we start. Have you heard about Tate?"

"Yes, very unfortunate, although it's been a while. Tate lost custody of her son. She was prescribing opioids, Prozac, and Zoloft for her patients as well as herself."

"Remember, she introduced us?"

"I didn't remember that. But let's get going with your reading. We have a lot of ground to cover. You know I'm a monologist. Save your questions for later. Can I start?"

I said, "Let's go."

He coughed, then snickered. "Your body is going to quit on you pretty soon. You've entered the infancy of old age." He took a long pause, snickered again, and let the weight of that sink in.

I found it difficult not to speak, but I knew that to interrupt would interfere with his flow. Conrad's method is improvisational. He rambles like a meandering river. He likes to get into a rhythm, like an NFL quarterback. Some would call it a trance. He falls back on parables and stories to emphasize each point. Often, he offers puzzles and riddles. The effect is Homeric, or what I imagine a session would be like with the Oracle of Delphi.

I mulled it over in my mind. *Is my body going to quit on me? The infancy of old age... What does that mean?* I thought, *I'm healthy. Things are no different than they've always been, at least as long as I can remember. I have a full head of hair, albeit I'm graying. I'm swimming, riding my bike, working, not overthinking about my body, as I always had. I've never had cancer or heart disease. Diabetes is still a possibility as it runs in my family, but not yet. I wake more often than not with an erection. My urinary stream is steady and reliable...not what it once was, but to my analysis, adequate. My concerns are external, what I am and am not getting. Habitual battles with colleagues at work. My position and place. My preoccupation is that I want more. I have several IRAs, which had been the case since my twenties with no plan for retirement. I've never taken medical leave.* Dying and old age seemed remote.

As Conrad spoke, I felt hollow, hungry, empty. I thought about that piece of San Jacinto cake the waitress was carrying. Why was I having this conversation? My brother died yesterday. Victoria was sitting at Sherman's. We needed to pack and get out of Palm Springs. Then I remembered I'd agreed to pay him three hundred and seventy-five dollars for what he was telling me.

He continued, "There are three cycles of life, each with its own calculus: youth, midlife, and old age. Saturn takes approximately twenty-nine and a half years to get around the sun. If you're lucky, you get three Saturn cycles. Most of us check out before then. From the astrological point of view, you've already entered the cycle of the elder."

The sun was high overhead and beat down on my head. The air was crisp. I felt a kink in my neck and a pang of insatiable hunger. I craved a piece of San Jacinto cake. My armpits were damp, sweat soaked my T-shirt, and there was the dank, earthy smell of ravens and crows flapping above my head.

Conrad said, "We pass through time in a logarithmic fashion. The final third goes much faster, and every year after that goes faster and faster."

Murders of crows and conspiracies of ravens lined the wires overhead and smudged the sky like thumbprints. One crow singled me out and dove so close I could feel the draft from its wings. As I walked, the bird perched on streetlamps, tormenting me. There was no escaping the racket.

I shouted, "Conrad, can you speak up?"

He continued, "The first Saturn cycle is when the individual seeks and finds out who they are. The right way to be young is to gather a vision. For example, let's say you meet two young people. One takes a job, the whole nine yards with benefits and a retirement package. The other takes off for Asia to go windsurfing. Which one do you want to have dinner with when they're forty? You get my point.

"The second Saturn cycle is about money, power, and sex. Between thirty and sixty, you make your stand and protect what you have. Say goodbye to that. You've left it behind. In the second cycle, there is an essential selfishness. You invest your energy in a career and have a family. Promises and neuroses rule the second cycle.

"The third cycle is about giving back. The source from where you draw your vitality changes. People get stuck in the middle cycle, hoarding and protecting. Most need a catastrophe to break them, to get on to the next stage. We fear old age more than death. Plastic surgery and dying your hair won't work. Here's an example: Hemingway, who achieved so much success in his youth and middle years, couldn't handle it. Electroshock treatment for depression fried his brain. He couldn't write anymore. He blew his head off with a shotgun while his fourth wife, Mary Welsh, slept upstairs. She, at first, declared it an accident. He was sixty-one, suicidal, and depressed. Why was a loaded gun so accessible? My question to you is different. Why did Hemingway fail to enter the third Saturn cycle? He'd mastered the earlier two spectacularly. And this brings me to you. There is something precious here if you get this right." He halted.

I looked up at the blackbirds huddled in the palm trees along Palm Canyon Drive.

"Your progressed sun opposes Saturn. It takes three hundred and sixty-seven years for the ringed planet to get around the sun once. So, most people never experience this phenomenon in their lifetime. That's why the third cycle is ripe with opportunity for you, and you're at high risk if you get it wrong. You don't have that much time left."

Best I could tell, I was twenty city blocks south of Sherman's. The downtown buildings had petered out. I passed a car wash, a mall, and a movie theater.

Conrad said, "The elder draws vitality in symbiosis from the young."

A photo flashed to mind, a wizened Mahatma Gandhi walking with his arms draped around two young girls. He called them his walking sticks.

Conrad said, "To get this right, you must offer your gift. You're getting it wrong if you say things like, 'Things were so much cooler when Hendrix was alive.' Don't become an old fart or a curmudgeon. Things weren't better when Jimi Hendrix was alive. Nothing turns young people off more. Your function is to be attractive to young people so you can give them your gift. Like mushrooms and fungi, it's about transmuting disappointments, failures, and fears. Rid yourself of poison and recover your ability to play.

"Also, you need to do something dangerous. You must do something where the outcome is uncertain. Powerful energies are at play. Like when a fighter enters the ring, even a sure bet can get knocked out. Look what happened to Mike Tyson with Buster Douglas. Uncertainty accompanies this transformation, and nothing corrects better than fear. You must know you could die trying. And everything must be on the line. Now's the time for heavy lifting. If you don't respond to the challenge, the screws will tighten with ruthless intensity. You've seen older people like this. They wither and die. They spend their days bickering and complaining, they go from doctor to doctor. They didn't rise to the occasion. I imagine you still look pretty good for an old guy."

I was feeling pressure to meet Victoria, pack, and depart. I felt overwhelmed.

He said, "That's all I've got. Any questions?"

I asked, "How do I know if something's dangerous?"

"Metaphorically, it will make you shit your pants." He laughed. "Again, Neal, I'm sorry about your brother. If there's nothing else, I've gotta go. Manly squeezes and one for lovely Victoria."

Radiant heat surged up from the sidewalk as the high sun beat down on my skull. A tall, lanky figure appeared like a mirage in the distance, an old man stooped at the waist with a distinctive hop. As he got closer, I recognized him—the guy who gave me the refund at the motel. He sported a straw Panama gambler's hat, green plaid Bermuda shorts, and an open Hawaiian shirt. His skin was weathered and furrowed like Methuselah, tan and leathery, the hue of the desert. His shoulder-length, wispy, white hair rippled like wheat in the breeze below his hat. He carried a wooden cane at his waist, holding it in the middle with his left hand. Our eyes met, and we nodded. When he stood up straight, he was six-foot-three or four.

He said, "Sure tough luck about your brother."

I said, "Thanks. He was sick for a long time. Also, thank you for the refund."

He said, "No problem. You'll be back next year."

"That's a good idea," I said.

"I'll be honest with you, I'm sure glad it's you, not me, heading into that snowmageddon. I grew up in Maine and still got some relatives back there. But I never looked back. Do you and your lady have overcoats and adequate clothing?"

"We shopped for some at Target."

"Don't take it lightly. I have an old, blue pea coat like Kerouac used to wear you can borrow. It'll fit."

"Kerouac. Thank you. I'm good."

"Are you sure? It'll keep you warm, and I don't need it."

"I'll be OK. And how would I get it back to you?"

"You could mail it and, as I said, you'll be back next year."

"Kind of you to offer, but I'm OK. Do you get out and walk every day?"

"I do most days. I don't own a car. I stay at the motel. I'm just helping out with the Christmas rush. My ex owns the place. I live in Big Sur most of the time."

"Big Sur?"

"I'll never retire. I do maintenance at Deetjen's and some at Calypso. I teach breath work, sell jewelry. Also, I do beads. I used to do bodywork, Rolf, and teach massage." He extended his hand and said, "My name is Earl."

I shook his hand, and he looked me in the eye. I said, "I love Calypso. That's where Victoria and I had our first date."

"Now, that's something. I knew there was something special about you two."

"We haven't been back for a while."

He said, "No place like it. What did your brother die of, if you don't mind me asking?"

"It was a heart attack, but he was ill for a long time. He drank himself to death."

"How old was he?"

"Forty-seven."

"I've seen that before. It's a hard habit to break once you get started. Most of my people are dead."

I said, "I've got to get back and pack. We're leaving for LAX in the hour."

"Don't worry too much about that. I saw that lovely little lady you're with putting the luggage in the car. You'll be on your way as soon as you get there. Best of luck to you, keep your cool. Families can bring the worst out in each other, especially when they don't know each other anymore."

I double-timed it back to the motel, crows and ravens circling overhead.

# PART II

# 28 DECEMBER, 7:12 A.M.

## (BUFFALO, NY)

*"All water has a perfect memory and is forever
trying to get back to where it was."*
Toni Morrison (1931-2019)

"**D**EADLINE," A DISTANT VOICE CALLED to me in a dream. It was Armstrong. Her voice was animated, rippling with excitement. She said, "Meet me at Goodbar in twenty minutes," and hung up. It was midnight. She was calling from the eleventh floor of Marguerite Hall. Her posse, the nursing students, known as the "Whore Corps," were carousing Elmwood Avenue. Whenever I was in Buffalo, she included me in these romps. On awakening, I reoriented myself—Armstrong's back in Buffalo and we're staying in her basement.

Home, that's what I felt when I opened my eyes. Armstrong's place is so much like my mother's. Delicate geometric frost crystals are etched on low-lying windows, icicles drip from rooftops, and steam spews from the footings of adjacent dwellings. A booming furnace blast causes the walls to shudder. Steam pipes ping, water boils and condenses. Home. Frigid outside, cozy and warm inside.

Victoria and I find ourselves snug and safe in a subterranean lair, a large, unfinished basement divided into three sections. It's downright tropical compared to the icy gusts of whirling sleet and snow outside. Vic slipped in after I fell asleep and buried herself beneath a pile of down blankets. Our little partitioned makeshift square has wall panels and a flimsy door. There's a padlock and hasp.

The walls are cluttered with posters and sports memorabilia. A trophy case is filled with medals for track and field and a greening bronze basketball trophy. Cheryl Tiegs's dark nipples greeted me. Her iconic pinup poster in a white mesh bathing suit faces the double bed. Next to it, broad, toothy smiles of Jim Kelly, Thurman Thomas, and Bruce Smith, stars of four consecutive unsuccessful Bills attempts at Superbowl triumph. And next to the bed, to my delight, a bookcase full of classics, holdovers from the previous resident's advanced high school English classes.

When I put my bare feet on the painted concrete floor, to my surprise, it was warm. I pulled a dog-eared paperback, Rilke's *Sonnets to Orpheus*, and walked to the bathroom in shorts and a T-shirt.

As I sat on the toilet, I read Rilke's lines:
"For among these winters there is one so endlessly winter
that only by wintering through it all will your heart survive."

While Vic slept, I explored the bunker. The spacious bathroom has a polished nickel eight-jet showerhead, the kind you'll find at the Greenbrier Spa in West Virginia and what I remember as a kid at the Buffalo Athletic Club. It pounds and soaks the body like an open fire hydrant. Around the corner, I came upon a dusty ping pong table with tattered net, rusty free weights, and a treadmill. Behind another door, a grimy stainless steel home brewery and a well-equipped laundry room.

Between the Civil War and the Great Depression, Buffalo was in its heyday. That's when they constructed grand fortresses like this. It's the kind of house my parents grew up in, and for the Queen City, it was the best of times. In high school, I had a friend who lived in this neighborhood. His place had a large, hidden room between floors accessed with a ladder through a closet. It had an eerie quality. He regaled us with stories of fleeing slaves huddled in the room, awaiting transport to Canada. Vic and I have landed in the soft underbelly of Buffalo's Underground Railroad.

Like in the house I grew up in, there's a coal chute plugged with cement. From my earliest years, this castoff had fascinated me. Why did it remain? Like so much of Buffalo, it has no function, built to last, and it's more trouble to remove than maintaining. It's a stubborn reminder of the past, like a keloid scar that never heals. No need to ever function again, the cover shouts out in rusty engraved letters, "Buffalo Steel," a rugged embellishment built to outlast the Apocalypse. This city is like that, hard fixed, bypassed by the St. Lawrence Seaway in 1959. Obstinate as steel, even though Great Lake freighters never call.

Back to yesterday, the man from the motel was right. Victoria had the car packed, and we got on the road. It surprised me that she wanted to make the trip to Buffalo at all. Mick's been such a thorn in our side, and I thought she'd bail. Yet here she was now, orchestrating the arrangements and offering to drive. Vic's a better driver than me, never distracted, even when doing a striptease. Always steady and self-confident, she never loses focus.

When we crossed the Union Pacific railroad near a Mobil station at I-10, the phone rang.

"Is that you, Deadline? You sound the same. I'm so sorry to hear about Mick." Like in the dream, it was Armstrong. Her voice is bright and melodic, full of the same vigor it was four decades ago.

Vic looked at me. "Who the fuck is Deadline?"

"Thank you, Strong. How did you find me?"

"Harvs called. She told me about Mick and that you and Victoria are heading to Buffalo."

I asked, "What are you doing in Buffalo?"

"I'm back. I bought a place in Canada and rent the upper story of a double on West Ferry."

I said, "My grandmother lived at 800 West Ferry. A guy in a suit and a white butcher's apron delivered her groceries. He had a key to her apartment and placed the items in her refrigerator and cupboards."

She said, "I'm only a couple blocks away. That's Buffalo's version of 'The Dakota.' "

I said, "Like something out of *Ghostbusters*."

"Yeah. You won't believe Buffalo. People want to be here again. It's a renaissance, and they're restoring all those magnificent buildings. Downtown is popping. There's a medical corridor in the Fruit Belt. Let's get back to your plans. Do you and Victoria need a place to stay?"

"We haven't worked it out yet. There's Mick's house. Pixie invited us. It will get awkward with my sisters. We also made reservations at Embassy Suites."

"Cancel them. I've got something much better. And you've got two choices. You can stay with me—I've got a guest room—or in the basement."

"The basement?"

"The landlords are in Winter Haven through April. They let me use the sub-level apartment for guests when they're gone. Their son lived there when he was in high school. It's even got a washer and dryer and an ironing board. I know you'll like that. You and Victoria are welcome to stay as long as you like. You can come and go as you please and come up to my place for drinks. The fridge is full. I have a fireplace and a large sitting room. I know there are a lot of people who want to see you, and you can entertain here."

I looked at Victoria.

She nodded and said, "Sure, let's do it."

I let out an audible sigh of relief. "I'm so glad we're not staying at Embassy Suites."

"Yeah, and we have a buffer between you and your sisters," Victoria said.

I said, "Embassy Suites, what a drag. I want to be with people. That's what Buffalo is all about."

"Well, then it's done," Armstrong said. "Show up whenever you want. I'll be waiting. Do you have your passports?"

Vic nodded.

I said, "Vic packed them."

Armstrong replied, "Cool, we'll make a day trip to Canada."

Victoria liked Armstrong, I could tell. The generosity of Armstrong's voice is contagious. Like Victoria, Armstrong's a ringleader, the life of the party. Also, Armstrong's a nurse. Between nurses, there's a sacred bond. Furthermore, both are cancer survivors who bounced back with energy and zeal. Victoria was springboard diving champ after Hodgkin's Disease at sixteen. Armstrong thrived after midlife ovarian cancer surgery, chemo, and radiation.

As we whipped down I-10, I said, "What the hell is Armstrong doing back in Buffalo?"

Victoria said, "Didn't she send you a Christmas card a couple years ago from Paris? You talk about her all the time when we go to the Clemente."

"Yeah, she lived in a sunny condo on California Street near Green Apple Books."

"What do you think she's doing in Buffalo?"

"I don't know. Armstrong left years before I did. After graduating from D'Youville, she moved to San Francisco and found her calling. She loved delivering babies, and her life revolved around being an obstetrics nurse. She sparkled when she talked about it, although she never had any kids of her own. Armstrong lived with a wild band of nurses near Golden Gate Park on Lincoln Way. When I headed west in my twenties, she welcomed me with open arms. I was broke and dirty, and she put me up. I had no idea what I was doing. When she went off to work, I'd scrounge around the city. I carried a tattered copy of Walt Whitman's *Leaves of Grass* in my back pocket and poked around Chinatown. Years later, we reconnected when I started working with the Integral Research Institute. She lived on Columbus Street near City Lights Bookstore. She and her husband put Scarlett and me up several times. It was a fantastic apartment with a spectacular view of the bay. I don't know all the details of what's happened since. Her husband died of a heart attack. She got cancer. She remarried and got cancer again. Last I heard, she was in Paris. She sounds the same."

Victoria said, "How did you meet her?"

"Through Harvs. They went to nursing school together. They'd come to Miami for spring break."

Vic's eyes narrowed and her shoulders cinched. "Is she an old girlfriend?"

I said, "She's a friend, a good friend. The sister I always *wished* I'd had."

"You know what I mean, Neal, or should I say, 'Deadline'? Did you sleep with her? And what's that 'Deadline' crap about?"

"We all had nicknames. It was a way of goading me into loosening up. I once told the Whore Corps I had a deadline on a paper and couldn't party. They've called me Deadline ever since."

"Whore Corps?"

"That's what they called themselves. They even had a song." I paused and realized I was gushing about Armstrong. And my answer to Vic's first question could change everything in an instant. I was traversing fragile ice.

A few months before, Victoria and I'd had a terrible fight. It was more than a quarrel. It was a breach, a pause, a reassessment of broken trust. She asked me to move out, and we had minimal contact for two agonizing weeks. The crux was that I'd lied to her about my relationship with Greta De Vos. It was a lie of omission convoluted by decades of friendship.

Greta and I had kept in touch since my early twenties. Letters, birthday cards, phone calls, and emails. There was always a Christmas card and carefully-chosen book in the mailbox on my birthday. Both of us were in committed relationships, living on separate coasts. Her husband and I would talk for hours on the telephone when she wasn't around. Her sister, Margo, also remained a life-long friend. Victoria and I visited Margo in New Zealand. There was never a hint of an affair or overt sex between us. Greta stayed in close contact with me through my three marriages. I visited her and her family whenever I traveled, and we'd remained penpals.

But the relationship didn't start that way. We were lovers. Victoria found out while reading my journal that described exquisite blow jobs and a detailed account of the hot and harried affections between two young people coming of age. I was unconscious of its effect on my relationship with Victoria. I'd never admitted it or told anyone. To this day, I think Greta, too, would deny it. And what does it matter at our wrinkled age? I bury my secrets. The only place I understand myself and tell the whole truth is in my journal. Victoria felt lied to, played for a fool, and I was angry she'd read my journal. We were at a standoff. Over time, I came to appreciate that a violation of trust by omission is as deadly as a direct lie. It simmers on a back burner, deferred. Victoria felt duped, and it could never sit right with her until I got it. No sideways truths or self-righteous defenses will ever work. And that's what I love most about Vic. I need her to be straight with me, even when inconvenient, even when it hurts in the short run. And I need to be straight with her. I learned a painful lesson. In fourteen years of marriage to Scarlett, both of us let lots of things slip by. We didn't confront one another but kept it all smiles. At first, they were little things, then an affair. It blew up. Given this background, I couldn't evade or lie about Armstrong. Not even a white lie.

I said, "Yes, I slept with Armstrong a few times in college dorm rooms and once in a motel in Key West. And yes, there was another time in Boston when we met as a group and shared a room. But we never 'slept' together. We pecked a couple times, and there's a deep affection between us. She's survived cancer and the death of her husband. Over a lifetime, we've supported each other through betrayals and disappointment. There was never 'a thing' between us but always love, respect, admiration, and ongoing concern. Harvs and Armstrong visited when I was a resident advisor at the University of Miami. We always had a great time."

Victoria said, "Is that the whole story, *Deadline?*"

My reply had to be concise, clear, and straightforward. It couldn't be vague. The gray area that accommodates twisted thinking was irrelevant. I knew even the truth might be suspect.

I said, "Yes," then paused. "There was a road trip. Harvs, Joel Rubinstein, Armstrong, and I crammed into a red Mustang and drove to the Keys. We picked up a hitchhiker and dropped him off at Marathon. We barreled down A1A with reckless intent, and in Key West we spent hours in the Hemingway house and rented a twelve-foot catamaran. Before fate intervened and blew us back to shore, we were adrift for three hours in the Gulf Stream. It was getting dark, and the girls were bikini-clad, teeth chattering. Harvs said she saw a large, triangular black fin off the bow. The task of getting to shore seemed hopeless, and there were no other boats in sight. Then the wind shifted. The only thing any of us knew about sailing was how to sail downwind. We swung out the single sail like a spinnaker. The sweet, harsh, cold onshore breeze drove us like a nail under a hammer to shore. Bewildered, when we reached the shore, the dock where we'd rented the catamaran was nowhere in sight. Shivering, hating the day we were born, we dragged the boat in shallow water to the pier. The proprietor charged us for an extra three hours and kept our hundred-dollar deposit. He was angry, with no concern for our lives.

"That night, we slept together across a king-sized bed in a sleazy, unembellished motel room, happy to be alive. Rubinstein didn't 'sleep' with Harvs. I didn't 'sleep' with Armstrong. And given our age and escalating hormones, I don't know why. We were all horny, and as for Rubinstein and me, we would have fucked a sheep. That's the kind of friendship I have with Armstrong. Not easy to put into words."

As I recounted the story, I lost track of time and space.

Victoria flipped on the air conditioner. When we reached the San Gorgonio Pass, it was ninety-six degrees.

Victoria's face brightened, and she gave me a half-smile, "Armstrong sounds cool. I like her voice."

I looked out the window at both sides of the freeway cluttered with thousands of white, whirling propellers.

I said, "These things always remind me of *The Empire Strikes Back*. The terrain's the same too. Is this the San Andreas Fault?"

Vic said, "You got it. It's where the wind blows hardest through a very narrow gap, the cold ocean wind forced across the scorched earth. That's why the wind farm's here."

"Do you think these things do any good? Can we wind farm ourselves out of the climate collapse?"

"That's what's advertised. Although, I've read they need back up from the grid. They don't work when the wind doesn't blow."

The desert stretched to the horizon before us, and hot, rust-colored, and brittle, frenetic turbines spun ineffectually. That morning, a spectacular sunrise glazed Mount San Jacinto in crimson, like Uluru, Ayers Rock, and I took it as an omen. Mick never saw Australia or the desert, or anything else for that matter. He dug in his heels, Buffalocentric, and refused to travel.

We parked in an outdoor lot at LAX. Towering palm trees swayed like hula girls in the brilliant sunlight. Both of us were ill-prepared for the inclemency ahead. Victoria had a lightweight down ski jacket from home, and I'd purchased a black, mid-length vinyl coat at Target. But no gloves, scarves, heavy pants, or hats. It hadn't been easy getting a last-minute flight to Buffalo. The best we could do was a three-hour layover in Charlotte. When we touched down in North Carolina, Victoria said, "Think we can find some winter stuff here?" We strolled interminable corridors, past pretzels, frozen yogurt, food courts, and familiar chains like Burger King, Sbarro, and California Pizza Kitchen.

Weary, we sat down at a Mexican taqueria, and Victoria ordered a margarita, then another. Maybe it was three. We talked and munched on chips, guacamole, salsa, quesadillas, and tacos. Victoria said, "I'm feeling a little better. Let's try again."

After leaving the taqueria, within a few shops we were accosted by a bright picture window with a massive teal banner, "FIFTY PERCENT OFF ALL HORNETS GEAR."

Victoria tightened her face muscles and wrinkled her lip. "What the fuck are Hornets?"

I said, "The basketball team. They're not very good."

Heavy sweatshirts, pants, and hoodies clustered the racks, while scarves and knitted winter caps hung from the ceiling. An ornate marquee above the door proclaimed, "Queen City News and Gifts."

Victoria said, "I didn't know they called Charlotte the Queen City."

I said, "They must've stolen it from Buffalo."

She said, "Look at this cool stuff. But the logo's got to go."

A cute young salesperson, a high school girl, bounced out the door. "How are you all today? Can I help? We have an outstanding after-Christmas sale. It ends soon."

I said, "I lived in Durham for years."

She said, "My daddy's people are from Burlington."

I warmed to her and said, "I did my preceptorship in Mebane."

She smiled wildly and shook her curly, permed hair. "We're almost cousins."

I said, "It's good to be back in the South where everybody's so personable and friendly."

Victoria rolled her eyes, marched through the door, and began to rummage through the gear.

The salesgirl said, "Where do you live now?"

"California."

"I bet it's beautiful there, but I could never leave, even though you've got the Lakers."

Victoria inquired, "Do you have gloves?"

"As a matter of fact, we do. They're in the back. Nobody buys them."

"Are they on sale too?"

"I can offer the gloves at seventy-five percent off."

She looked at the salesperson. "Do you have anything without the logo?"

"Sorry, ma'am, we do not. You're not a Hornets fan?"

Vic shook her head.

"You might like this line then."

She pulled a black hoodie with a discreet logo, "Buzz City," off the rack. We loved it, Buzz City, beneath it a smiley ultramarine hornet flapping its wings. Nothing flashy, no team name, nothing about Charlotte or hornets.

Victoria turned and said, "Let's do it. Grab what you think we need."

We each bought a hoodie, gloves, lined sweatpants, scarves, and wool beanies. When we boarded the plane with four shopping bags, plus carry-ons, the flight attendant said, "Looks like you two have done some shopping at Queen City."

Victoria said, "This is Buzz City." We looked at each other and roared.

On the final approach into Buffalo, we turned off the reading light and strained our necks to look out the porthole. The sky was black, but our eyes adjusted, and we could make out the massive, dark, frozen moonscape of Lake Erie. There was a faint dusting of gray snow with a bluish tint on rooftops.

The pilot banked the plane and said, "Those of you on the right can see the Peace Bridge. That's the neck of the Niagara River, where the waters from four Great Lakes converge. The five Great Lakes make up one-fifth of the world's water supply."

The Peace Bridge was iridescent, the colors of the rainbow dancing above the roiling waters.

Vic said, "That's awesome."

I said, "Those lights must be new. They do light shows like that at Niagara Falls."

"How far is Niagara Falls from here?"

"Seventeen miles downriver, a half-hour drive."

She said, "Didn't you tell me Mick went fishing there?"

I knew she was trying to cajole and cheer me up. I said, "You don't really want to hear about this."

She leaned her head on my shoulder. "Tell me all about it."

"I've told you about this before. Mick had waders, nets, poles, the whole nine yards. Even a drill and an ice shanty. He always caught his limit of walleye in winter, which are big fish and can weigh eight to ten pounds. He said the ice fishing was insane. The species are a little different above and below the falls. You can catch perch, bass, walleye, and even northern pike. His favorite fishing grounds were the lower Niagara, where you catch rainbow trout. He loved the solitude."

"And a case of beer."

"Yeah, that too. Once I asked Mick about his drinking. He was honest and said, 'I pour some vodka in a glass with Diet Coke and sip it. I forget everything and relax.' It didn't sound all that bad. In fact, it seemed pretty good."

She pushed her face against the porthole. "What happens to the fish when they get to the falls?"

"Some go over, get disoriented in the rapids. They can't swim back."

She said, "Does it kill 'em?"

"Most survive. They do better over Horseshoe Falls. Better to go left toward Canada than right around Goat Island. Many of us found that out during the Vietnam War. The American Falls is a rock pile. There was a seven-year-old kid who went over Horseshoe Falls in a lifejacket in 1960."

"Wow. And he made it?"

"Yeah, the *Maid of the Mist* pulled him out with a life ring. His name was Roger Woodward. We were the same age. It was a huge story. They called it the 'Miracle of Niagara.' The irony… he couldn't swim. Everybody was talking about it. It was on *The Today Show*."

"Wow!"

"The kid's father was a construction worker, and they lived in a nearby trailer park. His foreman took Roger and his sister out in a boat to celebrate her seventeenth birthday. Neither one had ever been out on the river and the boat was small and underpowered. They got too far downstream, beyond the point of no return. The boat filled with water, and they capsized in the rapids about a mile above the falls. His sister got pulled out a few feet before she went over Horseshoe Falls near Goat Island. She said it was like swimming in peanut butter. Roger catapulted over the falls, into the mist. The foreman went full force into the deepest part of the river. His body didn't surface for four days."

Vic said, "How do you remember all that?"

"It's especially vivid now that we're here. I can smell the

river. It's lime green after the falls. Its power is mesmerizing and makes you want to jump in."

The pilot announced, "Flight attendants, please prepare for landing."

The wing flaps lowered, creating a dragging sound, and the repetition of a dinging bell annoyed me. Nauseating diesel fumes filled the cabin. I began to sweat. I thought about Mick, how he was being dragged forward by his addiction, how he couldn't swim back. Nobody could reach him, and he was in free fall. He went over, swallowed by the falls. He didn't make it. I remember him best, as others do, as a darling, curious, bright-eyed, seven-year-old boy.

We arrived in Buffalo International at 1 a.m. and picked up the rental car. The Buffalo streets were under siege, as if a great army occupied the city. Subzero temperatures were a curfew foreign to us. A fresh powder of snow hid a treacherous layer of black ice. Both of us were cranky until we got to Armstrong's.

As pledged, Armstrong was waiting. Her huge, yellow house was the only one illuminated on the block. It screamed hospitality and Yuletide season from a dozen windows festooned with wreaths and electric candles. A brightly lit fir sat showcased on the second floor. "PEACE ON EARTH" in six-foot-high neon letters adorned the front lawn.

Armstrong greeted us with warm and cheerful hugs and showed us our quarters in the basement, then insisted we have drinks with her before we retired.

She said, "We have to take some time and catch up. How often do we get to do this?" The house smelled like fresh pine.

She's remained ever-stylish, tall, and slim. She was dressed in a black cashmere sweater, a white shirt, and slim-fitting, gray wool slacks. She put Victoria at ease and started the festivities with Tom & Jerry's.

She said, "Neal, help me. You still don't drink?"

I said, "No, but I'm thinking of taking it up this trip."

"Victoria, Neal always got crazy with the rest of us. And he didn't drink."

"He's on a natural high," Victoria said.

They both laughed and nodded.

It must be a Buffalo thing. Armstrong concocted the Tom & Jerry batter like my father. She directed me to break and separate the eggs. Then she instructed me to add superfine powdered sugar, vanilla extract, and powdered milk. She mixed a heavy dose of brandy with boiling water and folded it into the egg white concoction.

Victoria said, "Let me put the nutmeg on top. That's how my mother did it."

All the fatigue, aches, and worry slipped from our bodies. Time didn't matter. A light dusting of snow covered the church across the street, and lazy, plump snowflakes fell from the black sky.

"Elmwood Avenue," I said. "My father proposed to my mother at Cole's a couple blocks away."

"It hasn't changed much in seventy-five years," Armstrong said.

Her smile was irrepressible and infectious. She glowed under a thick cap of short, coiffed gray hair. It reminded me of when she went through chemo. Her face and spirit always remained bright. The fire began to play tricks on my eyes. Armstrong held up a bottle of Antinori Tignanello Sangiovese.

Vic said, "No need to call me. Pop a cork, and I'll come running."

Armstrong said, "Never underestimate the power of positive drinking."

They were giving each other foot massages at 3 a.m. when I lumbered down the three flights of stairs to the basement. I found my bunk and crashed without brushing my teeth.

# 29 DECEMBER, 6:37 A.M.

## (BUFFALO, NY)

*"The blood of the ancestors flows through the
chain of the generations and binds them in a
great linkage of destiny, beat, and time..."*
Oswald Spengler (1880-1936)

YESTERDAY, I LUXURIATED IN THE shower. The massive head pummeled me like a fire hose. I remembered soakings like this when I was a teenager—full tilt, steam clouding mirrors, turning the bathroom into a Roman spa. Back home, citing the drought, the landlord turned down our water pressure twice. It's a spit shower, quick and perfunctory. I have a friend who collects the shower runoff in a bucket for his garden. He says, "You waste five gallons getting it warm." But here, I can be extravagant and relish the abundance of the Great Lakes. They call it Adam's ale from the lower Niagara, and it cleanses every cleft and crevice. It had been a long time since I had a drenching like this.

As I was shampooing my hair, I felt Vic's breasts press against my back and I hardened in an instant. A warm rush spread from my thighs into my groin. She bent over, and I entered her from behind. We splashed like dolphins.

She said, "Hurry up. We've got to get to Mick's house."

I said, "This feels so good. What's the hurry?"

"I don't think they've made any arrangements for Mick."

I reached out to cradle her pendulous breasts that swung to and fro. I soaped her back and rump. The fracas and fray of our genitals at play drew the best out of me. I was energized, now ready for anything. We embraced full-frontal and our lips sucked, and she pushed me away.

She said, "Hey, we don't have time. Maybe later. We've got to get over there."

Armstrong had coffee brewing. The smell of her famous hot cranberry bread wafted down the back stairwell.

Vic said, "I guess we've got a few minutes."

We dressed and marched up the stairs. As we sat at the kitchen nook, I said, "Looks like everybody's in a pretty cheery mood today."

"You certainly are," Armstrong said. "Be pleasant until ten o'clock in the morning, and the rest of the day will take care of itself."

Vic said, "Who said that?"

"One of Buffalo's early luminaries. Three guesses?"

I said, "How far back? Give me a hint. Somebody recent?"

"Not too recent."

I said, "That rules out Ani DiFranco, Wolf Blitzer, and Tim Russert."

"Much further back."

"I have no idea. What do you think, Vic?"

"How about one of those presidents from Buffalo like Millard Fillmore?"

I said, "Or Grover Cleveland?"

Armstrong said, "Good guess. You're warm. He was famous for his aphorisms and maxims."

I said, "Mark Twain?"

"No, not that far back. Want me to tell you?"

We nodded in unison.

"Elbert Hubbard."

Vic said, "I know that name."

"He started the world-famous Roycroft artisan community in East Aurora," Armstrong said.

I said, "He made barrels of money at Larkin Soap, and for his second act, packaged the best ideas of the nineteenth century. He figured out how to distribute them to the masses."

Armstrong looked at Victoria, "He had a scandalous extra-marital love affair and a child with his lover. It was clandestine, then blew up and became front page news. His wife divorced him, and he married his soulmate. A bit like you two. They died together on the *Lusitania* before the US entered WWI."

Vic said, "My grandmother had a complete set of books called *Little Journeys* from Roycroft."

"That's the one," Armstrong said.

"Grandma lived in Santa Maria," Vic said, "and those books provided much of her education. She cut the pages with a knife as she read. They came with those uncut, untrimmed deckle edges. Many of the pages were still uncut when Grandma died."

Armstrong said, "That's the guy. He also said, 'Don't take life too seriously. You'll never get out of it alive.' "

Vic said, "We need to get going."

Armstrong handed me a long, wooden brush with a plastic scraper and said, "You better get started."

I said, "They gave me an ice scraper with the rental."

She said, "Have you looked outside?"

Vic and I pressed our noses against the tall, second-story windows. The trees and bushes jingled like glass wind chimes. The

Episcopal Church across the street dripped like Antoni Gaudí's La Sagrada Familia. Street signs, poles, and wires had been transformed into ornate ice sculptures.

Armstrong said, "I don't remember what kind of car you have."

I said, "A Prius."

"I hope it starts. Didn't the rental place have a Subaru or something with all-wheel drive?"

I said, "The guy said it wouldn't be a problem."

"Does it have a remote car starter?"

"What's that?"

"You press a button while you're in the house, and the car starts with the heater and defroster on."

"What a great idea. No, but it has a keyless door lock."

"Next time, get one with a remote starter."

Vic said, "Should we stay in?"

"You'll be fine. I've got some clothes that you might like. Give Neal fifteen minutes to scrape and warm up the car."

I said, "Fifteen minutes?"

The snow had transitioned into driving sleet and rain, and then it started snowing again. The Prius looked like an elliptical ice block with frosted, feathery windows. The doors and windows were frozen shut. To my amazement, the doors clicked open when I pressed the key fob. The door groaned like a submarine when I opened it, though. The engine started when I pressed the starter button. I turned on the heat, and the forced air was cold enough to make a penguin shiver. I got out and brushed away the loose snow on the windshield and chipped away at the opaque ice beneath it. I made little progress. I cursed Buffalo. Goddammit. Why would anyone build a city here?

Bam! I fell on my ass. Before I knew it, I was on my back, one of my legs under the car, and I was looking at treetops and a foreboding sky. Layers of clothing, a knit hat, and gloves had padded my fall. Undamaged, I felt ridiculous. Embarrassed, I looked around to see if anyone was witness to my folly. When I got to my feet, I thought, *How many words do I know for cold? Raw, frigid, penetrating, biting, glacial, Siberian?* None were enough. Buffalo inventoried them all and then some. The car sputtered, and I carved a porthole the size of a soccer ball in the driver's windshield. Big puffs of white smoke exited the exhaust pipe.

When Vic got in, she said, "Is this safe?"

I said, "Don't worry. The rest will melt."

I was channeling my father. I thought of him, how he'd refused to clear any more than a peephole on the driver's side. When he drove me to school on winter mornings, the interior was dark like the inside of an igloo. I had no idea where I was or where I was going. I was in his hands. He ran the defroster full blast, sometimes with the windows open. It was very uncomfortable because I was bound up in winter gear, unable to decide whether to zip or unzip my jacket. He insisted the ice and snow would melt, and it did twenty minutes later. He said, "Why waste your time clearing what's going to melt?" I heard his voice in my voice when I spoke to Vic.

The roads were slippery, and the visibility was poor.

Vic said, "To call this weather 'inclement' is an understatement."

I laughed and said, "Believe me, I curse it too."

Vic said, "Yeah, I saw you fall on your ass."

"Weren't you concerned?"

"No, Armstrong said you'd be fine. She said it happens all the time. People slip. She thought we'd embarrass you if we made a big deal out of it."

"She saw it too?"

"Yeah, and Armstrong said so did the neighbors. The lady next door called and asked who you were. We were both laughing so hard I almost peed. Get over it. How do you like my outfit?"

She wore a red, knee-length down parka with fur trim. Under it were the jet-black Buzz City hoodie and the ski mittens from the airport and above, a white Russian fur hat and a giant, check-print wool scarf.

"Is that Armstrong's stuff?"

"Well, most of it, and she has more. She has a whole extra room for clothes and dozens of hats. She said, 'There's no such thing as bad weather, only bad clothing.' "

The road was bumpy with chunks of ice and potholes. Vic pointed at a sign, Scajaquada Expressway, and said, "How do you say that?"

I sounded it out. "Sca-jack-wee-da."

She puffed her lips. "Sca-jack-wee-da. What a strange name. What does it mean?"

"It's named after the creek that runs through here, a Native American name."

"Like Yosemite?"

I nodded.

"How does anybody remember how to pronounce it?"

"They can't. My father, who lived here all his life, never got it right. He called it Ska-dak-it-dee, which always got a laugh."

The bigness of the day was upon us, a blustery wind, a massive, rolling dome of gloomy clouds. It was frigid, still, and dark, like Red Square in winter. I wondered what Vic thought of this jumble of Buffalo historical landmarks so familiar to me. I wished I were young again—nothing behind me, everything ahead. How many times had I traversed Scajaquada? Hundreds, maybe thousands. Now, this worming erosion, a road to nowhere, was to be seen anew through her eyes.

Victoria said, "It's weird this expressway goes right through the middle of the park."

"It sucks. Although, doesn't it remind you of Central Park?"

She smiled. "That's a stretch."

"The same guy designed it. Frederick Law Olmsted."

She giggled. "Ska-dak-it-dee?"

"No, Delaware Park. This is the centerpiece of Olmsted's parkway system."

The car heater had kicked in, and she'd removed her scarf and gloves. I noticed her cheeks were a rush of crimson. Her eyes flashed and bubbled like champagne. I wondered, was this the first time I discerned Vic's eyes were green, not blue?

She said, "Where's the art museum? What's it called?"

"The Albright-Knox, and it's fabulous. We just passed it. It's one of the most influential modern art galleries in the world. People don't realize how incredible Buffalo is..."

She pointed. "What's that?"

"The Buffalo History Museum."

"Cool architecture, like a little Parthenon."

"That's the idea. It's the only thing left from the Pan-American Exposition. Czolgosz's revolver is there."

"Who's Czolgosz?"

"Leon Czolgosz, the guy who shot McKinley."

"How long ago was that?"

"1901."

"That's a long time ago, Neal."

"Buffalo then was like Silicon Valley, more millionaires per capita than anywhere in the country. And it was the fastest-growing city in America, attracting the best and brightest. Promoters even touted the climate and summer breezes off Lake Erie."

She looked out the window. "Never thought of this weather as a selling point."

I objected, "Summers are beautiful here."

"I thought you said it snowed in May."

"Not every year. Buffalo has the sunniest and driest summers of any major city in the Northeast."

"Is that where they got the expression, 'a sucker's born every minute?' "

"That's P.T. Barnum."

"Same era, same idea."

"The Pan Am's when it started."

"What are you talking about?"

"That's when Buffalo's image got scuttled and, to outsiders, even the weather got worse."

She said, "The Buffalo Curse."

"How do you know?"

"Everybody does. I was married to a college quarterback. The Bills lost four Super Bowls in a row. I thought the curse was about the Bills."

"That's just part of it. The curse started long before that. After McKinley got shot at the Pan Am and died six days later, it went downhill. They bungled it, and Buffalo looked puffed up and stupid."

She said, "A failure for the ages."

"Don't rub it in."

"Is that why everybody's so down in the mouth?"

"Nothing ever went quite right for Buffalo after the Pan Am."

"I hate this victim crap." She stretched her neck, turned around in her seat, and said, "What are those spooky towers?"

"That's the Buffalo State Lunatic Asylum, or at least it was. It's a national historic landmark under restoration."

"Lunatic Asylum?"

"That's one of its names. When I was a kid, we called it 'Forest Avenue.' Like in, 'If you don't behave, you're going to Forest Avenue.' It still sends shivers down my spine."

"I can see why. It's scary."

"It's also called the Richardson Olmstead Complex and Buffalo State Asylum for the Insane. In the 1870s, there were no drugs or treatments for mental illness. People were locked away and forgotten. Buffalo was one of the first asylums, a campus, touting fresh air, exercise, and sunlight."

She said, "I read about that in Dorothea Dix's work. Even the rooms were small so people would get out and spend time with others rather than mope around."

"That's it."

"A peaceful refuge, like Calypso."

"Yes, but it didn't stay that way. It devolved into a mental institution that used electroshock and drugged people up on tranquilizers—a horror show. When I was a kid, there were stories about tormented souls hanging from the windows and howling at the moon."

"What's happening with it now?"

"They're turning it into restaurants and a hotel."

"What do you have against Scajaquada?"

"You pronounced it right!"

"It's not that hard, Neal."

"Just that my father never got it. I'm impressed. Don't get me started about Scajaquada. It chopped the park in half, families and businesses were displaced, a thriving community fell into squalor. My father grew up in this neighborhood where they ripped out a mile and a half boulevard of mature elm trees. One of my high school friends died in a motorcycle accident on the ramp near the Niagara River. And there have been lots of tragic accidents."

She said, "That's a shame."

"For years, various civic groups have been trying to get rid of it and restore the park to Olmstead's intent. Other than the name, I have no love for Scajaquada."

We curled along Delaware Lake. I pointed out Michelangelo's *David*, Larry Griffis's *Spirit of Womanhood*, and John Q.A. Ward's *The Indian Hunter*.

I said, "They built Scajaquada in the early sixties, same time the lake freighters stopped calling. My father said, 'The St. Lawrence Seaway shot Buffalo in one foot. Urban renewal projects like Scajaquada shot it in the other.' "

We took the shortcut through the Tudor estates on Nottingham Terrace and cruised the middle-class neighborhoods of North Buffalo. I parked across the street from Mick's house, wedged against a heap of ice and snow.

Vic shimmied across the driver's seat. Once on her feet, she slipped and caught herself, clutching my arm. We both took short steps and stabilized each other while ice crackled under our shoes.

She said, "This is rough. How many months is it like this?"

I shrugged. "This is the beginning of winter."

The aluminum storm door creaked, like it always had, as we entered the back hallway without knocking. A wall of radiant heat hit us like a blast furnace.

Cassie called from the kitchen, "Is that my baby brother and his darling wife from California?"

"Yes," we hollered in unison. We looked at each other and giggled.

Vic whispered, "Shit, here we go."

Cassie added, "Give me a moment. I'm on the phone."

Vic turned and said, "I'm roasting."

We hastily took off scarves, hoodies, hats, and coats and hung them in the narrow corridor.

I said, "It's hotter than two hamsters farting in a wool sock."

Vic broke up and said, "Where did you get that?"

"I've retained a few colorful expressions from North Carolina. A patient used to say it."

She feigned a Southern accent while slipping off a red Christmas vest and said, "It's like a steam bath in here. I'm going to take off clothes civility requires me to keep on."

I said, "You wore that wool vest under your hoodie?"

She nodded. "I'm sweating like a hog."

Both of us kicked off our shoes, convulsing with laughter.

We heard Cassie say, "Hold on," and bark at us, "Don't touch anything. It's under probate," and she returned to her call.

We entered the kitchen. Cassie had enthroned her immensity in the breakfast nook immersed in papers. Her tiny head was tethered to a twenty-five-foot yellow telephone cord stretching from an upright rotary phone on the wall. Her bare feet were planted and knees spread, straining the fabric of her muumuu. She toyed with a pair of gold flip-flops with her twisted toes and pushed them farther under the table near her walker. When she saw us, she pointed her right index finger at the ceiling, motioning that she'd be off the phone soon.

The house smelled like I remembered—a luxurious mix of bacon, eggs, and onions with a hint of boiled hotdog. There was a fine film of dust and grime covering the stove, oven, and adjacent walls.

Cassie said into the phone, "Let me speak to Father Kavanagh then. Tell him it's Cassie from the Islands, Mick Motherwell's sister." She covered the phone with the palm of her left hand and whispered, "Don't disturb anything. You can't take anything from the house." She rested her forearm on the shelf of her protuberant belly.

I studied her features as if she'd acquired an elaborate tattoo. Her once plump face had withered. Her chin was sharp, lips puckered as if drawn tight, like a leather purse. Her once alabaster complexion was ashen. Her head was no longer proportional to her body. It looked like it belonged to someone else. Everything from neck up had mummified as if shrunken by an Amazonian tribe, yet her large body remained stout and unchanged. I concluded that her inevitable decay was taking place from top down.

Her words seemed like bubbles leaking out from under water. I had trouble making sense of anything she said, preoccupied with her physical appearance and fixated on her collagen-depleted lips. I hated her in the same primal way I had when we were children.

And the plight of an unhappy family dynamic revived in an instant.

I gritted my teeth and barked, "What's the big deal? You don't want us to look around? Who put you in charge? And what the fuck is probate?"

She covered the phone again and said, "I'm the executrix, and I didn't say you can't look around, sweetheart. You can't take anything."

She curled her upper lip like my father, already dead three decades. He could rile me without a word. That same surly gesture at the margin of her mouth had resurfaced in her, and it had the same effect. Any rationality I maintained was forfeited. I went lizard brain.

These moments here were rare and precious to me. I knew this would be my last time to explore the house where I grew up. Mick was dead. Mick had kept everything in my mother's house intact after her death two decades ago. He called it "The Museum," and changed nothing. Like an archeological dig, all was intact, covered with layers of slime and dust from twenty years of living. The foundation beneath Mick's mess remained the same. It was the same kitchen table and four burly wooden chairs, with Mick's papers spread across the tabletop. He'd used it as a desk to pay bills. Beneath it was an olive-green tablecloth that matched the color of the fading paint. I visualized my mother cooking and doing dishes while talking on the telephone, her head wedging the receiver to her right shoulder.

Cassie, speaking into the phone, said, "Tell Father Kavanagh I need to speak with him right away. It's urgent."

She was wary of me. I felt her steely blue eyes on my neck. When she completed the phone call, she motioned for me to come and hang up the receiver. She didn't rise to greet us. We stood in an uncomfortable silence. She sat, her feet turned out, supporting the heft of her bulging ankles.

Then there was a ruckus, a rumble at the side door. Pixie arrived. We all listened in silence as if we had a dog's trained ears.

Pixie kicked off her boots, *bam, bam,* then entered the kitchen carrying several frosty plastic sacks of groceries and placed them on the kitchen counter. Her plump cheeks were flushed, blood-red with cold. She said, "Cassie, here's your change. It only cost me seventeen dollars and twenty-two cents. I used coupons." She handed Cassie a twenty, two ones, and a fistful of change.

Cassie said, "Thank you, dear. Let's put those things in the refrigerator and then come join us."

Victoria asked, "How's it going with Mick's memorial arrangements?"

Pixie stopped and put the bags of groceries on the floor. "It's all happening so fast. I'm glad you guys are here."

She started to cry.

Victoria held her hand, then rubbed her shoulders.

Pixie looked up at me. "I love that sweatshirt in the hallway. Is that a wasp? Buzz, Buzz, Buzz. Where did you get it?"

"At the Charlotte airport."

"Oh, I get it, a hornet."

Victoria said, "Getting back to Mick's memorial and burial, over the past couple years, my grandmother, father, and mother died, one right after the other. I know about the mortuary decisions. It takes a lot of planning. Don't let us get in your way. You two must have so much to do."

Cassie's right eyebrow rose and she said, "No, please go on, dear."

Victoria said, "Things like the casket, flowers, church service, wake, online condolences, and reception?"

Pixie looked dumbfounded.

Cassie's face was blank.

Victoria motioned for me to take over Pixie's shoulder rub and stepped forward.

She said, "I can help. I've done this before."

Cassie said, "Good, can you join us at the funeral home tomorrow?"

Victoria looked at me and nodded.

I was grateful she was there. Triggered by Cassie, I was ready to kill.

Victoria took a deep breath, "Are you OK, Neal, driving in the snow?"

Pixie broke free from my backrub and said, "It's too cold to snow."

Victoria said, "Then let's take two cars tomorrow."

Cassie said, "I'll ride with Pixie, and then you won't have to come back to the house. It'll save you some time, sweetheart."

Victoria looked at me. "We don't have chains."

Pixie contorted her face and said, "Chains?"

"In case of snow. For traction. We always do that at Tahoe."

Pixie laughed and replied, "We don't do that here. Chains? They'd wreck the roads, and they're bad enough already."

I said, "Let's take a look around."

Cassie stood, gripping her walker. "You know, darling, you don't need to hang around here. I know you have lots of friends and people you want to see and who want to see you."

"I'd like to look around. Mick kept this place like it was when we were kids. How often do you get to do that?"

Cassie repeated, "You know, Neal, you can't touch anything."

"What is this, a crime scene?"

"No, but this is the way probate works. You can't take anything."

"But it's OK if I look around?"

"Suit yourself if you must, but nothing is leaving this house. An appraiser is coming next week. I've taken pictures. I'll need every dime to settle the estate."

Vic said, "Neal, you promised to take me to Niagara Falls. Can we do that today?"

I said, "I'd like to check out the house."

She dug her fingernails into my arm.

I grimaced. "Ouch!"

"You promised you'd take me to the falls today. Thank you, Cassie. I know what you must be going through. We'll see you tomorrow."

As we dressed in the hallway, out of habit, I opened the sliding cabinet. I spotted a familiar Wiffle ball stained with red mud. My mother and Mick never got rid of anything.

I said, "Hey Vic, look at this. I used to smash this over the back fence."

She said, "Let's go."

I rummaged through scarves, gloves, and knickknacks. Nestled between a black knit hat and a baseball mitt flashed a bottle with a red label. The contents were as bright and clear as mountain water. It was Mick's stash. Holding it by the neck, I raised it above my head like a trophy fish. "Winner and still champion, Mick Fucking Motherwell." I heard Cassie's chair slide and her walker squeak.

She said, "Remember, Neal, this house is under probate. Don't take anything."

I slipped the bottle of vodka into the large exterior pocket of my coat and called, "See you tomorrow, Big One."

She called back, "I've asked you not to call me that. I hate that name."

I replied, "Oh, forgot about that, Biggie." I slammed the heavy wooden door behind us.

The ice crunched under our feet as we walked to the car.

Vic said, "You're making this worse. Why do you want to get in a fight with your sister?"

"What the fuck is probate?"

"Stop yelling. I'm not exactly sure, but it's pretty clear that she doesn't want you or anyone else to take anything from the house."

"Fuck her!"

Vic said, "Pull the car away from the snowbank. I don't want to crawl over the seat."

When I got into the car, the bottle pushed against the hand brake. I pulled it out and read the label. Kamchatka Vodka, 1.75 liters, 80% proof. The seal was unbroken.

Vic said, "We're not going to get through this, Neal, unless you cool it."

I said, "This is the cheap stuff. Mick ate frozen dinners at home, and the same was true for his drinking. He had an expression, 'It all gets you drunk. Why pay more?'"

She said, "You shouldn't have taken it."

I said, "Why can't we take mementos and keepsakes? What could this be worth to anybody? Mick told me he buys this stuff for ten bucks."

She said, "That's not the point. Cassie told us not to take anything."

When I got to the stop sign at the end of the street, I pounded the dashboard and screamed, "He was a drunk. I'm glad he's dead."

We drove to Niagara Falls.

# 30 DECEMBER, 4:05 A.M.

## (BUFFALO, NY)

*"I hate and I love. And if you ask me how,*
*I do not know: I only feel it and I'm torn in two."*
Catullus (c. 84-54 BC)

PARKED IN A MODEST LOT near Burger King. When I opened the door, freezing rain slapped me in the face. Victoria huddled under a shawl. We scrambled, slipping and sliding, toward a sprawling, one-story, red brick building. When I tugged the double-vinyl doors, a fierce blast of wind forced the doors open and I jammed my thumb. When I looked down, the force had shredded my glove.

"Mother of Christ," I muttered.

Vic feigned an Irish brogue and said, "Jesus, Mary, and Joseph."

My thumb hurt like hell, but I mustered a weak smile.

Once inside, a thick stench penetrated every orifice. I was reluctant to remove my hat and coat. The muddled aroma of formaldehyde, old furniture, and cut flowers made both of us gag. Vic looked at my hand and said, "You're not bleeding. It'll be OK. Good thing you wore gloves."

Holding my thumb, I limped up a long empty hallway, Vic a few steps ahead. I noticed two landings, each accessed by a single set of red-carpeted stairs. A maudlin guitar instrumental, "Here, There and Everywhere," played from ceiling speakers.

Out of nowhere, a short, plump man in his mid-forties appeared with blackened hair greased back into a stringy pompadour. He wore a crisp, white shirt that strained the buttons. A short, wide, black tie held by a gold clip rested on his gut. His dark, vested suit looked like it belonged to a younger version of himself.

He said, "If I may introduce myself, I'm Cleve Roberts. I knew the deceased." He shook my hand and winked.

His palm was sticky. He smirked as if he knew something I didn't. He stood too close. I noticed a band of rubbery sweat on his upper lip, and he reeked of a pungent cologne. Dots of white saliva gathered at the corners of his mouth. He dabbed them with a pressed linen handkerchief. He seemed unclear what he should do with his hands.

"It's such a tragedy when someone so young leaves us," he said. "Please join me in the arrangement room."

With excessive hand gestures, he directed us up one of the single stairways. He showed us into a white-walled room with no windows, where we sat in maroon wing back chairs. A print of Matisse's *The Red Madras Headdress* was fastened to an otherwise unadorned wall. It reminded me of my mother when she was young. It had an elaborate gold frame.

He asked, "Can I get you a drink?"

Vic said, "What are you serving?"

"Oh, nothing like that. I'm afraid all I can offer is water or pop."

We declined.

He said, "Do you want to see the body? I assure you, we've

handled Mr. Motherwell's remains with dignity and utmost respect."

Cassie burst into the room, rattling her purse and walker, "Sorry, darlings. I had Pixie stop. I needed a few things."

I said, "Where's Pixie?"

"Parking the car, sweetheart. She dropped me at the door. She'll be right in."

When Pixie entered, red-cheeked and harried, an attendant brought in a folding chair.

Mr. Roberts, situated in a wing-back, rose and said to her, "Would you like mine?"

"Thank you. This is fine." Pixie nodded.

"Let's get right down to business," Cassie said. "We don't have much time. The memorial service is on New Year's Eve. That's all I could get at the church. I want my brother, as would be his wish, to share the family plot at Mount Calvary. His place is alongside our mother. Of course, we want cremation."

Mr. Roberts walked out of the room and returned with a brochure. There were photographs of caskets and urns, but no prices.

Cassie pointed at an ornately sculpted, etched platinum urn. "I like this one. It's masculine, and it suits Mick."

Mr. Robert's said, "That's one of our most popular departure vessels. The other day, the family of a WW II vet who earned the Purple Heart selected it."

"Darling, would you be an angel and project how much this will cost?"

Mr. Roberts wrote down a number on a piece of paper and handed it to Cassie.

She gasped.

He said, "He'll also need a casket."

Cassie puckered her face and flushed. "Why does he need a casket if he's cremated?"

"There must be a vehicle to convey the remains."

Cassie looked around the circle. With an awkward grimace, she said, "I guess we don't need anything too elaborate. Do we?"

"It will be his final resting place," Mr. Roberts said.

"Oh well, then how much is this going to cost?"

"It's hard to tell. Each item is separate."

We looked at each other.

Mr. Roberts rose from his chair and left the room. When he came back, he handed Cassie another piece of paper.

She gasped and shook her head. "This far exceeds the funds at my disposal. Can we get something nice but cheaper?"

Mr. Roberts said, "A good part of that cost is to excavate the gravesite and inter Mr. Motherwell's cremains."

Cassie grimaced. "Do you have to dig a grave? Can't you slip it in the ground without undoing everything?" She winked. "Isn't it something we could do ourselves?"

The haggling continued for fifteen minutes, and Mr. Roberts retreated. He came back with a sheet of paper. It showed a plastic bag and cardboard box for the ashes. He assured Cassie the charge would be nominal. All Cassie's hopes of interning Mick in our mother's grave vanished.

Mr. Robert's said, "There will be a charge for the inurnment. Who will take the cremains?"

"I will," Pixie blurted.

Cassie, Victoria, and I looked at each other in agreement.

Cassie said, "Thank you, dear."

Mr. Roberts said, "Do you want to view the deceased?"

Victoria, Cassie, and Pixie shook their heads.

The funeral director's pasty smile had vanished. He frowned at the negative response.

I said, "Is Mick here?"

He said, "Yes. We have refrigeration units in this facility licensed by the State of New York. We embalmed and dressed him last night."

Pixie said, "I saw Mick after he died. I can't do it again, and he didn't look like Mick. He was so bloated and blue. Eeew!" Her eyelids flickered, and her lips squeezed tight as if she were eating something very sour.

The mortician said, "I assure you, we've concealed whatever putrefaction has taken place. We have skilled hands. He is ready for viewing." Mr. Roberts stood erect as he spoke with the pride of a conscientious craftsman. "I assure you it will not be like that. The deceased, in my professional opinion, is ready for visitation."

Cassie said, "Who permitted you to embalm and prepare his body? How much does that cost?"

He replied, "It's standard procedure. We intend to arrange all the obsequies. In answer to your question, yes, this has incurred another cost. We were not aware that you did not want to use our facility for a formal visitation. Chef Motherwell was a notable member of the western New York community. People will want to mourn his passing. Disappointment will prevail if there is no viewing, and it's not too late to change your mind."

Cassie said, "No, no. We don't want that."

"As executrix of his estate, it's up to you to decide."

"No, nothing like that. Please spare all expenses."

"Ms. Motherwell, I assure you, you will receive an itemized accounting of all our services."

I wanted to see Mick. The last conversation was so harrowing. I hoped he'd died well. How I'd miss him, and this would be the last time.

I asked, "May I see him?"

"That's why we prepared the body."

As Mr. Roberts led me down the stairs, I noticed a heart-shaped port-wine stain birthmark like the one on Cassie's arm, on the back of his neck. I had second thoughts entering the stark florescent lights of the basement and the thick stench of formaldehyde. The air was so close. It brought back an unpleasant memory.

I stumbled.

He said, "You OK? You're too big for me to pick you up off the floor."

I said, "I'm fine."

Years ago, when I was a paramedic in Florida, I became friendly with the medical examiner. He'd invited me, an eager student, to attend autopsies. I went to dozens and did fine. But there was an eleven-year-old girl who had died of a fatal skull fracture riding her bike, and when the medical examiner lifted her skull flap, everything went gray. I couldn't keep my eyelids open and broke into a cold sweat. I braced myself from falling and sprawled out on a stainless steel gurney.

As Mr. Roberts and I walked downstairs, I questioned what brought me here to view the remains of my brother. There had always been a competitive, aggressive edge between us. The cruel sadist most often surfaced in me when I was with him. Was I now the victor, like Achilles dragging Hector's dead body behind his chariot? My good soldier, my rival, now defeated.

Mr. Roberts said, "He's here at the end of this hallway."

Light-footed, he waltzed through a labyrinth of smaller rooms with stainless steel refrigerators. I followed. Mick was on his back as if sleeping. He had a serene smile. His honey-colored hair was combed to the side, and he was dressed in a three-piece suit.

I said, "All Mick needs is his chef's hat."

"We can provide one, but there's no need as there won't be a visitation."

It was Mick, but a different Mick without a beating heart and an overactive, agitated brain. He no longer needed to tamp down his anguish with alcohol. It was my dear baby brother who had challenged me at every turn. The brother I hated. The brother I loved. The brother I wanted dead. The brother I wanted alive. It was Mick, who had lied and cheated. Mick, who had made me laugh.

His features were swollen, as Pixie had reported. Restoration employing various waxes, creams, and plaster did wonders, though. Mick had swelled to three hundred pounds. His kidneys couldn't keep up with the toxins his body produced, and his liver failed. The official cause of death was a heart attack, but that was the tip of the iceberg.

There's a turbulent river that runs alongside this city. Twenty percent of the earth's fresh water squeezes through its tip, a mile-wide corridor. For thirty-six miles, it rumbles, rages, and roils. Near the end, rapids conclude in the thunder of Niagara Falls. The kidneys, like Niagara, control one-fifth of the heart's flow. Mick's flow was now ended. He loved Buffalo, and had vowed never to leave. His spirit is now free to ramble and roam these enormous glacial freshwater seas.

I wanted to touch him. Put my lips on his forehead. Hold him, embrace him, wish him peace in this farewell. The only child I ever reared, fretted about, and felt responsible for. I knew he'd departed, and his body was all I had left. Brothers, as do all siblings, share one hundred percent of their parents' DNA. If he were my child, it would only be half. Part of my package washes away with him. Where does the spirit go when the body dies? When these eternal lovers separate and flee? Beyond this life, do the body and the soul remember who the other was? Or do they march off oblivious? How do we navigate such divergent and disassociated waters?

To be honest, Mick looked better dead than alive. The last time I saw him, he was pale and puffy, his skin mottled. Diabetes had taken its toll. His feet tingled, and his toes couldn't distinguish hot from cold. A series of unsuccessful abdominal hernia operations had left him crippled. He had no stamina and bellowed a litany of aches and pains. He resented the gastric bypass operation that had shriveled his stomach and stolen his enjoyment of food. His agitation palpable, his moods dark, troubled, and confused, he never left the clutter of his house.

Yet even at his worst, he was good for a laugh. Mick found a way to laugh and to make me laugh. And I wanted to laugh with him again. As he lay before me, I could hear his antics. I wanted to joke with him. His high jinks were hysterical. He made up words and frittered with sounds. He loved to laugh and would drag me kicking and screaming into his powerful current. Alcohol was the only vehicle he had left. It was the only thing that rescinded the pain.

In Buffalo, the river never freezes. There's always snow or rain. Dark clouds never leave for long. Looking at Mick, I contemplated the most complicated relationship I'd ever had, and I was dry. Like at my mother's grave, I found no tears.

The funeral director said, "Are you ready?"

I replied, "Give me another minute."

"Take your time."

I needed to touch Mick. Like Doubting Thomas in the Bible, it required putting my fingers in his wounds. I pressed my lips to his forehead. Still, no tears. His skin felt hardened and cold, like my mouth pressed to a boulder, tossed aside by the ice age on Lake Erie's shore. There was no awkward smell. No seaweed. No gulls clacking. No blood traversed his veins. No haunting fog whistles blew. No arrival of ocean-bound craft. The lighthouse remained dark at Point Abino.

I pressed my cheek against his chest. No heartbeat. All his pain and suffering were gone. How have I survived this life, and why?

I said, "What about the tattoo?"

He stammered and said, "Oh, yes, the tattoo. It's near the amputated left ankle, correct?"

"Yes, on the left."

"Would you like to see it?"

"Well, yes, I would. Would that be too much trouble?"

"Trouble? Not at all. He won't mind." He snickered, and out-poured an involuntary snort.

He pulled off a black patent leather shoe held in place by a stumpy wooden pole and covered by a cuffed pant leg. As he pushed the pant leg up, the amputated bone became visible and was not the gory mess I'd anticipated. There was no blood. The wound was dry.

I asked, "How did you do that? Shouldn't the embalming fluid ooze and seep like blood? The amputation was only a few days ago."

"Everything congealed after he died. There was no open wound. Also, we have a few tricks of the trade, hemostatic agents and stuff like that." He nodded with half-closed eyes.

I said, "Amazing."

He said, "At the visitation, the amputation would have gone unnoticed, except to the trained eye."

And there it was before my eyes. The tattoo was intact: blueberry-blue, tall, cursive letters, "MOTHER." The surgeon had spared it.

The funeral director said, "Had enough? Don't you think it's time for us all to go home?"

I nodded.

With deliberate steps, we walked through the chambers. I could hear the loud *clunk* of our heels on the hard cold concrete floor.

He said, "The cremation is tomorrow."

I climbed the stairs behind the last human to be intimate with my brother's body. "What happens then?"

"We'll put the cremains in the lined cardboard box Ms. Moth-erwell ordered and give them to his fiancée."

I wondered if this was all Pixie would receive. So devoted to Mick through the worst of it. I'd asked Mick before he died if

Pixie would get the house. He said, "Cassie will take care of her. I promise you that."

Mr. Roberts switched off the lights at the top of the stairs. We entered the upper hallway with piped-in Muzak. This time, a clunky instrumental of Chicago's "Colour My World."

I visualized Mick at my grandmother's Chickering piano in the living room. He played a few bars by ear and had a deep heart-felt baritone like Terry Kath. He'd been playing that basic deliberate piano riff since he was three, and he whistled the flute solo. Mick, the performer, like Terry Kath, always touched the heart.

It was my birthday, 1978, when the shocking, senseless news of Terry Kath's death became known. Kath was playing around with a semiautomatic 9 mm pistol he thought wasn't loaded and blew his brains out. He was thirty-one. Chicago almost disbanded and never recovered the spark. Unlike the others in the band, Kath was self-taught. Jimi Hendrix said he was the best guitarist he ever saw.

The embalmer said, "It was a long night. I'm going home."

I blurted, "How do you know Mick?"

He said, "I ran around. Who *didn't* know Mick?" There was a smoky satisfaction on his face. He looked like he was sniffing a fond but forgotten memory. He said, "But those days are over. I knew him at the meetings."

"Meetings?"

"I've taken an oath of confidentiality. I can't talk about it. Mick was a funny guy. Let's get out of here."

Victoria was waiting in the arrangements room, looking at her iPhone. Pixie and Cassie had gone. She said, "How'd it go? I'm glad I didn't go down there."

I said, "The tattoo's intact."

"How could that be?"

"The surgeon didn't take it."

"You should have snapped a photo."

I said, "Oh well. Too late."

Victoria stood on her tiptoes, embraced me, and kissed my right cheek. The tenderness of her voluptuous body against mine aroused me. We fit. The deft placement of her sensitive hands on my shoulders reminded me I am alive. She smelled clean and fresh in opposition to the morgue smells. Is this where we all go after we die? A basement with fluorescent lights and humming stainless steel refrigerators? Then on to an incinerator or grave? Life doesn't end well for anyone.

Our shoes left soft impressions in the feather-like snow as we walked to the car. Plump, gussied up snowflakes fell like fat bridesmaids from the sky. Vic opened her mouth and called out, "Got one."

Melted snow covered her forehead and cheeks.

I said, "How do you do it?"

"Do what?"

"Make peace with Cassie."

She said, "You'll never settle anything by hurting someone's feelings."

The snow whirled on the ground like dancing angels, and she reached out her gloved hand. Gripping my bare hand tight, we walked to the car. I noticed a traffic jam at Burger King, where tempers flared. An overstuffed, middle-aged man in the drive-through, half out of his car, yelled, "Get the fuck out of my lane." I gawked, and he glared back at me.

Victoria tugged and pulled.

He yelled, "What the fuck you looking at?"

We bent our heads and bustled to the car.

We drove toward downtown on Delaware Avenue. The British burned Buffalo to the ground during the War of 1812, which gave rise to a radial street and grid system. It branches out like bicycle spokes. Delaware meanders through circles, parks, monuments, and neighborhoods by design, much like Washington, DC.

The wind picked up and the soft, engorged snow bunnies transitioned into a fierce, unrelenting blizzard. Gone was the crisp, sunny dreamscape of Squaw Valley or Yosemite. Wet, massive, icy clumps collected on the windshield. The wipers flailed. Blocks of slush collected and thumped in the wheel wells.

Victoria said, "Shouldn't we pull over? Why don't these people use chains?" She dug her fingers into my forearm when a large van passed and nearly sideswiped us.

I said, "We're almost there. This isn't unusual. People keep on trucking in Buffalo."

# 31 DECEMBER, 4:09 A.M.

## (BUFFALO, NY)

*"I'm never not going to be a guy from Buffalo."*
Sal Capaccio (1973- )

▌**I**T'S BEEN A LIFETIME OF Christ since I've been there."
"That's exactly why you should go," Armstrong said.
"It makes me sad."

Armstrong flipped a piece of cranberry bread onto my plate that emitted a savory puff of steam.

I broke off a crust and washed it down with a swig of orange juice.

As she poured herself a second mug of coffee, she said, "Let's do it. It'll be a road trip."

At first, I thought, *Like the old days, Armstrong always up for an adventure.* Or was she trying to divert me from going to the house? Had Vic talked to her about Cassie?

I gazed out the window from her breakfast nook. A white, snow-crusted surface outlined black asphalt streets.

She said, "Deadline, we should go. We can wait for Victoria to wake up, and she can go too."

"How long would it take?"

"It's just over the bridge. We'll be there in fifteen minutes."

"Even in the snow?"

"Yes, there's less traffic this time of year. All the lanes are open. I go all the time."

I said, "I want to spend some time at Mick's place."

"From what I heard, that might not be such a good idea."

"What do you mean?"

"Vic told me your sisters are paranoid that you're going to take something."

"All I want to do is check the place out."

"The trip over the bridge won't take long. You can go to Mick's later."

We sat in comfortable silence for fifteen minutes and spread out the *Buffalo News*. The paper had been on her doorstep since five that morning, and the newsprint was cold and crisp. I perused the sports page and stumbled into the local news. Two headlines captured my attention. The first, "One dead after a late-night shooting in Tonawanda," seemed routine, like something you might read in the locals of Detroit, Cleveland, or Chicago. The second, "Pizza delivery person robbed at gunpoint," felt unique, like something that could only happen in Buffalo. At midnight, a robber brandishing a gun took off with a pizza, cash, and a cell phone. The pizza delivery person, no gender disclosed, was carrying $17.23 and was not hurt. The thief remains at large, but the police recovered the pizza and cell phone.

I said, "There's a criminal on the loose. Got away with $17.23 and left the pizza and cell phone behind."

"That kind of stuff happens all the time around here. It's dangerous to go out alone even during the day," Armstrong said.

The smell of fresh coffee collided with nutmeg and cinnamon. I remembered my mother turning out dozens of fruitcakes in a production line. The fragrance of candied fruits, butter, coconut, maple, vanilla, and cake batter filled the air. Armstrong's meticulous holiday trimmings brought it all back.

Armstrong stood and started to tidy the kitchen.

I said, "What's the hurry?"

She said, "Check in with Victoria. See if she wants to go. Remember to bring your passports."

I descended the narrow back stairway. The furnace growled and pinged. Victoria was lights out in the bedroom with her head covered with a pillow.

I whispered, "Do you want to go to Canada?"

She didn't move, then rolled and said in a husky voice, "What time is it?"

I replied, "Seven-thirty."

She said, "Enjoy yourself. See you when you get back."

I said, "There's plenty of food. Armstrong made cranberry bread."

"Yeah, I can smell it."

I said, "There's fresh coffee upstairs, and the kitchen door to her place is open."

She managed a faint reply, "I can smell the coffee too. Thanks."

I found my passport, then bounded up three flights of stairs. Entering the kitchen, I said, "Victoria's staying."

"How's she doing?"

"Drained."

"Better she sleeps, then. Let's take my car. I've got a bridge pass. Do you have your passport?"

I gave her a thumbs up.

The frigid air snapped me to attention when I opened the front door. When we got to the garage door, the metal runners were ice-locked. I gave it several violent shakes before it yielded. Wood chips and flecks of yellow paint littered the fresh surface of snow.

Armstrong said, "Don't worry about it. They'll paint it."

The blue leather seats in her BMW were stiff and crunched when we sat.

She said, "They'll warm up. I turned on the butt-warmers."

My thick, brown corduroys were no comfort. It felt like my ass and thighs were bare.

I said, "What about the remote car starter?"

"I didn't think it was cold enough for that. I should've used it so you could check it out."

As she turned the key, *vroom, vroom,* the engine shuddered and refused to start. She tried again and it spat and sputtered with the same result.

I said, "Maybe we should hold off and do this another time."

Suddenly, as if on cue, Bavarian engineering prevailed. Armstrong's Beemer roared like a lion and sustained its intention.

She shimmied her shoulders and said, "This baby *always* starts."

White fumes and blue vapor expelled from the exhaust. With a heavy foot, she punched the coupe through a slim alley. We fishtailed and spun toward the three-story house next door. I rocked forward and braced myself, and we came to an abrupt stop at a dirty pile of snow left by the plow at the curb.

Clutching the dashboard, I said, "You almost hit that house."

Tossing her hair, she said, "I do this all the time."

I said, "That was too close. What's up with the alley?"

"It's the neighbors' driveway."

"So, your driveway connects with theirs?"

"It's a horseshoe-shaped driveway. I use it as a turnaround."

I loosened my grip and said, "But it's so narrow. You couldn't open a car door if you tried."

"The neighbors' garage connects to the house. They never get out of their car in the alley."

I said, "My grandfather had something like that. The garage

floor was a Lazy Susan and turned the car around, which seems a little safer."

Her roadster jerked forward and she said, "But not as much fun. There's no skill in that."

My heart was pounding. It felt like we'd navigated the Strait of Messina.

Within minutes, the battered majesty of the Peace Bridge jutted out above the bleak landscape. The sky, as always in December, was dark, threatening, and dreary. The Beemer hugged patches of black ice, and Armstrong locked a course along the riverbank like a race car driver at the Indianapolis 500. The heater rumbled and blew a robust gust of hot air. Frost and fog gathered on the windshield. Suddenly, I was sweating, belching, producing gobs of saliva, and felt an urge to vomit. I loosened my scarf, unbuttoned my coat, and pulled off my gloves. I focused on weathered and dilapidated buildings along the river. They reminded me of Venice from the Grand Canal. This spot, like the city of the Doge, possessed dignity. Though dingy and worn-down, it remains elegant, stunning, like a grande dame entering a ballroom in regal robes. The air was sharp, biting, and clear. I rolled down the window. The discomfort of being confined had overwhelmed me.

When I was small, my mother bundled me up in a snowsuit, scarf, boots, and gloves and pushed my father and me out the door. He never objected and accommodated her every whim. He told his customers, "I'm getting Neal out of Bernice's hair." Even as a five-year-old, I couldn't get my arms around it. How was I in my mother's hair? Like a buffalo, corpulent and well-insulated, my father possessed an immunity to the cold. He never buttoned his knee-length, wool overcoat. Even in subzero temperatures, he wouldn't use the car heater. He drove with a cracked window. He took me to lunch counters along the docks, train depots, seedy warehouses, and bars. I was his shadow, and he was proud to have me along. He called me "Champ." He even took me on cold calls, awkward and every salesperson's nightmare. With the gift of gab and familiarity, he handled most with aplomb. He was a natural salesman, big on small talk, remembering people's names and essential things about their lives. He made every client feel important although, even as a five-year-old, I sensed fraud and loathed him for it. It was so easy for him to bend and manipulate, then he'd build on it. I grew to hate him, and it embarrassed me how easy it was for him to pander.

Armstrong, sensing my distress, said, "Do you want me to turn the heater down? I can turn it off."

I nodded, and she flipped a switch and cracked her window.

Within seconds I sat up, revived, feeling better.

I said, "My grandfather made his fortune smuggling booze across this river."

"Prohibition was good for a lot of people in this town."

I shrugged and said, "They used small boats, undetectable to the authorities. I read somewhere that Woodrow Wilson vetoed the Volstead Act, but not because he was against alcohol. He didn't think anybody could enforce it."

"You got that right. And thank goodness, when the bridge opened in 1927, there was no way to keep alcohol out. It depends on how you look at it."

As we careened along the loping bends of the river, she pointed at the water intake, a round brick and concrete, red-roofed dome at the channel's center. It looks like it's moving because the water splashes white along its sides.

Armstrong observed and said, "Nothing matters more to a city than clean water." She paused, "And booze."

"Is that where slaves crossed?"

"No, that's farther down toward the falls, where the Rainbow Bridge is today."

"Slaves and booze, the story of the United States."

She said, "And of this river."

When I was a child, I was captivated by this very spot, where the Great Lakes squeeze their broad shoulders through a precarious strip and dash toward the Niagara Escarpment. The water roils and passes swiftly, enough to turn back the most competent swimmer. It's dangerous and violent, even on fair days. To a boy, it foreboded a storm, a prelude to the cataclysmic main event, Niagara Falls, a storm that never ceases.

I said, "Mr. Volstead made my granddaddy a millionaire."

She looked at me. "We're back to booze."

"The Eighteenth Amendment financed a legitimate business."

She said, "So after prohibition, he was flush?"

"Depression-proof."

While my grandfather prospered in his relationship with the river, it filled my father with thirst, cravings that wealth and success in business couldn't satisfy. He, too, traversed the Niagara in a small vessel. He was in utero—the son of an unmarried, nineteen-year-old Irish schoolgirl. When I acquired his birth records years later, I found a box checked "Illegitimate," and it hit home because that's how he approached his life. He felt misbegotten and responded to others in kind. He never grasped that he had the right to be here like everybody else. His most persistent message to me was, "Make people like you." And he tried extra hard.

When he married my mother, he'd weighed a hundred and fifty pounds. Within eighteen months, he'd ballooned to three hundred. My mother had wanted everyone to eat. She served enormous portions at each meal, and snacks were always available. She'd place a bulky, two-and-a half-inch-thick cold cut sandwich on rye, called a "Dagwood," slathered with mustard in front of me, and say, "That's not enough for you. You're still hungry." It was futile to protest, and she'd scamper to prepare another. Any time of day when friends came around, she'd roll out an enormous repast and serve until everyone felt stuffed. My father had aimed to please. His obligation was to eat the food she prepared, and he'd carried his burden in extra cargo and never fell short of that responsibility. His obesity was the butt of jokes, which he handled with generosity. He said, "If people don't tease you, it means they don't like you." He skirted the corners of ridicule from strangers and friends alike. He understood at his core that his work as a salesman required accommodation and agreement. He was a binge drinker, vodka and Coke, like my brother. The Irish river of blood runs deep. My father had been a bastard in the real sense of the word. Or a "love child." Depends on how you look at it.

His biological mother's residence was Fort Erie, Ontario. She'd transferred to a church-run hostel in Buffalo to have her baby adopted at birth by a German American architect and his disagreeable and barren wife. Their unhappy marriage had been prearranged by Buffalo's German community. I have no idea what happened to his biological mother. I've checked ship records and never found a clue.

He'd been an only child and treated more like a servant than a legitimate member of the family. There's an impulse to suspect that the German architect sired him, but my DNA supports a pure strain of blood that both his biological parents were Irish.

Armstrong's face twisted, and her gloved hands gripped the wheel. Semi-trailers stacked the third lane, waiting for inspection. We headed in the opposite direction unobstructed. The fast-flowing water hypnotized me, just like it had when I was a kid. I stretched my neck and, farther downstream, located the International Railroad Bridge. As we approached the center, three flags fluttered on either side—the stars and stripes, the sky-blue flag of the United Nations, and the red Canadian maple leaf.

I said, "When we were kids, we'd shout at the top of our lungs, "America, America, America, No Man's Land, Can-a-da."

She said, "We did too. We called the middle, Gonam's lamb."

"Gonam's lamb?"

"When my little brother said no man's land, it came out

Gonam. My father added the lamb, and it became a family joke. Gonam's lamb." She shifted her mouth and smiled.

I said, "You're shittin' me."

"Got you! You haven't changed a bit, Deadline. Gullible as ever."

I said, "What about the fish? Which side are they on?"

"They've got dual citizenship and circulate through Gonam's lamb." As we approached the Canadian border, she said, "You've got your passport, right?"

I rummaged through my pockets and backpack and began to sweat.

She said, "You have to have it now when you cross. Not like before."

It turned up deep in the pocket of the winter coat, wrapped in my shredded leather glove. I said, "Got it."

We waited in a line behind half a dozen cars. When our turn came, we rolled onto a tilted concrete slab with mirrors at ground level.

The Canadian border officer squinted. "Where are you going?"

Armstrong said, "Fort Erie."

"What's your business there?"

"To walk around, reminisce. My friend used to live there."

Pointing at me, he said, "What about you? Where are you from."

I said, "Gonam's lamb," and giggled.

He pursed his lips.

Armstrong said, "What he means, Officer, is Gorham Road in Fort Erie. That's where his family had a summer place."

"How long will you be?"

"An hour or two."

"Bringing anything with you?"

We both shook our heads, and he handed us our passports and waved us through.

As we pulled away, Armstrong said, "You can't do that any-more. It's much worse on the American side. Don't even think about it on the way back. They keep people stranded for hours."

When crossing this bridge, one submits. For the next fifteen minutes, Armstrong and I rode in silence. Though the language is the same, the landscape and temperament are not. Even squirrels have black coats rather than gray. Why is crossing this turbulent body of water so mind-altering? A rural rather than urban land-scape unfolds, forests of wet, leafless trees scattered with pine line the highway—a single house, a field, a farm, miles between inter-secting roads. And distance and speed are not measured in miles but kilometers. Here one enters a bleak, scant landscape, frozen and bare—frost on the windshield, frigid air whisking outside the car windows.

And this morning, back in Buffalo, where I'm writing, no one is awake. I'm sitting in the living room in a stuffed yellow chair, my feet on an ottoman, notebook on my lap. Peace and quietude prevail—time to follow the thread back to Melrose.

My mother's family had a summer place on the Canadian shore, located on the first beach across the border with a panoram-ic view of downtown. Extended family and friends decamped their city homes and descended on Fort Erie between June and September.

Grandfather had bought the property in the 1930s and chris-tened it, "Melrose." I've never discovered why. My parents and sisters called it the "Beach Place," "Mel," or "Canada." A vast disjointed rustic ramble, it was a panacea for a seven-year-old boy. Each generation made its contribution. Uncle Ernst had dug a funky outdoor swimming pool with a mud-menaced deep end. Not to be outdone, his brother, Sigi, had plowed a patch of dirt, conceived as a tennis court. Sunburnt, eroded, overrun with weeds, it sported a ragged net, neglected and never used. Uncle Artie had assembled a rope swing on a sickly elm attached to the bladder of a hot water bottle. The fart-like sound it made was so embarrassing, nobody would use it. He did his best to entice newcomers to try his whoopee cushion.

On the lake, there was a rickety dock with a dinghy. Melrose slept sixteen, with lodging for a half dozen more stragglers in high season. The rooms were slotted, like boxcars. The accommodations were stark with little ornamentation. We slept in single, damp beds, and there was only one bathroom with running water and a shower. There was a privy outside. We often took a bar of soap that doubled as shampoo to the lake.

Melrose was the antithesis of everything on the other side and only minutes away. Unlike my grandparents' place in the city, Melrose was freewheeling and never formal. It was self-service, no maid or driver on the premises. Everybody was welcome, including distant relatives, friends, and their friends. The first time I saw my grandfather smile was at Melrose. Also, he hadn't been wearing a three-piece suit. He'd sported an open, wide-collared linen shirt and baggy, gabardine pleated slacks. I'd never seen his neck before. His stern role as family patriarch seemed suspended. For years, I've hunted through family archives for a photo of him at the beach and never found one. The images left behind depict him as a shrewd Teutonic businessman, always in a tailored suit, pressed shirts with cuff links, vest, and signature striped bow tie.

Best of all, Melrose encouraged creativity. For kids as well as adults, it provided a loose and comfortable playground. Inventiveness was the top priority. Whether a project failed was irrelevant. Grandpa said, "Nothing goes to waste." The aim was to devise something offbeat, unconventional, and fun. Most everything was handmade. Grandfather had fashioned an enormous, whale-shaped latch that secured the front door. As a carving, it was a masterwork sculpted from a single piece of maple with a mirror-like lacquer finish. But it stuck and took two adults to lift. More often than not, everyone used the side door. In the living room, he'd installed an elaborate pulley system attached to the windows. The cables were frayed, tangled, and jammed. We conventionally opened the windows. Yet when he showed someone around, he proudly included both contraptions in the tour. He also conceived a lever window system in the attic. More successful with that try, it cooled the entire house on sticky summer days.

At Melrose, we woke to the smell of grease, butter, eggs, maple syrup, waffles, and pancakes. We ate sweet corn and juicy, red, ripe tomatoes from the garden and nearby farms. Neighbors sold vegetables at stands along the road. On rainy and foul days, adults played pinochle. My introduction to capitalism was at Melrose. Children absorbed themselves in marathon board games like Monopoly, Risk, and Careers. Grandmother was of the mindset, "Children are to be seen, not heard." Most of the time, kids moved among adults, but after dinner, she enforced strict segregation. The jokes and laughter from the other room got louder and raunchier. I'd craved to be part of it.

For a seven-year-old, it had been a Garden of Eden. On hot, humid nights, we'd slept on a wraparound screened porch that faced Lake Erie. Crickets and frogs chirped and filled the quiet spaces. The funky, dense smell of green algae permeated the stagnant night air. More stars than I could count filled the sky, and I discovered the Milky Way. Canada offered solitude, offbeat summer houses on deserted gravel roads. Some days, I'd swing for hours on a thick hemp rope that hung high from an enormous oak tree.

For me, though, the attraction was primordial. Two big concrete balls on square brick pillars formed an entryway to the lakefront. There were sandy fields spotted with tall grasses, wildflowers, and butterflies. Every nook buzzed with bees, ants, grasshoppers, beetles, and bugs. That's where I'd spent my time.

All the better if a stray dog tagged along. I savored the speechless company and wandered armed with a glass jar, collecting every living thing that crawled, slithered, or hopped. The earliest memory that still returns in dreams is poking plump, speckled fish eggs. They jiggled in the pock-holed granite reef, and my bare feet were bruised and bleeding, cut by the sharp corners of stone. If I only had one more day, that's where I'd spend it. We, the well-off white children of the Anthropocene, knew our fortuitous endowment. The industrial sprawl that paid for it lay at a safe distance across the water.

Armstrong said, "A penny for your thoughts?"

I looked up and noticed heavy condensation on the car windows with dripping streaks.

I said, "I'm thinking about the summer."

She said, "That's what everybody thinks about around here in winter."

"Do you remember my grandfather's place, Melrose?"

"Sure, the big house that burned down at Waverly Beach. Never been there, but I know lots of folks who have."

"That's what I was thinking about."

She asked, "What happened?"

"After my grandfather died, my grandmother began to drink. She fell, broke her hip, and never recovered."

"What do you mean?"

"She deteriorated, ended up in a nursing home for twenty years. Declared mentally incompetent."

"Is that why they sold the place?"

"The family sold it when I was nine. There was a big kerfuffle, and things were never the same again. The place burned down ten years after they sold it."

"I know how that goes. What were you thinking about?"

"Lizards, toads, frogs, beetles, snakes. I stalked everything that moved. The jar got cloudy, and black beetles died. I watched them with fascination, and it was like a gas chamber—a final dance and twirl. Like watching a fighter get knocked out, or a bull die in the ring. I'd pull them out and prod them with my fingertip to see if they could still crawl. Some did. I was their private audience and executioner."

"Boys will be boys."

"I loved to squish fish eggs on the reef. I was a destructive little boy. There were lots of flying green insects that chattered and coiled like rubber bands. I'd fall on them like a cut tree trunk. Timber. What a surprise when I felt the spiny movement of two grasshoppers cupped in my hands under my chest and belly. I liked to hold grasshoppers with my thumb and index finger on their sides and then toss them in the air and watch them fly. I always wondered where these high-fliers went in winter?"

"They're in Santa Barbara," she said.

"What made you come back, Strong?"

"When I couldn't get Lars to settle down any one place, I felt like I had stability here. My brother and his family live here. And I could afford it."

"Sure a big change from San Francisco."

"Also, I wasn't sure I wanted to go back to work in the hospital. That's the short of it. We'll talk later."

"It's amazing how well you've adjusted."

"Buffalo is home, and I love it here. It's the right combination of city and country."

I said, "Do you know what cured me of torturing insects?"

"Reform school?"

"Have you ever seen a praying mantis?"

"They're all over the place here in summer."

"At Melrose, one night after dinner, my father and some of my uncles were standing outback near a post and rail wooden fence. They were very quiet and whispering. I bounded out to meet them like an overzealous cocker spaniel, and they shushed me. They were watching something. It was one of those warm nights when it's comfortable in shirt-sleeves. The cool air hadn't settled in yet."

"Yeah, so what happened?" she said.

"I felt a presence I hadn't encountered before, then I saw what they were looking at—a huge, green insect hanging motionless on the fence. When I reached out to touch it, my dad pulled my hand away. He explained that praying mantises were helpful, not a nuisance, and they don't bite but eat annoying pests like mosquitoes and blood flies. He said it wasn't something to swat, trap, or kill. If you killed it or hurt it in any way, it would rain. In the worst way, I wanted to pick it up, hold it, own it, and make it my own. Like a shimmering, big, lethargic grasshopper, it glistened on the fence. I wanted to capture it like all the others. I wanted to put it in a jar."

"Did your dad stop you?"

"No, something shifted in me first. When I look back, it was at that very moment when my life became twisted and more complicated. Pancreatic cancer took my grandfather without warning that winter and that was my last at Melrose. My summer of mantis—tall, green fields, frogs, toads, fish eggs, and clattering wings."

She said, "We're here. There's the point. Let's get out and walk."

We parked near an abandoned building near the shore. It was bleak, washed out, colorless like a black and white photo.

She said, "That's the old dance hall that burned down."

I said, "Why does everything burn down around here?"

"That's true, we have a lot of fires."

A broken fence and frozen sidewalk led to the shore.

She said, "Walk over here, on the outside. I'm traditional that way."

I remembered Cassie's instructions when I was twelve to always walk on the street side when you're with a girl.

Both my hands were in my coat pockets and I shrugged, fending off the cold. Armstrong looped her right arm inside my left and clutched her gloved hands, pulling me in tight. She pushed her head against my shoulder like on *The Freewheelin'* Bob Dylan album cover. We walked arm and arm to the shore, where we stood motionless on ragged, white, glacial boulders. We pondered the chasm where Lake Erie funnels into the Niagara River. The worn, crumbling skyline in the distance was the same horizon I'd seen as a child from Melrose. When we began to shiver, we walked back to the car. Armstrong didn't let go of my elbow until we got there.

# 1 JANUARY, 3:12 A.M.

## (BUFFALO, NY)

*"The world of the family is very different for the first born,*
*the middle child, the youngest."*
Marge Piercy (1936- )

Y ESTERDAY, PIXIE CALLED EARLY WHILE Vic was asleep.
She said, "Cassie wants you and Victoria to meet us for
lunch before the memorial."

I said, "She's trying to keep me out of the house, isn't she?"

"Yes, but you know your sisters love that all-you-can-eat
buffet on Hertel."

I said, "The Chinese place?"

"Yeah, the New Dragon."

"That's been around since I was in high school."

"Same family owns it. The father died of stomach cancer last
year. They always bring a special dish to the table for us. They're
Mick fans."

I said, "I'm coming over to check out the house today."

"It'll piss her off, but what she doesn't know won't hurt her.
We're leaving soon because Cassie has to see a lawyer. Saundra

got here yesterday, and Cassie wants her to witness some probate papers."

I asked, "Is the key still in the garage?"

"Nothing changes around here."

"Tell Cassie we'll meet you at the church."

"What should I tell her about lunch?"

"Make up something, tell her we're going to Aunt Esther's. She wants to see us before we leave."

"I'll let her know." Pixie raised her voice and said, "Don't take anything. Cassie will have a fit if she notices anything out of place. She's been walking around the house with a Dictaphone and writing stuff down. She's paranoid. She's taking pictures. She'll have a conniption if anything's gone."

I said, "Dictaphone? That dates back to Alexander Graham Bell."

"It's big. She found it in the basement. It belonged to your father." She hesitated, "Did you take that bottle of vodka in the hall cabinet?"

"Yeah, but I didn't think you'd mind."

"Cassie asked me about it. I didn't even know it was there. Mick hid booze everywhere. Don't take anything. We'll see you at St. Margaret's at four."

Vic woke up with a jolt and said, "Who was that?"

"Pixie. She wanted us to have lunch with my sisters at a Chinese place on Hertel."

She rested back with her hands behind her head and said, "Let's skip it and get some breakfast."

I said, "I know a Greek place around the corner on Elmwood."

"Think it's still there?"

"My guess, it is. Things don't change much."

Standing in Armstrong's vestibule, we bundled in scarves, wool caps, and gloves.

I said, "I'd forgotten what a hassle it is to live here."

Vic poked me in the side. "Do I take that to mean you're not moving back?"

We laughed, and I pushed the door open against a foot of fresh snow. It blanketed everything, feathery and unblemished. The sky was an inviting, vibrant blue.

Vic said, "This reminds me of Yosemite."

I said, "I've never heard that analogy."

We locked arms, raised our boots high, and Vic broke into a goosestep.

She said, "This is fun. Let's do the angel thing."

I said, "Armstrong's neighbors will think we're nuts."

She plopped down on her back in a fresh, soft bed of snow, extended her arms, and made wings.

She said, "Come on, it's New Year's Eve. There's no such thing as bad weather, only bad clothes."

I knelt and flipped over on my back and pitched out my arms. A squeaky, cold powder reshuffled around my head.

She said, "This isn't so bad."

Her face flushed and rosy, both of us puffed big, white, steamy breaths. We dusted each other off and walked to the eatery, The Oracle of Delphi, and the lights were off.

I said, "See, it's still here."

A man in a long, gray overcoat and Russian fur cap with ear flaps was shoveling the driveway. He motioned to us, pulled a long chain from his pocket, selected a key, and opened a padlock. He pulled back a rusty metal security gate with a jolt.

Once inside, Vic didn't take off her coat.

I said, "Planning to stay?"

"After he turns the heat on," she said.

"I used to come here with my buddies, after pickup midnight basketball games. We'd meet at Baker Hall and play until dawn, then hang out and eat a huge breakfast. A Greek family ran the place."

The clanging sound of pots and pans came from the back. We heard a grill fire up.

She said, "Don't get your hopes up. Looks like this guy is the cook *and* the waiter."

Ten minutes later, a slim, short, dark man brought the menu. His eyes danced, and he brandished a toothy white smile as he said, "You like Greek food? Very healthy Mediterranean food."

I said, "Do you serve breakfast?"

"Sure, also delicious dolmades, moussaka, and kabob. You like grape leaves?"

"We weren't sure you were open," I said.

"Everything's ready."

"Was that you out there shoveling the driveway?"

He nodded. Without a winter coat and hat, he looked like a bird without feathers.

I said, "Are you Greek?"

"No, I am Ali from Jordan. This place mine now. Food is good."

He brought Vic coffee, and we ordered breakfast. Our meal consisted of stone-cold pancakes and stringy scrambled eggs. A jukebox in the corner played Fleetwood Mac's "Rhiannon."

Ali resurfaced. "Everything OK?"

I said, "It's cold."

"Let me take. We make it right. You like *mezze* plate, hummus, tzatziki, kalamata olives, dolmades?"

"Sure, I love it."

Vic nodded enthusiastically.

He said, "First, I bring hot pita bread."

Vic swayed her shoulders and sang, "I love this song."

Ali's face brightened, and his body twitched. "You like Stevie Nicks? Very popular in Amman."

Vic said, "Stevie rocks. She's a witch."

Ali swiveled his head. "Witch?"

"You know how she dances?" Vic stood and twirled, holding each end of her scarf like a cape.

Ali laughed. "That rhythm section son of bitch. Mick Fleetwood big foot on bass drum. John McVie, holy shit, train coming down track."

He vocalized, "Ca chew, ca chew," from the base of his throat.

I said, "They drive Stevie hard. You're right, that rhythm section has the bottom locked down. She rides it. I've never thought about it that way."

Vic said, "That's why it's called Fleetwood Mac, but they're nothing without the witch and Christine."

"*Alhand lilah.*" Ali wagged his head. "I was there May 19, 1980, Memorial Auditorium, downtown. Right here in Buffalo."

He scampered back to the kitchen and brought back two vinyl albums, *Fleetwood Mac* and *Rumours*. He said, "I play every day. Worn out. Skips a little."

He retreated to the kitchen, and we heard him conversing with someone, a female voice. A few minutes later, a steaming plate of pita bread arrived, searing to the touch. Then a *mezze* platter with all as promised, plus tabbouleh and a thick hunk of feta cheese, all interlaced with vegetables, tomatoes, and dried fruit.

My mouth watered.

A petite young woman in bright traditional dress accompanied Ali. She bore a plate of baba ghanoush with a broad smile that danced all over her face as she said, "*Mezze* means 'welcome.'"

Fleetwood Mac played on and, with both hands forgoing cutlery, Vic and I gorged ourselves. The young woman brought another basket of pita, and we mopped up every morsel.

When we asked for the bill, it was a pittance for pancakes and eggs, not a sumptuous Mediterranean feast. When we stood to leave, the young woman came out from the back and bowed. There were bountiful goodbyes. We shook hands with Ali and promised to come back. We left a generous tip.

Ali shook his head. "I can't believe, Mick Fleetwood. Holy shit. Big tom-tom, rhythm section. Think of me when you hear."

As we walked back to Armstrong's, I said, "That was such a good meal and baklava for dessert."

Vic put her hand on her belly. "Heavenly, what a flaky crust."

"Do you think it was homemade?"

"Of course. You can't buy anything like that in a store. I need a nap."

"Where did that young woman come from? Is she Ali's daughter?"

"Or his wife." Vic grinned.

I said, "Let's go to Mick's house."

Vic paused, raising her boots in the snow. "I wish your sisters weren't around."

"I've got some good news. They're not. And I know how to get in. The key's in the garage."

She tugged on my arm. "What's the deal with Cassie? You're acting like a child."

My back stiffened. "It's her fault."

"What do you mean? That Mick's dead?"

I nodded. "All of it." And I choked up.

She said, "Nobody poured vodka down Mick's throat."

I screamed, "She's a liar. All that sugary darling, sweetheart stuff…it's bullshit."

Vic kicked a frozen chunk of snow. "I know that, but we're only here for a few days, and you never need to come back."

"She enabled Mick. Why do you think she didn't call when he died? She can't look me in the eye. She's hiding something."

"Like what?"

"She's working a deal to sell the house and screw Pixie out of everything. She's lying through her teeth. She's ruthless. I know she's lying."

We walked the rest of the way to Armstrong's in silence.

When we got there, Vic opened the door and said, "I'll stay here and keep warm. This sounds like something you need to do on your own. Don't take anything. You'll piss Cassie off."

"Fuck Cassie."

I drove to Mick's ruminating about Cassie and how many times she'd steamrolled me and taken over my life. Like when my first marriage broke up. I was twenty-eight, heartsick, and shattered in a one-bedroom apartment in Dania, Florida. Aleida had walked out on me because she didn't want to follow me to Duke. It was a short-lived alliance of only two years. I felt like a failure, mournful and lost, and I hadn't seen it coming. Cassie showed up days later and moved in, not to help or support, but because she needed routine medical care. She saw an opening and wanted to use my connections. For two weeks, I drove her to dental and other medical appointments. She found a chiropractor and naturopath. She underwent nutritional counseling and treatments with herbs, massage, and acupuncture. Everything about living with her had been loathsome and repulsive. Her living standards were feral. She covered the small apartment in talcum powder, using it as an antiperspirant. A cloud of fine, white dust covered every surface and filled every crack. Anyone who entered would have thought we were snorting cocaine. Cassie's unwillingness to shop, cook, or clean proved insufferable. She complained, "Don't you have a girl to clean up? It's getting so cluttered." Shopping being her obsession, she stockpiled lingerie, loungewear, tights, bras, and sandals. Thank goodness my lease was up and I was leaving Florida for good, or she would have moved in.

Twenty years later, like a plague of locusts, she'd swarmed in on me again. Her partner had gotten sick with stomach cancer. Nowhere to treat him in the Islands, she'd solicited my help and brought him to Duke. After his surgery, she decided to stay and have an elective hysterectomy. He went home and left her in my care. She stayed for three tortuous months. And this proved to be the beginning of her love affair with Duke Medical Center. She participated in several Duke weight loss programs and bought a condominium. When Vic wanted to move back to California, Cassie dug in. She goaded me to divorce and stay at Duke. Again, knowing her imminent return to Durham, I fled with Vic, this time for the west coast.

As I drove through familiar neighborhoods, another, much earlier experience entered my purview. When I was seven, Cassie was sixteen, and I lay at the top of the stairs, bare-chested with my arms extended above my head. She touched my shoulders and stroked the sides of my chest. It felt creepy. She called my mother and Saundra and said something was wrong with my torso. She called it a "deformity." Already a competitive swimmer, my lats were bulky for a kid my age. My mother dismissed her complaint, but both of my sisters cackled cruelly, and I covered my chest. From then on, I kept my body covered in that licentious household.

When I got to Mick's, my obsessive thoughts about Cassie ceased. I parked on the street like I'd never left. Walking up the driveway, I noticed the ugly fissure in the white asbestos shingles at the back of the house, and it brought back the holy terror of my offence. I'd plowed my mother's Lincoln into it when I was fifteen, and I didn't have a learner's permit. My parents never repaired it as a warning. It took me many more years to develop the confidence to back a car out of that or any driveway. I postponed getting my driver's license until I was twenty-three. It felt crucial to touch the scar of my transgression. Something so important and damaging then didn't matter much now, but in some way, it still did. I ran my hand over the jagged crater with my glove. It was rust-colored and cracked, now a permanent feature of the house.

The neighbor's chain link fence post was still tilted. One could squeeze through to retrieve an errant basketball or frisbee. I sniffed the air, and it was cold and crisp, odorless. It blistered my

nostrils. The tips of my ears were numb. I could have been floating on an ice sheet like a polar bear at the North Pole. My mother
called it "nose hair freezing weather."

When I reached the garage, I feared it was locked. Mick had
replaced the sliding door with an aluminum overhead hatch.
I panicked and thought, *There's no way to get in the house if I
can't get the key out of the garage.* No problem. It rolled up like
a window shade, and the weathered *Buffalo Evening News* wagon
greeted me in the corner. Next to it, my Huffy snowblower and
push lawnmower. The house key dangled on a rusty nail. I left
my footprints in the snow, knowing it would reveal my trespass.
I wanted Cassie to see that this house is as much mine as hers. I
didn't have the desire to steal anything, although she could never
understand that. I admit, there was a greedy urge to claim something, but it was easy to overcome. The family things, paltry as
they seemed, affirmed our history and belonged to the house as
a composite. If I took something, it would erode the essence of
what my brother spent a lifetime preserving. Also, I didn't need
it...any of it. I wanted to swing through the house one last time
while the family legacy was still intact.

The back door was open. I didn't need the key after all. They
still don't lock the doors in this neighborhood during the day.
Neighbors keep an eye on each other. I hung my coat and walked
up two steps to the landing where, out of habit, I opened the
double refrigerator doors. There was an empty cardboard pizza
box, a few condiments, and nothing more. The flooring throughout the kitchen and hallway hadn't changed. It was the same retro
yellow brick, embossed inlaid linoleum that creaked, now more
soiled and stained, in places worn to the subfloor. On the kitchen
table, there was a complex bouquet. It had no odor. I touched it.
The flowers were plastic, arranged with care with branches, filler,
and berries.

As I turned the corner, there it was, "The Family Doghouse."

It had inhabited the same position my entire life. A twelve by six-inch, lacquered plywood plaque with six gold hooks. Below it read, "To stay out, obey the rules. To get in, try some she-nanigans." Each family member's name had been scripted by my mother's inimitable calligraphic hand. The five moveable dog figures read Saundra, Cassie, Neal, Mick, and CAM. Mine was in the doghouse, much like it always had been. In this family, I had a permanent place there and all the old feelings of worthlessness and sorrow came rushing back. I unhooked my figure, held it in my hand, and put Cassie's in its place in the doghouse.

When I entered the dining room, I shuddered at the clutter in such sharp contrast to my mother's meticulous housekeeping. As I looked closer, I recognized the underpinnings of her domestic regime. Beneath the rubble, as I suspected, Mick had altered noth-ing. He'd heaped his disorder on top of what she'd left behind. She'd followed a simple dictum with draconian zeal. "A place for everything and everything in its place." Mick had inherited a dif-ferent gene.

In this regard, I remember my mother coming home late and rousing me out of bed at midnight to wash a single fork left in the sink. She'd been out with my father for dinner and a movie, and I was babysitting my brother. Her fastidious home husbandry spilled over to the "girls" (mature women) she hired. She'd clean house beside them several days a week. Always a hands-on man-ager, she joined them for breaks and lunch. Among friendly patter, she prepared a midday meal that she took with her helpers at the kitchen table. Even when arthritic in her seventies, she insisted on washing the kitchen floors on her hands and knees. She saw it as a form of self-flagellation that she offered up to the Sacred Heart, a remnant of her Catholic boarding school upbringing.

My mother used the dining table for meals on holidays and special occasions, not day-to-day fare. It had three leaves and could expand to sit twelve. It served as her desk most of the time, a place to spread out, work on bills, and write checks. She sat on a padded, hand-embroidered, hinged piano bench. My father called it "Nefertiti's throne." I removed two of Mick's work jackets, a pair of pants, a belt, and a couple jerseys and lifted the piano bench top. The cover was still festooned with a faded garland of embroidered red roses. The hinge creaked like it had when my mother was alive. Though yellowed and dusty, everything inside was as if she were alive. Her long, blue leather business check ledger, stationery, and office supplies had remained all this time untouched. I came across a book of twenty-two cent stamps featuring the American bison. I read the inscription. "Once the thundering monarch of the plains, this animal was brought to the edge of extinction."

The sturdy captain's chair at the opposite end where my father had sat also remained. I could see him, his elephantine torso holding court, grinning and pawing at his nose with the knuckle of his index finger. Three matching, armless upholstered chairs were still stationed on each side of the table. The room itself was a repository of heirlooms. The tall mahogany cabinet melded into a corner. My mother had inherited it from her mother, and it appeared unopened since she'd died two decades ago—cloudy cut crystal from the old country that my mother had treasured lingered inside. Saundra's been trying to get her hands on it for years. The long, dark buffet stretched across the opposing wall. Silver candle-holders were only interrupted by Mick's colorful, stuffed toy exotic birds. I wondered if the lawyer's visit was to keep Saundra's covetousness at bay.

Mick had shielded my mother's lace dining tablecloth with a brown plastic cover and piled sundry items on it. A Phillips screwdriver, duct tape, foot inserts, talcum powder, and various electrical gadgets. Cardboard boxes, a broken lamp, a flashlight, paper towels, and toilet paper. Each chair shouldered coats and layers of zippered sweatshirts. It was a mess that somebody would have to excavate. The crystal chandelier hung without a glimmer, dulled by dust and cobwebs. My mother had said it traveled by boat under duress from Germany. It now served as a tie and bandana rack. Only one of five ornamental bulbs flickered when I flipped the electrical switch. The house, as Mick recognized, was a terminus of memory.

The *pièce de résistance* was behind the bar: a large, framed, sepia-toned photo of my grandfather, his right foot on the running board of a 1927 Pierce-Arrow roadster. Buffalo Pharmaceutical, his business, was displayed above him in the background. I leaned over the counter, steeped in my brother's paraphernalia, and studied my grandfather's face. Stained T-shirts, empty prescription bottles, expired coupons, and stacked videotapes formed a barrier.

My grandfather was much younger than I'd ever known him. He seemed smug and well satisfied with himself. His eyes were intense. He sported a turned down smile concealing his teeth. Dressed in a three-piece suit, bow tie, tilted fedora, and gold chain, he looked dashing. His wide-legged, baggy trousers emphasized the angle of his bent leg. He wore brown and white two-tone shoes. In his left hand, he held a cigar between his index and middle finger. It had a white plastic tip. Buffalo was booming, experiencing the most beautiful American bubble. There was no sign it was ever going to pop. People flocked to western New York for jobs, to raise children, and to put down roots. My grandfather was confident at the height of his powers: trains, ships, trucks, and automobiles bustled in and out of the burgeoning city. Frank Lloyd Wright, Louis Sullivan, and Henry Hobson Richardson came to Buffalo. The trinity of American architecture glorified the skyline of the thriving metropolis. Little did my grandfather know, this was Buffalo's most significant era of prosperity.

When I walked into the living room, I felt an immersion into even deeper chaos. There was a narrow, well-worn footpath lined with boxed, blue suede Puma athletic shoes. Large items like television sets and unopened appliances lined the path. Even so, my mother's furniture placement was consistent with memory. Over the years, she'd accumulated several really nice pieces, after the deaths of relatives. I recognized a pair of antique French, hand-carved chairs. Tottering Aunt Louise died at ninety-five, and this was her legacy. Deceased Aunt Helen's end tables flanked an overstuffed gold davenport. Matching outdated green glass lamps sat on either side. Under a raincoat, I discovered Uncle Carl's green marble chessboard. Carl, my grandmother's brother, a Jesuit in Berlin, had died before Mick was born. My mother had his bequeathal inlaid into an elegant wooden table. My grandmother's upright Chickering piano persisted against the vestibule wall. My mother's Hammond organ, with its accompanying Leslie speaker, packed the sunroom. In a way, nothing had changed with the exception that each room had a large bouquet of artificial flowers. The sticky, gold vinyl wallpaper was cracking and peeling. Aging brown streaks scarred its horizontal bamboo design. My sisters' portraits, done with an amateur's enthusiasm by one of my aunts, hung cattywampus on the wall.

I navigated the trail to the staircase and felt anxious, a disquietude in my gut. Mick's death changed everything. This was the last time, the only time, I'd walk through this bewildering maze again. Like seeing Mick's body at the undertaker, this was it. How many times had I climbed these stairs? Or had my father pursued me up or down in a rage? Or in fun, how many times had my brother and I jumped off the railing, onto the gold couch? I stood on the landing and looked out the window. I remembered how Saundra had shattered the glass with a hairbrush. She threw it at my father from the bathroom in a rage. I looked down at the snowy driveway and across to the gray, two-story house twelve feet away. When I was fifteen, I watched a beautiful young woman undress in front of that window. Her amber pubic hair was thick and transparent in the scant electric light. Then her boyfriend ravished her and turned off the light. I stood next to a three-foot painted statue of Jesus as the Sacred Heart. Beneath it, I drew my hand across a set of Funk and Wagnalls encyclopedias. Growing up, these were the only books in the house. I heard the rumble of a car engine followed by voices. It was Cassie, Pixie, and Saundra.

The back door opened and Pixie called, "Neal. Neal."

I was silent.

"Neal, we know you're here. Cassie says it's OK if you look around. Just don't take anything."

I didn't respond.

Pixie bounced up the stairs and said, "Cassie forgot her purse. Don't worry, she's not coming in. We saw your car out front."

I said, "That's a relief. I mean, that she's not coming in."

Then there was a commotion, and I heard the back door clap and a loud shrieking voice.

"Neal? Neal. Where are you?" Saundra trudged up the stairs, gasping for breath, and met me on the landing while Pixie was in the bedroom.

With an evil glare, she said, "We're getting a buck."

I said, "What are you talking about?"

"Mick and Cassie have it all worked out. We're getting a buck."

I said, "A buck?"

She came so close I could smell her foul breath. "Yeah, nobody's getting nothing."

"What about Pixie?"

Saundra moved toward the stairway, stared down her witchy-beak, and said, "She'll be dealt with in due time."

Pixie called from upstairs, "I've got Cassie's purse. Let's go, or we won't have time for lunch before the memorial."

Halfway down the steps, Saundra turned. "If you want anything, you better take it now because you're not getting anything once we read the will." She rumbled down the stairs heavy-footed, holding the railing.

Pixie appeared on the landing.

I looked at her. "So, what's going on with the house and the will?"

She shrugged. "I don't care. My mother didn't raise me to be greedy. Did you notice the flowers? Mick made them."

I looked around. "I didn't know he had an interest in that kind of thing."

Pixie shrugged again. "He bought all this stuff. It's expensive. You should see the basement. I don't know what to do with it."

Saundra called from the living room, "There's a lot of things you don't know, Mr. Big Shot. Take what you want...last chance."

Pixie trotted down the stairs and joined Saundra. They made their way to the car and Cassie waiting in the front seat. Pixie hopped into the driver's seat, and Saundra in the back. None of them looked up as I waved a clumsy goodbye.

I looked down the stairwell. So much scattered there. On the wall was a photo of Mick toting a quart of Southern Comfort up the stairs. He was a toddler, his tiny hand gripping the neck of the bottle. Even then, Mick made everybody laugh at parties, his antics immortalized in this photo. He'd raised an empty bottle to his lips, extended his neck, tasted the last drop, and said, "All gone."

Another memory flooded in. I was thirteen. It was a Saturday night in January, and I had a friend over for Bocce's pizza. An elderly babysitter, Mrs. Moore, supervised us. My mother had sent my father home drunk in a yellow cab and stayed out for dinner with the Ryans, a young couple I adored. They reminded me of John and Jackie Kennedy. After this incident, I could never look them in the eye again.

The cabby had rapped on the front door. We were in the kitchen, and it took a while for us to respond. Then the cabby yelled through the mailbox, "Your father's sick."

My heart raced. When I looked out to the street, the cab door was open, and my father was vomiting in the snow by the curb.

The cabby said, "He can't walk. I can help you get him inside."

I put on my boots and walked to the street. The smell of his vomit made me wretch. My father had also thrown up inside the cab.

The cabby said, "Let's get him inside."

My father looked at me with big, helpless, dumb eyes. The cabby, a slight man, and I did our best to prop his arms over our shoulders, but he was dead weight and foul. He was sweating and had torn his overcoat. His fly was open. His feet and ankles weren't communicating. There was no way we could get him in the house without him helping us. He had to walk.

I slapped him in the face and screamed at the top of my lungs, "Walk, you motherfucker! Don't you know the neighbors are watching!"

He came to and glared at me, but didn't raise a hand. With all our might and his assistance, we pulled him up the slippery vestibule stairs. The cabby left me at the front door. It was up to me to get my father up the stairs to the bedroom. If he fell back, he would crush me, but I'd known it was the only way. So, I put my right shoulder behind his ass and pushed, and we reached the landing. He was reeling, but I found the strength to drive him to the top of the stairs.

When we got to the bedroom, I screamed, "How could you! Cornelius, how could you!" It was something I'd heard my mother say many times.

I helped him take off his pants and he hit the bed, snoring, asleep in an instant. His boxer shorts were stained with shit.

When I went downstairs, I told my friend my father was sick

and with an awkward look, he went home. Mortified, I was grateful he never mentioned it again. The cabby came back and asked for twelve dollars. Also, he asked for a soapy bucket of water and rags to clean his cab. I don't know what he was going to do about the foul smell. Mrs. Moore, shell-shocked, was no help. She never returned.

I went to the basement and ran hot water with Lysol in a bucket. It steamed in the frigid air. I looked for my father's wallet and couldn't find it. I scrambled to find eight dollars in change from my paper route. There were a few silver dollars in my piggy bank from my grandfather. I gave it all it to the cabby.

He said, "You're all right, kid."

As ashamed as my father made me that night, he made me proud the next day. Neither he nor my mother would ever admit he had a drinking problem. His wallet was gone. At first, he blamed the cabby for robbing him.

I said, "He didn't do it. He's a nice guy."

My father then called the cab company where he knew the owner and said to the dispatcher, "I was drunk. I lost my wallet."

That simple admission cleared things with my father and me. I had less respect for him, but I thought he handled the situation like a grown-up. His alcoholism, and both his and my mother's denial of it, never resolved. They both took that lie to the grave. He continued to binge and drink without remedy or admission. He never joined AA or was willing to talk about it, like it was a secret protected from most parts of himself. He'd have to be very drunk to acknowledge it or sobered by an incident as vile as that night to own it.

I stood on the landing—there were only five more stairs to the top. I thought about my father on that drunken night. How had I gotten him up there? The second floor was dusty and dirty, but nothing was out of place. More artificial flowers lined flat surfaces—azaleas, geraniums, calla lilies, garlands and wreaths, peonies, poppies, sunflowers, and roses. There were lots of roses, my mother's favorite. I thought, *How many people my age get to revisit their childhood home?* It's the way I remembered it, a Brigadoon, unaltered by time. I fantasized that I'd buy it and keep it this way. Everything I touched exposed a hotbed of memory.

The first item I encountered in the hall was an antique pull down desk. My mother had covered it with the same thick, sticky vinyl wallpaper as downstairs. When I opened it, there were two square cardboard boxes inside. I shook each like a maraca, and a gritty, granular, sandy substance was inside. I opened one end, and some gray dust got on my fingers. The contents at first stupefied me. Then I remembered Mick had talked about bringing The Boys home. They were the cremains of Terry and Jerry, but the boxes didn't state which one was which.

Two familiar, rectangular, antique picture frames hung on the opposite wall—a series of photos of my parents as toddlers. My father's hung on the top and my mother's below it. The images recorded two preschoolers standing, smiling, jumping, playing with blocks and toys. My mother had a large bow in her hair and she was holding a doll, and my father grasped a stuffed lamb. Although my parents were six years apart, the images matched up like they were twins.

Throughout my childhood, those photos had bewildered me. I couldn't imagine either of my parents as children. I remember a mind-bending conversation with my mother when I was eight as she sat on the side of my bed.

"Who are the children in those pictures?"

"That's your father and me. Can't you tell? Don't you recognize us?"

"But you're so small."

She said, "That's how it works. Little people grow up. You won't be little for that much longer. Although I wish you could stay like this forever. I could eat you up."

I asked, "Did you know Dad then?"

"Of course not. We were children."

"Then how did you get in the same pictures?"

"They're different photos taken at different times."

"But they look the same."

"That's because the same studio, the Bliss Brothers, took them."

I said, "Do you remember?"

"No, I was too small."

"Does Dad remember?"

She said, "I don't think so. I've never asked."

"Why did you put them up on the wall?"

She said, "Neal, you're asking too many questions. It's time to go to sleep. Our parents gave them to us when we married and moved out. It was my mother's idea that we hang them together, and they've been in that spot ever since. It's called a coincidence."

I studied the photos again. I knew it wouldn't be long before they'd be removed and sold by Saundra at a swap meet.

When my parents were children, Buffalo was the tenth-largest city in the United States. Both were born and grew up during a gilded age. They stood on big shoulders like Carl Sandburg's Chicago. Buffalo was relevant and underwent a reversal of fortunes during their lifetime. Buffalo fell to the sixty-eighth largest city in the country. It was an old and tired metropolis, but it hadn't died. My brother's blind faith in his town survived in this crumbling house. A brittle bundle of palm fronds drooped over the picture frames. Crumbling and encrusted, they trembled with heat rising from the floor vent. My mother couldn't throw a blessed object from Palm Sunday away. These fronds were two decades old. On his entry, the crowd welcomed Jesus into Jerusalem, waving these giant, hand-like leaves. The Sunday before Easter is the celebration of martyrs and the triumph of the spirit over flesh. The Jews greeted the end of forty years of wandering with palm fronds.

Muslims associate the palm with paradise. In ancient Egypt and Mesopotamia, the spiky plant was the symbol of immortality. Here in the household of my birth, they remain placeholders to Buffalo's glorious past.

I knew my time in the house was over. It would never be the same. Mick's memorial was in a couple hours. I stuck my head in each of the three bedrooms, all a jumble of memories, all broken down, worn and full of clutter. Yet everything I remembered remained in place. The bathroom looked the same as the rest, dingy and dirty, not close to the meticulous cleanliness my mother administered with a bleached toothbrush. I wondered how a family of six survived the cramped conditions. My mother wouldn't let any of us use the shower. It was a bath only household because she didn't like the soap scum on the walls. My father, my brother, and I showered at the Buffalo Athletic Club downtown. My sisters and mother washed their hair in the tub. The area was meager, smaller than I remembered, with very little room to turn around.

It struck me again at how much everything had stayed the same. My parents' framed marriage license clanged on the back of the master bedroom door when I opened it. Mick and Pixie slept, as my parents did, in the same modest double bed. There was no alteration in the arrangement. Black and white photos of both grandfathers hung on the wall. The oval mirror on my mother's vanity was smoky with age and dust. Her jewelry case unmoved, a cold cream jar sat encrusted next to it on the counter. The green nap carpet was suffering and worn. I wandered to the tiny closet where my mother dressed. The door was ajar. Dozens of cardboard hat boxes lined the shelves. It smelled fetid, like a thrift shop. My mother's clothing had sat unworn for twenty years, crammed on hangers on a single closet rod.

There was no room for Mick's or Pixie's clothes. It made sense why they tossed them in piles around the house. They lived in my dead mother's house like guests.

Deep-seated in the closet, I heard an incessant *tick tock*. When I turned to locate the source, it vibrated and rang. Startled, I jumped, then sprang toward the sound. In both hands, I gripped an old-time, key-wound alarm clock. Like trying to secure a slippery trout out of the water, I almost dropped it and scrambled to find the off switch. Once quiet and tame, I admired its generous boldface. A sturdy mechanism with lots of moving parts, it was an instrument from a forgotten age. The broad sweep of its hands delighted me until I observed the time. Two-thirty. I thought, *Shit, Mick's memorial is at four.*

I'd been poking around the house for three and a half hours. I verified the time on my phone, and the old timepiece was accurate to the minute. It filled me with questions. *Who left it here? Who wound it up and set it? Why is it in my dead mother's closet?* When I turned to go, I observed my mother's mid-length, sheer nightie hanging on the back of the closet door. I thought, *Why didn't he burn that?*

My entire family history splashed up against my face. I'd never made the decision not to drink or take drugs. Unconscious, it occurred and came from an internal source, one more concrete and settled. *Why me, not Mick? So much talent. A reservoir of ability to make people smile and lighten up.* In Mother's ragged nightie, I saw his demise.

Too much happened yesterday to write it all down now. I'll pick it up with Mick's memorial tomorrow.

# 2 JANUARY, 4:20 AM

## (BUFFALO, NY)

*"I do not believe that sheer suffering teaches.
If suffering alone taught,
all the world would be wise,
since everyone suffers."*
Anne Morrow Lindbergh (1907-2001)

THOUGH IT HAPPENED THE DAY before yesterday, the details remain vivid. Late for the memorial, I bolted from Mick's and raced across town on the Scajaquada. The asphalt was black and slick, and a sliver of sunshine peeked through a dark cloud. Once a cop pinched me here for driving seven miles over the speed limit, so I slowed down. My chance of getting to Armstrong's with time to spare was slim. I fretted Vic would be chomping at the bit. She likes to be early. My getting a ticket on the way would make it much worse. I slowed down and took in the sights.

The stately Buffalo Historical Museum loomed ahead. Delaware Park emitted a worn and weathered dignity, and I absorbed its haughty hopefulness. The museum, a remnant of the 1901 Pan American Exposition, maintains an enduring regal pomp. The Pan

Am by all accounts was a disaster, a money pit, and a knockout punch to Buffalo's global aspirations. Most of the structures were temporary, fashioned from wood, chicken wire, and plaster. But not this one, a reproduction of the Parthenon. It had been constructed of Vermont marble and built to last. Its original design, like the New York State Building, oozes permanence and durability. Regardless of the season, it's a landmark, like Venice's Salute, its pale white face reflected in the man-made Mirror Lake.

It's impossible to underestimate the fiasco of Buffalo's World Fair. It set the stage for all future disappointments. It's why the region has a chip on its shoulder. Never good enough, always second fiddle, a runner-up. Its ambition to emerge supreme among Great Lakes metropolitan cities had been thwarted and never realized, a second-class status its citizenry never shook. The Pan Am was Buffalo's opportunity to shine in its own right. To cleave itself from the Big Apple and transcend its lakeshore brethren, like Chicago did after the Columbian Exposition in 1893.

The Pan Am suffered from low attendance. To boost numbers, organizers awaited the arrival of President McKinley in September. His stopover proved catastrophic, and a series of bungles and miscues ensued. The "City of Light" earned a new sobriquet, "The Buffalo Curse," analogous to Murphy's Law, "Whatever can go wrong, will go wrong in Buffalo."

On September 6, an anarchist shot McKinley twice in the abdomen at close range. The first bullet grazed him, and the second penetrated deep into his gut. In the days before antibiotics, an abdominal bullet wound was almost always fatal. The president's best hope relied on the renowned local surgeon, Roswell Park. Park, an expert on gunshot wounds, was in the middle of a complicated surgery in Niagara Falls, so a gynecologist with little background proceeded. Despite hundreds of thousands of electric light bulbs on buildings, the treatment center lacked electricity. A mirror reflected waning sunlight, and retractors weren't available. The surgeon probed with his fingers. The second bullet was never located, and the incision was closed with silk thread without a drain. Furthering the folly, the X-ray machine, displayed for the first time at the Pan Am, wasn't deployed.

The president's robust constitution allowed him to rebound a bit after surgery. To make things worse, local physicians leaked optimism for the president's recovery. Roswell Park returned to Buffalo but refused to intervene. Ironically, he saved a woman suffering from an abdominal pistol wound two weeks later.

The eyes of the world were on Buffalo. McKinley died September 14 of gangrene and blood-borne infection. The vice president, Teddy Roosevelt, took the oath of office the same day, in Buffalo.

Bad luck and bumbling are my hometown's fate. Excuses and complaints—it's a city consigned to the art of premature ejaculation. It has earned a reputation for bad weather and bush league. A blizzard swept town center smack in the middle of the Great Lakes wind corridor. Coined in the '60s by a sportswriter, the moniker "Armpit of the East" stuck to Buffalo. In the '90s, when the Bills lost four consecutive Super Bowls, pundits mocked it. And when the team stopped winning, they ignored it. Buffalonians hate ridicule, but irrelevance is much worse. It's a place always trying to prove its worth—a mindset of significance. Thus, the term "Buffalo Curse," and it started with McKinley and the Pan Am.

Through the years, when I say I'm from Buffalo, strangers quip, "Buffalo's a good place to be from." Even if they've never been there, they offer, "Get a lot of snow up there."

Why do Buffalonians like my brother live and die by Buffalo? As I meandered through Delaware Park, I realized that I did too.

After I left the park, the traffic crawled on Elmwood Avenue. A plethora of frustrating streetlights and pedestrian crossings tested my nerves. I wished I'd left Mick's earlier. When I parked on the street out front, I saw Victoria staring at me out the front window. Before I closed the door, she called down from upstairs, "I'm ready. Where the hell have you been? The memorial starts in twenty-five minutes."

I said, "It took longer than I thought to get down Elmwood."

"Did you get enough of the house?"

"I wanted to stay longer."

"You didn't take anything, did you?"

"No, and that part was easy. There's nowhere to put those memories."

"Put your coat on and let's go. Armstrong is going to meet us there."

I said, "You should have come. It was amazing. My mother's clothes were in the closet, and her nightie on a hook."

"That doesn't sound good. What will happen with all that stuff?"

"Saundra will peddle what she can at the flea market and dump the rest. Cassie will commission her to sell the house, so she gets the real estate commission. It's all kickbacks and bribes."

Vic said, "Glad we're not involved. I'll drive."

"Saundra showed up and threw me a line that we're all getting a buck."

Vic turned. "They were there while you were poking around?"

"They stopped back for a few minutes. Cassie forgot her purse."

"What do you mean 'a buck'?"

"It means Pixie's fucked."

As we turned the corner out of the driveway, my phone buzzed.

Vic said, "Who's that?"

"It's an 805 number I don't recognize." I answered, "Hello."

"Neal, sorry to bother you again, but this is an emergency, and I don't know who else to call."

It was PJ.

She said, "My urine's red. What should I do? It's never happened before."

I said, "Do you have the urge to pee? Is there any pain or burning when you urinate?"

"No, I'm fine."

"Any red blood in the stool? Are the stools dark?"

"No, nothing has changed. I've got a few bruises on my belly where my mother gave me the shots, but they're almost gone."

"Are your periods normal?"

"Haven't had one, but no change."

"What was your last INR?"

"Two point seven a couple days ago, and Katie said it was good. She told me to stop the shots."

"Has your diet changed?"

"No, same, all raw foods. I juice carrots, apple, and celery. I went to the farmers market yesterday." She paused. "I bought some beets."

"Are you juicing the beets?"

"I did it today."

"The red urine is from the beets. It should clear in the next couple voids. If not, go to Urgent Care."

"I will. How stupid of me. Thank you, Neal. I hope I'm not calling at a bad time."

"No, I hope that's all it is. We're on the way to my brother's memorial."

"Sorry to hear that. My condolences to you, your wife, and your family."

I said, "Thanks so much."

Vic said, "I could say something, but I won't."

I slumped in my seat.

She raised her voice. "What the fuck! You just took a work call. We're on the way to your brother's memorial. I'm incredulous."

I met her objection with silence.

She turned the car into the parking lot. "I've resigned myself to it. But take note, you stupid son-of-a-bitch. It pisses me off. Let's get on with this."

We parked behind a monolithic concrete structure.

Vic regained her composure and said, "Is that the church?"

I said, "No that's a pile of concrete. It's a lot uglier than I remember."

She said, "What are you talking about?"

"That's the church school. My Great-uncle Seymour designed it."

She said, "Didn't your dad's father build that famous theater across the street?"

"Yes, Seymour, his younger brother, and partner built a string of impressive theaters throughout the city. The one across the street has been operating since 1920. It's under restoration. The others have been torn down or abandoned, especially on Buffalo's East Side. The irony is that Uncle Seymour designed and supervised the construction of this abomination forty years later. It's right across the street."

She said, "It's not that bad. It's functional."

"A cheap, ugly building, and it hasn't aged well."

She asked, "Where's the church?"

"Behind it. The theaters my grandfather and Uncle Seymour built were works of art. Both of them were contemporaries of Frank Lloyd Wright. Palatial buildings with marble staircases, stained-glass windows, Neoclassical foyers, murals, and a proscenium."

"We don't have time for this now, Neal. Why are you dragging your feet?"

"Some people don't know what a proscenium is, and it's kind of hard to explain. It's the arch or around the stage that creates the illusion that the actors are in a different reality. They built the theaters during the age of vaudeville. All kinds of live shows traveled through Buffalo then. My grandfather's specialty was designing ornate prosceniums."

"That's great, Neal. I'm glad one of his theaters remains."

"The rest are dilapidated and scheduled for demolition."

She said, "That's how a lot of stuff looks around here."

"This hasn't been a school for years. There aren't enough kids going to Catholic school anymore. They're converting them into condos and apartments."

"Let's get in the church. It's time."

I said, "We still have a few minutes, don't we?"

"It's 3:55," she replied.

I said, "My grandfather died before Mick was born. I saw Uncle Seymour a lot when I was a kid. He was very tall and wore a long, camel hair coat to his ankles. Enamored with Frank Lloyd Wright, I once asked him, 'What do you think?' He dismissed Wright, saying, 'His draftsmen do all the work.' To him, an architect did his own drawing. There was a big gap in age between my grandfather and Uncle Seymour, twenty years."

"Like with you and Mick," she said.

"Mick and I are eleven years apart and never shared a common livelihood. Uncle Seymour and my grandfather were unique."

"Are you delaying this? Let's go."

"My grandfather took my father everywhere, even as a newborn. He bundled him up in swaddling clothes. Relatives tell me my grandfather put him in the car and took him to building sites in subzero weather. Things got worse between his folks after my father arrived. They didn't interact. They slept in separate bedrooms. I guess that wasn't so unusual then. It was up to my dad's father to raise his adopted kid himself."

I felt a hand on my shoulder and when I turned, Dr. Schwab grabbed my right hand and shook my arm up and down."

"Dayton Schwab, DDS, at your service. Remember me?" He

broke into an odd, electric smile. "We all knew this day would come."

A thick, cold gray Lake Erie sky extended to the ground, and I shuddered from the cold. Dr. Schwab wore a traditional, three-quarter-length herringbone topcoat and a black ambassador cap. His eyebrows clinched, his face darkened, and with an awkward chuckle, he said, "He was too young. I warned him. We all did. He never got the message."

I nodded, and he gripped my hand tighter. I noticed his pale, ungloved hand. I pivoted and said, "Dr. Schwab, this is Victoria."

He blushed as he dropped my hand, then quickly grasped hers, although not with the force and persistence he had mine. "All the way from California. An all-American Californian girl. Bet you can't wait to get back."

She curtsied a bit and said, "Dr. Schwab, nice to meet you. I've heard a lot about you."

He said, "I hope it's all good."

With a mischievous grin, she said, "Well, not all of it."

He exploded into a loud, single, forced laugh, then said, "I like you. Best we get into the church. Don't want to keep the monsignor waiting." And he walked away.

Vic poked me and whispered, "Was that Mick's sponsor?"

I nodded and said, "Yeah, that's the guy."

As we walked in, the pungent scent of burning incense got so high in my sinuses that it tickled my frontal cortex. I sneezed and my eyes watered. It had been years since I'd been in church. My antagonistic relationship with the clergy and nuns came streaming back. I'd had enough Catholicism for a lifetime. My contemporaries, who endured the same fate, say, "It wasn't that bad. It's all for good." As for me, it was wrong, a misstep, a failure. And it had done me no good. I'd deleted the whole church thing from memory once I left Buffalo. When my parents died, it was perfunctory. My mother had no service for my father. The grip of his loss hit me over ensuing months, then lessened over time. I was thirty-one, assuming my first job with responsibility, and married to Scarlett. In essence, I'd found my own life. My mother's service six years later was at our neighborhood parish church. And, although hard to admit, there was gladness as well as grief. She left so much wreckage behind, extending to Saundra's children, that a cheer went up inside me. My mother could no longer abuse me, my brother, or anyone else. And now, due to my heritage, I was back in a Catholic church for the saddest day of my life.

I felt a hand on my shoulder and thought, *Dr. Schwab again?* When I turned, Cleve Roberts shook my hand.

With a half-baked smile, he said, "We knew this day would come."

And in an instant, I recognized the connection. Cleve, Dr. Schwab, and Mick were drinking buddies and later shared abstinence at AA. Both bubbled with an incestuous glee. They'd admired Mick and wished they could imbibe as he did, drench the darkness of their souls and follow him to certain death by alcohol. I got the sense from both that drinking oneself to death was far better than living sober. They had, in an odd way, admired Mick's commitment.

The church filled like a poured cup of tea and soon swelled to the brim. It didn't matter that Mick was reclusive and drank without restraint for the last five years. His popularity hadn't waned.

As we took our places in the front pew, Vic whispered, "In Buffalo, it's acceptable to drink yourself to death."

I nodded in agreement and whispered, "I think it's true everywhere."

Hundreds of people filled the pews, and dozens more stood in the vestibule and aisles. My father, after his acquaintances started dying, became obsessed with the obituaries. He tracked how many people showed up at funeral homes and memorials. For a well-attended funeral, he'd say, "The entire First Ward turned out." And if sparse participation, "Not even the widow showed." Mick's memorial, in these terms, registered as "First Ward." My father had no burial rites because my mother nixed them. She freaked out, fearful of greedy undertakers and lawyers. The outpouring of love and affection for Mick on this day felt like it was for him and my entire family. I was grateful Cassie let it happen.

Our immediate family gathered in the front right pew with me sitting on the aisle next to Victoria, Pixie next to her, then Cassie and Saundra. At 4 p.m. sharp, a deep voice from an unseen male in the choir loft sang Cat Stevens's "Wild World." The vocalist pressed rudimentary notes on a thready organ while his tragic tone bounced off the vaulted ceiling and reverberated against the stained glass windows. On the bench next to Pixie, I noticed an unmarked cardboard box, like the ones in the antique pull-down desk. Mick's cremains. At that moment, I wished my brother's memorial could last forever. A sharp mix of flowers and incense filled the air. I savored every moment, every word, every Gregorian gesture.

After the song and a few minutes of silence, the monsignor entered flanked by two altar boys. We all stood. They genuflected together and lit the candles. He proceeded with the Mass. Vic, who isn't Catholic, and I, a long-lapsed one, received Holy Communion. I thought, *What the hell, this is for Mick.* I wanted to embody every aspect. I remembered how the sticky wafer felt on my tongue mixed with saliva. Was this the body and blood of Christ? It didn't make much sense to me then or now.

When the Mass was over, the monsignor stepped down from the altar, clasped his hands in front of him, and rocked back and forth. Then he walked toward the front pews, and a quiet hush enveloped the room.

With a calm, metered voice, he said, "I knew Mick, not well, but when I was the chaplain at St. Alby's, I helped coach the swim team. Mick was deceptive. Guys would look at him and think, this kid has no chance. He wore a tiny speedo bathing suit. He had a big gut hanging over it. Once in the water, though, Mick usually won. He said to me once, 'Father, I wish I looked better in a bathing suit.' And I said, 'Why don't you lose a little weight?' and he replied, 'Father, my real calling is cooking, and I've got to taste whatever I make. I can't give that up.' That blew my mind. Here was a fifteen-year-old kid who already knew what he wanted to do with his life."

Pixie let out a God-awful shriek. Vic stroked her spine. Cassie clutched a handkerchief and whimpered. Saundra rolled her eyes.

The monsignor held a pregnant pause and walked toward us. "Cassie Motherwell, Mick's sister"—he nodded in her direction— "asked a couple of Mick's friends to speak. We will also leave time for others to say something as well." He raised his hand high above his head, extending his index finger, and pointed to someone in the back. I strained my neck to see.

Marty Mack rose from the middle pews. When he walked, his boot heels clicked on the terrazzo floor such that every step echoed. He carried a crumpled piece of paper in his right hand. When he mounted the steps to the pulpit, he stumbled, caught himself, and proceeded to the top.

A gasp reverberated throughout the assembly, followed by an audible sigh of relief.

Marty, an older man and not related by blood, had provided avuncular guidance to Mick. He'd befriended Mick when Mick was doing shoeshines at the Buffalo Athletic Club. Mick had been twelve at the time, too young to get working papers. He'd figured out an angle, a way to pick up some extra cash. Marty admired his enterprise. They were from different worlds, but something had clicked. Marty followed Mick's career and remained a loyal friend. After my mother died, Mick spent holidays with Marty and his wife, Geri. They didn't have children or other entanglements and adopted Mick as one of their own. Marty was an engineer who maintained steam boilers and could fix anything. He was hands-on while the household where Mick and I grew up had been hands-off. My mother had always employed a handyman for the most straightforward mechanical repairs and carpentry.

When Marty reached the microphone, he took a deep, exhausted breath, then coughed and cleared his throat. Though I didn't know him, the cadence was familiar. He was like one of my guys, with a thick Great Lakes industrial accent. I imagined Coleridge's ancient mariner and how he might speak if he were an American. Marty came from generations of stevedores in South Buffalo, with ranks of relatives who had unloaded and packed the barges for lake travel. It was a profession that had all but dried up, but the pride of an honest day's work remained.

He expressed himself with care, accounting for every syllable as he said, "Mick could've written his own ticket. My wife, Geri, and I were watching the Food Channel the other night. We saw a guy who called himself a celebrity chef. I turned to my better half and said, 'Ms. Geri, Mick was doing that twenty years ago.' She nodded her head and agreed. In my book, Mick was the first TV chef. He was ahead of his time. He had a celebrity personality. He loved to cook, but most of all, he wanted to make people laugh, make them like him. He was always fun to be around. I'll miss him so much, and I know Ms. Geri feels the same." He fought back the tears and said, "Mick could've written his own ticket."

The church hushed and stilled as Marty's heels clapped back to his pew. Ms. Geri reached out and handed him her frilly handkerchief when he arrived at her side.

Dr. Schwab stood without hesitation. He and his spouse had camped in the first bank of pews across from us. When he walked up the pulpit steps, his black suit shimmered. He sported a gold handkerchief in the jacket pocket that was almost as shiny as his golden hair, greased and piled high on the top of his head. A starched white shirt, gold cufflinks, and a black tie completed the ensemble. Once established in the pulpit, he looked like Captain Ahab observing a vast and open sea.

He angled his face with a toothless sneer, saying, "Mick was a Bills fan." He waited for a laugh.

The stillness was awkward and uncomfortable.

"I'm not sure if you heard about what happened at the courthouse last week." His eyes searched the room for a response.

Heads lowered and eyes looked away.

He wrinkled his brow and smiled. "A seven-year-old kid challenged a court ruling over custody. His parents beat him, and supervision was awarded to his aunt. He told the judge his aunt beat him too. The judge reconsidered and asked the boy to propose who he'd recommend. After two recesses, the judge granted guardianship to the Buffalo Bills. The judge and the kid concluded that the Bills weren't capable of beating anybody."

Silence and nervous shifting, then somebody in the back snickered.

Dr. Schwab pointed his index finger toward the back. "See, somebody got it. Mick was a good guy. We all know that. He made me promise I'd tell that joke, so I did."

A few scattered laughs trickled through the church.

"As you know, Mick was funny and a very talented chef. He also, like you, loved our Bills. Here in Buffalo, the Bills are integral. They're part of our DNA. It's a significant loss to our community when someone as young as Mick passes away. Please join me in the Lord's Prayer."

A drone of muffled voices echoed off the wall and high ceiling. "Our Father who art in heaven, hallowed be thy name…"

My mind drifted, and I thought about all the Masses I'd accumulated in my life. When I was a kid, it seemed like every day. As an altar boy, I served Mass at the neighborhood Carmelite convent as well as my parish church. I can still hear the cloistered nuns' ethereal voices as they maintained their anonymity behind the thick, red velvet curtain. It was titillating to hold the gold plate for them when they received Holy Communion, their faces screened off from everyone else. There was talk among us that the Carmelites were ugly and had disfigured faces, but there was no truth to it. Altar boys stood by a small, square opening and got a fleeting glimpse, sometimes a nun's profile, more often only her mouth, chin, philtrum, and tongue. Once a priest was drunk in the vestibule and put his vestments on backward. Nobody else noticed, but I giggled with the other altar boy throughout the service. We wore black cassocks and short, white surplices that had thick wads of stitching. The Carmelite nuns had darned the garments until there was little fabric left, the same vestments repaired for generations. They threw nothing away.

On cue, I mumbled with the rest, "And lead us not into temptation, but deliver us from evil."

Dr. Schwab returned to his seat.

The monsignor stood with open arms, his black chasuble hanging like obsidian wings. With gesticulating fingers, he called forth his flock. "Who out there would like to speak? Come up to the front so everybody can hear you."

One of Mick's coworkers, a short, shy, stout woman, made her way to the altar. With a robust Hispanic accent, she said, "He was always so funny in the kitchen. I loved it when he said, 'You know it!'" She imitated Mick's high-pitched squeal and said, "The real high voice went right through me. In a *good* way. We laugh a lot. He took good care of me at work."

A lean prep cook, no more than twenty, said, "Heaven just got a little bit more fun, and the food just got a whole lot better."

Then came a neighbor, Romano Giancarlo, a boy I remembered, now a man who, like Mick, had remained in his family home. He lived a few houses away. Dressed in a dark three-piece suit, I didn't recognize him until he spoke.

Romano said, "Mick, I have to confess that I flung the rock

that hit your kitchen window. It was an accident, and I never told anyone. I heard you were in your highchair, and your mom was feeding you baby food. I was trying to see how many fences I could toss the rock over. Thank goodness, no one got hurt. But I remember your mom running outside to see who did it. Many years later, I found out that the stone that came through your window upset two different baby foods. The combo sensation agreed with you so much that you'd only eat it that way. Bite-size pieces of chicken mixed in Swiss cheese and ham. Voila! Cordon bleu. I'm proud that I was, in some way, inspirational in your career choice. Mick, you were a super chef."

Reminiscences of this kind went on for over an hour. There was a steady stream of well-wishers. In my bag, I carried the bottle of Kamchatka. I'd planned to pull it, like a rabbit out of a hat, and declare, "This is what Mick loved. All that was important to him." But I couldn't do it. Why tell the truth when it's so easy to avoid? I was in league with his AA comrades. I respected his commitment to hard drink. Was it a wasted life? Wasn't it what Mick wanted?

Cassie, Saundra, and Pixie joined me in remaining mute. No family members spoke at the memorial. My friends, like Armstrong, also stayed silent. They hadn't known Mick, only what a burden he was to me. No one mentioned that Mick was an alcoholic and a reclusive hermit who shut out the world. And that as long as he could manage, he'd lived alone with his bottle. As his health declined, Pixie moved in and became his supplier. She'd said he whined, cried, and made such a fuss that she had to buy him booze. She gave her life over to caretaking, cleaning up after him, and temporizing his moods. Cassie had enabled Mick from afar and bankrolled the operation. Her sin is more egregious. She'll recoup her investment with interest when she sells the house.

When the eulogies ended, Victoria, Cassie, Saundra, Pixie,

and I marched down the long aisle. We took slow steps and, in procession, observed mysterious, yet familiar faces. Curious, wet eyes stared at us, and we gazed back. It was a life review, recycling relatives, friends, neighbors, and acquaintances.

We stood in the church vestibule and shook people's hands. Mrs. Ryan, now a widow and recluse, covered her face with a shawl. The encounter rekindled the shame of that night when I was thirteen and my father was sent home drunk in a taxicab. Two six-foot-tall great-grandsons propped her up on either side. She held my right hand in both of hers, like a round loaf of Italian bread.

In a whisper that made me strain my ears to hear, she said, "He had his problems, but I loved Mick."

I looked into her eyes and searched for the glamourous young woman I once knew.

She leaned and kissed me on the cheek. "You still got it. Don't get old."

I felt her facial hair as she brushed against my face. Her soft, wrinkled palms trembled. On her feet, she wore house slippers, her ankles red and pitted, incongruent with her tiny body.

It was a rare brew of friends and family, one generation giving way to the next, all in a prelude to what I hoped would be a raucous Irish wake. But Cassie would have none of it. My idea was to open Mick's house and let people drink up his leftover booze, and that's what most expected. When I told mourners there would be no wake, their disappointment and anger were palpable. Cassie, Saundra, and Pixie retreated to the house, and Vic and I organized a meet up at a local bar.

When we left the church, forty people followed us in a caravan to Cole's. Vic was in a party mode, and everybody loved it.

She stood up on a barstool and said, "You ever played Buffalo?"

My friends from Buffalo, to my surprise, shook their heads and said they'd never heard of it."

Vic said, "We play it—"

Armstrong interrupted, "Come on, me with a drinking game? I don't need encouragement."

Vic said, "I know. I know."

Armstrong said, "Please."

Vic said, "You find out which hand people use for drinking. So if your right-handed, you have to drink with your left. If, at any point, you drink with your dominant hand, anyone in the group can call, 'Buffalo,' and you have to drink it all."

"Oh, this is a bad game for me," Armstrong said.

Vic said, "No matter what time of day. No matter what drink and the best part is when you're with a group of people on a three or four-day trip."

Armstrong said, "Um, hmm."

Vic said, "So, if you're going out to drink and someone takes a sip of their Bloody Mary with the wrong hand, you say, 'Buffalo,' and the whole thing goes down. Even if it's first thing in the morning."

"I couldn't play," Armstrong said.

Vic said, "You will think about this all night."

The bartender said, "What about if you're ambidextrous?"

Vic said, "If you have equal dexterity with both hands, then you pick."

I said, "Or you can make it more difficult and carry your drinks a different way, on the top of your head."

Vic laughed.

Armstrong said, "Or if you have drinks in both hands. No matter what you use, you're going to get called for 'Buffalo' and you have to drink."

After that, the party was on. "Buffalo," was shouted every few minutes, again and again.

The bartender said, "Where did you get this from? I've never heard of it."

Vic said, "I used to play it all the time in the dorms with my boyfriend, who was the quarterback at San Jose State."

I said, "And Jack Elway, the coach, complained to the team that she outdrank the offensive line."

Faces from decades ago, once so familiar to me, stared back as if in a dream, albeit more wrinkled, gray, and wizened, recognition evident in their eyes. It was a joy to be in this company again. We hadn't changed. Our hearts were pumping, and we were sharing the same air again. It was a life review—friends, cousins, schoolmates, swim team members, and their children.

And they'd all turned out for Mick. It was a long line of memories, waves of recurring flashbacks. Many faces I'd never see again.

I did a double-take when I saw him across the room. He was at a round table in the corner surrounded by young people. Garbôn, how could this be? The madman, the rebel, the antichrist who had made my father's blood boil, always a volume of James Joyce or Nietzsche on his person. The genius, the linguist, the poet, the consummate rule-breaker, the vulgarian. The slob. I'd tried to contact him for years. No one knew what had become of him, and here he was hiding in plain sight. I walked over while watching his every move with keen interest.

He said, "Buffalo, buffalo, Buffalo, buffalo, buffalo, buffalo, Buffalo, buffalo."

The group around him, all a little tipsy, giggled.

A tall fellow shouted, "Buffalo, buffalo, buffalo."

He retorted, "It's the longest one-word sentence. And the grammar's correct."

A sassy young woman countered, "But what does it mean?"

He said, "Buffalo is a noun, an adjective, as well as a verb. So why don't you give it a try?"

A squat, bespeckled girl said, "How do we know you aren't buffaloing us?"

He said, "OK, Buffalo is a city, a buffalo is a bison, an animal, and to buffalo, someone means to hoodwink them."

A beautiful young woman with long, auburn hair shouted, "I got it! How many buffalos in that sentence?"

He said, "Eight."

She said, "The buffalo from Buffalo who are buffaloed by buffalo from Buffalo, buffalo other buffalo from Buffalo."

He said, "Yes," and reached for a massive stein of beer with his right hand.

In unison, the group shouted, "Buffalo."

And he chugged the whole thing. Garbôn was still enormous, bigger than life, actually the shape of a bison, with a substantial upper torso attached to spindly legs. He had a wild head of woolly, now silver hair and a scruffy, thick, white beard extended to his temples.

With beer foam on his upper lip and beard, he looked up at me.

I said, "Thanks for coming."

We shook hands, and I reached over a chair to hug him. From afar, we gave each other a soft pat on the back.

He said, "I had to show up for Mick. I saw it in the paper."

I said, "Do you live here?"

"Yes, I have a dental practice in Williamsville."

"Wow. How come I haven't been able to find you?"

"I don't know. I've been here except for dental school in Boston. How long have you been away?"

I said, "You've got a point."

He said, "This is my son, Michael, and his sister, Jennifer, is over there with her mother."

A tall, lanky, shy twenty-something reached out his hand. I glanced across the room at a ravishing, dark-haired coed surrounded by a group of young men, her slim and elegant mother by her side, holding a drink.

He said, "I'm going to hang around for a while so we can talk. The kids are going to a New Year's party, and Midge has to run out and check in on her mother. I'll catch you later."

Vic waved, and I walked back to meet her at the bar. I hadn't seen Garbôn since we were in our mid-twenties. The last time was in a lock-up psychiatric unit at Erie County General. He called for me—he was mad, frothing at the mouth, low on lithium. I hadn't been able to locate him since. At the time, we were confidants and he influenced me like nobody else. It was a turbulent friendship, dangerous, dark and stormy, a love affair of intellect involving many crack-ups, breakups, and reunions. He lived on the edge, and I followed.

Garbôn learned to speak, read, and write fluent German in high school. He never visited Germany but sought out local native speakers. Obsession is an understatement, his powers of concentration, scary, like Rasputin. His memory and recall were superhuman. He recited Molly Bloom's soliloquy from *Ulysses* at will. At the University of Buffalo, he'd learned Hungarian during his freshman year. My father hated him. He felt he was a bad influence. Garbôn had a trust fund and endless cash flow. He could do whatever he wanted. He followed me to Miami during my first year, and it was only then that I got a real glimpse into his mania and torment. I'd never seen the downside, where he would sleep for days and not answer his door. Our friendship had always been up, never down. He left Miami after a semester. Now, to see him here with a successful profession and family was curious. How could it end this way? Two of his brothers took their own lives, and his family home was a haunted place, affluent and macabre. I remember a large print of Edvard Munch's *The Scream* in the family room. It felt like a model for what everybody in the family was feeling. But here was Garbôn, alive, well, a productive member of the middle class…another mystery of Buffalo.

Victoria said, "Who's that big, loud-mouthed guy you were talking to over there"—she pointed—"with the beard?" She puffed out her cheeks, shrugged, and rocked side to side. From the base of her throat, she gurgled, "Buffalo, buffalo, buffalo."

"That's a pretty good impression of the mighty Garbôn. It blows me away that he showed up."

She said, "Then who's the tall guy standing near the door? I'm getting the two mixed up?"

"Godzilla."

"Don't any of your friends have normal names?"

I said, "Godzilla's his legal name. He'll interrupt anybody midsentence if they call him anything different."

"What's the deal?"

"In his twenties, he left Buffalo and went to New York to become an actor. His agent, blown away by his strapping physique, said, 'You look like Godzilla.' He took it, ran with it, and abandoned his given name. Ever since, he blows a cork if anybody calls him anything else."

"Weird. What's his real name?"

"Stanley Krakowski."

She giggled. "Hey, Stellllaaaahhhh!!! Hey, Stellaaaahhhh!!"

"That's Kowalski, Stanley Kowalski."

She said, "Got to admit, it's an unfortunate name. Makes sense he prefers Godzilla."

I said, "Don't tease him about it. He's sensitive."

"He looks like a pretty big dude."

I stood up straight, pulled back my shoulders, and pushed back my hair with my hand. "You should've seen Godzilla in high school—the perfect V. Huge chest and shoulders, ribbed abdomen, machine gun biceps, tiny waist. Girls and their mothers huddled to watch him take off his sweats at swim meets."

"Was he on your team?"

"It goes much further back. There was never a time I didn't know Godzilla. We were born the same year, on the same street. His mother and my mother pushed us as newborns in strollers under big elm trees. That was before Dutch elm disease blighted the domed avenues of North Buffalo. Godzilla was slow and awkward as a child. Other children sensed he was different. He got frustrated and was prone to fits of anger and violence. He was big for his age and much stronger than other kids. He drooled. He didn't fit in and was never what you would call a normal kid. Expelled from St. Aloysius in third grade and forced to attend another school, he was an outcast, always an oddball. Our friendship resurfaced in high school. We won the 100-yard relay in the citywide swim meets two years in a row. He turned up again after my mother died, and this time he never left. We're like brothers, albeit he is a strange, massive, super muscular brother who behaves in peculiar ways. He has eccentric preoccupations, like surfing on Lake Erie in winter and swimming across the lake in chains to protest the Tiananmen Square massacre. And beware, he gets riled up at the drop of a hat."

"I'll look forward to that." She grimaced. "Both these guys sound like lunatics."

I nodded in agreement. "Certified maniacs, my best friends."

She said, "Who are your other two friends at the bar, Caligula and Attila the Hun? Give me a sentence or two, not a dissertation, so I'll remember their names."

"The one on the right is my childhood friend, Mark Rotolo. A finance and securities lawyer, he practiced in the same downtown firm for thirty years. He loathes Buffalo and dreams of leaving. Like quicksand, Buffalo has only pulled him deeper. He calls it 'Brutal Buffalo.' "

"How about the other guy? He's cute. Looks like a nice guy."

"Rudy O'Malley's the most irrepressible and positive person I know—the product of two social workers who raised twelve children. He followed his parents into the same profession. He works at the VA and maintains a robust private counseling practice."

The party dwindled, although the bar and restaurant were heating up. Drinking establishments are open until 4 a.m. in Buffalo. It was New Year's Eve, and people were heading off to other events. One after another, friends and relatives came over, hugged Victoria and me, and wished us well. Plans to get together were proposed, all knowing it would never happen. Dr. Schwab, sipping soda water, said, "We should do this again sometime," then departed into the cold night with an arm draped around Cleve Roberts, Mrs. Schwab, a little tipsy, trailed behind.

A handful of my hardcore friends remained, none in a hurry to leave.

Armstrong said, "Let's welcome in the New Year at my place."

She didn't finish her sentence before, like a squad familiar with the drill, everyone headed for the door. Some loaded into cars, and Victoria and I walked. As we meandered up Elmwood Avenue, a big, fat blood moon climbed above the city rooftops.

With a puff of steam pushing out, Vic said, "You seem pretty excited."

I said, "This is the real deal. These are my closest friends. Except for Garbôn, we've all stayed in touch."

She said, "After fiesta, they call this a *tardeada*, the after-party where the family and friends, the intimates, hang out to celebrate the event."

"I thought it meant a party in the afternoon."

"It's a Santa Barbara thing, a mix of Spanish and Mexican culture. You've got to be part of a charmed circle to get invited."

I said, "This is as charmed as it gets, and it won't happen again. Did you notice how everybody bolted for the door when Armstrong announced it?"

She pointed to the sky. "Once in a blood moon. I've heard you talk about your buddies. Give me a little more detail? Like, who's Harvs?"

I said, "She's Armstrong's best friend from nursing school."

Vic opened her arms. "Of course, the Whore Corps?"

"A bonafide charter member. Through Harvs, I met Armstrong. Harvs lived up the street, and we went to grade school together."

"But she introduced herself to someone at the church as Fiona."

"Most people don't know that's her name. There's a funny story. One night when I was home from college, my father walked downstairs in his boxer shorts. Harvs was sitting at the kitchen table. He opened the refrigerator, looked over, and said, 'How're you doing, Harvs?' and walked back upstairs. The next day, he asked me where I was going, and I said, 'Hanging out with Fiona.' He looked at me with puzzlement. 'Who the hell's Fiona?' he said. Nobody knows her name."

Vic asked, "What is it?"

"Fiona Shauna Harvey."

Vic said, "She's the chick in the sailboat in Key West."

"Now, you're up to speed. Harvs wants people to call her Fiona. It doesn't work no matter how hard we try. You call her what you like, but she'll answer to Harvs."

When we got to Armstrong's, eight of us sat across from each other on puffy, yellow flower couches between the fire and Christmas tree, overlooking the idyllic country church across the street. Soft Christmas music played in the background. How did we all survive? My sadness for my brother mixed with euphoria that my friends were together again.

Harvs shook her highball and clinked the ice. "Hey, Strong, why don't you put on that old Peter, Paul and Mary album we used to play over and over in the dorm? It has the cover photo of them dressed up as Bonnie and Clyde, holding machine guns."

Armstrong said, "You mean *Album 1700*?"

Harvs puckered her lips, took a sip of her drink, and nodded.

Everyone shouted, "Buffalo," and she chugged it.

Armstrong shuffled through a stack of worn cardboard album covers and pulled it out. When she placed the needle on the LP, it crackled. For a moment, we sat hopeful and unsure if anything would happen. It was very nostalgic, the thin line we all crossed when we settled into careers, mortgages, and families. I looked around the room, and we were reliving those halcyon days.

Garbôn in his earlier incarnation dominated and turned people off. In his twenties, he was uncouth, disheveled, unshaven, and brilliant. Now he was a new man, a professional with a family, yet I couldn't be sure. I feared things could get ugly fast.

Mark shifted in his chair. "Garbôn, I heard you talking about Buffalo. Do you know where Buffalo got its name?"

Garbôn coughed and blustered. "There's no discrepancy. The city got its name from the small trading settlement, Buffalo Creek. That dates back to 1780."

Godzilla chimed in, "That's not the question. Where did Buffalo Creek get its name?"

Garbôn said, "An acute observation. The American bison roamed the midwestern plains in the 1800s, but nowhere near Buffalo Creek."

Armstrong said, "I'm going to open another bottle of wine. Red or white?"

"Let's try a red," replied Victoria.

Godzilla said, "Yeah, you're right. The creek was named by those early French fur traders in the 1600s. They could have seen some bison.

"It's well documented that bison were extinct in this region long before then," Garbôn said.

Rudy O'Malley jumped in. "What about the Iroquois and Neutral tribe who lived here? Buffalo Creek's a mispronunciation of a Native American word. Their word for beaver is very close to buffalo. Or it might commemorate a great Seneca chief named Buffalo."

Victoria said, "I can tell we're getting into one of these Scajaquada discussions." She shouted across the room, "Armstrong, what other kinds of music do you have?"

"Come take a look. Play anything you like."

Mark said, "The name is an anglicized form of the French expression *beau fleuve*, translated as beautiful river. You know how the French Canadians barbarize French. Every other word is a belch-like stop or guttural groan." He made a deep sound in his throat, like a bullfrog, and said, "Buf-fla. That's how *beau fleuve* in the French Canadian tongue sounds to an English speaker's ear."

Garbôn said, "What about the story about horses slaughtered and passed off for buffalo meat? The epithet, 'buffaloed,' stuck."

I noticed Mark and Godzilla were beginning to nod off. Harvs was looking at her mobile phone.

Armstrong said, "Everybody's staying until we finish this bottle of wine. Nobody gets out of here before midnight."

I stood up and stretched. The mood had shifted. There was no consensus on what to do next.

Rudy said, "Let's take a walk around the neighborhood."

The group followed him down the stairs, once again part of the same organism. It started snowing. Rudy threw a snowball at Garbôn, and he threw one back. We walked along lonely, narrow lanes among Tudor mansions and weathered iron streetlamps. We picked our way along the slippery sidewalks, kicking lumps of ice like soccer balls. Then we reached a dark and hidden place, a clandestine Victorian circle.

Harvs said, "That's one of the Frank Lloyd Wright prairie houses."

An enormous frozen lawn led to a conservatory, and farther

behind the house was a horse stable. These homes were relics of the past. If only we could turn back time. Between Civil War and World War II, Buffalo was humming on all cylinders. Philanthropists, industrialists, entrepreneurs, and successful dreamers lived here. Was their vision or ingenuity any different than ours? "Shuffle Off to Buffalo" was on the tongue of the nation. The song was introduced in the hit musical film *42nd Street* in 1933. These homes felt like shells left behind by mollusks.

We resumed the merrymaking after we got back to Armstrong's.

Rudy said, "I saw this done at a conference. Let's go around and name our favorite song, why we like it, and how it has influenced our life."

Armstrong said, "I'll start. 'Stop, Look, Listen (To Your Heart),' by Marvin Gaye and Diana Ross."

Garbôn injected, "The original was done by the Philly rhythm and blues group, The Stylistics. Also, there's a nice cover by Johnny Mathis."

She stood with a drink in her hand. "I'm not sure. I was living in San Francisco, working, enjoying life. There were so many surprises. I miss the surprises."

Armstrong nudged Mark, whose eyelids drooped.

He said, "Favorite song, right. Creedence Clearwater, 'Lodi.' All the things I planned to do before I got stuck in my job and everything else. There's a fabulous line I can't remember at the moment, but it's about the disconnect.

Godzilla sang, "If I only had a dollar..."

"That's it! For every song I've sung."

Everybody joined in, "Oh Lord, stuck in a Lodi again."

Mark added, "What we dream and how it turns out like shit." He looked at Victoria.

She said, " 'No Man's Woman' by Sinéad O'Connor. The title

speaks for itself. I'm sick of men running everything. I wish I could stand up to patriarchy like Sinéad."

Garbôn said, "Look what happened to her. She got crushed."

Godzilla leaped to his feet. "She has bipolar disorder and attempted suicide on her thirty-third birthday."

Garbôn squinted and gave him a grave look.

Godzilla was winding up. "She did. Also, she looks like shit. She got fat. And that bald head thing doesn't work on somebody who looks like that. You know what I mean, a matron, an older woman who's going gray. She should shut up and take better care of herself and her family and go to the gym."

Victoria rolled her eyes.

I braced myself.

With a composed voice, Vic said, "That's what I'm talking about and why I like the song. Have you read her open letter to Miley Cyrus?"

Godzilla said, "I like Miley Cyrus."

"Of course you do. She's young and sexy."

"I like her music, too, and her video, 'We Can't Stop.' "

"Well, Sinéad told Miley that it's not cool to send that message. It's not OK to be a prostitute. It's dangerous because women have value beyond sexuality."

"Why?" Godzilla laughed and looked around the room for support.

Nobody laughed.

Victoria said, "We aren't playthings, just objects of desire."

Armstrong coughed and said, "Does anybody need anything? Let's do some shots."

Harvs said, "I'm up for it."

Victoria said, "At the same time, I love the way Sinéad sings 'I Believe in You.' That's the other side, the feminine at its best. It doesn't need to be all-out war and militancy." She punched me on the thigh and indicated it was my turn.

I said, "That's a hard choice."

She shifted. "Get on with it, Neal. If you could only take one song to an island, what would it be?"

"OK then, 'We People Who Are Darker Than Blue' by Curtis Mayfield. First, it's long and intricate, at least the way he performs it with Henry Gibson live at The Bitter End. There's a wailing saxophone that kills me every time I hear it. Sometimes I listen to it several times in a row. I remember how bad and lonely I felt in high school and how Curtis Mayfield made me feel better. Gave me hope. The cities were burning down, and he sang in that sweet calm voice." I looked at Garbôn.

He said, "Neal Young, 'Heart of Gold.' I like the line, 'I've been in my mind / It's such a fine mind.'"

Godzilla interrupted, "That's not the lyric. 'It's such a fine line,' not, 'fine mind.'"

"I like it the way I hear it, so I'll keep it that way," said Garbôn. "Does anybody know what the Beach Boys are singing? 'I wish they all could be California girls,' or, 'I wish they all could beat California girls?' You get it. It doesn't matter what the lyrics are on paper. It's how you hear it and what it means to you."

Rudy said, "Mine's a little song by Crosby, Stills, Nash, and Young. 'Find the Cost of Freedom.' I listened to it in Colorado. I'll never forget my two years there. On my own, I was working a long way from my family and Buffalo, which was liberating. Sometimes I wish I would've stayed. It's from the live double album, *4 Way Street*, and it features Stephen Stills. I identify with the loneliness and resolve in his voice."

Rudy looked at Harvs, who was falling asleep but said, "Not sure. I'll go with 'Gimme Shelter.' I saw the Stones last year, and they were awesome. Unbelievable. But on the original, you hear this crazy break in the female backup singer's scream."

Garbôn said, "Merry Clayton. She belts out, 'Rape, murder.'"

Harvs said, "The third time her voice cracks and Mick Jagger responds, 'Whoa.' It makes me remember Korea. What was I doing in the military? It was such a mixed bag. I wished I could scream like that. That song brings me back."

She looked at Godzilla, who looked away. He reached for a shot of tequila with his right hand.

When his elbow went up, the group bellowed, "Buffalo!"

He said, "Shit, I'm drunk already."

We tormented him, "Drink, drink, drink."

He lifted the shot glass above his head, showed it, and brought it to his lips, then downed it in a single gulp followed by a shudder. He said, "What were we talking about?"

Harvs said, "Your favorite song?"

"Oh, yeah, it's got to be Jimmy Buffett's 'Son of a Son of a Sailor.' I never get tired of it. When I was younger, it was, 'A Pirate Looks at Forty.' I also was a pirate two hundred years too late, but I'm a long way past that now."

Victoria pulled a curled Jimmy Buffet album off Armstrong's shelf. A gray cover featured an older Jimmy Buffet with a broad mustache, ascot, blue blazer, and captain's hat. She put the needle on vinyl, and we hummed along and sang the words we could remember.

Midnight came, we kissed and hugged, and toasted with full glasses. It was New Year's Day. One by one, like falling leaves, we dispersed and reentered our respective lives.

# PART III

# 3 JANUARY, TUESDAY, 8:06 A.M.

## (SANTA BARBARA, CA)

*"you know that the saddest lies*
*are the ones we tell ourselves"*
Lucille Clifton (1936-2010)

V IC'S FUMING, THE BEDROOM DOOR shut tight, and I don't dare enter. I'm wearing a T-shirt, no pants, shivering under a throw blanket in the living room, writing in my notebook. We quarreled on the plane, and all hell broke loose at LAX.

Yesterday started in a snowstorm. The Prius, still at Cole's, wouldn't turn over. Something about a frozen fuel line. Mark Rotolo said he'd get it back to the rental place. Although hungover and exhausted, Armstrong insisted on driving us to the airport. Sticky, wet snowflakes clung to every surface while some melted on impact, forming a sludgy gruel. The windshield wipers beat madly, like a hummingbird's wings. Visibility reduced to instinct, Armstrong remained unflappable and piloted her craft like Charon. We advanced crosstown on the Kensington Expressway through what looked like a cloud of cream of wheat.

From the back seat, Victoria said, "Are you sure they're flying today?"

"Looks like it's a go," Armstrong said. "Haven't heard anything different."

When we got to the loading zone, Armstrong popped the trunk, jumped out of the car, and helped us extract our bags. In a matter of minutes, her ankle-length, red wool coat was nearly white, gummed in snowflakes. The wind howled, and ice water dripped down our cheeks. We hugged.

She said, "I better go. I'm not very good at this. I hate goodbyes."

She slammed the door, revved the engine, and roared off into the whiteout.

Victoria looked at me. "They can't be flying today."

I said, "I checked the flight before we left, and it's on time. No delays."

"Ridiculous. This is ludicrous. You can't see your hand in front of your face. Do you think it's safe?"

We checked in, and the agent directed us to wait at the gate. Our soggy bags and gear at our feet, we settled into comfortable chairs.

I said, "This is a pretty cool airport."

Vic scowled and scanned the suspended fifty-foot glass ceiling, the only barrier between us and the lake-effect gales that whistled above our heads.

I said, "This is a significant improvement from my days in Buffalo. It's fun watching a blizzard from this vantage point."

She scrunched up her face. "Thank you, Mr. Narrator. Do you have to say out loud whatever comes into your head? I pay attention to what you have to say. Can't you shut up sometimes? I'm on overload."

Snow accumulated in waves, and the tarmac transformed into

a battlefield. A half dozen huge, tank-like snowplows matched the intensity of the storm.

Victoria grimaced and said, "Nothing's getting out of here today."

I said, "They're doing a pretty good job clearing the runway."

Ten minutes later, an announcement came. "Passengers on American Flight 3503 for Dallas, please report to gate five for boarding."

Vic studied me in the very bright interior created by the white snowfall reflecting off the windows. She said, "You look tired and old. I see wrinkles I've never seen before."

I didn't reply, and we wheeled our bags to the gate. Then I turned to her and said, "Not only the weather's harsh in Buffalo."

She said, "Just saying. You're the one who wants the microscopic truth."

We didn't speak or look at one another until we were in flight, an hour outside of Dallas.

She said, "You need to divorce your family."

Her statement jolted me.

"Say something," she said. "We need to talk about this."

I said, "I don't like them much either. But divorce? Mick's dead. My sisters are all that's left. What does that mean?"

"Cut them off and don't respond anymore. Break the cycle, move on with your life."

I said, "You're looking for a simple answer to a complicated question. I can't *cut off* my family."

"Why not?"

"That isn't how my father raised me. I'm stuck with them."

She leaned in. "Didn't work that way with Aleida and Scarlett."

"That's different. You're talking about my ex-wives. They're not blood."

"But it's over. You paid Scarlett off and haven't heard a word. Why not the same with your sisters?"

I said, "It pissed me off that Cassie didn't invite anyone back to the house after the memorial. Mick has a full bar. What are they going to do with all that booze?"

Vic interrupted, "If you haven't noticed, they didn't call to check on us or say goodbye. When are you going to get it? They don't love you, Neal. Your sisters are toxic to both of us. I can't take it anymore. I've had enough."

I shifted in my seat, looking around to see if anybody was listening. In a muffled voice, I said, "How can I cut myself off from my sisters? They're family."

Vic was in attack mode, homicidal, unyielding, and unwilling to let it go or back down. "You want Cassie calling you and, when you don't answer, putting you on speed dial every thirty seconds? If you let her, she'll continue to show up for medical treatment wherever we live. Can't you see it, Neal? They only bring you down. Mick is gone. You're free. You've paid your dues."

Again, I was silent.

She said, "To make this work, you've got to feel it in your bones. Do it for us, if not for yourself. It's unhealthy. We can't live a good life with them in it."

I said, "If you don't have family, what's left? Friends can never take the place of family."

"Neal, there's no choice here. You're done with them or done with me."

I squirmed and my jaw tightened. "You're giving me an ultimatum?"

"It's more than that, Neal. I love you. I didn't sign up for this dysfunction and drama. I didn't grow up that way. I put up with it while Mick was alive, but not anymore."

We changed planes in Dallas. Through disembarking and re-boarding, we never spoke a word. I was seething. Cassie and

Saundra, despicable, both of them…but how can I cut myself off? And who was Vic to tell me to do that? I couldn't back down. I thought about Viet Nam. What were we fighting for there? Honor. I was defending my sisters, whom I loathe. Neither one of them has shown any love for me without asking for something in return.

Vic in the window seat, me on the aisle, the middle seat vacant, we ignored one another for the entire flight. Cleared to land at LAX, the bang from the plane's belly when the landing gear dropped broke the silence. Then ten minutes later, the screech of the brakes signaled we'd touched down. When the bell rang to deplane, Victoria jumped to her feet and jockeyed for position. She grappled with pulling down her carry-on from the overhead.

I stood and put a hand on her bag and said, "Let me help?"

Her eyes narrowed, and she pulled it away and the bag crashed to the floor with a loud thud. When I attempted to pick it up, she pushed me away. "Let go. I don't need your help." Then she weaved like a halfback through a crowd of passengers waiting in the aisle.

I lost sight of her. A young woman with two small children strained to get a folded stroller out of the bin in front of me. The smell of diesel and baby spit-up filled the air. I sat back down in my seat.

The woman pointed and said, "You're tall. Can you help me reach that?"

I ignored her, snatched my bag from the overhead, and pressed forward through the plane, bumping into people as I went. When I got to the gangway, I started running. Pulling my carry-on behind me, I sprinted through the airport, conjuring up a vague idea of where we'd parked the car. The keys were in my pocket. I saw Victoria outside and darted in front of a moving bus, then across a six-lane highway, dragging my bag behind me. Horns honked, brakes screeched. A furious man in a truck pulled up beside me and screamed, "What are you trying to do, you stupid motherfucker, kill yourself?" He roared away, and I wanted to die then and there. I ran and ran and ran. I'd lost my family, my brother was dead, and Victoria threatened to leave me. In the madness of LAX, acres of parking lots, and heavy congestion, my suitcase bounced and wobbled as I ran, dodging traffic, my heart beating like a piston. I wanted to die. I was begging a car, a bus, a truck to put me out of my misery. I lost contact with Victoria, found the car, loaded my bag, and took off. I drove to the gate to pay, stopped, thought twice about it, and turned around. When I circled back, she was sitting on the concrete parking stop in the space where we'd parked the car under a single stark streetlamp.

She said, "Give me the keys."

I resisted.

She repeated, "Give me the keys."

I acquiesced.

Victoria drove ninety-six miles, two hours and five minutes, back to Santa Barbara. We didn't speak a word. My right hand clutching the passenger door handle, I thought, *open it, end it*. I imagined myself as roadkill. Wouldn't it be better that way? When we got home, we unpacked without speaking a word and went to bed, me on the couch, her in the bedroom.

Sunlight's streaming through the Venetian blinds, not warming yet. The air is chilly, nothing like western New York, but too cold to get up. Bright and cloudless, the sun gushes through the smallest cracks. The snow-eclipsed sky of the Great Lakes is far behind me, yet the travails of Buffalo aren't over. If it had been my idea to nullify my relationship with my sisters, I'd be all for it. Under these circumstances, I'm fighting for something I don't want. And worst of all, I've dug in.

In his early twenties, Mick had led the Buffalo police on a high-speed chase. They apprehended him in the Forest Lawn Cemetery. My father knew a judge and got him off. The incident swept under the rug, Mick went on with his reckless life. The same rage and unpredictable demons flare up in me now. Where the fuck would I be if I couldn't write? Is it in my DNA, like my father, to go bat shit crazy? A wild bull out of control? Faith and longevity in marriage comes down to a matter of forgetting. A short memory pays off. There is no forgiveness for how I behaved last night. But I have faith that Vic, in time, will forget what I did.

My parents dying was one thing, my brother, another. All the clichés don't come close to explaining my anguish. Are there words for it? Gloom, heartbreak, despair, wretchedness. The torment in my gut, the sadness on waking? When my parents died, I didn't cry. It was a relief. My father's heart had been hanging on a few thin muscle fibers after a catastrophic heart attack. There was no viability left. My mother's brain had been ravaged by stroke. These were natural causes that came in consequence of time. They'd lived a life, and Mick hadn't. His potential has been spent. I'm angry, full of rage, and I can't find tears for Mick either. Can I find words? Will words lead to grief, a cleansing cry from the heart?

Before we left for the airport, Garbôn called, and we talked for an hour while Victoria and Armstrong had coffee. It was like old times. How did he reenter my life? Looking back thirty years, my ex-wife, Scarlett, walked in when Aleida walked out. The scene, a post office in Fort Lauderdale. Standing behind me in line, Scarlett said with a Southern drawl, "You're Neal Motherwell." I nodded. She said, "I'm Dr. Hart's medical assistant." We talked for two hours. I confided in her what had happened with Aleida. I told her about my acceptance to Duke. She said, "You've got to go. My sister and brother-in-law graduated from Duke." It felt scripted and preplanned. Who sent Scarlett? I didn't think I could survive without Aleida. She played such a significant role in my reaching for Duke, and then she said it was my destiny, not hers. Living alone, after Aleida left, I had panic attacks. Cooking rice one night, I forgot about it and left it on the burner, and the apartment almost went up in flames. Scarlett put out the fire. Then Duke, divorce, marriage, a new religion, new friends, and colleagues. Six months later, Aleida called and wanted reconciliation.

And what about my layoff at the hospital? I'd finished a doctorate at fifty and found my dream job, all my talents employed. I'd attained my avocation, and they paid me for what I wanted to do most—writing with people who needed to express themselves, a way to commune with one another in a supportive way, beyond the medical model, where I fit in best. Over seven years, it grew by leaps and bounds. Hundreds of people and their families participated. It also allowed me a place to open up and write out my confusion, turmoil, and agitation. I applied the hands-on principles I'd learned at Duke and San Francisco. Everything made sense until one day when my boss's assistant pushed a piece of paper across her desk. It was the banking crisis of 2007 and, in an instant, it was over. Then, two weeks later, a vice president came and offered me the job back.

I'd already moved on with Vic to Santa Barbara. It took years to get over the loss. What triggers me? Could I have avoided the meltdown at LAX? Why did I blow a gasket? Is there some reason I couldn't suck it up and let Victoria fume? What's so competitive in me where I refuse to follow? Wouldn't restraint have been better this time? If only I had the strength and endurance to let it prevail. I can be such an asshole. I crave the fireworks. Had I not acted like a jerk, would I have anything to write about today? Is it our slip-ups that lead to enlightenment? Only by admitting and acknowledging do I have a chance to change. Most of my destructive stuff is done out of ignorance. If I write it, does it mean I admit it? That's what I advocated at the hospital writing groups.

With Garbôn, after thirty years of separation, it feels like not a day has passed. Both of us remain turbulent and unresolved. On the outside, things look pretty good. He's married, the father of two college-age children, and responsible for people's teeth. He also sent me an email. He woke last night in tears. His mother took his cat away when he was twelve and gave it to another family. The excuse? His sister was allergic to cats. It was all a lie. He hid in a closet, clutched the cat close to his face. His mother took the cat and gave it away. He never got over the grief.

The story seemed too close to my own. In fact, it seemed like the same story. After a knockdown battle with my father when I was eleven, I crawled into a closet. I was shaking with tears. I don't remember the reason for the fight, but the humiliation sticks with me.

My mother flushed me out, coerced me to apologize to my father. She said, "You'll be a better man for it."

My father was belligerent, a massive hulk, four times my size. Why was it me who had to apologize? I was a child out of control, and he was an adult. His violence revolted me.

I did apologize, and I remember saying out loud, "I'll be a better man for it."

It stuck in my craw that my mother possessed that kind of persuasiveness and could bend my will.

Am I a better man for it? I didn't have the strength to defy her. I did have the power to defy my father. What would have happened if I'd said no to my mother, if I'd refused her demoralizing demand and stayed in the closet, defiant and weeping? If I'd spat in my father's face rather than extending my hand? Would I be a better man for it?

My father, like Lake Erie, was a tideless inland sea, calm most of the time. It was his violent, unpredictable storms I feared. The same rage, fury, and erratic eruptions endemic to the Great Lakes permeated our home. Outside the household, he was a sunny day to all who knew him.

One of Mick's spectacular moments took place when he was

eleven. He was skippering a 19-foot centerboard sloop called a Lightning at summer camp. A storm came up, and the gates of hell opened. Black clouds, gale-force winds, and five-foot waves. What started as a calm day flipped in a microsecond, and four small kids were his crew. Mick yanked the tiller, tacked, and turned the craft to shore. He opened the jib and rode the squall safe into the harbor. When he landed, the waterfront staff clapped and cheered. Mick was a hero.

He loved to talk about it, and it became a standard part of our telephone conversations.

He'd say, "Remember the Lightning?"

On cue, I'd reply, "How did you do it?"

"Don't mess with me. No rain, no wind, no heaven or hell, no exhalation. There's no wave tall enough to flip my craft, nor thwart my destination. Don't mess with me, please. I ain't no tease. You're playin' with the best. I guarantee you won't be blessed."

Now Mick is dead, and he'll no longer weave his myth. My sisters are alive, and they'll sell the house and everything in it. They'll abuse and cheat Pixie. Money-grubbing, untrustworthy liars. Their greed is outdistancing their selfishness.

My sojourn in Buffalo is over, and I'm back in the clinic tomorrow. Yet nothing is the same. Mick's death broke the detente with my sisters. Vic wants me to sever my relationship with them, and I know she's right. There's no going back. But I'm not ready. I can't let go, and I can't back down.

# 4 JANUARY, 4:35 A.M.

## (SANTA BARBARA, CA)

*"It is an easy thing to talk of patience to the afflicted."*
William Blake (1757-1827)

N O CHANGE WITH VIC. WE adhere to a strict code, one of silence and contempt. Cohabitating in a tiny space, invisible and inconspicuous, tests one's resolve. The battle lines are drawn. As if we are one creature split in two, we don't brush into one another in the kitchen or the bathroom. We limit all contact to an expression or a glance, albeit an irritated or hostile one. We move beneath time, neither ready to talk. We know the whereabouts of the other, as if we have built-in sonar, like a bat. Only a well-worn relationship, like bruised leather, allows for such a regimen.

As a youngster, Vic had worked her family's cattle ranch. Her father worshipped her and delighted in her company. As an adult, when she visited, her mother was jealous. Nothing made Walter happier than spending time with Victoria. The relationship was one of silence and respect. The two alone, quiet in a room, created a space where anxiety couldn't enter. Though he had four sons, Walter regaled Vic's prowess as a wrangler and proclaimed her the best of the bunch. He cherished Vic. At the dinner table, with her brothers and their families in attendance, he captivated us with stories. They had a special bond. In the field on horses, he said he could communicate with her from a football field away. All it took was a click of his tongue or a raised eyebrow, and she knew which way to move the cattle.

Buffalo was so toxic and cruel, my family's feculence exposed. Bleak and harsh, loud and panicked, nerve endings frayed. Vic didn't grow up that way. We need a break from each other. It was a relief to go to work yesterday, to do something familiar and helpful, to escape the conflict.

When I walked into the clinic, three patients were in the lobby, and one waited in the exam room. Katie was in the workroom, hunched over her desk in concentration. I focused on the back of her head, a stylish, short, thick scalp of silver.

She asked, "How are you, and how is he?"

I said, "It's been a rough week. It looks like we've got a full house."

She said, "Oh, good grief. Jeez, Louise. Let me scope out the scoop."

Only then did I realize she wasn't talking to me. She had an earpiece in and was speaking to a patient on the phone.

She said, "I don't know. I don't know. Good gosh."

And that's how I felt.

We exchanged a glance, and Katie managed a frazzled smile. When she hung up the phone, she turned to me. "I brought an extra sandwich. It's in the fridge. Also, there are oranges from my yard on the table."

I said, "Thanks. I didn't bring lunch."

She swiveled her chair and looked at her screen. "Thought that might be the case."

Then it was off to the races until midmorning, when several patients canceled and the phones went quiet. The waiting room became a ghost town. I knew we'd pay for it later.

I grabbed the sandwich from the fridge and a couple of oranges and went outside to eat lunch on a bench in the parking lot and enjoy the comfort of a warm day, no jacket required. A balmy ocean breeze clattered the palm fronds. Bright sunlight streamed through a flourishing angel's trumpet tree. Its big, yellow, pendulous flowers provided much-needed shade. A thick, saucy perfume drifted over me, and some of its enormous blossoms fell to my feet. That's when Pixie called.

She said, "Me and your sisters wanted to make sure you got home OK."

I said, "Everything's OK. I went back to work today."

She said, "Another blizzard dropped a foot of snow after you left."

"We saw some of it on the way out. What's happening at the house?"

"I went shopping today. Can't seem to keep enough food around."

I said, "Yeah, with Cassie there. It didn't look like there was much in the fridge."

She said, "I didn't buy much today, but you'll love this. My bill was two hundred and four dollars. I saved one hundred and twenty-six dollars and, with coupons, I only paid seventy-eight. And you'll love even more what I did last week. Last week, my bill was three hundred and thirty-nine dollars and thirty-six cents, but I saved two hundred and fifty-five dollars. I paid eighty-four dollars with coupons."

"If I save five bucks with coupons, I'm impressed," I said.

She laughed and said, "It's a skill."

"Do you pull them out of different newspapers and magazines?"

She said, "I cut the coupons out in the Sunday paper. But my mom and I share, 'cause if there's a coupon for something I use and Mom doesn't, she gives me hers, and I do the same. Mom doesn't eat granola bars. I eat a ton. Stuff like that."

I said, "With Cassie around, you probably go to the store every day."

"Since she came, I've spent four hundred and eighty-two dollars on groceries, and that's with coupons."

I said, "Sure weird that Mick's gone."

"He was my guy," she said.

"I know."

She said, "I never told you the cookie story. You'll laugh. It's funny. I went to Strong Memorial every day for seven and a half months. Every day."

"So it was that long. Wow."

"If I didn't go, Mick would call me twelve times a day crying."

"Wasn't he intubated most of the time?"

"Sometimes. But, um, the times he was…"

I said, "Conscious."

"He just wanted to get out of there, just wanted to get out of there in the worst way. He wanted to go home. That was his thing. He wanted to go home. So he's like, 'I want some cookies.' I said, 'OK.' I left at seven in the morning every morning to see him. I got home after eight o'clock every night. I have to do the laundry. I have to, you know, find something to eat, you know, to do the regular stuff, pay the bills, blah, blah, blah."

I said, "How long a drive is it to Rochester?"

"Hour and a half each way. So, I stopped at the store and got him Keebler cookies, the ones with the peanut butter cups in them. They're pretty good. He wouldn't eat 'em. He says to me, 'What in the hell am I supposed to do with these?' I told him, 'Don't eat them, then. You're good.' He says, 'You know, Pix, you got me too spoiled. I don't eat cookies from the store. I only eat cookies that you make.' "

I said, "Sounds like Mick."

"So here I am, two o'clock in the morning and I can't sleep. I'm making stupid cookies for him."

"What kind would you make?"

"Oh, he was fussy. He was spoiled, but…. He liked brownies with chocolate chips in them but no frosting and no powdered sugar on top. He liked chocolate chip cookies, but he'd like not a lot of chocolate in them. He'd always say, 'extra batter.' "

I said, "I'd like just the opposite, more chocolate."

She said, "I don't like chocolate, so I don't make cookies like that."

I said, "I pulled out some old videos yesterday and watched four or five clips of Mick on *Good Morning Buffalo*. He made omelets. I had no idea where he was going with it, and neither did the host."

She said, "That's Drew Kahn."

"Was he at the church?"

"Sure was. You shook his hand."

"Now that you mention it, I met him in the receiving line. I didn't put it together. A tall guy was wearing a sweatshirt."

"That's him."

"In the video, he's very dapper in a suit."

She said, "You won't see him in a suit now. He's a professor at UB."

"He and Mick had a wonderful rapport. It came through even after all these years. They kept up a steady banter. Mick cooked the onions, garlic, mushrooms, and peppers in the pan first and then stirred in the eggs. He said, 'to let it thicken.' He used the word 'coagulate.' "

She said, "Coagulate, yeah, that's what he'd say."

"The host said, 'Most people would cook that in two separate pans.' "

"And Mick said, 'That's the mistake you're making.' "

I laughed and said, "That's what he said. After the omelet set up, he flipped it like a pancake. He added mozzarella, provolone, and Swiss cheese, let it cook, and folded it. I'd never seen an omelet cooked like that before."

She said, "That's how he did it."

"Mick said he did four hundred and seventy-five of them on Mother's Day at the Hyatt."

"That's about right. What else did you watch?"

"He made coquilles St. Jacques, seafood pesto, and venison hunter's stew."

"What about Mother's sweetbread?"

I said, "That too."

"What about Hawaiian chicken paradise?"

"Yeah, that was there. And there were more. I can't remember the others. Mick also did a *Taste of Buffalo* promo. He was talking a mile a minute. I couldn't understand him."

She said, "That's Mick."

"What about Cassie and Saundra?"

"Saundra took down the dining room chandelier. The plaster and wood chips were everywhere. She did it herself with a Phillips head screwdriver, couldn't wait to get it down. She was huffing and puffing. It left a huge hole in the ceiling. She almost dropped it on the table. She couldn't get it down fast enough and refused any help. She also cleaned out the crystal cabinet. We never used it. Saundra wrapped it in newspaper and put it in her car. There's no room to sit, and the trunk's full too. She's using Mick's car to get around."

"I thought Cassie didn't want anything moved."

"I guess she changed her mind. There's a liquidator coming tomorrow."

I said, "How come Cassie doesn't call me?"

"I don't know. Your sisters are always out. Saundra drives Cassie around. You know, Tim's on hospice now. I sit with him during the day."

I winced at the mention of Saundra's tyrannized husband.

She said, "He's not doing well."

"I knew he had prostate cancer, but that's been going on for years. I didn't know it had gotten that far along. Saundra didn't say anything at the memorial."

She said, "That's why he wasn't there."

"I should give him a call."

"He sleeps most of the time, and a nurse comes in the afternoon. He doesn't eat much. I baked him snickerdoodles, which are his favorite, and he nibbled on them. He tried to pinch me on the butt. I told you that story about him stealing my bra when Mick and I were on vacation with them in Florida. He's a pervert."

"Why isn't Saundra with him?"

"She says she's too busy with Cassie and the house. Mick's got huge medical bills, over a million dollars from Strong Memorial alone. Your sisters are trying to work it out so the state pays it. Mick didn't have any money. Cassie and Saundra are finagling with a lawyer to keep the house."

I said, "How long are they staying?"

"I dunno."

"All I saw in the refrigerator was an empty pizza box."

She said, "Cassie orders Bocce pizza, but she doesn't get a normal pizza. She gets triple cheese, double pepperoni, double mushroom. It's so thick I can't eat it."

"She used to fold the pizza in half, so she doubled every bite."

She said, "Still does that. Did Mick make chicken parm?"

"I didn't see that clip."

"That was his signature dish. He always whipped it up when my parents came over."

I said, "I make it too. Maybe I'll make it for Vic tonight."

"I didn't know you cooked."

"Only on special occasions. The best way to Vic's affections is through her stomach."

"Are you in trouble with Vic?"

"Not exactly. It's getting better."

"I don't know how she tolerated Saundra and Cassie. She's a saint. I'm glad she was here. Tell me how you make your chicken parm?"

"I dip the chicken breast in egg batter."

I heard her sigh. "You don't prep it? You have to butterfly the chicken breast and bread it first with flour. You skipped the whole first step."

"I sprinkle breadcrumbs and pan-fry it in olive oil."

"Mick always used panko breadcrumbs for a lighter crust. But wait a minute, you don't put the chicken breast in cellophane and pound it?"

I said, "No."

"Mick always used a cooking mallet. That's the whole point." She giggled.

"Makes sense," I said. "I've never done that before."

"That's what makes the meat so tender, so it melts in your mouth. What you made wasn't chicken parm, but breaded chicken with tomato sauce. What kind of pasta did you use?"

I said, "Bow tie."

"Mick always used angel hair pasta. OK, here's the deal. There are three steps. First, butterfly the chicken breast. Then, flour with salt, pepper, and Italian seasonings and dip it in egg batter. I like to add a little water, then bread it with panko breadcrumbs. I use Italian style. Step two, pan fry it and finish it in the oven at 325 degrees for forty-five minutes so as not to dry it out. Finally, add tomato sauce at room temperature. Be generous with fresh mozzarella over the top and cook until the mozzarella melts. I don't make my sauce from scratch the way Mick did."

"Got it. Can I call you next time I make it? It seems complicated."

"Sure thing. I hope you won't be needing to make a peace

offering to Vic anytime soon. I'm with Tim, and the nurse is at the door. I'll call you soon." She hung up.

I sat on the bench and examined the sagging tubular trumpets as they fell, each a husky, golden bell, half-closed with a pink lipstick fringe. If ingested, angel's trumpet is poisonous and can paralyze and induce hallucinations. Such a tangy, robust scent that seduces while masking its deadly intent. A couple days ago, I'd be sitting in a heated apartment looking out at ice and snow.

Hungry, I attacked the peanut butter and jelly sandwich on home-baked bread. It tasted better because Katie had made it. What a doll. She knew it was my first day back. The oranges were juicy and easy to peel. Satsuma mandarins are a joy of winter in southern California. I chuckled at the thought of Saundra smothered in plaster, her thick, short bob of gray hair covered in white dust. She ached to unmoor my mother's chandelier. I marveled at her industry. How did she wrench that old light fixture from its sturdy anchorage with a screwdriver? What drives her? It can't be money. She's always broke, robbing Peter to pay Paul and the IRS fast on her heels. And there's not a sentimental bone in her body, so she won't keep it or cherish it. She'll sell it and fabricate a story on the spot to inflate the price. It's the frenzy of the marketplace Saundra craves. She's greedy for it. She lusts to get something over on someone. She's obsessed with knickknacks, bric-a-brac, and *objets d'art*, all as a catalyst. She's addicted to the stress.

And it's in that drive that she and Tim found their nexus. But first, there was Leslie. My recollections would be incomplete without his mention. He's more than a footnote because Saundra's children bear his name. Over the decades, he proved discreet—a precision instrument for Saundra's nefarious ends. But I'm getting ahead of the story. I was eight at Saundra and Leslie's wedding, a memory so murky, but some details remain indelible, like a bloodstain on a white sheet.

It was a big family affair, a sunny day at St. Mark's Cathedral followed by a reception at the country club. I pelted the bride and groom with a fistful of rice as they raced to the car. Uncle Sigi caught it in a photo—my eyes pierced and lips tight, like I'm trying to knock down a batter with a fastball as a rain of rice rushed out of my right hand. I'd heard someone whisper in the vestibule, "That Leslie seems funny." I'd chewed on it. Leslie never made me laugh. Another murmured, "Italianized." Another cackled, "He's Greek." Leslie was odd, not funny, a tall, thin man with a droopy widow's peak. Always wore a puckered look, like he was about to sneeze. Clothes hung long on his skeleton like a manikin. And his ancestry was Scottish.

Leslie carried himself high in the shoulders, hands adrift. He walked with a wiggle, not a confident stride. Never direct but always pursuing an indeterminate course. Years later, Saundra confided that at nineteen, she'd never been with a man. Following the restrictions of the nuns, she'd never ventured a kiss. Her first child, Leslie, Jr., was the product of a single act of intercourse. She'd pressed Leslie to make love to her during their honeymoon in Hawaii. They never conjoined in sexual union again.

They'd met at Buffalo Airport, where they worked as ticket agents for United Airlines. Leslie had second thoughts and, at one point, called off the engagement. Cassie intervened and convinced him to go forward. Leslie was later convicted of embezzlement and fired and disgraced and took up childrearing full time. That's when Saundra discovered her sex drive, which was prodigious. She had dozens of affairs and got pregnant with her second child. Saundra never revealed the suitor, and, in those days, highly accurate DNA testing wasn't available. I was always taken aback by my father's reaction as she was seeing men in his circle. He said, "It feels strange to call your daughter a whore. But that's what she is."

The second child, Dwight, took Leslie's surname, and Leslie stayed on as household manager and nanny. The arrangement suited everyone until a phone call came for my father. Leslie had approached a male police officer in the downtown Greyhound bus terminal. Arrested and held for lewd and lascivious behavior, my father couldn't get him off. I remember Leslie weeping so loudly my father held the phone away from his ear. The scandal led to divorce and, for Leslie, a downward spiral. Saundra carried on as if nothing happened. The last time I saw Leslie, years ago, he was toothless, living in a dive above a bar on Chippewa Street. He was washing dishes to make ends meet. Soon after, he died by a gruesome suicide, throwing himself off a skid row building in the dead of winter.

But that was a lifetime ago. Saundra's story gathered momentum when she was still young, hot to trot, and Tim carried a gun. Leslie was homemaking and raising the kids. He shopped, vacuumed, and packed lunches, which allowed Saundra to kick up her heels.

Some men crave a Harley or a low chassis Chevrolet, but Tim lusted for a smooth operator. He was a wheeler-dealer, an engineer of deception, a swindler, a master of the sleight of hand. He wanted Saundra to be Barnum to his Bailey, Bonnie to his Clyde. He became Saundra's accomplice, co-conspirator, and partner in crime. She sold low-end real estate, and Tim made shady loans. They worked on volume and quantity, never quality. She was the doyenne with him behind the scenes. Tim massaged the paperwork, and Saundra closed the deal. Together they bamboozled young and old. Starter houses with mold and foundation problems for newlyweds. Budget condos a stone's throw from Love Canal in Niagara Falls to elderly widows with social security. I'll never forget Tim's dreamy eyes. I was fifteen when Tim took me aside and said, "She's a thoroughbred. She can run." I thought he was talking about a racehorse until he added with enthusiasm, "Your sister can sell anybody anything."

Saundra and Tim were a dream team, a status most appreciated by my family. Tim weathered Saundra's murderous outbursts. Rather than us, he was the punching bag to her foul temper often displayed in public. Once, on Mother's Day at the Buffalo Athletic Club, I saw her push him up against a wall and slap him silly in the cloakroom. I was in my early teens and stayed out of the way. She let out a blood-curdling scream. When they returned to the table, they were all smiles as if nothing had happened. My father, in a coarse whisper, said to my mother, "I don't know how any man can take it. Why doesn't he hit her back? A man can't let a woman get the upper hand." My mother replied, "No other man would have her. Let's be grateful." Cassie let out a sigh. "Imagine where we'd be if Tim weren't around." Saundra could blow a gasket at any time, and Tim could absorb whatever she delivered. And we counted our blessings.

After Leslie's departure, in a limp-dicked tough love way, Tim took on her boys. But it didn't start that way. Tim was a single, hypermasculine career parole officer. In the beginning, he bowled Saundra over with his testosterone and male prowess, and as I said, he holstered a gun. She had other suitors, but eventually, only him. Over time, like Japanese water torture, she asserted control. There was never a doubt in my mind that he loved her, and I wasn't alone in wondering why.

Saundra and Tim, once married, regardless of earnings, were always in debt. They drove a yellow Cadillac convertible with whitewalls and lived in the suburbs. Tim had two children from a previous marriage who visited on weekends. My father said, "They're playing a shell game. It's only a matter of time before they get caught." He confronted them. "Why don't you put something away for a rainy day?" Saundra's reputation as a pariah was well earned. She harassed my father, ever in a crisis, and pushed him to the limit. He used up all his favors with friends, business associates, and judges to exonerate her. And Tim abetted her behavior. When he pleaded with me to give them five thousand dollars because the IRS was closing in, he said, "You don't want to see your sister go to prison, do you?" Like a fool, I complied. I still have the hand-scrawled promissory note he wrote that rescued the two of them from jail time.

Mick is gone, and my sisters are all that's left. This is my family. As a kid, I wondered how I could share the same DNA. Mick's hallucination was prescient. He saw Saundra gathering all my mother's possessions. Now Saundra's moved in and she's taking whatever she wants. When Saundra whispered to me, "We each get a buck," her stale breath had hung on my face. She'd repeated the phrase several times, like a mafia hitman, with hand gestures. She's found a way to get what she wanted.

Some years back, I stayed with Saundra and Tim in their dreary trailer in Lockport. A lonely gravel road led to a bleak habitat accessed through a flimsy aluminum door. Once inside, I was engulfed by a pervasive odor, antiseptic, like in a hospital. It turns out Tim, as he advanced in years, became compulsive, a germophobe. He sanitized my hands on entry. The guest room was no bigger than a closet and cluttered with kitsch. There were no curtains. He said it was "a milieu for microorganisms." Outside, a thirty-foot streetlamp beamed in my face. An annoying, pink and yellow cuckoo clock hung on the wall. Each tick and tock jolted me, and then an ass-kicking hoot on the hour. I heard the two of them down a long hallway turning, farting, snoring throughout the night. I decamped before they stirred orange juice in the morning and never returned.

Both Saundra's sons are living underground without a glimmer of a happy or productive life. Fifteen years ago, Leslie, Jr. developed a heroin habit. He helped Saundra and Tim with the flea market business. While Saundra and Tim were in Florida, he sold everything, even the best stuff, to pay his debts. Saundra disowned him. Last I heard, Leslie, Jr., is living on the streets of New York City. There's been no word of him for years.

Dwight, a few years younger, started a family with his high school sweetheart. They had three children before either reached twenty. Dwight loved guns and signed up for the first Gulf War. He came back altered, and the couple split. In a fit of rage, Dwight kidnapped the children. Picked up by state troopers with a trunk full of automatic weapons, it's a mystery why he's not serving time. Dwight's partner and the children steer clear of Saundra and Tim. When I asked Saundra about informing them about Mick, she said, "Why bother?" I argued, "They're my godsons, they should know." She glared at me. "*I* made you their godfather. They're dead to me now. Stay out of my business."

So, this is my family. Are they worth fighting for?

Vic hasn't muttered a word since we got home. On the plane, she said, "Divorce your family." Why the beef? It was a strange term to use in this regard. What is it to divorce? Is there such a thing as a legal dissolution with my family, and does that include my city? I looked it up. Divorce means to have no more legal bonds or debts connected to the other as once it had been in a marriage. Isn't that already the case with my sisters? There's nothing left, nothing binding. What about the emotional strings? They don't call or return my calls but rather, go through Pixie. What's important to me is my relationship with Vic. I know my sisters are miscreants and scoundrels. Now they've reentered our life, and they're pressing my buttons. How do I work through this? I know Vic well enough and where and when she needs space. It's comfortable to be silent, nothing resolved.

Twenty years ago, after prepping Easter Sunday family brunch, Mick was driving drunk. He knocked down a street pole and power line. The roof of his Ford Explorer crumbled and crushed his pelvis. The investigation showed he was driving over sixty miles an hour within the city limits. He also suffered a concussion and lacerated spleen. The hospital called Saundra, and she went to the emergency room. She reported from outside that she could hear his blood-curdling screams. "I have no family. I have no family. I have no family." He'd repeated this phrase until they put him under and wheeled him to the operating room. He would never walk the same again or without pain. The north side of the city was dark for hours. He didn't get a speeding ticket, lose his license, get jail time or probation. Like my father, Mick had friends in high places. Was this Mick's attempt to divorce his family? Was his final word on the matter the manner of his death?

# 5 JANUARY, 3:35 A.M.

## (SANTA BARBARA, CA)

*"The canal likes to think that rivers exist
solely to supply it with water."*
Rabindranath Tagore (1861-1941)

L AST NIGHT, VIC SAT DOWN next to me on the couch. Co-habitation and poor memory prevailed, and we proceeded as nothing had happened. We both remained tepid but friendly, minding our manners and on good behavior.

She said, "What're you watching?"

"The evening news."

"What's happening?"

"Patrick Swayze's pretty sick."

"I heard about it. He's got stage four pancreatic cancer."

"It's a miracle he's alive, and he's still working and making a TV series in Chicago. He gets chemo on weekends. Barbara Walters is interviewing him tomorrow. Do you want to watch?"

She nodded and looked toward the kitchen. "I started a juice cleanse."

"I saw the carrots, apple, and ginger next to the sink."

Her eyes flashed. "Did you check out the fridge?"

I sauntered into the kitchen and swung open the refrigerator door. "Celery, parsley, arugula, romaine lettuce, kale, and cabbage."

She said, "Did you see the Swiss chard and beets?"

I rolled open the hydrator drawer. "Oh yeah, they're here. Pretty good idea after my sisters."

She said, "I gained six pounds."

"Me too. I mean, I gained weight. I haven't the courage to get on the scale. I couldn't live that way, all the pizza, pasta, and bread. It's delicious, but I've got to get back on track."

She stood, walked to the kitchen with an elegant sashay, and revved up the juicer. It whined, spun, and growled. Our cottage smells like fecund earth after a fresh rain. I appreciate what she was doing to restore our shattered personal ecology.

She shouted over the rumble, "Do you want me to make enough for you?"

We sat on the couch, sipping raw carrot, apple, and ginger juice, and watched the news, neither of us ready to talk or engage in a skirmish. Not ready to smoke the peace pipe either.

Buffalo stirred my darkest memories and, like Vic, I'm purging myself of toxins. I'm determined to excavate everything through writing. Find every person who has meant something to me and write them a spontaneous personal message. Each needs to know that Mick is dead. A predator has been set loose, and I'm not sure if I'm its hunter or its prey.

Despite the digital revolution, I'd retained my three-by-five address card cases. They form a road map of the places I've lived, worked, and put down roots. The cards are different from the contact list on my phone, albeit it bears the same information. Rough and worn, they speak out loud. Mementos of broken attachments are easy to trace. I don't want to leave anyone or any part of my life out. I want to inspect each element and remember each phase. It's tactile as I touch them, some cards with the addressee's handwriting. Shuffling through the deck takes me back to when those friendships and attachments flourished. Thank goodness I didn't throw them away when the information age engulfed me. Like the green marble chess table in my mother's living room, some tattered remnant of my past remains. Like my brother, I harbor what's vital to me.

A couple weeks before Mick died, Vic and I wandered through the Santa Barbara Art Walk and met a Native American artist, Buffalo Feather, who left a deep impression. A master illustrator, woodcarver, and sculptor, he renders the American bison. We talked for forty minutes. He said that as long as a tribe could hunt buffalo, nobody went hungry, and everybody stayed warm and sheltered.

I said, "Abundance?"

He shook his head. "That's a white man's notion. Wouldn't enter a native person's mind. Abundance leads to a different kind of hunger. Greed and hoarding. Nobody can ever get enough when there's too much. The buffalo symbolizes harmony and the ability to share. Enough, not too much."

I bought a hand-painted greeting card. Buffalo Feather's contact information was on the back, and I called him yesterday. I told him about Mick and my project to connect with people from my past.

He said, "It's good to build bridges between the living and dead. If you want to find yourself, look to your past."

I ordered a hundred cards, and he showed up at the cottage on his bicycle ten minutes later. It was expensive, five bucks a card (and he told me he gave me a significant discount). It felt weird to fork out five hundred dollars in cash to a guy on a two-wheeler.

When he departed, he said, "Buffalo is big medicine, power, strength, stamina, freedom to roam."

Now I have another explanation of how my hometown got its name. In the early nineteenth century, Buffalo was the frontier. It took a rigorous, two-week overland journey through the wilderness to get there. Settlers came seeking the bounty of the west. It wasn't abundance they asked for, but enough to feed themselves and their children and scratch a living from the new land. Many, like my ancestors, found too much, more than they needed, and fought over the spoils like jackals.

Last night, I addressed the first forty envelopes and included a copy of Mick's obituary from the *Buffalo News*, a wallet-sized photo of Mick in his chef uniform, and his Mass card. My goal is to fill the white space of each card with whatever comes to me, unconstrained and free. Like Allen Ginsberg—first thought, best thought. I won't ponder it. I'll let whatever issues forth find its way to the page. No logic. Scary, personal, naked. Quick pen strokes. No cross-outs or corrections. Keep the pen moving. If I misspell a word, no matter, keep going. The aim is to capture the ebb and flow of my mind like I do in my journal. And I'll send whatever I write. Like Abelard and Heloise, no thinking, write from the heart. Some will be easier than others. I'll announce Mick's death and reconnect with significant people in my life.

And there's the flip side. Mick held me in a state of panic. I talked to him every day. What am I going to do now with my boring life bursting with overeating and despair? I miss Mick's calls. How I wish the phone would ring, him drunk or well into his cups, dialing from that sad household. I miss his phone calls and his need for me. In some way, my life ended with his. He slept in my mother's bed, and I could picture his exact location. I miss his friendship and camaraderie. My brother is dead. There will be no more phone calls.

Will Vic's juice fast and my diligence to reconnect with people bring a new order to our lives?

Each time I say Mick is dead, it communicates something to me on a deep level. It says Mick is gone, something I don't yet believe or fully embrace.

Mick is dead. I say it to myself again and again. It's a constant reminder that he won't be calling, and I won't be calling him. I force myself to use the word dead, not "passed away," because "passed away" couldn't be further from the truth. He's more alive now than ever. He dominates my every thought.

Mick is dead. He is relevant. Everything else is immaterial, inconsequential, unnecessary. Everything else is lifeless. It's Mick who is alive. I wish I'd recorded Mick's phone calls or kept his voice mails. Not a single remnant of his high-spirited, high-pitched, squealing, and irrepressible voice survives. If only I could talk to him now.

The Great Lakes cover a landmass half the size of California and contain twenty-one percent of the world's fresh water. When I was a kid, a 400-million-year-old predator threatened the native fish population. The sea lamprey swam up the human-made canals and breached the closed system. The lake trout that weighed up to seventy pounds (and made such delicious eating) were almost wiped out. Commercial fishing came to a halt. Long before Sigourney Weaver uttered, "Get away from here, you bitch!" Buffalonians understood the bone-chilling threat of alien life forms.

The sea lamprey, a sleek, foot-long tube without a jaw, that only weighs a pound or two, had upset the heterogeneity. The lake ecosystem couldn't combat it. The lamprey's faceless mouth is almost impossible to detach once it takes hold. Razor-sharp teeth cut and chew while anesthetizing its victim with an anticoagulant. Blood flows in only one direction, into its rapacious mouth. Furthermore, the sea lamprey can hitch a ride on a motorboat going fifteen miles per hour. This alien creature drove a stake into the heart, assaulting the Great Lakes from within. The stable ecology that had evolved over ten thousand years was changed forever. It's a similar disruption to what I feel now that Mick is gone. A foreign invader has colonized my vitality. My homeostasis is spinning. His absence strikes a blow to a place never penetrated before.

The Great Lakes now receive ongoing chemotherapy with a lampricide. Lamprey that breed in cold running streams are currently under control. Recrudescence will recur if scientists withhold the poison. So, it's not as satisfying a solution as Sigourney Weaver's obliteration of her alien.

The sea lamprey was only the first wave of ocean invaders to disrupt the fragile balance. Quagga and zebra mussels pave the Great Lake beds, sucking the very life out of the water. The mussels arrived in the ballast water of freighters from Eastern Europe. Also, phosphorous-fed seasonal algae blooms can smother Lake Erie, which remains a huge problem today. Ask anybody in the western basin, cities like Toledo, where algae threaten the freshwater supply. Samuel Taylor Coleridge's *Ancient Mariner* said it best: "Water, water, everywhere, Nor any drop to drink." Lake Erie is shallow and empties and refills every two and a half years, so it serves as the canary in the coal mine for what might be in store for the rest. In my lifetime, scientists estimate that Lake Erie has aged fifteen thousand years.

Before work yesterday, I slathered my face with shaving cream. I was stressed and trying not to cut myself.

Victoria said, "Neal, all your energy is going out. It would help if you pulled in. Have you thought about why you behaved that way at LAX?"

As I pulled the razor across my face, I said, "I'm late for work. Can we talk about this tonight?"

I looked in the mirror and examined my face. I looked like my brother on a bender—confused, bloated, weathered, my eyes wild and chaotic. A flush of rosy acne had broken out on my cheeks and in the creases of my nose.

She said, "You're gonna have to figure this out, Neal, and I don't think you're gonna find any answers in condolences."

I blurted, "Everybody treats me like nothing's happened. No one's even said, 'Sorry to hear about your brother.' Even Kate didn't say anything. That's why I hate this goddamned place. Nobody gives a fuck."

Then there was silence, and she walked away.

After I washed my face, I called into the other room, "Do you have any of that cream for acne rosacea?

She said, "There's Finacea and metronidazole in the cabinet beside the sink."

"I can't find it."

She walked into the bathroom and pointed. "You're looking right at it."

As I walked to work, I thought about my days at Duke—long, lazy Friday afternoons with nothing to do. Spring rising from the black soil, the smell of robins' eggs and heavy dew. I worked at the new, state-of-the-art cardiac rehab center that overlooked the stadium. Little did I know how lucky I was, and this would be the best job I'd ever have. The patients were gone, my work was done, and I'd call Mark Rotolo at his law offices in Buffalo, and we'd chew the fat. The cafeteria in the building made fantastic oat bran muffins. Fresh-baked, hot out of the oven, they delighted the palate as well as the soul. My clinic offers no reprieve, only more patients and more paperwork, a treadmill that keeps escalating. The faster I go, the more work there is to do. Our boss pulled up a scene from *I Love Lucy* on her iPhone at a recent meeting and viewed it with sardonic laughter. In the scene, Lucy and Ethel are working on a conveyor belt at a chocolate factory and can't wrap the confections fast enough, so they frantically stuff them into their mouths, hats, and blouses. She said, "Like you and Kate, hamsters running on a wheel."

It pleases me that I can still perform at this level, though. When I was at Duke, there was so much insecurity and fear that I'd blown it and made a wrong decision. At this stage, I've seen the same thing over and over again. If I'm not lazy or sloppy, it's easy to get it right. I got the impression when I saw Rudy O'Malley in Buffalo that he was working at his craft the same way. He has a busy private practice. He helps people deal with the hurdles of life—grief, anxiety, freak outs, worry, the pain inflicted by children and lover's betrayals. Human beings twist themselves into knots, and Rudy unties them.

In the clinic yesterday, Paul Harvey, 77, a former banker, asked me, "Can I talk to you about something else?"

I said, "Sure."

"I'm having more senior moments."

"What do you mean?"

"Even with a group of friends, I don't talk anymore because I forget what I'm trying to say. I'm embarrassed, so I listen and smile. My wife covers for me."

"Can you remember things from the past?"

"I'm muddled about it. Everything's foggy."

"Have you spoken to your doctor about this?"

"Yeah, he gave me some pills."

"Aricept?"

"I think that's it. All it does is make my mouth very dry. Is there something else?"

He's getting a neurological consult next week. Depression can do this, and as I'm finding out, so can grief. There is not much I can do for him. I felt connected to his situation. What happens when memories die? Will Buffalo become a blur?

These days, I'm lackadaisical at work. I'm pulling myself through, like I have a steel bit in my mouth. Memories besiege me. Some I wish I could forget, like my second marriage, and then there are others, more mixed, buoyant and unresolved. Sadness strikes at random.

Last night, as I thumbed through the stack of index cards, I lingered long and hard on one. It was dog-eared and yellowed with time, the name and address written by someone else. The navy-blue ink had faded, and it was hard to read. The script was large, well-defined with curled, soft, ladylike edges.

Years ago, at work, I'd ordered a three-and-a-half-inch, light-gathering acrylic dome magnifier. At the time, I wasn't quite sure why. I've never used it or needed it. Now I don't have that job anymore, but I kept the magnifier, and here was the perfect opportunity to use it. So, I passed it over the card and read, Wendy Peterson, 4504 Kingston Cr, Mississauga, Ontario. There was no phone number. At the bottom, it said, "Come see me in TO, Wendy."

I hadn't seen or heard any news of Wendy since my sixteenth summer. Except for one important episode, she was a girl and I was a boy, and that was the awkward extent of it. It was my first season on staff at St. Jean-Baptist Camp on Lake Simcoe. Sixty miles north of Toronto and run by the Christian Brothers, it became my refuge. I did my first seven-week stretch as a camper when I was eight and went back every summer after. My father and Mick also spent summers at St. Jean-Baptist. Both were campers, but neither made it to staff. More than anywhere, summer camp shaped me. I met people who mirrored my consciousness and connected deeply with my Canadian cohorts. It was a new twist, a different outlook I hadn't encountered at home. Looking back, it was therapy, a place I felt accepted and understood.

Also, it was an escape from my mother.

My mother trotted from the bedroom to the bathroom un-clothed. Around the house, she wore skimpy, threadbare, knee-length nighties with no undergarments, her nipples and breasts exposed. Even when I was a teenager, she insisted on a goodnight kiss. To her, this consisted of coming into my bed and hanging her body over mine. She gave me full access to her breasts. No kiss ever took place.

The whole family was always in my parents' bed, where we

watched television. As a five-year-old, I remember my mother's wet tongue in my ear and her nibbling on my earlobes. Thank goodness it didn't go any further than that. I've often wondered what happened between her and my brother.

Before I took off for camp that summer, my father pleaded with me to cut my hair. I wanted to grow it out. I'd worn a brush cut since I was a kid. It was a point of rebellion, and I needed to push back. It was shaggy but no more than an inch long. He said, "Neal, it will fall out if you leave your hair that long."

When I ignored him, he got caustic and said, "You look like a girl. I'm not sure if you're my son or my daughter. He called me 'Cassie Anne.' "

At that point, I was too big for him to manhandle, so he offered me twenty dollars. I refused.

My father loved the brush cut and as a youngster had forced me to wear it with religious zeal. Throughout my childhood, he took me to Leon the Barber. He'd tell Leon he wanted it "clean," which meant shaving my skull, so it was white with no trace of hair. My father called me "Soupbone." He told the story over and over again, and it embarrassed the hell out of me. In an obnoxious way, my father combined everybody's given name with bone. He took the first name and attached bone, so I was Nealbone or Cornbone. Leon, after he shaved my head, said, "This isn't a Nealbone. It's a soupbone. To my good fortune and my father's dismay (and not for his lack of trying), nobody else picked up on it. But my dad persisted on calling me "Soupbone" until the day he died. He told the story at the most humiliating times.

My father liked the short, military look, which I couldn't understand as he'd never served in the armed forces. Once I got old enough to decide, I started growing my hair out and he hated it. It came to represent our violent opposition to one another. He was a Republican, and I emerged as a liberal socialist. The hair on my head protested everything I loathed about my father and America.

Before going off to camp, my father implored me, "Do this for me, Neal. This one time. Do this for your dad."

And I fell for it. My father took me to Leon at the Buffalo Athletic Club, who took the electric clippers and scalped me. I remember tears welling in my eyes, and fighting back the indignity.

When Leon finished, I stood up, ripped off the tunic, and ran to the showers, then to the pool. I was mutilated, humiliated, and betrayed. It was more than the hair that he'd taken. They'd taken my dignity. And I vowed never to trust my father again.

He said, "It's only hair. It'll grow back."

My mother agreed with him and said, "You won't even notice in a couple weeks."

But I did notice, throughout the day and during the night. I rubbed my scalp when I woke up and remembered the injustice, how this was against my will. I was resentful and angry that I'd gone along with my father. I dreamed about my hair growing back. I spent my days willing the denuded follicles to express themselves. I remember the shame, nakedness, and despair. It took a long time to heal. How awkward and dorky I felt in the company of girls because my head was shaved to the bone like a soupbone.

Wendy was a big-boned, Canadian schoolgirl with a short crop of red hair and large, plump breasts. She had freckles on her face, chest, and arms. She was taller than me, a little clumsy, and a bit shy. Her accent was soft and melodious, so different from what I'd heard at home. I would listen in amazement at the way she politely shaped words. It was a summer of pairing off at camp, the way angelfish adolescents do in an aquarium. The boys arrived a week early to set the place up, and I was on the waterfront crew. I worked long hours at the docks with Brother Xavier. He was a hard-drinking, no-nonsense Christian Brother who was well-built with a hairy chest. He always had his shirt off. I wore loose-fitting sweatshirts to cover my hairless, flabby rolls. The tops of my feet got sunburned furthering my foolishness.

During swim periods, my post was the farthest raft from the grassy beach. It was one hundred and fifty yards offshore. The spot was known as "the reef" because below it was a formation of submerged rocks. The water was murky, cold, and green, and about thirty feet deep. The wooden platform swayed and creaked with every wave. Especially when the wake of a motorboat jostled it, I'd stand arms folded across my chest, balancing best I could. It was my first job, an assignment. I wore a black, cut-off sweatshirt with a whistle slung around my neck from a braided lanyard. I was self-conscious in a soft, cotton-brimmed hat. Those who made the swim were often panting. Some would call out in a euphoric way, "I made the reef! I made the reef!" Canadian glacial lakes make one giddy. The swimming season is so short, the water so frigid that it feels like a baptism. Swimmers would hold the steel bars on the raft, rest, catch their breath, and swim back.

Wendy had been different. She had a powerful, efficient, long, clean stroke. When her hands entered the water, there was no splash. Her broad shoulders, strong arms, and hands churned, making an independent wake. Any extra weight she carried on land provided ballast, and she crested high in the water. She was a creature of the lake. When she reached the raft, I'd extend my hand and pull her up to the wooden platform. My agenda was not to miss the spectacular display. Her breasts popped out for an instant into full view, like lake trout jumping from the water. She wore a baggy, one-piece orange bathing suit that she never seemed to change.

That summer, Wendy did more than swim out to the raft. She saved me. It was brief and unexpected, and never parlayed into obligation or further intentions. It was fun.

One night, a dozen counselors were sitting around a campfire. She slipped under an upside-down red canoe and waved for me to join her. At first, I thought she must be motioning to someone else. Then once I crawled under, I wasn't clear about her purpose. The earth was cold and wet. In an awkward motion, I rolled toward her, and our lips met. It was a long, undulating, unhurried kiss. She pressed her tongue into my mouth, and I felt like it struck my spine. I could feel her hurt, all the pain of her life, and all the pain of mine. I didn't want it to end, and she stayed. We kissed and pecked for an hour. Her lips and saliva tasted salty, as if a small cut yielded blood. My blood mixed with hers. I'd never felt anything like it. She showed me how to unhook her bra and helped me. I slipped my hands under her shirt and cupped her humongous breasts. I felt hunger, a surge in my groin. I felt better than I'd ever felt in my life. She wasn't my mother. Wendy was the first girl I made physical contact with and caressed.

Then there was *rap, rap, rap*. Brother Xavier knocked hard on the top of the canoe with a flashlight handle and said, "Curfew." He shined a bright light under the boat and said, "Get out."

It was dark, and the group scattered. I masturbated with a whole different intention that night. I'd touched a girl, tasted her lips, felt her breasts. It was different than I'd imagined or anyone had told me it would be.

It is these silent and secret acts, unheralded and unadorned, that alter a life. No one remembers the red canoe on the grass by the dock at Lake Simcoe but me (and maybe Wendy). The camp is defunct. It's a provincial park now. I remember the girl of the lake, the creature from the deep, who swallowed me. Who took pity on the twerp with a shaved scalp. She overturned yet another cruel act visited upon me by my father.

My hair grew back, and I never let my father tell me how to cut it again. My relationship remained complicated with my mother. She continued her sexual visitations at night. And to this day, I'm confused and don't understand her intentions. Like the lamprey, she couldn't let go of her prey. Sexual abuse by a parent is complex, full of shame and guilt. With a few highballs on board, a different person entered my room each night with demands I couldn't meet. We were not equal, the sexual encounter not consensual. As an adult, she bore the responsibility. It's taken years for me to let go of my part in it. Aroused, I hated myself. If there is a silver lining, it's that I understand another's humiliation and shame. I don't want to hurt anyone the way she hurt my brother and me.

# 6 JANUARY, 4:28 A.M.

## (SANTA BARBARA, CA)

*"I used to advertise my loyalty and I don't believe there is
a single person I loved that I didn't eventually betray."*
Albert Camus (1913-1960)

A CERTIFIED LETTER ARRIVED YESTERDAY. THE return
address on the envelope—Stasia Wypijewski, P.C., Attor-
neys at Law—made my skin crawl. She's the same attorney
who handled the fiasco of my mother's estate twenty years ago.
The legal proceedings took five years, and it was twice that long
before my brother and I spoke to each other again. As it turned
out, Wypijewski enjoyed a larger share of my parents' estate than
the rest of us combined. It ran through my mind, why would
Cassie hire her again?

There were broad shifts in my brother's temperament after
my mother died. One day he'd be easy, euphoric, enthusiastic,
and fun, and the next sullen, depressed, moody, and irritable. The
gaps widened the more he drank. As time went on, he dug in his
heels and demanded that he keep the house without a mortgage. A
costly legal battle ensued. Wypijewski escalated and inflamed the
situation, making it even more toxic.

A wave of nausea came over me as I signed for the certified envelope and held it in my hand. It brought back everything that had happened twenty years earlier. The week my mother died, she'd survived the first stroke but lost her ability to speak. Cassie dropped everything and flew in from the Islands. The doctor warned me that this was the first event in a fatal sequela and that my mother wouldn't last long. If I wanted to see her again, he'd advised me, come home immediately. Scarlett was recovering from a pneumothorax, and I chose not to heed his words. A few days later, my mother had another stroke and returned to Sister's Hospital on Main Street. Scarlett was home and out of danger, so I flew to Buffalo. Scarlett couldn't get on a plane due to her collapsed lung. By that time, she'd had enough of my family anyway. Her medical condition was a good excuse to stay home. I'm so appreciative that Vic stuck with me in spite of my sisters and made this trip.

When I got to Buffalo after my mother's second stroke, I wished I'd heeded the doctor's advice and come home sooner. Mick showed me the workbooks my mother was using after her collapse. She'd always valued words, and the precision of using the right one in any situation was crucial. My mother was a hard worker and diligent in everything—the best she could do after the stroke was a grunt. The workbooks were full of squiggly marks connecting words and pictures. I remember the word duck and images of animals in the adjoining panel, a duck, a squirrel, a seal, and a deer. She had connected the word duck with a picture of the deer. My brother's eyes were full of tears when he showed me these tragic exercises. I wish I could have been a better brother to him then. I was unable to be supportive and understanding. He was out of control, lit on vodka, smoking marijuana and snorting coke, and he made a scene. He howled at my mother's memorial. Tears, mucus, and saliva sprayed in every direction. At one point, the priest interrupted the service. Cassie and Saundra escorted

Mick outside. His bloodcurdling screams saturated the proceedings. People acted as if they didn't notice.

During my mother's final days, my sisters asked me to meet without my brother. They chose Parkside Candy, an old-time soda fountain across the street from the hospital that maintains the priggish atmosphere of Victorian Buffalo. It's a chocolate confectioner that dates back to the 1920s, and shiny glass cases filled with delicacies encircle the interior. They serve ice cream, soups, and toasted wheat sandwiches. My grandparents could have courted there under brightly-lit, high, arched ceiling with the soles of their shoes on the same black and white tile floor. I hadn't been there since I was a kid.

We sat in a large, open space at a sturdy wooden table in vintage maple side chairs. The meeting's goal was for my sisters to tout family unity, and Mick was excluded because they said he was unprepared for such grief. He needed our support and guidance to make his way in the world. I ordered a chocolate milkshake delivered in a thirty-ounce stainless steel cup, poured thick with plenty of extra on the side. It was so rich my lips puckered, so cold it gave me a brain freeze. Cassie and Saundra spooned a chocolate parfait and a banana split and sampled from each other's bowls. It didn't feel any different than before Mick was born. When I was seven, my teenage sisters often took me out for a treat. Parkside Candy was a good choice, a Buffalo tradition since 1927.

Cassie said, "After Momma's gone, we've all got to stick together. We can't let anything get in the way of that."

Saundra shifted in her chair. "Family's what's most important."

And for a brief moment, I wanted to turn back the pages and believe them, but I knew their promises were lies. From the time I was a child, both my sisters manipulated me and everyone else. Sitting there, courting my naïve younger self, I knew it was a ruse. To what end, I wasn't sure, but their words fell flat, like a fish flopping out of water. I wanted to believe they were sincere and kind and had everyone's best interest at heart, but it had never happened before. With them, I'd never had a family life or could trust anyone who looked out for me without a hook. I slurped the last few drops of my milkshake, making a loud, obnoxious sucking noise at the end.

When I'd arrived in Buffalo, my mother was getting palliative care in a regular hospital room. Intubation withdrawn, she had an IV and a telemetry monitor only. A "Do Not Resuscitate" order was in place. Cassie stayed with her throughout the night. There was no cot in the room. She sat upright, crammed in a narrow reclining chair the width of an airplane seat. Cassie's stamina was remarkable. My brother and I came the next morning.

Cassie said, "Darlings, thank you for coming. Now that you're here, I'll run down to the cafeteria. They're serving pigs in a blanket, one of my favorites. We don't see them much in the Islands."

Mick and I each took one of her arms and pulled her out of the chair. It was like removing a cork from a wine bottle.

Mick said, "How'd Mom do last night?"

Cassie said, "I think she's doing a little better." Then she put her hand on my mother's shoulder and said, "That's my little mother. There, there."

My mother was unresponsive.

Mick said, "Do you think she'll get better? When can she come home?"

Cassie replied, "You never know. God is good."

I said, "Did you get any sleep?"

"A little, here and there."

The heavy smell of her sweat filled the room. She glowered at me, "It's about time you got here." Then she left the room.

Mick and I stood on either side of the bed. Our mother was unrecognizable. Her facial features were withered and distorted and her lips cupped tight around her gums. Her upper and lower dental plates had been removed. Her hands were curled into balls. With each slow breath, there was a sigh and her lips flapped. She gurgled. I didn't want to touch or kiss her. She felt foreign to me.

Mick and I had nothing to say to her or each other. He whimpered. I was stone-faced.

When we stepped out of the room, there was a huge ruckus, bells and alarms going off. A nurse came rushing down the hall and closed the thick oak door. My mother had straight-lined. I'll never forget the panic in Mick's eyes.

When the nurse came out, I asked, "Is she gone?"
She nodded.
Mick screeched, whooped, and wailed.

I wrapped both arms around his shoulders and braced his trembling. I held him as tight as I could and said, "I love you, and I'll be there for you no matter what," and I meant it. And it felt like he knew it too.

When Cassie wandered back down the hall a half hour later, we were sitting on a bench in the hallway. Covered in a white sheet, my mother's body was wheeled on a gurney by a hospital attendant to the morgue. Neither one of us, caught up in our own grief, had thought to find Cassie in the cafeteria.

I slit open the certified envelope from Stasia Wypijewski with a dull silver dinner knife. Inside was a letter addressed to Saundra and me attached to Mick's will. My name was spelled wrong and corrected with blue ink. There was no legal mumbo jumbo, and the message got right to the point. "Your sister, Cassie, has retained me to represent her as Executrix of your brother's estate. Cassie inherits Mick's residence and all property." Further, the will cut Saundra and me out by name. It was specific. "Nothing under any circumstances to go to my brother, Neal, or sister,

Saundra." That's what Saundra had meant at the house when she said, "You're getting a buck." There was no mention of Pixie.

My jaw tightened and popped. I felt hurt, rather than angry. It's a familiar emotion when dealing with my family...disappointment. It smells like rotting fish and bears a moribund, greenish hue, the same sickly feeling I get when I view photos of myself as a gawky teenager.

The dispatch asked me to sign a waiver. Otherwise, I'd need to appear at the Surrogate of Erie County to protest. Wypijewski used the word probate, and it tipped me off that Cassie had been in league with her all along. On further examination, the document was sixteen years old, unchanged. Written four years after my mother died, when Mick and I were estranged, and Pixie wasn't in the picture.

As I read, Mick's last wishes got worse. If Cassie failed to survive him, it stipulated that the funds go to Mick's high school. He wanted to establish a scholarship in his name. The upshot was that Pixie, Saundra, and I were excluded under all circumstances. I know how Mick loathed Saundra, and it smarted seeing my name lumped in with hers. The exclusion of Pixie was a crime for which Cassie will rot in hell.

I faxed the documents to Mark Rotolo, then called him and said, "Is this bogus?"

He said, "Well, first of all, as you know, Wypijewski is a bottom feeder. We have a lot of them up here, lawyers that advertise on billboards promising to set their clients up for life. Like folks who slip on a banana peel in the supermarket. They advertise on TV, radio, and scatter pamphlets around church lobbies. They're ubiquitous. Wypijewski's pretty old now. I didn't know she was still around. She's an evil harridan, one of the original slimeballs."

I felt a sinking feeling in my gut, one I couldn't articulate. My skin got clammy, the way it had when my mother made her visits at night. I was anxious, hurt, and afraid. I made a joke. "Maybe she came out of retirement for this one."

"You never know with your sisters."

I said, "This doesn't include Pixie."

"No doubt Mick and Cassie were in cahoots and set it up that way. Pixie and Mick weren't married."

"But engaged. Pixie waited on Mick hand and foot when he was sick."

He said, "She has no right to anything. Cassie can kick her out of the house at any time. Pixie should have gotten a lawyer and something in writing. There's nothing you can do to help Pixie's case now."

I said, "I thought at the very least Mick would leave the house to Pixie. Where is she going to live?"

He asked, "Who was the executor of your mother's estate?"

I said, "Mick and Cassie."

"I've seen this before between unmarried siblings. When your mother died, they made a pact that the survivor would get everything. That's the document Wypijewski is presenting now."

"Why the fuck do they want to push Pixie out?"

"It's about the money and it's in the courts now. Cassie has chosen to take off the gloves. That's why she's distanced herself from you. She thinks you want Pixie to get something."

I said, "The letter directs me to sign in agreement. What should I do?"

"I'm sorry, Neal. Cassie made this stick. I don't think there's much you *can* do. You can slow things down, but this looks airtight."

"What was Mick thinking? He wasn't a prick."

"Look a little deeper. The person without a prick is behind this one."

I shouted, "Cassie."

"The document's well-executed. *Fait accompli.*"

I said, "Buffaloed again. What about Pixie?"

He said, "That's up to Cassie."

And when it comes to betrayals, I'm not immune, and this one I conferred on someone else, my second wife, Scarlett. Rather than having the courage to walk away, I sabotaged my way out of a fourteen-year marriage. Rather than having the courage to walk away, I kept a foot in it, though I knew full well I couldn't resist the groundswell with all good intentions and willpower. Scarlett had no ambition, and I hated her for it. Her only commitment was to organized religion, of which I wanted no part. But I wouldn't admit it and, at the time, couldn't articulate it. A new life was coming, and Scarlett and the Bahá'ís weren't part of it. It took me years to concede that we all betray. We all lie, and we all are lied to and deceived. There are no angels. We're all human, capable of the best and the worse. The most important thing one can learn is what one wants and stay true to it. There are no bargains, no fire sales. One has to pay the price.

At thirteen, when I read Albert Camus, my response was visceral. The setting, Algeria, the French language, philosophical abstractions, all went over my head. It didn't matter. Camus pulled me in. He became my hero and role model. When I learned about his chaotic romantic entanglements, it annihilated me. His second wife, Francine Faure, attempted suicide in response to his womanizing. His novel, *The Fall*, characterizes this relationship, the man who fails to come to the aid of a drowning woman. The collateral damage Camus caused, I vowed never to create in my own life. I featured myself as an uxorious type and played that role with Scarlett. Our life together was sexual and sweet, but never with enough depth to hold.

I tried on different relationships with women as friends, innocent enough. The marriage had failed to satisfy my inner longings. I've always had a fascination for women, how they move, how they point their toe when they stand. It's an insatiable curiosity, the other half of me unfulfilled. Women are shapeshifters. Their bodies create new life, something I'll never do. Women are not equal to men. They're far superior. I didn't want to hurt Scarlett, but I caused more heartache by letting her down easy, and that was for me, not for her. I was a coward, and I played the Motherwell game of half-truths, the same as my brother and sisters. I was hanging onto the childish notion that I could have both my wife and the new woman. I strung Scarlett along. I lied, and she believed me, and she still hates me for it. Like my brother wanted my parents' house, I felt entitled. I was unwilling to face facts.

During that time, I remember talking to my boss on the telephone. He was on my side and disliked Scarlett.

I said, "Yes, we're going to counseling. Who knows, maybe we'll work it out."

There was dead, stone silence on the other end.

He said, "Once you go to counseling, it's over."

Cleary, I was drowning. I'd already slept with another woman. I couldn't admit it to Scarlett or myself that our marriage was over. The rapids I'd entered were too swift. No matter how hard I tried, I couldn't swim against the current. We were long past reconciliation. For better or worse, Scarlett and I had become one in many ways over the years. We knew what each other was thinking and ate the same food. We shared the same fears, aspirations, and superstition, and slept and woke in the same bed. The parts of us that had coalesced were indistinguishable. Why did I suppose I could have both? I still don't understand my ignorance. I'd already pressed the demolition button. The walls of the house had collapsed. What remained was smoking rubble, like a locomotive had roared through the living room. There was nothing to rebuild. Both of us were devastated, wishing it were different.

Divorce rips everything apart. It's like an exploding cow. Everything is bloody, bloated flesh flying through the air. Body parts hang from walls. That's required. Let no one tell you any different. The Greek poet, Constantin Cavafy, was right when he said, "Half the house must come down." I paid the price, watched it fall to pieces. The dust finally cleared, but my betrayal to myself left an enduring scar.

When I finally left Scarlett, she said, "This is coming at a bad time. You know my abandonment issues." She stopped eating. Her frame was rib and bone. If she turned sideways, she'd fall to earth like a feather—a hunger strike due to abandonment. And I was abandoning her. The word stuck in my gut, and I knew nothing about her as she withered away to a shell.

Little did I know it was my inner fear too. That's why it's still with me, how I walked out into freedom and how Scarlett suffered. The word abandonment was too big, too crushing like an elephant or a whale—a monster. Had she finally put words to it? Was it me that forced it through?

I saw the wrinkles on her face. She was changing, and my hair was peppering gray. It was from the bellows of the whale that this blowhole pushed through. I was walking away. I was saying different things, going to a counselor with her, trying to patch things up. It was never a direct "no." A new epoch was calling me—a wild thread and needle pulling through a new passage. I acted like I didn't know it. I was abandoning her.

My brother lied to me about Pixie. He said he'd taken care of her when he took no responsibility. He left me, his most loyal friend and confidant, nothing, not even good thoughts but rather, direct exclusion. Why do I feel shame, like it's my fault? What had I done? He hurt me because I loved him.

Cassie and Wypijewski are behind this. Saundra's along for the ride to pinch whatever crumbs she can.

And what about Pixie? She loved Mick, and now she's being steamrolled by Cassie, who won't give it to her straight. I prefer Saundra's crass truth-telling to Cassie's swarmy ways.

# 7 JANUARY, 4:12 A.M.
## (SANTA BARBARA, CA)

*"The source of all humor is not laughter, but sorrow."*
Mark Twain (1835-1910)

CAN'T BELIEVE IT'S COME AROUND again, and he won't be there. Mick's birthday was huge, and it's happening in a few days. My father boasted, "Twenty-three years of child-bearing, all with the same woman." Mick was the climax, the focal point of the experiment, and his birthday was bigger than Christmas. There was nothing more important to us as a generationally-challenged family. And Mick loved it.

In later years, after my parents died and my sisters and I scattered, Mick continued to celebrate his birthday with reckless abandon. He took excursions to Nassau and Freeport and gambling forays to Puerto Rico, where he'd visit Cassie. One year, he flew friends from Buffalo to Las Vegas to drink, wager, whore, and take a hot air balloon ride. He was a high roller and when it came to a party, nothing was held back. He spent ambitiously and was always the life of the party. But this was before he drank full-time and restricted his activities to the house.

The last time I saw him, he was a recluse, an acropolis of hair, a greasy mustache, a bloated face. In short, a mound of adiposis, too beleaguered to walk without assistance. His abdomen, protuberant and distended, had the firmness of a watermelon. Spider angiomas tattooed his neck, face, and arms. Pencil-thin arms and legs could no longer support his corpulent torso, and he had droopy boobs. As a joke, he cupped his plump bosoms with both hands and said, "What do you think of these?" An E.E. Cummings line comes to mind: "how do you like your blue-eyed boy Mister Death." He was end-stage, but even then, I couldn't see it. Cirrhosis disrupts the testosterone/estrogen ratio. Male alcoholics develop breasts. To me, he remained the curious, fun-loving, grinning, smirking, beaming little Mick who tickled everyone's funny bone.

But worse, he suffered tempestuous mood swings. He couldn't dial himself in or out. His mental health deteriorated. He thought he could hear my parents walking, talking, and flushing the toilet at night. He never left the house. A myriad of diseases ravaged his once beautiful face, mind, and physique. He was crippled in every respect, yet still a young man.

Today, a hard rain's pelting the roof. It looks like I won't be riding my bike to the beach this morning. Yesterday, I cycled through a dense fog. And what a surprise, when I got to Butterfly Beach, it was gone. As far as the eye could see, weathered tan rocks the size of bowling balls had displaced the abundant sandy shoreline. Butterfly Beach was ravaged. A capsized sloop with a broken mast foundered on its side. Nearby, an enormous brown body, half-submerged, bobbed in the brine. It revolted me, a dead sea lion lifeless as rubber. Palm fronds and branches littered the roadway.

The only thing that hadn't changed was Phil Zelinski standing at the concrete lookout, his battered old Mercedes parked on the curb a few feet away. Phil's a recurrent fixture here, and he was wearing a rumpled captain's hat. Outside the clinic, I see him often when I get down this way.

I called out to him, "Phil, people are going to start calling you the mayor of Butterfly Beach."

He lifted his sleeve and exposed his right bicep. An ornate tattoo with a surfboard declared, "Butterfly Beach, Santa Barbara."

I said, "Hell of a storm last night."

With a toothy smile, he nodded. We stood and inspected the devastation. A desolate, half-mile strip stretched to the cemetery cliffs. A cold, salty wind tickled my nostrils, and I sneezed several times in succession.

Phil stepped back. "Hope you're not catching something. Don't give it to me."

I pulled out a red bandana from my pocket and wiped my nose. "It's vasomotor, a reflex. It happens when the temperature shifts."

We resumed our silence staring at the ruin.

I said, "What happened to the beach?"

He pointed. "It's out there."

I said, "Do the Army Corps of Engineers dredge the sand and pump it back onshore?"

He wrinkled his lip. "These rocks have been here for ten thousand years." He laughed. "The sand's the interloper."

We stood speechless, like soldiers observing the aftermath of a bloody battle. Lazy waves lapped the shore.

With a surly grin, he added, "Usually, only tourists ask that question."

I felt ridiculous, a ragamuffin in my sweatshirt and knee-length cotton shorts. "Tourists?"

He scratched his chin. "Neal, a monsoon and howling winds strafed the beach last night. It's a natural occurrence. It happens now and then. Give it some time. The waves, currents, and tides will wash all the sand back and you'll have your beach again."

The concept was foreign to me. When I worked as a lifeguard in Florida, huge bulldozers pushed mountains of sand around. Otherwise, the beach would wash away.

I said, "What about beach renourishment?"

"What's that?"

"You know, sculpting the beach, filling in erosion."

"It's not necessary. It's a natural thing for sand to move around. Enjoy it, walk, check out the tidal pools. Play like Ed Rickets and John Steinbeck. Earlier, I saw some sea hares, purple urchins, and kelp crabs. An octopus is guarding her eggs." He pointed toward the tide line.

I locked my bike and proceeded south toward Summerland.

When I lived on the east coast, the beaches were under constant reconstruction. Things are different here. Nothing to fix, the tides bring the sand back. There's a natural order. Mick is dead. Ravaged, like Butterfly Beach, I've had my career at Duke. Always under constant duress and reconstruction, there's nothing for me to do now except wait for the tides and currents to renew me.

It was tedious picking my way around uneven rocks. Pretty soon, I discovered a deserted retreat. The sky was dark and foreboding as I sat on a comfortable stone slab and called Pixie.

Before I could get a word out, she blurted, "When Mick went into the hospital, he told me he was sorry. He didn't think he could spend Christmas with my family. That's about the nicest thing I ever heard."

I said, "It means so much to me that you loved Mick so much. I'm blown away by your strength and endurance. Mick couldn't have done it without you."

Pixie blurted, "Medicaid's picking up Mick's hospital bills. So, the state won't be taking the house as collateral."

I said, "That's good, isn't it?"

She said, "Your sisters will sell the house, and I'll move out."

"What are you going to do?"

"I'll live with my mom for a while and find an apartment in Lockport. My grandmother said I can stow some of my stuff in her garage. That's if there's any left. Saundra already sold my bed."

"What? Your stuff isn't part of Mick's estate."

"I don't know. Saundra thinks if it's in the house, it belongs to the estate. I'm not going to fight with your sisters. They've gone a little crazy."

I said, "And they've got that scum bag lawyer, Stasia Wypijewski."

"You got that right, and do you know how much Cassie eats? It's disgusting. She downed six extra-large Bocce pizzas in the last eight days."

I said, "Are you sure Mick didn't write another will?"

"We never talked about it."

I said, "When I asked him, he told me he'd take care of you."

She said with a strange, flat affect, "Guess not."

"How could that stand up? It makes no sense. Whatever he has should go to you."

"I didn't take care of Mick for money. My mother taught me not to be greedy."

I said, "This isn't right." I paused because I could feel her resistance, then said, "By the way, how is your mom?"

"Very well, thank you for asking. What's happening with you and Victoria?"

I said, "We had dinner last night with some new friends, a lovely couple who live on the Riviera. I always avoid going up there. The narrow, winding roads make me car sick, and I always get lost. It feels like a hassle, and before last night, I couldn't understand why anybody would want to live there. I've changed my mind. Their place was paradise."

"Isn't that where they have all those fires?"

"Yes, and like with the hurricanes on the North Carolina coast, they rebuild the houses right away. Their place is a real beaut. Very natural, nothing too fancy, surrounded by big sycamore and magnolia trees. They have a large, succulent garden in front of the house with cacti. In the back yard, they have lemon and orange trees, figs, persimmons, and cherimoyas."

"What's a cherimoya?"

"It's a spiny, green melon. It's heart-shaped, looks like an avocado but bigger. It has a creamy custard inside. Some people make cocktails with them."

"Sounds weird."

"I'd never seen one before I came to Santa Barbara. They had all the windows open, and we sat on the balcony and watched the sunset."

"What about mosquitos and bugs?"

"The windows didn't have screens. I guess they don't have flying insects up there."

She said, "Was it that warm?"

"It was cool but comfortable, kind of like Crystal Beach in the summer. They gave us blankets to put over our legs after the sun went down. You could see the Channel Islands. We sat on the balcony and pointed out landmarks near our cottage. All the red roofs and old Spanish architecture looked spectacular from up there."

"Who are these folks? I've never heard you talk about them before."

"I met Jim Axelrod as a patient about a year ago after he had a blood clot. We've gone to a couple yoga classes together and had breakfast a few times. I told him about Mick. He's a nice guy. I'm glad he reached out."

She said, "He sounds nice."

"His wife, Martha, he calls her, Marti, is a fantastic cook and host. Jim is a strapping, athletic fellow who spends every free moment surfing. He has seventeen surfboards and runs a construction company. Martha and Victoria hit it off like they were college roommates. They have so much in common. The evening got off to a flying start and ramped up as the sun went down. Victoria and Martha both have four brothers and exchanged stories. Also, both were homecoming queens in high school. Jim and I couldn't get a word in edgewise. At one point, he said, 'Do you want us to leave, so you two can get the party rolling?' Things loosened up as the wine began to flow. As we watched the sunset, Martha said, 'You know how they make those red roof tiles?'

"Victoria and I shook our heads. Then Jim said, 'Marti, you're not going to tell that story again. I'm not even sure it's true.'

"Vic said, 'With some kind of machine.' Marti replied, 'They do it that way today. But the original tiles in medieval Spain were fitted over women's thighs. That's why they're different sizes.' Jim shook his head. 'Bet you didn't know that?' "

Pixie said, "I've never seen a red tile roof. Tell me what that lady made for dinner. Mick would have loved it."

"Yeah, it was an amazing meal. Marti started with guacamole with chilies, chopped tomatoes, onion, garlic, and cilantro and served it with homemade tortilla chips hot out of the oven. The main course, seared ahi and broiled prawns over cucumber noodles, cooked to perfection. They drank champagne and local red wines, and I downed River City root beer from Sacramento."

"What about dessert? You don't have dessert in Santa Barbara. Everybody there is so slim and health-conscious."

I said, "Well, Marti rolled it out, and I don't know how she stays so trim. She made a flaming thing with ice cream, and it was delicious."

"Baked Alaska?"

"I'm not sure. She splashed it with dark rum and lit it."

Pixie said, "Ah, bombe Alaska. It's a sponge cake, vanilla ice cream, and meringue. Did she cover it with a strawberry syrup?"

"Yes, how did you know?"

"I used to make it at the Lancaster Country Club."

I said, "She sent us home with a bag of fresh-baked chocolate chip cookies. But the funniest thing happened on the way to the car. They insisted on walking us down the steep hill with a flashlight, and Marti confessed why she wanted to meet us. She said, 'Do you know Grant Houseman?' I said, 'Sure, he's an infectious disease doc at our clinic.' She said, 'He's a good friend. I went to high school with him. He thought Jim might be a closet gay and run off with the male nurse at the Coumadin Clinic.' Jim blushed. We all stood under the full moon and branches of the huge sycamore trees and howled. It was the first belly laugh I've had since Mick died.

"Adding to the fray, Victoria said, 'Neal's a physician assistant, a PA, not a nurse.' Marti replied, 'I know Neal's much more than a nurse.' Vic got ruffled and said, 'Nursing is an independent profession. I'm proud to be a nurse.' The three of us continued to roar. Even Vic cracked a smile. Jim was red as a beet."

Pixie said, "That's why you like coming back to Buffalo. You've got so many friends here."

I said, "That's true. I've moved so much. It's nice to be around people who know me, people I can trust. It's good to laugh. It's wonderful to laugh. Last night came out of nowhere. New friends and lots of laughs."

After I hung up with Pixie, I walked down the rocky shoreline and thought about my father. Thirty years ago, he had a massive heart attack on the Fourth of July. He'd been across the river in Fort Erie, feasting with a group called "The Philosophers." He ruptured his left anterior coronary artery, the "widowmaker." Besides an open bar, "The Philosophers" indulged in lavish smorgasbords. Lobster Newburg was a standard offering, with its luscious buttery sauce. They also served up hot dogs, hamburgers, baby back ribs, potato salad, corn on the cob, and garlic bread. And because it was the Fourth of July, everyone partook in a slice or two of apple or cherry pie (or both) with ice cream à la mode if preferred.

My father had reveled in it. A week after his coronary, he succumbed in an intensive care unit in Buffalo. The instant we heard the news, Scarlett and I drove to Buffalo. We were in Johnson City, Tennessee visiting her family for the holiday. When we arrived, the cardiologist said, "Your father is a powerhouse. Anyone else would have expired in twenty-four hours."

He hadn't needed to remind me my father was strong and unbreakable. I knew my father's demise was cumulative. It was a lifetime of binge drinking and over-indulgence that brought him down. He was only sixty-nine years old, and it felt like a great tree had fallen. There was no time for a transition. He didn't linger (and that's how he'd wanted it). The fatal blow took place in Fort Erie, where his unwed mother hailed from seventy years before. He went over the river to Buffalo to be born and back over to Canada to die.

My father tipped the scales between two hundred and seventy and three hundred pounds during most of his adult life. I know his weight because he weighed himself in the locker room of the Buffalo Athletic Club. I watched him standing naked, his massive paunch protruding over his genitals. He'd squint with his right eye closed at the sliding weights on the bar. When he stepped off, he'd push the balance bar to the left with his thick right index finger. When I was old enough to read numbers, I kept a mental record of his weight and reported it to my mother. I'd say, "Dad weighs two hundred and seventy-seven pounds today." His weight was the same as Tom Sestak, the outstanding defensive end of the Buffalo Bills. I teased my father when the Bills got clobbered, "Why don't you get out there and help them out? You're as big as Sestak."

He'd grin. He'd lost seven teeth, including two front ones, playing football in college, and wore a dental bridge. It was easy to imagine him plugging the line and sacking quarterbacks. He was an imposing figure with broad shoulders and stout biceps. His protruding midsection was hard, not flabby—not a soft beer belly but an iron-clad fortification that anchored him as an immovable object. His automobiles were engineered to accommodate his intumescence. The front seat was always pushed back, eliminating the rear seat so that he could fit behind the steering wheel. His massive upper body was supported by lean, spindly legs and tiny, quick feet. Like a bison, he was the composite of two different creatures. His enormous presence never wavered, even in the sunset of his years.

There had been all kinds of jokes about my father's corpulence inside our household and outside. It was a constant source of embarrassment to which my father seemed immune. When confronted, he'd pat his swollen mass with both hands and say, "It's all paid for." Cassie would mimic him by pushing her belly out and saying, "I'm Cornelius Arthur Motherwell. I carry a lot of weight around this town." It always got a laugh until I did it in front of him and he pounced on me, crushing me beneath his girth. I learned his limits. He could be pushed, but only so far.

The irony is that my father hadn't always been obese, although I only knew him as fat. When he married, as photos will attest, he was lean and trim. He fit the profile of the average American male, five foot ten, and one hundred and fifty pounds. How he gained such a mass during the first year and a half of marriage and never shed it remains a mystery. He carried the burden of an extra eighty percent of his lean body weight over his entire adult life. He'd been an athlete. He had a football scholarship at the University of Florida, where he played wide receiver. He was a distance swimmer who specialized in cold water endurance swims in Lake Ontario. He wasn't fast but as the cardiologist said, he had incredible stamina.

He grew up watching water shows at the Buffalo Athletic

Club in its early years, the 1920s, years of opulence and embellishment. The natatorium was state of the art, the best in the city. It was tiled with high, serrated ceilings, a spectator gallery, and spotlights. The construction paid close attention to detail and ornamentation characteristic of the day. The 1927 Whispering Jack Smith hit, "Me and My Shadow," was the theme of my father's aquatic act. In the 1930s, he donned a black bodysuit and swam underwater while another swimmer swam on the surface. His most famous partner was the visiting Olympian, Johnny Weissmuller. Weissmuller swam on the surface for four continuous lengths—one hundred yards. My father kept pace beneath him on a single breath. Even at the height of my competitive swimming career, I couldn't duplicate more than half that feat, and I tried. So did my brother.

My father never told me about Johnny Weissmuller. The oral history of his physical prowess came to me through others. His contemporaries were always forthcoming with new tales. My pick (and knowing him, it's easy to believe it happened) is the infamous mile swim. I've heard it in many renditions, and all corroborate. It goes like this: He was at his favorite watering hole, the Buffalo Athletic Club bar overlooking Niagara Square. He was a regular almost every afternoon. The consummate salesman, he made his best deals there. He sold paper goods, mostly cups, by the train car full. I never put together how much of that enterprise happened at the bar. But from an early age, I recognized that his job was people. And the people he knew were the way he made his living. He hobnobbed with judges, lawyers, and businessmen. "It's the people you know" was his most overworked maxim. Relationships were everything to my father, and he cherished his reputation.

In those days, the saloon was on the third floor. Elegant dark wood-paneling rose two stories, and velvet drapes framed the McKinley monument, the central hub of Buffalo's radial street system that Joseph Ellicott designed in 1804. Someone asked my father if he was still doing any swimming. My father said, "I can still swim a mile." Nobody believed him, and a guy named Dick Plumber challenged him. He said, "That's seventy-two lengths. I'll bet five hundred you can't do it." They had another drink, and Plumber needled him, "If you're lucky, you can do ten lengths. Look at the size of that gut. Why don't you show us you're not a liar? I've got half a grand that says you can't do it."

The noise level increased as the watering hole filled. Lawyers and judges filed in after a day in court downtown. More level heads were pleading with my father not to do it. "CAM, you're tipsy. You couldn't do it if you were sober. Lose some weight, work out, then take the bet."

Plumber said, "You're a liar. You can't do it."

The intensity of the confrontation heated. As patrons drank more, they made more bets.

My father loosened his bow tie and stood, then he removed his suit jacket and unbuttoned the cuffs of his shirt. The entire bar emptied and followed him down the stairs. He pulled off his clothes as he went. Poolside, he removed his slacks, shoes, and underwear, and dove into the water. It was a men's club. No bathing suits were necessary at the BAC in those days. When he dove in, he created a huge splash. Heaving, huffing, and puffing, he began the slog. His style was never smooth. On the surface, he was sloppy, a herky-jerky motion. His biceps slapped the water's surface, and he never perfected the smooth stroke that creates a pocket in the armpit from which to draw a breath. But even with these limitations, he was formidable because he was relentless.

At that point, onlookers weren't sure if they should call it off or call an ambulance. He sputtered, slowed, but never stopped. My father told me a story of how when he swam in Lake Ontario, it was so cold his suit came off and he didn't notice. He wouldn't quit. As word got around the club, more spectators joined in and made more bets. The even money was that he'd have a heart attack or come to his senses, give up, and pay the wager. But he lumbered on. And as he got to lap sixty-five, Plumber moved to the back of the crowd and slipped out the door. My father finished the mile swim to applause but no payoff.

My father was a peculiar man to live with because he was even-tempered most of the time. Whether sober or drunk, his temper, once breached, was like Vesuvius overflowing. He had a litany of juicy anecdotes and well-worn philosophical sayings. For example, his response to me graduating from PA school at Duke was, "Doctors bury their mistakes." And in describing his tumultuous relationship with my mother, he'd say, "Can't live with 'em, can't live without 'em." It's easy to conjure up memories of my father in the Buffalo Athletic Club steam room. He was adept at discussing the finer points of Buffalo politics or the Buffalo Bills (that are the same), concluding his statements with, "Am I right, or am I wrong?" What I appreciate most about him is that he was a man who was willing to change his mind and admit that he was wrong. He could always relate to someone on a personal level—like he did on the racial issue.

In the late 1960s, African Americans couldn't join the Buffalo Athletic Club. My father, ultra-conservative and a George Wallace supporter, opposed integration. He was up in arms and said he would never sit in a steam room with a black man because he couldn't stand the smell. Under legal pressure, the Buffalo Athletic Club admitted a black judge. Within a couple weeks, my father and Judge Howard were palling around, taking steam baths together. He forgot all about his racism. He never commented that black people smell different again. Although this was a tiny step, it was one I applauded.

Unlike me, I don't remember my father ever sitting around the house depressed. He was a man on the move and, as a youngster, I was often under his care. I learned early that my mother wanted me out of the house. She had strict routines she didn't wish to alter. She made it clear that it was my father's parental duty to take me with him, much the same way I did my brother years later. He loved to drive. He called on customers all over the city with me in tow. I still have a fascination for the seediest parts of town, especially near the waterfront. He introduced me to every kind of person. His final stop was always the Buffalo Athletic Club bar. Sometimes I'd sit with him as he banged the leather dice cup with force on the bar and wager. It bored me, and he'd excuse me and let me go off to the pool where I would create games, dive for rings, and explore my buoyancy.

On Friday nights, he'd find an excuse to drop a letter at the airport. He called it "his report." He'd explain, "New York needs this right away." What this involved was driving through the heart of the African American ghetto, a taboo and hidden world, dark and foreboding, mean streets full of danger. My brother was a baby, and my father took only me along. He allowed me to roll the windows down a crack, no more. Smoky aromas, fried chicken and barbequed ribs, wafted in. A throbbing, dirty, bass beat accompanied by drums, electric guitars, and organ spilled out of honky-tonks. It was a private world cut off from the white churchgoing families who lived in pillboxes with manicured front lawns. People loitered in the streets, laughing and whooping it up. And they had style. I loved the way women and men strutted their stuff—elegant black people in wide-brimmed hats and yellow suits, with no barrier to their desire. I'd ask my father to explain. Regrettably, like me, he was an observer, a European extract who lived in a prison of decorum and middle-class. Ebony eyes followed us, and I peered back through the closed car window. Dark faces opened and flashed exuberant teeth. Extraordinary, these people had broken out of the humdrum. William St. was popping on payday. My father would point out barbershops with envy, said they were open until midnight. I could tell he longed to be part of it, get out of the car, and join in. But he never did. Instead, we plodded our slow, gawking pace toward the airport. The exotic sights, sounds, and smells of William St. were behind us in a flash.

Friday nights with my father were predictable. He always had an urgent letter for someone in the Big Apple that needed special handling, and I rode along.

He ate enough to sustain three men. My mother encouraged this behavior, saying things like, "CAM, you hardly ate anything." And she'd serve him up a second plate, which he'd consume as if it were a snack. He also ate strange things like white bread with milk coated with granular sugar. My mother attributed this kind of behavior to his deprived upbringing. I'd say, "He was never in an orphanage." She'd reply, "It wasn't easy for him." Food was love, and my mother piled it on in heaps.

Although my father never engaged in routine exercise, he remained vigorous throughout his life. He was rarely sick. On occasion, he had the flu. I never heard him complain about his health. He got up very early in the morning and was energetic throughout the day. He never took a nap. In short, he was a dynamo.

Like my father, I overeat to fill an empty void. My hunger is never satisfied. The family refrigerator, always filled to capacity with cold cuts, liverwurst, salami, and sausage, was never fulfilling. Meals were a time of turbulence and frustration. There was always an argument and yelling at the table.

Last night when I got home from work, Victoria said, "Why don't we go to restorative yoga? Maybe it'll make you feel better."

The Santa Barbara Yoga Center is a half dozen blocks away, but Victoria and I were bickering. It took forever to get there. She said I was walking too fast, and she asked me to slow down. I felt like a horse under the control of a rider. I wanted to gallop, and she forced me to trot. As we reached the corner, we stood for an entire sequence while the stoplight changed because she didn't want to cross. The light was green, turned yellow, then red, and green again. I was seething. As we coursed through alleys, the final flickers of sunlight sparked, and the neon lights came up on the Arlington Theater. When we crossed State Street near the Bank of America, a woman in a beat-up van turned in front of us, forcing us to jump back. She parked at an angle, slammed the door, and bolted to the drive-up teller, brushing by us without a word. The parking lot was empty.

A small man in a gray uniform said, "You'll have to pay five dollars if you want to park here."

She said, "I'm parking short term. Can't you see I'm using the ATM?"

She shuffled through her purse, looking for something. The contents fell on the ground. As she squatted and picked them up, she yelled, "I'm not paying five bucks to park for five minutes."

He said, "You'll have to pay five dollars or leave."

She replied, "Fuck you, you son of a bitch."

He curled his lip and snickered.

She gave him the finger.

He said, "You'll have to pay five dollars or leave."

That's when I went off and started yelling at the top of my lungs, "You fucking Nazi. You fucking Nazi. You're a Nazi."

Victoria said, "Enough, enough, Neal. What are you doing?" She grabbed me by the arm.

I screamed again, "You fucking Nazi!"

And he was now getting it from both ends of the parking lot.

The woman screamed, "That's what you are, a fucking Nazi. Nazi, Nazi, Nazi."

The parking attendant walked toward me. It was dusk, and I hadn't seen his face. As he came closer, I saw the hurt in his eyes and his wrinkled frown. It was only then that I got a grip. With my yoga mat under my arm, I walked away.

Victoria was upset. She tugged my arm and in a hoarse whisper barked, "You're going to get us killed. He could be carrying a gun."

The Santa Barbara Yoga Center, like much of downtown, has a stylized, futuristic feel. Something ancient and modern, like Charlie Chaplain's *Modern Times* or Fritz Lang's *Metropolis*. It's housed in a two-story square structure painted yellow with ionic columns, and the building was constructed in the 1920s as the First Church of Christ, Scientist.

As I sat in the yoga class, the tall, pony-tailed graying male instructor said, "Breathe in. Fill yourself with peace and love. Breathe out. Let out all the stress that has accumulated during the day."

I wondered about my mental state. My lack of control. Was it a knee-jerk reaction, an opportunity to blow off steam? Had the pressure of the day gotten to me on top of the constant quibbling with Victoria about how fast or slow we walk? Was the parking lot attendant an innocent bystander subjected to my rage? At first, it felt like a joke. Did the woman's stress infect me? She was chaotic and disorganized, but what did that have to do with me? There was no thinking, no filter. It was as if I were drunk. I said exactly what I wanted to say: "Fuck you, you Nazi." Only after I'd lain for seventy-five minutes of gentle yoga did I return to baseline. Breathing into my heart and putting my body in restful positions, I thought about my anger. It went back a lifetime. I thought about my father, who hung on a thread. My father's rage was palpable at home with his family. Anything could trigger it. Outside the house, he was affable and brought a smile to people's faces. They couldn't feature his violent personality, he kept it so well disguised and camouflaged.

*Am I channeling my father?*

On the way home, Victoria was clearly incensed, the evening ruined. She said, "I'm not going to put up with this."

My mind was going back again and again to the parking lot attendant's eyes. He looked hurt and pitiful. I felt shame.

# 8 JANUARY, 4:18 A.M.

## (SANTA BARBARA, CA)

*"The patient loves her disease.*
*She doesn't want to be cured."*
Erica Jong (1946- )

YESTERDAY WAS A WASH. I collapsed—fever, a wildfire raging inside me, flushing and burning. Then, like a Siberian cold snap, I shook and trembled as if standing naked in the tundra. My only escape was sleep and more sleep. I soaked three T-shirts, every muscle and bone sore and aching. The thought of food made me nauseous and intensified my affliction. I wanted to die because I didn't have the energy to live.

Now my back hurts.

Conrad called. Without a hello, he said, "Victoria tells me you tried to walk in front of a bus at LAX. And what the hell happened between you and some poor parking lot attendant yesterday?"

"I flipped out."

"Do you remember what I told you?"

"Something about a Saturn return on steroids."

"What are you going to do about it?"

"I'm out of clinic next week. I'm going to Duke for a PA re-certification meeting."

"Cancel it."

"Why?"

"Neal, you need something bold, preposterous, outrageous…"

"Dangerous?"

"Yes, dangerous, threatening, treacherous…whatever words you choose. Do something risky. Jolt yourself out of your comfort zone. What about Calypso?"

I said, "Visit my sister in the Caribbean?" I sang, "Day-o, day-o. Daylight come and me wan' go home."

"Yeah, yeah, Harry Belafonte. You know I'm talking about Big Sur. Victoria tells me you've been there…"

I said, "I found a therapist, although it was a little disappointing. All she did was watch me fill out forms, sign a disclaimer, and collect my copay."

"Neal, you don't need therapy. You need something radical, a quantum leap, a breakthrough. Talk therapy's fine for maintenance. That's all I have for you. Give my best to Victoria."

He hung up.

I said to Vic, "Why did you get Conrad involved?"

She glared at me. "You've got to do something. This is bad. This isn't business as usual."

"He wants me to go to the Calypso Institute."

"Take my car."

"Don't you want to go with me?"

"Neal, this isn't about me or us. Let go of the marriage and do this for yourself. Come back to me whole."

"What do you mean?"

"You're fucked up. It has nothing to do with the marriage. It's your mother…it's the Motherwell thing."

"But what about North Carolina? I can't cancel that."

"You can make it up some other time."

I said, "Let me think about it."

"No. Call and make a reservation now. You're floundering. Things are much worse than you think. You need help and not from me. I'm not your shrink."

After Conrad called, I noticed a strange, crusty taste in my mouth and a metallic smell. My nostrils picked up an odd scent of something familiar, acrid, and sweet. It took me several fits and starts to identify it. It smelled like Coppertone suntan lotion, and this transported me back to South Florida. That was before anybody used sunscreen and a disgusting layer of oily, blue bubbles was acceptable on pool surfaces. In those days, we were going for the darkest, deepest, most luxurious tan.

In my half-sleep and discomfort, memories of my brief marriage to Aleida flooded in. A union so condensed and abridged, what I remember most is the trauma of the divorce and with it, the zeitgeist of the '70s: Vietnam, the draft, the peace movement. Over three million dead in Southeast Asia, jungles deforested by Agent Orange and herbicides. Monks and peace activists self-immolated on street corners. And, of course, there was Studio 54, the Bee Gees, and disco. In this stupor, Aleida's words from the past century surfaced in incredible detail. "It's your destiny. You have to go." She was talking about Duke. Like Victoria's insistence, there had been no discussion. In the final phase of the breakup, Aleida and I went to a counselor. It was a female who sided with me. Aleida said, "I'm not going to North Carolina. Why don't you fuck her?" I pleaded with Aleida to reconsider. We signed papers. Six weeks later, it was done. Divorced. She stayed in the Sunshine State, and I departed for North Carolina.

Before Aleida, there were other crushes, passions, and obsessions.

Girls were always the motivating factor, but with her, there was commitment. I expected to spend the rest of my life with her, and it didn't work out. It broke my ego, shattered my sense of myself. Why couldn't I hang in there like my parents had?

The marriage was dead, executed like a soldier by a firing squad. Aleida was nine years older, the same age as Cassie. The match lasted two and a half years, the parting swift and traumatic.

We lived in the back of a one-story brick duplex next to an empty lot with two scraggly mango trees that yielded small, stringy fruit. Everyone ignored the trees, but to me, it was a windfall. Here I was, a kid from Buffalo with unlimited access to tropical fruit. I'd never seen a mango before coming to South Florida. After peeling the skin, the scrawny, yellow matrix of the fruit barely yielded a bite, but I could suck the sweet juice and use my front teeth to scrape the pit. The juice dribbled down my cheeks and a sticky, gold residue stuck to my hands and didn't wash off. The essence remained on the tips of my fingers throughout the day (and sometimes into the night), which I often brought to my nose and revisited. The hairy pulp stuck in my teeth, even after flossing.

As I lay febrile and sweating, other episodes surfaced. After dinner one night, Aleida and I were fighting. She'd fallen asleep on a futon in the living room, and I was in the bedroom. Half asleep, I sensed some commotion next to the bed. When I looked up, a small, slim, black man was going through my pants pockets. I stood up, raised both arms above my head, and started screaming, "Awwwwwww!" I chased the intruder to the door, shrieking something unintelligible at the top of my lungs. He ran into the shadows. When my bare feet hit the sidewalk, I stopped. I realized I wasn't wearing a stitch.

The next day, a neighbor told me he saw some clothing strewn in an open lot across the street. I recovered my pants and wallet.

Everything was there except the cash, eighteen dollars. Even my credit cards were intact.

It turned out the guy was a petty thief with a drug habit well known to local police. He'd entered through the kitchen window. The landlord put iron bars on all the windows the next week. Aleida and I never discussed it. The bars seemed enough of a deterrent, and the rent was cheap. All this while Buffalo was enduring "The Great Blizzard of '77."

I loved the simplicity of Dania Beach. A single bedroom, a narrow hallway, a bathroom, and an orange shag carpet. The only accouterments were the futon and a leather rhinoceros ottoman anchored near it. There was nothing of value. We sat on the floor. The neighbor, a hulking, disabled African American security guard named Willie, patrolled the walkway. He peered in our windows, turning his stiff neck in a brace like an owl. Aleida often walked naked between the bathroom and the kitchen. When I'd see Willie on the prowl, he'd say, "OTJT," then pause a beat and laugh. "On the job training, nothing like it."

In Florida, my objective was to get in shape and reload. I worked as an ocean lifeguard and ran to the beach with a backpack filled with everything I needed for the day: a beach towel, swim goggles, and a wheat germ smoothie. It amazed me how simple life could be.

Aleida's reality was different than mine. She was miserable as an elementary school teacher and forced to commute twenty-five miles inland. Her parents, Polish Jews who had fled the Holocaust, gave her few career choices. They pushed her to excel. She earned a master's degree at Stoney Brook and immersed herself in a career she loathed. She smoked pot and put the time in at a job she despised. She pined for summer break and holidays. She didn't want to struggle with it anymore. She needed a man to support her. She said she aspired to a white picket fence, a home, and a baby—things I wasn't ready for, at least not yet. And, as it turned out, never would be.

I met Aleida in Buffalo before she moved to Florida. We were working at a residential center for emotionally disturbed boys. The center consisted of two rundown, post-antebellum mansions on Buffalo's millionaire row. With time, these palatial estates had yielded their marquee addresses to social programs. The clientele consisted of tortured, distraught, anguished children without a thread of an ability to cope. These were the lost, rejected, and abandoned, pariahs of the school system. Their mental health was fragile, and they freaked out with minimal provocation. And on occasion, it got scary because these youngsters possessed super-human strength. I've seen an eight-year-old heave heavy wooden furniture with the force of King Kong. Like Holden Caulfield, our task was to catch and protect them from themselves. In polite par-lance, they were slow learners, and we all knew that they would never learn. The majority moved on to lifelong incarceration. But that didn't stop us. It proved to be the most crucial time of my life for making lifelong friendships. And Aleida was part of it, but in a fringe way. She wasn't a counselor or one of the guys. She was a professional, the remedial reading teacher.

My position was bottom rung, the night man. My assignment, and my only value, was to stay awake all night. It consisted of turning a key every hour to alert an outside security service that, indeed, I was awake. On a few occasions, I slumbered and was jolted by a phone call that returned me to my duty. I comforted kids who had nightmares and changed pee-soaked beds. Most of the time, I read James Joyce, T.S. Eliot, Walt Whitman, and dabbled with my poetry. Aleida and I had little contact. On first meeting at one of the center's many social events, my eyes fix-ated on the dark circles under her eyes. So black and profound, I found myself staring. Tall and attractive with an athletic body, she had thick, obsidian hair. I liked that she had wiry gray shoots she didn't attempt to conceal. Her voice was husky, soft, gentle, and low. It flowed like molasses or snow melting in the sun, and she had a natural calming effect on children. She possessed the patience of Job, something that proved essential in assisting me to get my life on track. Her presentation was sophisticated, but it was clear that she was carrying a heavy load. From others, I learned that her live-in boyfriend had died. Rumor had it that he was a bad boy, obstreperous and alcoholic, a grown-up version of one of our wards. She'd lived with him for ten years and was grieving the loss.

Yesterday, in the fit of my discomfort, Victoria came in, fluffed the bed, and changed the sheets. Her motto was, "Comfort the disturbed, and disturb the comfortable." Having a nurse in the house is a huge advantage. She spritzed my back with lavender water, which proved to be a godsend. It quieted the inferno. She also sprayed behind my knees. During intermittent periods of wakefulness and sleep, I found myself flailing. I spoke in tongues, a kind of delirium. It flung me back in time, immersing me back into my transition from my parents' house.

Before Aleida, there was Brooksville. After I graduated from the University of Miami, there was a huge hiccup. In late August, I found myself in West-central Florida. Smothered by humidity, tormented by mosquitoes, snakes, and vermin, I came to my senses. It all started during my final semester, when I'd seen a sign at the U of M placement office: "Do you want to be a hero?" Inflated and delusional, I applied. It was a reformatory for boys who had committed hideous crimes. Too young for the penal system, the camp was an alternative to prison for troubled youngsters. The program emphasized a back-to-nature approach that appealed to me.

I'd studied Rousseau's noble savage theory and felt I could

make a difference. Upon arrival, it was nothing like I expected. Spanish moss dripped from live oak trees in a vast and isolated wilderness. The delinquent kids lived in the same tents with the counselors. I feared one might thrust a knife through my chest as I slept. The conclusion of the psychologist at my final interview was, "A guy like you, with these kids, they'll eat you up and spit you out." But that's not what deterred me. It was a six-foot black snake that slithered across the footpath while I was walking to my tent. I knew right then it was time to shuffle back to Buffalo. The sticky, humid wetlands of the Deep South weren't for me.

I'd missed Vietnam by a hairpin turn. The draft ended and switched to an all-volunteer army in my last year of college. Kent State behind us, Saigon fell in 1975. The jig was up. The lie exposed. We lost the war, and the communists won. What was I doing in Brooksville?

I found out later, Brooksville commemorates an assault. Its eponym was derived from Preston Brooks, who nearly caned his colleague to death on the Senate floor in 1856, and it remains one of the most antagonistic and repulsive events in American history. So brutal and relentless was the attack that Brooks shattered his weapon, and the country was so divided that Southerners sent Brooks dozens of replacements with messages like "Good job," and "Do it again." His victim, Senator Charles Sumner of Massachusetts, suffered PTSD and brain injuries. Sumner, an abolitionist, spent three years recovering. Later, he became a significant force, along with Lincoln, in reshaping American views on slavery.

Congressman Brooks resigned after the attack and got off light with a three hundred dollar fine for assault. Reelected by his South Carolina constituents, he met a hideous end the next year from a croup-like illness. He tried to rip out his own throat in order to breathe. He was thirty-seven. The melee inflamed passions on both sides. Civility and moderate voices dismissed, extremism became the order of the day and led to the Civil War. The reason for the mugging: Brooks was enraged by Sumner's inflammatory anti-slavery speech. Sumner, a brilliant orator, had gone too far. He insinuated sexual activity between owners and slaves and mocked Brooks's second cousin, Senator Andrew Butler, a slave advocate. Brooks felt that his gentleman's honor was at stake. So went the Civil War. So went Vietnam. Pride always comes before a fall. Brooksville wasn't for me.

My father picked me up at the airport. It was my first attempt to get away from my family and Buffalo, and I'd failed. My shoulders slumped as the fat man drove me home, back to my childhood. I said to him, "What I really need now is a father."

He sat silent.

That only further intensified our hostile relationship. Four years away and a college degree hadn't gotten me very far. I was stuck, and I knew it. What a mistake my first job in the wilderness had been, with kids who had murdered parents and babysitters. My attempt to be a hero and save the world was a disaster. So ingrained in me, like so many of my generation, I can't say no to folly. Now I was back in my bedroom with the blood-red corduroy bedspreads—the bed my mother made for me each day. I didn't drive. I walked or took the bus. The refrigerator was full of cold cuts and delicious treats. I was outraged when my mother demanded rent.

In Buffalo, I took writing classes at UB with Leslie Fiedler. He told me, "What can I say? Keep writing. Give me more." At the time, I was scribbling cryptic poems, fragments. All my closest friends worked at the center while deciding what to do next. On my nights off, I played pick-up basketball until two in the morning, then closed down the bars on Elmwood Avenue. The ritual was followed by breakfast at a greasy spoon or a donut place at sunrise. The heaving bellows and fire ovens of Bethlehem Steel still lit the skies along Lake Erie, covering the ground and cars with a fine, black soot.

I liked my job because I had the entire night to read and write. And I loved my friends. I slept all morning and worked as a life-guard at the Buffalo Athletic Club in the late afternoon. My shift at the center started at nine in the evening. I got off at eight, and Aleida didn't come to work until nine the next morning. We had no cause to interact. But throughout the night, I fooled around on her typewriter that had large font. It was fun to see my poems in large letters. One morning, I left a poem behind in the typewriter carriage. "I, the disgusting one, who revolves around the sun. Transparent in my loneliness, forever stubborn in my desire." The next day, I found it in my mailbox with a note. "Keep this up, and you'll be joining Mr. Pound as the most wanted man in America, A."

For three years, I was in and out of my parents' house. They kept my room, albeit when I was there, they demanded rent. I also rented a dilapidated room on the eighth floor of the Buffalo Athletic Club. That summer, I was managing a boy's summer camp in Allegheny State Park and came home for a few days to pack and get ready. I was lying in my parents' bed watching television. Aleida showed up with a Saran-wrapped plate of chocolate chip cookies. Her gambit was that she was visiting a neighbor across the street and thought she'd say hello. My mother, without hesitation, sent her upstairs. She sat on the bed beside me and said, "Are you writing anything? Wanna cookie?" I took a bite and retched because they were hard and burnt to a crisp. I put the charcoal-braised cookie back on the plate. She said, "I didn't say they were any good."

There was little contact with Aleida that summer. We didn't write. She called me once through the switchboard, and I don't remember why or what she said. It surprised me that she'd found me. I had a girlfriend at the camp. Aleida's voice was always persuasive and flowed like maple syrup, especially on the phone. I loved to listen to her talk. When the camp closed, I went back to the night job at the center and worked afternoons at the pool. My mother did my laundry and kept the house quiet so I could sleep in the morning. She always made me lunch. I took the bus and walked downtown on days it wasn't raining. My father continued his sales trips, away two or three nights a week. Mick was also home, an adolescent. Saundra was married to Tim, and Cassie was already in the Islands. Mom's nighttime visits to my bedroom ceased.

Autumn was brief, and winter rolled in with ruthless certainty. The trees were bare overnight, and snow came. After bar-hopping with friends on Elmwood Avenue one night, Aleida and I were left standing alone next to a donut shop at 5 a.m. in the morning. A bright red neon sign flickered, "We Never Close." We pressed our noses up against the frigid window. The baker was drizzling thick, bronze glaze on the hot maple bars.

I said, "Do you want one?"

Her rich brown eyes sparkled. "Do you think I should?"

"Why not?"

"I have a sugar addiction."

It was the way she wrapped her tongue around the word "sugar" when I fell in love. I knew she meant it. And she was sugar, she loved sugar, and I wanted more.

I said, "You look great."

"I lost twenty-five pounds after Beau died," she said.

I said, "Let's split one."

She nodded.

We argued about who was going to pay.

She said, "I make more than you."

But after extensive debate, she allowed me to fork over a dollar.

She said, "How are we going to divide it?"

"Why don't you take a bite and then I'll take a bite?"

"What if I take a bigger bite?"

"Which end do you want?"

She said, "Why don't we do it at the same time and meet in the middle?"

Soon our frozen faces pushed together. The sugary sweet maple frosting led to a gush of kisses covering foreheads, cheeks, and lips.

Aleida pulled my goatee. She said, "I've wanted to do that."

We fell back into a tall snowbank, laughing, my hands exploring her body through scarves and wool. Aleida invited me back to her flat on Forrest Avenue, a short walk. She changed into a long, brown Moroccan tunic, and we lay on a Persian carpet. When I reached for her breasts, she pushed me away and said, "You can't touch my muffins." The rooftop rattled gusty winds that blew snowdrifts against the windows. I slept with her all morning and into the afternoon, though she'd made it clear, no sex. At sunset, I got up to go home. She said, "Can you take the garbage out?" It smelled musty, like earth worms, rotting zucchini, and chard. I deposited the bag in the dumpster and walked three miles home, feeling no pain in the freeze, as if I were drunk. I marched with elation across lumpy, white ice clumps. I looked up at the big oak tree in Delaware Park and shouted, "I love trees." I beseeched the gods that I'd never fall out of love. Never separate from the feeling when all the world, the entire sphere of madness, glows with a blank face, and I am parent of every smile.

After that it was full-on with Aleida. I had two other girl-friends, Emma Jean in Toronto and Emma in St. Catharines. At first, I tried to maintain contact with both. Aleida wouldn't have it. Also, she wouldn't tolerate my bullshit. I talked and talked about New Zealand and how I wanted to live there. Emma Jean was born in Wellington, and her family put me in touch with friends. By the time I met Aleida, I had pen pal relationships with several Kiwi families. I read everything I could get my hands on about New Zealand with the relish of a savant and brought it up in conversation. "Did you know the Treaty of Waitangi is the first agreement between European colonists and native people where no blood was shed?" I was in touch with the New Zealand embassy in New York and Los Angeles. Aleida was amenable to immigrate with me. She leaned hard on me to make my dream a reality and made it clear she'd settle for nothing less.

My cousins in California convinced me that I could use their place as a base and, from there, work my way to New Zealand. I had the idea that I could catch a freighter in San Francisco or Los Angeles. At the same time, Aleida would leave the center and move to Florida to be closer to her aging parents. We agreed she'd meet me in New Zealand once I got established. I met little opposition from my mother. My father wondered in a naïve way how I'd get home for holidays. They both understood my resolve, and I was on my way.

On February 17, 1976, I placed all my belongings in a backpack and headed west. I took buses and hitchhiked. In Detroit, I picked up a new Buick Riviera drive-away and drove to Torrance. The car was a beast, firecracker orange with an astroroof. Its 205-horsepower, 455-cubic-inch V8 engine guzzled gas. I picked up hitchhikers along the way, who chipped in for fuel.

In Canoga Park, Dinky welcomed me to his grimy, one-bedroom barrio apartment. He shared everything. I encountered a generosity that I'd never experienced before or since. His California king, Chevy El Camino, and Doberman pinscher were mine at my choosing. Anything was OK with Dinky. More than once, he tried to persuade a girl who was visiting to let me do her as well. He never charged rent and would never take any money, but he could be obnoxious and a cruel tease. He modeled his rapid-fire banter after Don Rickles. When he was drinking, his verbal assaults became intolerable. But generous in describing Dinky's character is an understatement. No one has ever treated me so unconditionally. We lived cheap. We had a third roommate, a teetering, middle-aged Mexican landscaper named Robert. Robert slept on the couch. Sad and lovable and alcoholic, Robert had a heart of gold. Dinky and I were often broke and without money for food, and Robert would waltz in with a bag of burritos.

Dinky and I had little in common. Books, film, and culture were of limited interest to him. Our mothers were sisters, and I never doubted the bond of blood, but he couldn't understand my enthusiasms and drives. He'd say, "I don't know where you get your energy." During the week, he painted houses. On weekends, he barricaded himself in his bedroom with curtains shut. He'd say, "It's been a hard week, and I need to be alone. Leave me alone." As far as I could tell, he'd watch porn, *The Three Stooges* and *Here's Lucy* reruns, masturbate, and drink beer. Before entering this voluntary isolation, he'd hand me the car keys and say, "Have a party." I'd drive the LA freeways and dream about getting to New Zealand. After a year of working landscape and construction jobs, I was no closer to the Land of the Long White Cloud and I hadn't saved much money.

Aleida was in Florida, and we were at a stalemate. We'd lost daily contact, and my attempt to get to New Zealand had stalled. The low point, I got pneumonia and ended up in the hospital for a week. The entire enterprise withered, going nowhere. LA is the land of dreams, inflated fantasies, and nightmares. One of Dinky's favorite words, "Bummer," describes my situation. I'd reached rock bottom.

But then, a pivotal event. Dinky and I lived on the second floor. A young woman had moved in a few doors down and she asked me over to fix a dripping faucet, and we ended up on the couch necking. I called Aleida and told her it was over between us. The next night, the girl asked me to go out with her to a bar. We met an older man there. She handed me her car keys and said,

"I'm with him. Take my car." I can still hear those keys jiggling from a yellow rabbit's foot.

That night, I packed my gear and took a red-eye to Miami. It took me months before I could call and tell Dinky what happened.

He said, "Man, why'd you split?"

"Remember that chick who lived next door?"

"Yeah, Chloe. She's still there."

"I thought we had something going. We went out. We met another guy. She handed me her car keys and told me to hit the road."

He laughed. "She's a pro. He's her pimp."

Beaten and lost, back in Miami at twenty-five years old, I stayed with friends near campus in Coral Gables. It took a few days before I worked up the courage to see Aleida. I remember my friend waiting in the car outside her apartment in case she threw me out.

When Aleida opened the door, she smiled and said, "I thought you'd show up. What took you so long?" She threw her arms around me, and things resumed as if we were never apart, except she insisted that I find a job and I had no idea where to start. I thought about working at a bookstore. I had delusions of writing and working as a bookseller like Hermann Hesse. A week later, she exploded when she found out I'd skipped an interview at Barnes & Noble. She bared her teeth. "I'm not going to support you and all your big ideas. I had enough of that with Beau."

I screamed back, "I'm not some fucking broken-down drunk." She was crying. I slammed the door and hitchhiked to Ft. Lauderdale. It seemed like we were at the end.

I'd heard about a city ocean lifeguard job and showed up for the competition. The conditions were miserable with heavy winds, onshore swells, and a Portuguese man o' war warning. The beach was a minefield cluttered with purple, gas-filled bladders. So many, it was hard not to pop them like bubble gum out of spite. To my surprise, the trial wasn't called off. Only six candidates turned up, and two decided not to swim. I had no other prospects. I knew I'd be heading back to Buffalo if this didn't work out.

The captain of the beach patrol was short, slight, wiry, military-erect. He had long, wheat-colored hair that was heavily bleached by the sun. His given name was Sterling St. James, but most addressed him as Sterl. Behind his back, they called him "The Little General," "Napoleon," or "Boner Part."

Using a bullhorn, he shouted, "You'll start together here." He pointed to a slick, red-painted lifeguard stand a few feet away. "Nobody takes off until I blow the whistle. If there's a false start, I'll call you back. Do it twice, and you're gone." He stood firm, brazen, wearing the tiniest G-string of a bathing suit. He braced his bare chest and shoulders as if to defy the cold wind. His hair fluttered. He lowered the megaphone and pulled one of the candidates aside. Squinting, he pointed out at the ocean. "See that buoy out there?" The guy shook his head. At first, I didn't see it. The waves were massive, coming in sets. Seeing anything offshore was a tribute to better eyes than mine. He leaned over at his hips and said, "See what I'm talking about?"

No one nodded.

"Take my word for it. It's out there, about a hundred and fifty yards. You'll see it when you get there. Keep swimming until you do. Touch it with your hand. I'll be watching with binoculars. If you don't touch, you're disqualified. From there, swim to the pier, touch the second buoy, and swim straight to the beach. From the fishing pier, you'll run back here." He handed each of us a long, red float with a rope and harness. It started to rain. Using the megaphone, he said, "Everybody got it? Any questions?"

Someone asked, "What's this for?"

He put the megaphone aside. "That's a torp, and it's your best friend. You don't go out on a rescue without it. You'll wear it in the water so I can see you swim with a harness under these conditions. This ain't no freestyle relay."

"What if one of us gets stung by a jellyfish?"

"First off, don't worry about the person next to you. I'll take care of that. We've got meat tenderizer in the kit. If you're in so much pain you can't swim, we'll come get you. Any other questions? You can leave your gear in the shack." He pointed to a small, dilapidated building and then looked around and sneered, hands behind his back.

We stripped off our sweats, piling them in a heap on a wooden bench in a damp, puddled room with a slick, glossy floor painted green. It smelled musty and made me sneeze. The surface was cold and sandy. I was out of shape, fluffy, carrying an extra fifty pounds from California. I hadn't been in the ocean since I left Florida. When we got to the starting line, there were four of us. Everyone looked scared and anxious, like they'd never done this before. It was before the physical fitness craze and triathlons. We lined up, and when the whistle blew, we flared our feet in the sand, and pushed off like horses. The guy who asked about the torp tripped and fell. Once in the water, I felt comfortable but winded. I stroked as hard as I could, long fingers pulling from shoulders. I paddled out to the buoy, touched it, and stroked my way to the pier. I caught a wave into shore that almost took me into the timber. When I looked back, I could see splashing behind me and none in front. I knew I needed to be ahead when I hit the beach. I was slow as a snail on land. When I stood, my legs buckled like the jellyfish. I was soggy and started to run. It was two football fields away. Huffing and puffing, I lumbered to the lifeguard stand. A strapping young woman with long, stringy, sunbleached hair was close behind. She'd been stung across the face.

At eleven that night, The Little General called and offered me the job.

I said, "Why are you calling so late?"

"Heather turned it down. She's taking the job in Hollywood."

"But I won."

"She would have cleaned your clock if she hadn't been stung. I hope you're planning to lose some weight."

I assured him I was.

He added, "You're a blob."

The position didn't pay well. It was like being a private in the army, and The Little General never let me forget it. But staying fit was part of the job. We swam in the ocean, ran on the beach, and lifted weights on company time every day. I built muscle and lost fat and learned new habits. The city offered medical benefits and other incentives. Ocean lifeguards were the first to take courses in the new emergency medical field. For Aleida, her father, and me, it became a family affair. They took preliminary courses like first aid and defensive driving with me. Once enrolled, I found I liked it and had an aptitude for picking it up. I'd never taken a science course in college. No one in my family had done anything related to medicine. In the past, I'd get queasy around blood and body fluids. I passed out when they drew blood for the lifeguard position. Little did I know I was on a career path that would support me for the rest of my life.

My twenty-sixth birthday was fortuitous. I completed the coursework and passed the emergency medical technician boards. The next step, paramedic, was new and only offered in Miami. I commuted and got the first-hand experience at Jackson Memorial Hospital, one of the busiest emergency departments in the world. The walls, at times covered in blood and excrement, both scared and titillated me. The shrieks of human suffering echoed off the walls. Babies being born, heart attacks, mutilations, alcohol-related shootings, drug violence. I immersed myself. In contrast to my time at Jackson, I rode the physician-staffed ambulances in posh Miami Beach albeit, in all cases, I was an observer, a bystander.

Driven to learn more, I signed up for extra shifts. Proximity to the dark shadow of human suffering satisfied a curiosity long un-requited. It fed me. It wasn't so much that I wanted to do good as I wanted to be part of it. I was doing it to save myself. It was for me, not them. It was a calling, a rite of passage, a point of destiny.

The episode I remember best at Jackson came in my early days. Six students huddled in a tiny patient treatment room the size of a cubby. An inexperienced doctor was attempting to intu-bate an elderly man during a code. The man's family—his wife, daughter, and grown grandchildren—were waiting outside the door. The intern tried again and again and brought back red blood on the laryngoscope and tube. After each attempt, he'd squeeze an Ambu bag attached to the hose. A nurse listening over the patient's stomach with a stethoscope said, "Air." I thought she was saying error. It meant that the intubation tube was in the esophagus, not the trachea.

It was a quip, a fast communication shorthand, so the doctor tried again. The group worked with ferocious intensity and wouldn't give up despite no patent airway. Members of the team took turns compressing the chest. The weary neophyte physician pounded the patient's sternum. The EKG remained a flat line. It felt like there was still life as they hammered away at a bag of flesh without a heartbeat. Forty minutes into it, everybody sweating, a voice spoke to me. It was as if I were communicat-ing with the dead man. I watched his essence rise and exit along the white-tiled wall, like ether. It wasn't scary or frightening. I muttered as if channeling his voice, "He's home now." And soon after, the frenzy stopped. A nurse pulled a white sheet over the patient's face, and the medical team relented. It was this kind of real-life drama that I craved—commerce with unseen spirits. An occupation that took me far beyond the voyeurism of television and my ordinary life, and I wanted to be engulfed. I'll never forget the look on the youthful doctor's face. Exasperated and defeated, he put his failure behind him and moved on to the next case.

The most bizarre episode, and the one Aleida and I came to regret, was how we got married. It had seemed like a good idea at the time. Things were going well enough, and we had income. Yet both of us were dissatisfied with our jobs and where our lives were going. We were in love, and I didn't see anything beyond Aleida. It was the first marriage for both of us, precipitated by a bar mitzvah. Aleida's brother, a dentist in Saddle River, New Jersey, was throwing a huge family bash. Relatives were coming in from everywhere for the event. His brother's wife asked Aleida if she was bringing someone. Aleida said, "Of course, Neal," to which she replied, "Are you married?" Aleida answered, "Yes." A week before the bar mitzvah, we got married in Ft. Lauderdale with her parents as our witnesses. Little did I know it was the beginning of the end.

When we got back from New Jersey, Aleida had an idea. She'd heard that the Eastern-rite Catholic Church ordained married men. She thought it would be great for us and a way to get to New Zealand. We started attending St. Basil's Byzantine Rite Church in North Miami. Looking back, it wasn't as crazy an idea as it seems now. We were part of the Woodstock generation. The sounds of the '60s were being drowned out by disco. I'd grown up Catholic and Aleida a Jew, but our real affiliation was to some other calling. The vocational dalliance with the priesthood only lasted a few months and ended. There was no decisive turning point. It wore off.

Neither one of us had given up on New Zealand. We scrimped and saved and blew it on a bone-chilling summer there, our last as a couple. It wasn't the cause of the breakup, but it sure let the air out of the tires. Aleida's contribution was her cherished summer vacation from the classroom. Days before we departed, I passed the paramedic board exam, intending to find employment down under. I was in touch with Aleida's help with emergency medical services on both the North and South Island. We appeared on an

Auckland radio talk show during our first week, and I rambled on and on about what it was like to be a paramedic in the US. Full of youthful exuberance and hubris, I was a student and never practiced. Both of us were overwhelmed with the Kiwis' tolerance and politeness.

Not helping matters, our summer down under is winter, and frigid, more cutting than we ever expected, and it dragged on and on. It was rare to find central heating. Shivering, we often sought out public buildings like the public library for warmth. We deflected plans to explore South Island job opportunities and spent those valuable weeks in the Bay of Islands seeking radiant heat and sunshine. We found that the Bay of Islands is a picturesque vacation district devoid of employment opportunities except for picking kiwis. We made lots of friends, and people were ever supportive and helpful, but both of us wanted to come home. Our New Zealand interlude proved to be a dalliance, not a geographical cure. It was clear we wouldn't stay, and the turning point was *The Last Waltz*, a film we'd already seen in Florida that came a year late to New Zealand. At the time, everything took months and months to get there, and some pop culture milestones never arrived at all.

A few weeks before we left, we joined a rowdy crowd at a bar in Auckland. A single tube of white light cut through the smoke and darkness and projected the film on a white sheet draped on a wall. When patrons stood to get a beer, their shadows blocked the screen. No one cared. The vamped-up electric sound system filled any gaps. For me, the effect of seeing The Band on stage at the Winterland Ballroom in San Francisco was hypnotic. Everybody in the pub wished they'd been there, hooting and hollering for each super act Robbie Robertson brought to the stage. I swelled with pride as an American. I wanted to be in the music, not six thousand miles away. Raunchy rockabilly performers like Ronnie Hawkins reminded me where I came from and where I belonged.

When The Band performed "It Makes No Difference," a song that to this day splits me open, a pure wail and sad lament, written by Robertson and sung by the late Rick Danko, it expressed the emotion I felt that frosty summer in Auckland. Although my commitment to Aledia proved temporary, my devotion to rock and roll and America was visceral.

In one line, Danko rips his voice wide open and yelps, "Stampeding cattle, they rattle the walls." It shook my rib cage so hard, it felt like the hoofs rumbled on my heart. Levon Helm and Richard Manuel's whiny country harmony vocalize Americana and Robertson's guitar teeters an edge, like cocaine addiction. The penultimate saxophone solo by Garth Hudson at the end never fails to bring me to tears. My choice was to be an American and accept the chaos, lies, racism, warmongering, waste, and stupidity. Not because I was born an American but because I now chose it. And this proved to be the most important decision of my life.

Upon return, Aleida picked up where she'd left off, smoking weed and loathing every minute of her wretched job. Walking on the beach and time off for weekends and holidays offered some solace, but we were growing less interested in each other's lives. What once was easy became strained. Both of us looked forward to time away from each other.

I returned to the beach, passed the firefighter exam, and got hired by the City of Oakland Park. At the fire station, I convened poetry readings. Lawrence Ferlinghetti's "In a Time of Revolution For Instance," was a favorite. Ferlinghetti read at the University of Miami when I was a student and dazzled me. My colleagues loved the punch line, "…in a time of revolution for instance / she might have fucked me."

On the beach, a friend came up with the moniker, "Lifebard." It fit as I was passionate about literature and the healing arts. I brought poetry to the fire station, and I've used it as a handle ever since.

Enter Dalton Smith. When Dr. Smith drove into the parking lot in his red Corvette, nurses swooned. He sashayed through the hospital doors like Shaft. And there were different exotic sports cars every day. Maserati, Porsche, Shelby Mustang—he changed his ride like most change shoes. Photogenic, charismatic, a bachelor, he had emergency room contracts all over South Florida. Fire departments like mine engaged him as medical director. More than a businessman, he wanted to provide top-notch emergency room medicine. He had a long, friendly Southern drawl. Our group met with him twice a month for continuing education to review our work in the field. He trained paramedics on how to write proper medical notes. He demanded each report follow the SOAP formula: subjective, objective, assessment, and plan. He grilled us until we got it right.

He read one of my notes to the group at a meeting and said, "Motherwell, you're pretty good. Have you ever thought about becoming a PA?"

I said, "No," paused, and embarrassedly said, "What's a PA?"

He laughed. "Does anybody here know what a PA is?"

Nobody raised their hand.

He said, "It's an acronym for physician assistant or physician associate. It's a new field. PAs work under a doctor's license. They can do almost anything a doctor can do, even start a practice. It started at Duke University after the Vietnam War. I'd put my money on it. It's going to be big. It's the future."

I said, "Where's Duke?"

He said, "Durham, North Carolina. Up there in tobacco country. You know, Tobacco Road, Bull Durham cigarettes, but that's not what they're about anymore. They call Durham the City of Medicine now. There's a doctor up there named Eugene Stead, chairman of the department of medicine. He started this thing. Dr. Stead's a graduate of Emory, my alma mater."

He changed the subject and resumed the meeting. When it

was over, as we were milling around, he said, "I've been thinking about this. As you know, I've been very blessed and fortunate to achieve success on many levels. You can only have so many cars, take so many vacations, and own so many houses. If one of you were to apply to Duke and get in, I'd like to make it possible for you to go. I want to do that for someone."

I told Aleida, and she started researching PA schools. And when she undertook a research project, she left no stone unturned. She called my parents, who adored her. My mother would often say, "God love you. You're the best thing that ever happened to Neal. He's a dreamer." My parents were very proud that I hadn't ended up on "the junk heap," my father's choice expression for long-haired hippies and ne'er-do-wells. Complicating matters more, Aleida's parents were fond of me and saw this as a life-altering opportunity.

I remember the phone call with my folks. Aleida said, "Dr. Smith's right, Duke's the best. They only accept forty people a year, and they get six or seven hundred applications. If Neal can pass chemistry, he's got a chance. They're looking for people with experience. He'll get preference."

I took chemistry at the local community college, applied to Duke, got an interview, and got in.

Dalton Smith was true to his word. He sent me a check for a thousand dollars with the note, "Tell me what you need, and I will make up any shortfall." There was no contract, and he never asked me to sign a loan application. I took student loans as well and made a verbal commitment to pay him back. And then he also assured me that there'd be a job waiting for me when I got back.

I was ecstatic. At twenty-eight years old, it felt like my first success. Everything I'd tried so far had ended in failure and disap-pointment, even New Zealand. I'd play James Taylor's "Carolina in My Mind" over and over again. I knew every pause and nuance of that haunting tune. I dreamed of a new life in an open place.

At first, Aleida planned to join me in Durham, or at least was paying lip service to it. One day, driving home from the beach, she was sullen and dark. I played "Carolina in My Mind." She started to cry, slammed the cassette player, and turned it off. At that moment, I knew she wasn't going. Big tears flowed down her cheeks. I tried to remedy the situation and withdrew my acceptance letter. She moved out to her parents' condo who were in North Carolina for the summer. There was no way to save the marriage.

Two short scenes I remember: A week before Aleida moved out. We'd been swimming in the ocean. When we walked out of the surf, she said, "What do you think those people over there are thinking?" I looked and saw a young couple sitting under an umbrella. It didn't look like they were looking at us. I shrugged. She said, "That old lady with that young stud—she must be paying for it." Another time, she served breakfast in the nude. When she sat down, she said, "You didn't even notice." I said, "Have you done something different with your hair?"

When I woke from my reverie, I canceled my spot at the conference. To my surprise, the registration office refunded my fee. Next, I called Calypso and spoke to a helpful young man named Casey. He said there were three workshops this week: A Gestalt marathon, a pelvic floor workshop, and Dangerous Writing. The Gestalt workshop was full, and the pelvic floor workshop was for women only.

He said, "That's all we got this week. There's one spot left in the writing workshop, which I'm sure will fill. Everything, as you know, is first-come, first-serve."

I said, "My brother died. I'd want to do the marathon. I've done Gestalt before, and I need it."

He said, "I'm sorry, Mr. Motherwell, it's full, and I'm doubtful a place will open up. How about this? If you sign up for the writing workshop, I can book you a room and waitlist you for the marathon. If I were you, I'd keep checking. You might get lucky."

I asked, "Is there anybody on the waiting list?"

"Currently, there are five. Let me check... Well, it's six or seven. It's one of our most popular programs."

"Don't you do Gestalt workshops almost every week?"

"We do, but it's this leader, Zephyra Capistrano. She only comes twice a year. People signed up the same day we released the schedule eight months ago. I met a couple earlier today who have been coming to this workshop for twenty-seven years."

I said, "You don't leave me much choice. Sign me up for Dangerous Writing."

I gave him my credit card number.

He said, "At this stage, your payment is nonrefundable."

How is it I'd never heard of Zephyra before? I imagined a mysterious Egyptian queen like Nefertiti or Cleopatra gowned in flowing robes, wearing a crown.

Conrad hadn't been explicit. He'd said, "Go to Calypso," and, "Do something dangerous." I'm going to Calypso. At least the title had dangerous in it. Can writing be dangerous?

It will be strange to be there without Victoria. I've never been to Calypso without her. She'd said, "Let go of the marriage and do this for yourself. Come back to me whole."

I'm on my way.

# PART IV

# 9 JANUARY, 5:23 A.M.

## (CALYPSO INSTITUTE, BIG SUR, CA)

*"Call it a clan, call it a network, call it a tribe, call it a family.*
*Whatever you call it, whoever you are, you need one."*
Jane Howard (1935-1996)

I T'S EARLY. THREE STRANGERS ARE snoring in the beds below. I'm sharing the room with four other men. For the time being, one of the upper bunks is still empty. I've got the top bunk closest to the picture window and was lulled by the roar of breaking waves all night. Now, there's commotion. Ed's standing naked, squinting at the floor, holding a flashlight. I met Ed last night. He took the top bunk kitty-corner to mine. He looks over at me scribbling in my notebook.

In a heavy whisper, he says, "I lost my glasses."

I look up. "Can I help?"

"No, but I'll have to move this dresser and desk. Think I'll wake anybody?"

"Looks like they're out cold."

So far, no sunrise. A gray, waxy rim of light skims the horizon.

I watch Ed out of the corner of my eye and keep writing. He's taking drawers out and dragging the desk and dresser across the floor. Ed's tall and slim, at least six foot four, and like the biblical Esau, his body is jacketed with thick hair. He sports a well-trimmed gray beard. The weight of his head seems too heavy, and his spine is curved like a willow. At the first meeting, I noticed his soft, drooping eyes were the color of brown sugar. A thoughtful man, he told me he was seventy-three, but he looks fifty. Even standing bare assed in this ridiculous scenario, he maintains a regal presence.

Now he's on his belly on the floor, wedging himself behind the bunk. The guy in the bottom cot, only inches away, doesn't flinch. His lips are motionless, like a comatose patient under anesthesia. Ed resurfaces and stands triumphant with a wide smile. He raises his right hand, holding the spectacles. "Found 'em!"

I'm distracted, but I keep my pen on the page, shaping words, while tracking Ed. He's careful, quiet, and meticulous. First, he reinstates the dresser, then the desk. He pulls on an oversized green T-shirt. It's tattered, with a torn collar, the image of Ram Das with the inscription, "Be Here Now." He shimmies into a pair of skinny jeans and doesn't bother with underwear, then laces his boots and tramps out the door. There isn't a peep from the bunks below.

Now that Ed's gone, I can get down to it and get some writing done while everybody's still sleeping. And there's so much to write. My mind's exploding. Yesterday was a full glass that brimmed over the top, and I drank every drop.

First light is cresting across the Pacific. I'm propped up with pillows, facing the ocean and backlit by a single dim light bulb. I can see the dark outline of the brown, bubbly, otter-infested kelp forest below. There's salty spit on the picture window from the storm.

I remember in detail the ocean cruise to Cuba I took with my parents after my first communion when I was seven. I'd slept in a top bunk like this one. My corpulent father had long pauses between breaths. I can hear my mother shrieking, "Cornelius, Cornelius, you're not breathing." She'd flail and slap his back and shoulders. He'd roll over with the insouciance of an elephant seal and say, "What are you talking about? I'm not even asleep." That cruise took place before my brother was born.

Shipboard, confined to a small, cramped compartment, I felt safe. My berth had a small, built-in shelf that I filled with toy soldiers and dinosaurs. And on that trip, I acquired a hand-painted figurine of Fidel Castro. For a flash, El Comandante was a liberator, not a scoundrel. Dressed in cap and military fatigues, the figure had a white dove on his shoulder, a man of peace. Fidel became my patron saint. I remember the poverty-stricken street vendor where we bought it, and her hungry child begging for food along the Malecón in Havana.

Each bunk at Calypso is supplied with the same kind of little built-in shelf. Rather than toy soldiers and dinosaurs, I've assembled books: *Ulysses*, *Light on Yoga*, and *The Art of Losing*. There's also room for my notebooks and my favorite fountain pens.

To someone else, this space might seem cramped. I'm grateful that the bed is long enough, and my feet don't dangle. The varnished plywood ceiling is only a few feet from my face. I can place my hands flat on the ceiling with my elbows bent. It feels like a coffin, but I don't feel claustrophobic. Instead, I'm safe, like a child with my parents. Even though I share this berthing with four other men, it feels private. Everybody here is working on something. There's an internal struggle, like a divorce, a death, the loss of a job, the end of a career...for some, changes they're not ready to make. Everybody's in transition. It's not weird or awkward for me to be scribbling in a notebook at dawn. Frankly, nobody cares.

Yesterday, the sun was breaking through the fog when I left Santa Barbara. The sky darkened, and it began to sprinkle at the railroad bridge in Gaviota. That's when I switched on the intermittent windshield wipers. In San Simeon, it turned into a steady rain. The slapping sound of the windshield blades became persistent. Two violent downpours followed, then a debris flow at Mud Creek stalled traffic. Flagmen directed the motorists into a single lane. In spite of the obstacles, Victoria's Honda S2000 was supreme, a real joy on the wet and winding roads. Snug, its low center of gravity made it reliable on every turn. The vinyl convertible top fits tight and didn't leak a drop. It's six years old now and only eighteen thousand miles, still looks and drives like new. Painted Laguna Blue Pearl, the interior blue leather is still crisp. The gearbox is tight and smooth. Why Honda stopped making this dazzling roadster, I'll never know. It revels in switches and hairpin turns. Massive waves rolled across the horizon, and the ocean spray splintered like waterfalls. Huge rocks surfaced and submerged like sea monsters.

In the middle of the night, I soaked in the Calypso hot tubs. My hair's still wet and smells like sulfur. I woke with clarity. There's an unwavering belief that something will work through me and change. My anxiety, disquietude, and malaise are temporary, something better is ahead.

I'm staying in "Ephesus," a brown-paneled, prefab modular building two hundred feet above the baths. Each building is named after an ancient Greek city, temple, or literary theme. Henry Miller called ancient Ephesus the heartbeat of the world.

The grounds saturated when I arrived, I geared down and descended the steep driveway. There was a muddy stream flowing down the asphalt, and the blacktop was very slippery. My windshield wipers still flapping, I stuck my head out the window at the guard house, smaller than I remembered, a little turret with a sliding glass window, to check-in. A young woman stepped out. She held a clipboard, and I couldn't see her face obscured by a hooded raincoat.

"What's your name and what seminar are you taking?"

"Cornelius Motherwell. Dangerous Writing."

"You're not on the list. Let me call the front desk."

Before I could speak, she turned and walked away and talked to another young woman, who ran out to the car. "Neal, is that you?"

I opened the door, and she threw her arms around me. There were tears in her eyes. I hugged her back.

She said, "I was so sorry to hear about your brother. How are your wife and family?"

"PJ, what are you doing here?"

"Neal, I could say the same. And what's this Cornelius stuff on your registration? I wasn't sure it was you."

She turned to the other girl and said, "He's OK."

I said, "What about MIT?"

"I'm taking a semester off, maybe a year. I applied for Calypso work study and got it. I need a change of pace. I'm working here at the gate, and I'm in charge of the hot tubs at 1 a.m. when outside people come in."

"Are you OK?"

"Yeah, I got one of those home blood monitors, and I call my number to the clinic every two weeks. I feel fine, especially since I got here. Her bright smile flashed. "Neal, you're all set. Check in with the office about your accommodations. You can park over there." She pointed up a steep, muddy hill.

As I pulled away, I called back, "What seminar are you taking?"

She shouted, "Zephyra Capistrano."

The parking lot was a mucky swamp impossible to navigate on foot. I stepped into one puddle, then another, and gave up any attempt to keep dry. Bedraggled, soaked to my knees, I trudged toward the office schlepping my gear. As I drew closer, I heard what sounded like a relentless metal claw scraping concrete. A woman using a walker passed me on the sidewalk. Her hair was damp, the color of fresh-cut cantaloupe. She operated her custom-made walker with aplomb. Her elbows supported her weight. She walked on the tips of her toes, skimming the surface like a water bug. A tall, burly man and two attractive young women accompanied her. She stood upright with a sense of dignity and determination. Her tenacity and grit struck me. I wondered what had brought this motley group here? What an effort it would take to bring this entourage to this remote location in the rain.

I walked into the office. A scraggly, middle-aged man with long dreadlocks was in a heated discussion with the clerk.

The man wore a sleeveless, rain-blotched suede vest, open chest with booming biceps. He said, "The catalog says the food's grown on the grounds."

"Yes, we grow most of the vegetables and all the greens on the grounds," replied the clerk.

"But what about the other food?"

"We have a full raw salad bar at lunch and dinner that comes from the gardens to the table. You'll have to ask the chef about the entrees. I don't think we use canned goods. Wait, I take that back. I saw them making pasta with canned tomatoes last week."

"Let me explain. I am a locavore. I need to know. Food that's not local is a disaster. It's picked unripe, stored for too long, and handled over and over. It's lousy for the environment. It's not fit for subsistence."

The youth cringed. "I'm pretty sure almost everything we serve here is local."

The man's face reddened. "But do you *know*? Who can tell me? It's unsustainable to truck food over long distances. It makes sense, it's better for the consumer and the environment when food is local."

"I can assure you we make every effort to serve healthy food.

You can leave your recommendations in writing here." The young man pointed to a wooden suggestion box on the counter.

"Who can I talk to about this? Healthy food is essential, not just for physical well-being but for the mind and emotions as well."

"If you leave your concerns in writing, management will get back to you." The attendant reached for a piece of paper and said, "Here's…"

The man ignored him, picked up his heavy backpack, banged it on the counter, turned, and strapped it to his back. He took the paper from the clerk and walked out the door. When he turned, I noticed a colorful mural tattoo that covered his right shoulder. A mushroom-shaped rocket ship rose from his massive bicep. The moon, stars, and Saturn with its rings were represented in a vivid spaulder. The inscription read, *"Dulce Periculum."*

The clerk looked up and asked me, "Checking in?" His skin was youthful, untested, smooth and unwrinkled. He wore a ribbon band fedora and sported a light, blond beard.

I said, "Do you know Latin?"

He nodded. "I took three years of honors in high school."

"What does *dulce periculum* mean?"

His eyeballs rolled to his forehead, like he was reading a dictionary in his forebrain. Then he said, *"Periculum* means peril, liability, risk, or danger."

"What about *dulce?"*

"I'm not sure in Latin, but in Italian, *dolce,* means dessert, the sweets at the end of a meal."

I said, "Danger is sweet."

"That's pretty close." He turned toward his computer. "I was in Tuscany last summer, and the Italians say, *"Dolce far niente."* It means ' The sweetness of doing nothing.' "

I said, "That's what we do here."

He smiled. "Hardly. How can I help you?"

I said, "Has anything opened up for Zephyra?"

He said, "You're Cornelius Motherwell. I spoke to you last night. I'm Casey." His eyes dampened, and he added, "I'm so sorry about your brother. That must be devastating." He checked the computer. "Not for 'Open Your Heart,' still nothing, and there's a waiting list. But the instructor can let you in. She's on the grounds. She might be willing to make a spot for you."

"What does she look like?"

"You'll know when you see her. She has ALS. There'll be a bunch of people around her."

"Did she walk by a few minutes ago?"

He said, "Didn't see her. She's usually with her husband, a tall guy."

"Shit, I've blown it."

"Don't worry about it. You can ask her at dinner."

"But the conference starts tonight."

"You can still make the switch tomorrow."

"ALS? Do you mean Lou Gehrig's disease? I thought people don't live long with that?"

"Some do, like Stephen Hawking. Zephyra's a twenty-nine-year survivor."

"Twenty-nine years?"

He nodded.

As I walked to my cabin, a burst of sunshine skirted through an intimidating, dark cloud. A spotlight illuminated a patch of the emerald-green lawn in front of the lodge. I found my bunk, put my bed together, and stowed my gear. It was time for dinner, which filled me with anxiety. At full capacity, the lodge is a madhouse. There are never enough seats to accommodate everyone, and the first meal of the week is always frenetic. Last night was no different. When I walked in, people were scurrying in every direction, pots and pans clanged, dishes crashed—a city of voices, all talking at once. I looked around at masticating mouthfuls, people shouting, others waving their arms. Someone signaled for me to sit with them. I waved back, then flushed, embarrassed because I didn't know them. They were flagging someone else. Trays, dirty dishes, and utensils piled up in front of the bus station, a dingy wet window. The dishwasher couldn't keep up. Near the beverage station, someone spilled a glass of milk. The work study person summoned to mop it kicked over a soapy cleanup bucket. The floor was as slippery as an ice rink. I stepped around it, stood in line, filled my plate with brown rice and tofu curry, and went in search of a seat. At Calypso, like summer camp, you join a tribe. Cramped, long wooden tables encourage family-style meals that provide no privacy. And for the most part there are no rules. It's every person for themselves. The place is always in the weeds.

When I sat down at a crowded table, everybody was looking around. It was the losers, people alone, who hadn't met anyone yet to share a meal. I noticed a bench was missing on the other side, creating a space. When I raised my fork, the man with the dreadlocks and tattoo stood over me panting, holding his tray.

His eyes narrowed and he said, "Who moved the goddamn bench? I was sitting there. That's my coat."

I looked down. There was a long, black, double-breasted gabardine trench coat next to me. I said, "Why don't you sit here? I'll find another spot." I stood and walked to the other side of the room, moved a short bench, and sat down.

Within a minute or two, a woman sat next to me. She was very close, and it was uncomfortable. I couldn't raise my elbow to eat without touching her. I said, "Is this your seat?"

"It was before you moved the bench. I got up to get some tea."

I said, "Sorry," picked up my tray, stood, and spied an empty seat a few tables over. An attractive, middle-aged woman wearing dark-rimmed glasses sat on the other side. I said, "Can I join you?"

She smiled and teased, "No," then nodded yes, and said, "It's open. There's plenty of room."

She had shoulder-length, thick black hair, a cleft chin, and chiseled facial features, by all accounts a handsome woman. She giggled when I sat down.

"Thanks, I didn't think I was going to find a seat."

She said, "It's always like this the first night. Wild. It'll get better. You been here before?"

"Yes, my wife and I had our first date here."

"I've never heard that one before. A lot of people meet here, but a first date?" She raised her left eyebrow above the frame of her glasses and looked out the window. "I'm gonna try that. I'm between relationships." She jutted her chin and clenched her teeth. "The last one ended ten years ago. He's the father of my three girls. They're teenagers now. I've been coming to Calypso a couple times a year ever since."

I said, "Where're you from?"

"St. Louis."

"The Gateway City. I've passed through but never spent much time there. I have friends who went to Washington University."

"That's where I met my ex. Have you ever been on the campus?"

"Yes, but it's been long time."

She said, "We're divorced. We're still friends. That's not exactly accurate. I tolerate him. Before the kids, we worked at the same law office."

"Are you a lawyer?"

"A paralegal, although I haven't worked for years. Jim, that's my ex, took up with a temp secretary named Jade after our third child. He had the gall to want to keep both of us. He married Jade. We've all adjusted. He pays the bills. I've been out of the work-force since."

"What do you do with your time?"

"I take care of the children, although, if I'm honest, that doesn't take much anymore. I travel and come here."

"What workshop are you taking?"

"Dangerous Writing."

"So am I. I'm signed up, but I want to do Zephyra's."

"Me too, but it's full. I'm on the waiting list. I've done it a dozen times. I wouldn't have gotten through my divorce without Lady Z. I would have murdered my ex without her. I was so god-damn angry. I've learned that living well is the best revenge. Not that I wish Jim affliction, but I must admit I took a little pleasure after his rotator cuff surgery last year. Jade took off with her girlfriends on a romp to Spain. He called me because he got constipated on the painkillers."

"*Schadenfreude?*"

"The Germans do have a way with words. You could say that. There's pleasure in his misfortune. I'm taking care of myself now. By the way, my name's Joyce."

"Neal."

We shook hands.

"*Schadenfreude.*" She raised a glass of red wine.

I clinked it with a glass of water. "*Schadenfreude.*"

She said, "Do you wish evil on anyone?"

Before I could answer, the table swelled with activity. One by one, like swallows filing into a belfry, a group of people gathered and sat down around us. Everybody knew Joyce, and everyone knew each other. They slapped high-fives and swapped stories. It was a family reunion. They hugged and kissed and told each other how great it was to be back together again. It was better than a family reunion. There was no baggage, no feuds.

And nobody told me to move.

An athletic, middle-aged man embraced Joyce and sat down. He had short-cropped gray hair and a friendly, assertive smile, but up close revealed a weathered and troubled look. He reached out his hand, "Hi, I'm Dan."

Joyce jabbed him in the ribs. "Dan the Man."

The noise level was deafening.

He shouted, "Where are you from and why are you here?"

"Santa Barbara. My brother died."

"I'm sorry. You're in the right place."

I said, "Too bad Zephyra's workshop is full. I could use it."

"Let's talk to Z. She'll let you in. I know she will."

Joyce said, "The workshop's full. I've been calling for weeks. There's a waiting list, and people waiting beyond that."

Dan said, "You never know. It's worth a try."

I said, "I need this bad."

Joyce sighed.

A man with a white beard bear-hugged Dan from behind and tossed him side to side like a rag doll. Dan stood, and they embraced. It felt like an Italian wedding. Dan's meal was in a riot with the constant interruption of well-wishers. He patted each on the back and shared belly laughs. In the mayhem, he tapped a guy on the shoulder sitting a couple seats down, then pointed at me and shouted, "This guy's from Santa Barbara."

The man stood and said, "I live near the Mission."

I yelled, "I'm not too far. I'm downtown."

Dan said, "Over the past twenty years, I've been to twenty-five of Zephyra's workshops. And that's my best friend, Jerry. I met him here. We've also done Zephyra's training together in Baltimore."

Jerry walked over and shook my hand. "We're neighbors."

He pointed out his petite, silver-haired wife, Ann Claire, sitting at the other end of the table. She waved, then frowned. He disclosed that he met Ann Claire at one of Zephyra's workshops a dozen years ago.

Dan said, "What do you do, Neal?"

"I'm a PA."

He said, "I'm a psychologist."

Jerry said, "He's too modest. Dan still holds AAU records for the hammer throw at Northwestern. He got two world records at the gay games a couple years ago."

"Gay games?"

"The Gay Olympics. Never heard of it?"

I shook my head.

Jerry replied, "It's huge, and more athletes compete than in the Olympics. We went to Amsterdam in 1998 to watch him."

Ann Claire listened with cautious intent but stayed seated.

Dan leaned back with a modest grin, toyed with his fork, and ate nothing. His wide shoulders filled his tight-fitting gray Henley. Bulging thighs crowded his baggy cargo shorts. At Calypso, Dan was a god, and the man knew it. He puffed out his chest, pulled back his shoulders, and took in the adulation.

He nudged me and pointed at Zephyra in the next room, sitting with a group of seven or eight people. He said, "Let's go over there, and you can talk to her. I'll introduce you."

I said, "I saw her earlier. That looks like a private party or a staff meeting. Why don't I talk to her later?"

He stood, tugged my shoulder, and walked toward Zephyra and her entourage. I followed him, my nerves on edge. Eight people sat at a small round table near a bank of dark windows. My palms sweated and my heart raced. My ears were full of the noisy cafeteria and the crashing waves below. The windows hung close to the cliff. At that moment, I wanted the workshop more than anything in the world.

All stood, except Zephyra, and hugged Dan. Zephyra stared through half-closed eyelids as if in a trance. As if she were probing with an alien capacity, a mind-meld. She tilted her head. With the gentleness of a butterfly, Dan placed his lips on her forehead. It was a grand reunion.

Dan said, "This is Neal. He wants to talk to you about something." And he walked away.

Others at the table made polite excuses, picked up trays, and departed. The man in the cowboy shirt, Zephyra, and two young women remained with their eyes focused on me.

The man pointed to an open chair and motioned for me to sit. He reached out his hand, "I'm Ned Capistrano. These two young ladies are Sally Jeffers and Gloria Esperanza. They work with Zephyra, and we couldn't do it without them."

Zephyra mumbled something.

Ned said, "Zephyra says these two keep her glowing."

Both women giggled. Gloria halved a Brussels sprout with a knife, speared it with a fork, and Zephyra opened her mouth like a baby bird waiting in a nest. Zephyra chewed.

Ned leaned forward.

I said, "My brother died. I want to be in your class."

Ned said, "We'd love to have you, Neal. But we're already past full, and there are a half dozen others already here on campus who are on the waiting list. It wouldn't be fair to them."

My heart sank. "Please, this is really important. I need this."

Zephyra said, "*Norton wio tonne shear am yo too botvik.*"

I didn't understand a garbled word. She had a green, leafy remnant of Brussels sprout on her chin and spittle at the corners of her mouth.

Ned said, "She says you can join us. But most likely there won't be time for you to do personal work. If you accept those terms, you're in."

I jumped up and danced around as if I'd won the lottery. "Yes, I agree. I want to be in the workshop. Thank you. Thank you, Zephyra. I'm good in groups. You won't be sorry."

I hugged Ned and each of the ladies, then leaned and kissed Zephyra on the forehead the way Dan had.

She tittered.

I hugged her and felt her chest vibrate.

Ned said, "Show up tonight at the Epidaurus House at seven-thirty. There'll be a short introductory session. We'll take care of the paperwork tomorrow. Remember, you won't be doing any personal work with Zephyra. I don't want you disappointed."

"I'm not. I mean, I won't be. I understand. Thank you. I can't thank you enough." I walked back to the table where Dan and the others were sitting.

Dan said, "So, what did she say?"

"I'm in. I can participate, but won't do any personal work…"

"Great! She'll make time for you if that's what you want."

Immediately there was a stir as Joyce stood and said, "I've been on the waiting list for *six weeks*. And now you won't be in Dangerous Writing. That's not fair." She stormed across the room toward Zephyra's table.

I watched, and to my surprise when Joyce arrived, her demeanor changed. She hugged Ned and Zephyra, sat down, and sipped a glass of wine. She started to laugh, although at first, I thought she was crying. Ned, Zephyra, and the ladies joined in. There was howling, bodies shaking. Joyce slapped her hands on her knees and tears streamed down her cheeks, and it was infectious. I started to laugh. Joyce was still gabbing with Ned and Zephyra when I left the lodge.

Calypso hangs on a thin strip of habitable land between Highway 1 and the Santa Lucia peaks. A steep creek-cut canyon divides the campus in half. It was getting dark, and a solemn red-orange glow crept across the horizon. The heave of the night was all around, like the planet had taken a deep breath and inhaled Calypso into its lungs. The air oozed with the scent of musty pine, and the creek ran high with rain. I crossed the footbridge. At Calypso, everything is accessible by foot. There's no need to carry a wallet or ID. Calypso provides everything—food, drinks, materials—no money exchanged. First names (or nicknames) only apply. The torrent streamed and echoed off the tall, dark trees like a hollow drum. I heard high-spirited voices behind me. Epidaurus House ahead, I saw the light. I'd dressed in my Calypso uniform of loose-fitting drawstring hemp pants, a long-sleeved T-shirt, and sandals. Over my shoulders, I carried an intarsia cardigan sweater with a shawl collar. It's a favorite of mine with an elegant Southwest Native American vector design that is always in season in Big Sur. I never get to wear this outfit at home.

I removed my shoes and entered the long, rectangular meeting room. The thick, blue plush carpet felt good on my bare feet. I noticed a stack of mattresses next to the fireplace. People sprawled on large, colorful corduroy pillows on the floor. Others stood and interacted, exchanging embraces. I sat down on two cushions and crossed my legs.

"First time?" a raspy voice inquired.

When I turned, a woman with winter-white hair hovered next to me. Though she was standing, her head was level with mine.

I said, "I've been here before, but not to this workshop."

She plunked down next to me. "Nervous?"

"A little."

She said, "This is my eighteenth time."

"Why do you keep coming back?"

"This is my tribe."

We shook hands and she said, "I'm Lucille from Grover Beach."

Ned walked in and adjusted the sound system. He played the soft, stripped-down guitar and voice of Patty Griffin singing, "Be Careful." In contrast to the informal way people arrived, there was reverence and stone silence. The entire group stood like in church. The people on each side of me reached for my hands. Everybody knew the words and sang along. Then Zephyra made a grand entrance clanging her walker. She stood tall and regal like a queen. She sang each word while making contact with every eyeball, emoting with each participant. Several people broke down and she lingered, her eyes watered, and tears rolled down her cheeks. I felt the same sense of wonder and exhilaration as when an opera singer sustains a high note. At the same time, I felt squirmy, and it was too close. My palms sweated, and I looked around the room and counted twenty-seven adults. Most were crying, even men like Dan and Jerry.

When the song ended, Zephyra said, "Look around."

This time, I understood her garbled speech, although Ned repeated every word. Each eyeball scanned the room. I gazed back at others, and they at me in a way that made me uncomfortable. People nodded approval, passed their gaze to the next person, and smiled. The most awkward was with PJ. We knew each other in a different context. Then there was Dan the Man and Jerry and Ann Claire, veterans of the process. And my roommate, Ed, and there was Joyce, her big doe eyes full of tears. Zephyra had found room for her too. The technique seemed so simple: play a song, stand in a circle, and hold hands. I felt disarmed of resentment and anger, at least at that moment, but was anxious about what was going to happen next. My armpits were drenched. I felt relieved when my neighbors let go. We remained standing.

Zephyra asked each person to say their name and what song defined what they wanted from the workshop, and then to repeat their name.

Several people asked to pass and didn't say their names at all.

I was nervous and couldn't grasp the instructions. When it was my turn, I said, "Neal, and I'd like a little help from my friends." But I forgot to repeat my name, so the entire group shouted, "Neal," which embarrassed me, and I bristled.

PJ said, "I feel buried, a landslide."

Dan said, "I'd like to get down to the heart of the matter."

Jerry sighed and quietly said, "What's that song by Leonard

Cohen?" He looked around the room. "You know, where for the light to get in, there needs to be a crack.

In a chorus, the group responded, "Hallelujah."

His diminutive spouse, Ann Claire, standing next to him, shrugged. "I can't always get what I want." She put her face into her hands and started to cry.

Then it came around to Joyce, who took her time, and the room got quiet. "Respect, that's what I want."

I had no idea what this had to do with anything, but under Zephyra's spell, it was profound.

When the group sat, Zephyra remained upright. She stood like Muhammad Ali, defiant. She refused to rest between rounds and gained momentum as the evening progressed. Erect with her forearms on her walker, she addressed the group, and Ned repeated every word. "We can't make our contribution to society until we make it right with ourselves. Nelson Mandela said, 'One of the most difficult things to change is not to change society—but to change yourself.' This often has to do with our parents. It's up to each of us to correct our ancestry."

I thought about my parents, how they got madder and more alcoholic with age.

Zephyra's energy and drive were relentless. She seemed to grow larger and stand taller as she lectured. "Many mothers don't know how to love. They've abandoned what it is to be female. Too many are petty and small. They leave their children incomplete. Unnurtured children aren't able to take care of themselves. Imagine a chimpanzee. We know the work of Jane Goodall, and she makes it clear. The infant can't develop and grow to take care of itself without exquisite mothering. And we are the same. For those of us without kind, caring, and nurturing mothers, we are at a loss to live a healthy life. That's why you must develop a compassionate mother within. To do that, you need to know your needs and how to provide them for yourself."

She nodded to Ned, and he cued another song. We stood and held hands. Zephyra and Ned joined the circle. It was a slow dirge with an eerie guitar, and everyone seemed to know it. The words had to do with never leaving anyone behind. Hands moved from palms to shoulders, and the group swayed as a single unit. When I looked around the room, I saw less vexation and brighter, lighter, smoother faces. Smiles and laughter replaced frowns, fear, anxiety, and indifference. What did other people see when they looked at me?

I walked back to the cabin, poleaxed, alone via the waterfalls and roaring current. The ink of night revealed a canopy of stars. Then it started to rain.

# 10 JANUARY, PREDAWN, OH-DARK-HUNDRED

## (CALYPSO INSTITUTE, BIG SUR, CA)

*"...easy is the descent to the underworld, but to recall one's steps
...this is the art, this is the work."*
Virgil (70-19 BC)

EVERYBODY'S ASLEEP. A COLD BLANKET of fog settled in last night. The cabin's dark and damp. Steady snores mix with a choppy swell. The sound of gravel raked from the beach and spit back up again comes with the regularity of a metronome. Eight thousand waves strike the Big Sur coast every day. I have no idea what time it is, and it doesn't matter.

Today would have been Mick's forty-eighth birthday. It's also the day I left Buffalo thirty-four years ago in a snowstorm and never looked back. I'm in profound grief. The take-home message from Zephyra's sessions was "get out of your head."

She said, "Get into your body. Don't think. Do something. Move, laugh, cry, stretch, breathe. You need to know you're there for yourself come hell or high water." And coming from her, it meant something. She suggested that we take a good look at the past. She led an exercise where we wrote down and shared the first time we were betrayed.

I wrote about when I got kicked out of high school. A painful, low watermark I haven't thought about for years, long buried in a festering memory hole.

Victoria had said, "Come back to me whole." Is this what it's going take? To write out the hurtful memories, to reassemble my past?

Mick's death gutted me. At best, I've been compensating, keeping my anxiety and neurotic behavior at bay. I've never done this kind of thorough assessment. How does one recover the pieces? I was never whole. I trust Zephyra. Why not here, now? There's everything to lose and everything to gain. What would it take to revisit those memories?

There was a handwritten sign outside the classroom door: "Shift happens. Life belongs to those who live."

Big Sur. The first time I heard those two pithy syllables I was fourteen, in high school. Even now it's agonizing to revisit. I was awkward and scared, short for my age. My body was soft and flabby. Late to puberty, I was obsessed with body hair. There wasn't a trace on my face, under my arms, or within three feet of my crotch. I'd stand naked in front of a mirror and examine my armpits and genitals, imploring a single hair follicle to break through the shiny surface. My complexion was angry, splotched with honey-crusted acne. I pleaded with the gods of loneliness to let my balls drop. My pecker looked like a mushroom, retracted, ineffectual. My voice was so high that I was often mistaken for my sisters when I answered the telephone. I loathed PE. I'd stay up nights scheming how to get out of it. When forced to take part, I'd shed my clothes while keeping my genitals covered. I held my body in contempt. Rolls of pale fat dripped over my belt, and my unmuscled chest drooped like saggy breasts. There was no escape. I cut gym class whenever I could.

And looking back, what I dreaded most was the shower room—a steamy corridor with eight rusty spigots that spit water from a grungy, brown tile wall. There was no privacy. I'd face the wall, soap up, and conceal myself. Everything was on display, the room filled with electricity. Hard-muscled buttocks, ball-laden scrotums, and hair, lots of hair. Hair everywhere, sideburns, mustaches, beards, chest, armpits, balls. Fresh testosterone blooming, and I didn't have a fuzz. I was a freak. I felt like everybody was watching me. Stuck in time, locked in a smooth, hairless, child's body, while everybody else was sprouting manliness.

The PE teacher was a Welshman named Brian Victory. Later, he became my swim coach. I hated him then but became friendly with Ol' Vic before I graduated. Before I reached puberty, we were at cross-purposes.

He'd shout, "Now, boys, into the showers. Everybody. Get on with it."

I'd cringe and try to dress so I could slip out.

He'd reprimand me, "Motherwell, where's your dignity? What kind of stink-dog are you? Get in the shower." Ol' Vic also taught health. He explained personal hygiene in detail and how important it was for a man to wash his genitals. He demonstrated on a diagram how to retract the foreskin and clean the head if we weren't circumcised. I couldn't relate on either count. The locker room smelled of the chlorine that wafted in from the pool, infused with body odor and cologne. I kept my showers very short, but bullies tormented me, flicking me with towels.

I studied a thick medical book at the downtown library to research my condition. The best I could come up with was that I was a hermaphrodite. I implored all the forces of God and the heavens to help me. All I wanted was some delicate trace of pubic hair, some faint sense of a mustache, and for my balls to drop. I took this shame with me into every encounter, my eyes always focused on the floor. I didn't want anyone to know (but felt like they did).

They could humiliate me at any moment with a simple word or gesture. I felt like everyone knew the raw truth. I was hairless, my gonads undescended, not a whisker on my chin, and my manhood feckless. I watched my brother go through the same prolonged ascent to puberty. He, like me, was seventeen or eighteen before he expressed any physical signs of manhood.

In the schoolyard and halls, I heard "Motherfucker" more often than "Motherwell." I began to respond as if it were my name. My tormentors reached me at every juncture, always lurking around a corner or in the bathroom. When the teacher called on me in class, someone would jab me in the ribs from behind. When I stood, a chorus would chant, "Mother," followed by a hiss formed with the top teeth on lower lips, creating a farting sound, "FFFFF." Then a rip of derisive laughter. For them, the joke never got old. Every day, petrified, scared, and anxious, I walked blocks out of my way to avoid hangouts, always skirting looming fields and unsupervised streets. I had a few acquaintances but no defenders or confidantes. I had little interest in the classroom. My grades were marginal, an edge I cut too thin, and I flunked out after midterms in my sophomore year. Fear ruled me, and my only purpose was survival—to get through the day, remain invisible, and avoid further humiliation.

For the first year and a half of high school, I attended St. Alban's Collegiate Institute, an all-boys private Catholic school known to locals as St. Alby's. It was a boot camp where Christian Brothers imposed corporal punishment. For me, the only bright spot was my homeroom teacher, Brother Patrick O'Donoghue, better known to the boys as "Knuckles." Brother Patrick was in his sixties, graying around the temples, a fixture on campus. I liked him, and he took an interest in me. Although, Pat didn't put up with any nonsense, he metered out discipline with the detached insensitivity of an executioner. And at this stage of his career, he was irritable and easy to anger.

Further shortening his fuse was the change brought about by Vatican II. During my freshman year, English replaced Latin in the Mass, and Pat made it clear he felt betrayed.

He said, "Folk music and guitars usurp the nuance and elegance of the liturgy. Why disrupt the language of antiquity with such a debased vernacular?"

As an altar boy, I'd memorized the Mass in Latin and sympathized with his anger. Smothered in incense and Gregorian chant, Latin was mysterious and cultish. The language of the Christian martyrs formed a safe coalition among Catholics. We felt aligned in this mystery. After the changes, the veil of secrecy was torn away—we no longer belonged to the same club.

Vatican II ripped the lid off. Nuns removed their veils, and we realized they had hair. The Christian Brothers dropped their vocational names. In New York State, the names started with A, B, and C. For example, St. Alban's had an Aelred, Barnabus, and Calixtus. When Barnabus became Sam Riley, it didn't carry the same gravitas. In the coming years, an exodus took place. All the youthful and energetic Brothers I knew abandoned the order. Some rejected religion altogether. Many cobbled together new lives as lay teachers, bankers, and insurance salesmen. Some married and had children. Others found their sexuality as gay men. The motto of the Christian Brothers dates back to the mid-seventeenth century. In Latin, *Viriliter age* came from David's twenty-seventh psalm. In this era, the Brothers pressed the English translation, "Act manly," and oft repeated it in the classroom without the adverb, "Act like a Man." It was an absurd directive in the chaos. Vatican II signaled the changing of the old order and sweeping in of the new.

Brother Patrick's general appearance was neanderthal, but taller. When he entered the classroom, his shoulders filled the doorframe. His long, thick arms fell to his knees. He had humongous hands that, when clenched, formed wrecking balls. His nose was purple and bulbous with spider veins, and he was quick to temper. We knew to watch out when his pale face blotched red. He arrived each day in various stages of dishevelment, always an indelicate gray stubble, a stray plume of silver hair jutting out in a pesky cowlick. Unkempt, wiry hairs protruded from his nose, and bushy eyebrows crept over his horn-rimmed glasses. He breathed exclusively from his mouth, coming and going like a freight train. He wore extra wide, battered black Oxfords and was always heavy afoot. His cough or sneeze was sudden and violent, like a whale clearing its blowhole. He stooped a little. Upright though, like a grizzly bear, he was imposing. And standing up straight, he looked every bit the six-foot-four Jack Dempsey of his youth, albeit he'd added fifty pounds. Attired in his religious habit, a long, black robe and oversized white collar, he looked like a giant panda. And like the bamboo munchers at the San Diego Zoo who seem adorable and harmless, Pat could leave a very nasty bite.

I walked to school alone, about a mile and a half, and only if raining, took the bus. I rambled and enjoyed the walk more than school. It's where I found time to compose myself and unwind. The snow and icy wind didn't bother me. What I dreaded most were the fights at St. Alban's. Suddenly chaos and violence would erupt in the gym, corridors, or bathrooms. Across the street, there was a designated war zone—a cinder block paint shop where guys could settle scores in the parking lot, often in front of a howling, bloodthirsty crowd. But the conflict I remember best occurred in the classroom, fisticuffs between Brother Pat and a student named Raymond Abdul. I've never written about it. However, it traumatized me, and the memory remains vivid. There were many witnesses, a whole classroom of adolescent boys. Do they carry the same scar?

It was mid-February when the fiercest polar winds ripped Lake Erie, and even the most ardent Buffalonians become disheartened. When the tyranny of winter gashes a hole in everyone's heart, when a geographical cure is on everybody's mind, Florida, the Caribbean, Mexico, Hallelujah…anywhere with blue skies and sun will do. It's when native western New Yorkers are punch drunk from the blistering cold and dream of sunshine on their neck. And to relieve themselves of winter jackets, long underwear, wool socks, and gloves. It's been too many months without naked flesh, and everything is shriveled, gone internal and dormant. The first vestiges of spring are still months away. When the frigid air is clear, cleansing, petrifying, and devoid of all smells.

Ray Abdul was angry, an outsider. He was short and thick, with a mat of black hair covering his body. He combed up a tall pompadour with grease that emphasized a low forehead between the top rim of his browline glasses. For all practical purposes, Abdul was already a man. He moved like a bowling ball through crowded hallways. There were rumors he tortured cats and carried a knife. He was part of a large family. His parents were from the Middle East and owned a popular grocery in North Buffalo, where he and his brothers worked. It was a big deal for him to be at St. Alby's, the first in his family to enter a private Catholic school. He was the eldest son, and his family and community expected big things from him. He always sat in the back row and cracked jokes, blurting out wisecracks. He was never a good student. He pressed the Brothers hard and, most of the time, got away with it.

It was a dark, bitter day with thick cloud cover. We all knew more months of cold weather were still ahead. When I got to the classroom, the bell rang. My face flushed, my feet were icy, and I sensed a different mood.

Brother Pat entered the room, and we stood. He said, as was the tradition, "Let us remember that we are in the holy presence of God." Then he put his books and papers on the desk. "How are you today, gentlemen?"

We replied, "Very well, Brother."

He wasn't satisfied. "I said, how are you today, gentlemen?"

We shouted, "Very well, sir!"

He continued, "That's better. Now sit down. I want each of you to sustain that fervor throughout the day. Mr. Abdul, what's the definition of fervor?"

Abdul slumped at his desk and didn't reply.

Brother Pat said, "Anyone else?"

Michael Halloran, a tall, skinny kid with a delicate, high voice, jumped out of his seat, waving his hand.

Pat nodded.

Halloran exclaimed, "It's a strong feeling of excitement and enthusiasm, sir." Midway through the sentence, Halloran's voice broke.

A ripple of laughter erupted throughout the room, and a loud snort came from Abdul.

Pat said, "Yes, yes, that's fine. But does anybody know the origin of the word? What are its roots? Words, like people, come from somewhere and have a soul. They have layers of meaning. Each of you needs to understand that."

Halloran waved his hand again, fluttering his long, silky fingers.

Pat ignored him, leaned against the blackboard, and crossed his arms. "What are your thoughts, Mr. Abdul?"

Abdul slumped farther into his seat, and Pat waited in awkward silence. Abdul rustled in his chair. Pat walked toward him.

"Maybe Italy or Greece," Abdul mumbled.

"Yes, it's Latin. Go on."

Abdul shuffled his feet and brushed his fingers through his greasy hair. He began to sweat.

"Can someone help Mr. Abdul?"

There was an uneasy hush.

Halloran raised his hand again.

I kept my eyes straight in front of me. My feet were soaked, warm and cold at the same time, and a puddle was forming from my frozen boots on the floor. I noticed blood beginning to rush to Pat's face.

Pat said, "Mr. Abdul, from where does your family hail?"

"You know, Brother, the Middle East."

"Where in the Middle East? Where are your roots?"

"You know, Lebanon."

"Do they speak English there?"

"Yes, but also French. Arabic is the official language."

"Do you speak Arabic?"

"No. I hear it around the house. I can understand it. I can't read it, if that's what you mean. It's a different alphabet."

Pat turned and walked toward the front of the room.

Abdul made a face, shrugged, and did his best Gomer Pyle impersonation. "Surprise, surprise, surprise."

There was a sprinkle of uncomfortable laughter that Pat ignored. We'd seen Pat pushed too far before, and most of us feared the consequences. But a rogue contingent relished the spectacle and egged Abdul on.

Pat continued, "Now, we're getting somewhere. Fervor, as Mr. Halloran elucidated, has to do with excitement and enthusiasm."

Abdul, modulating his voice like an Irish whistle, imitating Halloran, blurted, "Excitement and enthusiasm."

The classroom roared.

Pat said, "Enough from you, Mr. Abdul."

Abdul said under his breath, again modulating his voice, "Excitement and enthusiasm."

Everybody around Abdul got the giggles.

Pat's face reddened, but he brushed off the horseplay. "Yes, the origin of the word is from Latin, but of course, that was two millennia ago. Most recently it came to us through Old French. The meaning today, as it was in the fourteenth century, is pretty close: heat, enthusiasm, ardor, and passion. It's even spelled the same. But what about the Latin? That's what you boys need to know to be successful in life. Any Latin scholars in the room?"

No one raised their hand. Even Halloran sat mute.

Pat said, "The Latin root means to bubble, to boil, to be hot, to glow, to burn. I want you boys to burn."

Abdul blurted, "Burn, baby, burn." Under his breath, he snorted, "Up against the wall, motherfucker." And he continued to snicker.

Pat grabbed a piece of chalk and rifled it at him with high accuracy, hitting him in the chest.

Abdul stood and demanded, "What's that for?" He shook his big head of black hair and settled back into his chair, then mumbled under his breath, "You don't scare me, fascist motherfucker."

From twenty feet away, Pat riffled another piece of chalk. This time it bounced off Abdul's narrow forehead.

Abdul bolted upright and bull rushed toward Pat but stopped dead in his tracks a couple feet from him. That's when some higher decision-making operation reached his cerebral cortex.

Pat slapped him, *crack*, across his right cheek.

Abdul pushed Pat's shoulders with both hands and screamed, "You can't touch me!"

Pat, red as a tomato, dribbles of thick, white saliva at the corners of his mouth, went into a controlled rage as if a bell went off in the boxing ring.

Abdul opened both hands in front of his chest as if to say, *I don't want any part of this*, and cried out, "I'm sorry, Brother. I'm sorry, Brother."

The classroom went limp, all the air sucked out of the room. And it happened so fast nobody protested or made a sound.

Pat slapped Abdul on the left cheek with a well-timed right cross as if to say, *I can do anything I want. Game on.* Then, he fought on instinct.

Thirty of us watched Knuckles in silence as he pummeled

Abdul up and down each aisle. Abdul's glasses flew across the room. For Pat, it was target practice. He reached deep from his hip for some shots. Others came in rapid combinations, like working a speed bag. Abdul offered no resistance, although he was game, and stayed on his feet and moved his head. Though wobbled, Abdul refused to go down. Pat worked him like a heavy bag. Punch, punch, punch, duck, overhand right cross, left hook. Ray took one shot, then another, every blow from a different angle. It was a massacre, sliced and diced by a professional.

We watched a gruesome, bare-knuckle street beating, dumbstruck. Abdul, defenseless, took a repetitious and relentless drubbing. The carnage went on as if in slow motion without bell or intermission. Pat fought up and down a second, then a third aisle. When he reached the door, he grabbed Abdul, now limp and bleeding. The *coup de grâce*, he threw him like he was a garbage can into the hallway.

He shouted, "Now get yourself to Brother Anselm's office for some real discipline."

We all feared Brother Anselm, the school vice principal, a wizened, thin-lipped bureaucrat. His puckered face looked like he'd sucked lemons. We called him Brother Death because he bore a likeness to the "Angel of Death," Josef Mengele. To this day, I can hear Brother Death's high, hysterical voice, scolding a student. "How would your mother feel if she heard about this?" Whatever Anselm might dispense would be worse than what Abdul got from Pat. It meant a meeting with your parents and suspension or expulsion.

No one stood. No one spoke. No one aided Abdul. Shell shocked, we withdrew into silence after watching the gory spectacle.

Panting and exhausted, Pat composed himself. He drew a white handkerchief out of his pants pocket and wiped his brow.

His robe torn, collar buckled, and large sweat stains under his armpits, he said, "So where were we, gentlemen?"

Halloran raised his hand.

Pat nodded.

"We were discussing the etymology of the word fervor, Brother."

Pat said, "It's imperative these cold winter days to defend ourselves against spiraling negative thoughts. There's a tendency to get cranky. That's when you must be fervent. I don't care how dark it is or how cold it is outside, even if we don't see the sun for weeks. You must remain positive, and thus become a beacon for others."

The bell rang and Brother Pat said, "Saint John Baptist de La Salle."

We responded, "Pray for us."

"Live Jesus in our hearts."

We said in chorus, "Forever!"

The twenty-five-minute homeroom period concluded. A dirty, brown puddle of ice melted under my desk, I gathered my books and hastened with the others to our first classes.

Abdul never returned to St. Alban's. After the melee, there was little mention of him. Exaggerated stories emerged, most taken as hearsay and confabulation. Some said he went to public school. Others that Brother Pat broke his nose, or that Abdul pissed blood for weeks after the thrashing. But the subject was taboo because we all feared the same fate. The consensus of silence was that Abdul got what he deserved. The Brothers maintained a firm hand, and that was their contract with the boys and their parents. Abdul broke the code and got lippy. Insurrection at St. Alban's was always met by superior force and squashed. It was an unwritten principle, and no one dared talk about it.

Like so many mysteries, I found out years later that Abdul transferred to Christian Brothers Academy. Brother Death designed the plan. CBA, is a military boarding school in Albany for troubled boys. It touts a one hundred percent college admission rate. Like all the Brothers' operations, it's expensive and, for Ray Abdul, it was a step short of reform school. I knew he got screwed, shipped up the river. As one kid said, "Military school sucks so bad it makes everything else seem easy."

Albany and Buffalo share abysmal winters and not much more. As the crow flies, two hundred and sixty-one miles separate them, a four-and-a-half-hour drive on Interstate 90. In February, one confronts as bleak a tundra as any described in *War and Peace*, where icy crosswinds prevail, the likes of which curled the toes and turned back Hitler's army. Strange bedfellows, these municipalities, connected by a trench begun in 1825. Colonial Albany, priggish, the oldest European settlement in New York State, conjoined with obstreperous Buffalo, a dirty hinterland on the western edge. When I showed Victoria a map of the state, she said, "Buffalo couldn't be farther from New York." And it's accurate on many levels. Albany's a stone's throw from New England and sits pretty on the Hudson, a hundred and forty-three miles north of New York City. On the map, the three cities form a right-angled triangle. The Big Apple sucked its trade up the river, bent like a straw into the Erie Canal, opening the Great Lakes. The colonials first experienced the expanse and vast distances of North America through Buffalo. The two cities, at best, endured a marriage of geographical convenience. Today, New York City dominates, Albany rules, and Buffalo's star has long faded. Like Abdul, Buffalo is an outcast, a wannabe, an upstart. Albany remains an insider, the state capital, integral to its dominion.

After Abdul left that winter, we read Conrad's *Heart of Darkness*. I couldn't help but draw the parallel between Abdul and Colonel Kurtz. Both a little crazy, gone upriver never to return. And when I learned of Abdul's fate, it came full circle. He never finished high school despite CBA's one hundred percent college admission rate. He joined the Marines while still a teenager and stepped on a landmine during the Tet Offensive. He'd only been in Vietnam a week and came home in a body bag. It haunts me. Was it that horrible beating in front of his classmates that took him down?

One of Pat's homeroom exercises was to show an image, read a quote, and write it on the blackboard. One day, he projected a slide of emaciated, naked dead bodies stacked against a steel-gray sky, a mass grave at the Nazi Bergen-Belsen concentration camp. He wrote, "Cruelty is a part of nature, at least of human nature, but it is the one thing that seems unnatural to us." Under it, in his flowery cursive script, he wrote, Robinson Jeffers (1887-1962).

I remember it like it was yesterday. In a gruff, bellowing voice, he'd said, "Think, boys. Think. What does this mean? Dialogue with each other. Please don't ask me. Be bold. Don't hedge. It's up to each of you to figure it out for yourself. A successful life starts with using your mind. You must become critical thinkers."

Viewing the photo repulsed me, and the words affronted me in a way I hadn't felt before. I was sick to my stomach. The hair on the back of my neck stood up. I felt a sense of disgust and hopelessness. I didn't fully understand the meaning of the words but grasped the absurdity. When we broke into small groups, the room fell silent. Football season was over, so there wasn't much to occupy our chatter. There was a lump in my throat.

Pat harangued us, "I want to hear you boys talking to each other. You must dialogue."

The bell rang, and we rushed off to our classes. The image alongside Jeffers's pithy observation rocked my reality. Through Pat, I became acquainted with Robinson Jeffers, Big Sur, and the horror of the Holocaust.

My parents read the local newspaper. Other than a set of Funk and Wagnalls encyclopedias, there were no books in the house. The extent of the household's reading materials was the current *Life Magazine*. My mother displayed it on a love seat in the living room. And always, a bathtub-soaked *Reader's Digest* sat next to the upstairs commode. In grade school, I recognized my inclination toward words. I got caught up in rhythms and rhymes in poems like "Casey at the Bat" and "Gunga Din." But Robinson Jeffers's poetry was different, and it didn't rhyme. His long sentences were musical but didn't connect. There were no simple conclusions like, "…the mighty Casey has struck out." His words smarted and stung like the image of Bergen-Belsen, and I wanted more. The Holocaust and Robinson Jeffers weren't on my radar before Brother Pat. After that, I probed my mother's German ancestry and, through Jeffers, I came upon the harsh wonder of Big Sur.

After Pat's presentation, I started examining my roots. Why did my father call my mother a Nazi? An earlier incident came up in vivid detail, and I started to dream about it. When I was ten, my mother sent me to the basement to fetch a can of tomato soup. It was a task I didn't relish, because I wasn't fond of the rickety stairwell. It creaked with every step and scared me to enter the dark, damp, lifeless hole. At the bottom of the stairs was a rusty refrigerator that gasped and hummed. Bulging, white-washed plaster walls crumbled on the floor in stone-size chunks. When it rained, water ran unobstructed across a smooth, gray stone floor. There were primitive, hand-cut gutters to catch the runoff, and a black iron cast drain that smelled like rotten eggs and glugged. Hidden in the corner was an alcove called the fruit cellar where my mother kept canned goods. It was always grim and dark inside, except on rare sunny days when a small, square window let a sliver of light through. The fruit cellar had a squeaky door that made me cringe.

To switch a hanging, bare light bulb on, one had to yank a

long, slippery string. The line dangled like a cobweb in the dark. On that day, a ray of light beamed from the window, and I spotted a big, white canvas bag with the imprint of an ocean liner. Curious, I opened it. Inside was a red banner with a black, cross-like symbol with arms bent at right angles. It was longer than a flag, more like the long Roman banners I'd seen in *Spartacus*. I wrapped it around my shoulders and ran up the stairs. I stretched out my arms as if I had wings, tripping in excitement, yelling, "Superman! I'm Superman!"

When my mother saw me, her face blackened, her eyes darkened, and she became fierce. "Where did you get that?"

"In the fruit cellar."

"What makes you think you can take anything you want?"

"What is it?" I started to cry.

"Where's the soup?"

"I forgot."

She slapped me hard across the face. "You're always getting into things." She took the banner and folded it.

"Momma, I'm sorry."

She said, "This is something other people wouldn't understand. Why can't you leave things alone?" She sent me back to the basement to bring the tomato soup and said nothing more about it that day.

After my father died, I visited my mother every summer. Scarlett had no interest. I made the trip alone and stayed in the room I'd inhabited during my teenage years. My mother would lie in bed at bedtime, propped on pillows, sipping Southern Comfort, and we'd talk. I poured her drinks like my father had, following his instructions to make it stiff. And I sat in a lazy boy while she nibbled on a Hershey bar she kept by the nightstand. She was a good listener, and getting her to talk about herself until she was well into her cups was out of the question. On one of these occasions, we discussed Germany and the Holocaust.

She said, "Do you remember your grandfather?"

"Not very well."

"Now, there's a man who knew how to get things done."

I said, "I thought he was a tyrant."

"Well, that might be true. But isn't that what the rest of us need? I like a man who takes charge."

"Do you believe that?"

"How else do you think we have any order in the world? Most people are sheep, and they follow. My father built a business with a hundred and fifty-two employees. He drove a Pierce-Arrow. Do you think anyone could step into his shoes? He took our whole family to Europe, to the Olympics, first class."

"When was that?"

"1936."

I said, "The Nazi Olympics?"

"It was the happiest summer of my life. I turned eighteen." She blushed like a schoolgirl. "We spent the entire summer touring Germany. And sixteen glorious days in Berlin."

"But there was outrage around the world. The Nazis made brutal attacks on Jews. Why didn't you ever talk about this?"

"After the war, nobody talked about it."

I said, "Wasn't there an international boycott?"

"I know, I know, but the Germans pulled it off. It was outstanding, the most spectacular Olympics ever. And I was there."

"What about the protests?"

"We didn't see any. I heard about three swimmers, Austrian girls, Jews, who refused to take part. The IOC banned them for life." She added, "You've never seen anything like the *Kurfürstendamm*. That summer was magic."

I said, "I remember a huge, framed photo of an ocean liner over the bar in the dining room when I was a kid."

"That's the *Europa*. It held the speed record for transatlantic crossings. It wasn't easy for my father to get tickets. He planned it years in advance. The *Europa* was the Blue Riband champion. He loved the competition. He said it judged the superiority of nations. And Germany was the best. He followed it every day in the newspapers." She started to well up. "Stomach cancer ate him up. There was nothing they could do at Mayo." She hesitated and dabbed a tear from her eye with a handkerchief, then said, "He loved the Blue Riband."

"It's a German ship?"

"The best, fastest, and most efficient. The most luxurious too. The women wore beautiful gowns and men dressed in tuxes at meals, perfect gentlemen. And everything was done with etiquette and according to protocol. No riffraff. Every meal was spectacular, magnificent place settings. Seven-course meals, each done with panache. All the waiters wore white gloves." She paused. "I drank schnapps for the first time. My parents didn't know. Uncle Artie and I did it below deck."

"What happened to the photo?"

"It's in the attic."

"When did you move it?"

"Some years back. Your grandfather's portrait hangs there now."

"I'm glad Jesse Owens showed Hitler that the Aryans weren't the master race."

"Jesse Owens was the most successful individual athlete," she said. "He won four gold medals. Germany got thirty-three. The United States came in second with twenty-four. By all accounts, the Berlin Olympics were an enormous success. The hardware's a small part of it. It's the pageantry, the spectacle. The Germans were always hospitable and friendly. I'll never forget it. What a summer to turn eighteen!

"We strolled the Unter den Linden every night and met people from all over the world. I did see Jesse Owens one night. The only word I can come up with to describe him is sublime. What a smile, he moved like a cat. His own country treated him much worse because he was a *Neger* than Germany ever could. Americans discarded him like a dog when he got back. But Berlin, for those two weeks, it was the center of the universe. Music, art, culture, and such pomp and razzmatazz. The streets were lined with banners, swastikas, eagles, and Olympic flags. From the tops of buildings to the ground, everything was a sea of red."

I said, "Flags like the one in the fruit cellar?"

"You remember. Uncle Artie and I brought back all kinds of souvenirs. Everything about the Third Reich was new and impressive. Berlin, what a thrill, a wondrous place. I wish those two weeks lasted forever. Berlin was clean, orderly, and safe. You could walk anywhere."

I said, "Incredible. If you're not a gypsy or a Jew."

She said, "You're not! Why are you spoiling this for me? Can you imagine a hundred and ten thousand people all packed into the new *Olympiastadion* for the opening ceremony? The Germans invented the torch relay."

I said, "You mean the Nazis."

She said, "Doesn't matter," and dismissed me with her hand. "I can still see the German boy, Fritz Schilgen, so handsome, fit, tanned, muscular, and blond. How gracefully he ran into the stadium and stood in silence and paused before he lit the flame. My heart was in my mouth. Everyone held their breath. Rather than individuals, we were one great organic mass. We stirred with the same spirit—what a beautiful thing. I never felt anything like it again. Then, the Hindenburg crossed low over the stadium trailing the Olympic flag. And Fritz is still alive, a fit man in his nineties."

I said, "This is wrong. All wrong."

She continued, "When the Austrian team entered, they saluted Hitler. There was a clap from the heavens. It sounded like thunder. How can you spoil this memory for me?"

"What about the Holocaust? And it got so much worse. The Olympics were Nazi propaganda."

"I don't care about that. I cherish the memory of the games. I thought then my life would be more like that, traveling, experiencing the world. How did I end up here, in Buffalo, back in this house? With your father. With children. When I was in Germany, I was where I needed to be. I could have stayed. Your grandfather offered me a trip around the world if I didn't marry your father."

"Do you regret it?"

"I have lots of regrets. What do you know about regrets? I had responsibilities." And then her eyelids began to fall, and her breath softened. She slipped into a fitful sleep.

Her bedroom was chock-full of Northern European artifacts, dust-free and meticulous. Photos, paintings, and decorations all occupying the same position I remembered from childhood. The double bed and television were rooted in place, a formal black and white portrait of her father next to her bed. Her face strained in sleep.

At that moment, I saw that this hardened stoic woman my brother and I called the Nazi was dying. Slowly and by small degrees. Her skin was sallow, deep crevices around her mouth and chin. Her hair, teased into a chestnut-colored bouffant, was thinning. Even her signature widow's peak that once reached toward her eyebrows had receded. We never discussed the Nazis, the Holocaust, or the Berlin Olympics again.

My mother's parents spoke German in the home, as did my father's adopted parents. As a small child of four or five, long before my brother was born, we always had a German housekeeper. My earliest memory is of a large, handsome woman with enormous, soft breasts like goose down pillows. Her name was Gundi, and she stood on stout legs and smelled like baked bread, powdered sugar, and Lysol. Her hands were rough as sandpaper. Gundi had cared for me since my parents brought me home from the hospital. She'd speak in broken English, caress my face, and say, "Neal, what good big boy." Then pause, "Like *apfelkuchen*?" My eyes opened wide, and then she'd envelop me in her arms, "Now, only one piece. Your Mutter don't like *fett werden*." She'd rock me in her arms, ripples of joy shaking her body like Jell-O. I adored Gundi and ran to the door to greet her when she arrived.

My mother approached homemaking with Teutonic single-mindedness. She employed Gundi five days a week and insisted on working right alongside her. I can still see Gundi and my mother on their hands and knees scrubbing the kitchen floor. The two of them, rumps high, slouch-shouldered, up to their elbows in suds. It reeked of ammonia, and the smell repelled me.

When Gundi moved to Cleveland to live with her sister, I was seven and it was traumatic. A significant loss for me and a momentous shift in our household. For weeks my parents talked about her replacement. I heard my mother say, "Only a girl from the old country will do." My father retorted, "Better if she's fresh off the boat." I didn't know what "fresh off the boat" meant. I envisioned a boat between the old country and the port of Buffalo on Lake Erie. I wondered how and why people were trafficked there.

When the interviews began, a string of applicants paraded through the living room. My mother sat each candidate in an oversized, brown-striped velvet wingback chair, stood in front, and asked questions while my father read the newspaper in a chair across the room. One poor girl, no more than seventeen, wilted under cross-examination. She cringed and became flushed.

My mother said, "Did you ever take anything from your employer?"

Fresh beads of sweat formed on the girl's brow and she wrung her hands.

My mother said, "Did you ever take anything?"

The girl twisted in the chair and twirled her long, blond hair with her index finger. She scrunched her pale, freckled face like she was going to sneeze.

My mother repeated, "Did you steal from your employer?"

The girl exclaimed, "*Ich würde Ihnen niemals was stehlen!*"

The exchange that came next sounded harsh, like they were shouting at each other. Later, I found out they were speaking German. The girl had said, "I would never steal anything from you." It had never occurred to me that my mother spoke German.

The girl said, "*Nie, gnädige Frau.*" (Never, Madam.)

When the interview concluded, the girl stood, curtsied, and said, "*Danke, gnädige Frau.*" (Thank you, Madam.)

She didn't understand English, and I wondered if that's what it meant to be fresh off the boat. Her fear was palpable, and my mother gave her no wiggle room.

My grandparents were the first generation born here, not "off the boat." They all grew up on Buffalo's East Side, in a German-speaking neighborhood called the Fruit Belt. The district took its name from a cluster of streets: Lemon, Orange, Peach, Cherry, Grape, and Mulberry. Early German immigrants planted orchards and gardens, thus the street names. Arranged marriages were common, and vocations passed from generation to generation. Humboldt Parkway, the grandest of Buffalo's boulevards, ran through the Fruit Belt. The parkway was two hundred feet wide and meandered for two miles, a green space designed by Olmstead, lined with three hundred mature elm trees. The fate of Humboldt Parkway rested in the hands of burgeoning automobile usage. After World War II, traffic was abominable. People were moving out of the city, into the suburbs, and wanted quick access in and out of downtown. There was a clamor to do something about it. Funding was available from the state to improve the highway system. Demolition of Humboldt Parkway began in 1958, displacing hundreds of families. A subterranean concrete trench, the Kensington Expressway, split the Fruit Belt in half.

It eviscerated the community and further divided it by race. The inner city crumbled. Talking about it with my parents, I learned that what they missed most were the trees. No one appreciates the convenience of the expressway with such nostalgia. The Kensington Expressway cut the heart out of their city.

In this regard, I always felt robbed, like there was another Buffalo, a lost gilded age I never knew. It slipped away from my parents when they were children. The loss has always saddled me with melancholy and longing. Could I save my city buried beneath dilapidated buildings and boarded up storefronts? The inner city streets were decaying and riddled with crime. Once one of the wealthiest cities in America, now one of the poorest. In my bones, I understood the antecedent. The Victorian boom town of yesterday was part of me, a dinosaur skeleton I could excavate. I longed for what I couldn't see. Wherever I traveled, like a ghost with a heavy scent, my city hung over me. Anyone who grew up in Buffalo understands this feeling. I celebrate it with expatriated Western New Yorkers, strangers I meet in faraway places. "You're from Buffalo?" "Me too." "Holy shit, where did you grow up?" Caught up in its spell. Too many things to talk about, endless experiences to relive. We'll jaw on for as long as the present company allows. Ted's Hot Dogs, Anderson's Frozen Custard, Crystal Beach Amusement Park (which closed in 1989), Sherkston Quarry (which, like Crystal Beach, is across the border in Canada), Letchworth State Park…the list is ever expanding. I discovered long ago that I can't turn my back on Buffalo. If I do, I pay a stiff price. I mortgage my soul.

And I blame this curse on Frederick Law Olmsted, the master builder who constructed New York City's Central Park. Buffalo courted him to duplicate the same success in 1868. Instead, Olmsted designed three parks interlaced with something new to America, parkways. Olmsted layered his interconnected park system over Ellicott's radial angles and curves. The park reached into the city. And through the first half of the twentieth century, the metropolitan area flourished. Buffalo was a city of green belts. The streets were lined with trees and broad boulevards. Large, well-kept homes graced the avenues. These are the images that permeate my earliest memories. Buffalo, a city like Paris, with vast democratic spaces that belong to everyone. A town where people feel like they belong. Olmsted called Buffalo the best-planned city in the world. Every resident absorbed it and assimilated it into their internal geography.

After the Civil War, Buffalo was at the center of America. The push west went through the Queen City. Before Cleveland, Detroit, and Chicago, there was Buffalo—a dynamic nerve center humming with grand visions, culture, industry, and trade. So different than the dilapidated forgotten metropolis I grew up in a century later, a period when some questioned if Buffalo should exist at all. Always I sensed Olmsted's presence, alive in what remains of the park system. And the innovative architecture of Louis Sullivan, H.H. Richardson, and Frank Lloyd Wright.

A prescient local lawyer, William Dorsheimer, brought Olmsted to Buffalo. His aspiration was that public lands, like art, would cultivate a higher civilization. In the age of Walt Whitman, Buffalo was a city of promise and light. A century and a half later, despite butchering, much of Olmsted's cityscape remains. More or less, Olmsted's palate remains intact and still informs residents. Tells them that regardless of race, color, or religion, they belong. The park system is the soul of Buffalo. Painful as it is, the tragedy of Humboldt Parkway didn't destroy the well-laid foundation. The division of Delaware Park by the Scajaquada Expressway maims it, but it still breathes. Enough Olmsted remains. Buffalonians share a lasting sense of place.

At fourteen, like most, I staged a rebellion, although my storm of self-discovery was subtle, silent, and secret, and it wasn't evident to my parents or even me. I found that when absorbed in a book, no one tormented me. Reading became my portal, as well as an escape—a place to forget my problems. I'd close my bedroom door and remain transfixed for hours. Most of all, I enjoyed reading in a warm bathtub with the door locked. My chief lieutenant in this insurgence was Brother Patrick. He became my Che Guevara. He not only suggested books but supplied them, and his loan policy was for keeps. Pat never demanded a volume back. Pat's approach was, "Better a book in hand than collecting dust." Albert Camus, *The Stranger*, Pearl S. Buck, *The Good Earth*, and *The Autobiography of Malcolm X* are still on my shelf. During this period, Robinson Jeffers solidified his place as my soul poet. To Pat, books were medicine, the right book could offer a cure, and I banked on him being my specialist. And it was fun. It channeled my energy inward and gave me hope for an independent life far away from my parents and St. Alby's. Though I'm not as generous as Pat, to this day, I follow his axiom. There's nothing more satisfying than giving a young person a book, no strings attached. It might well provide the key to their future.

As a young man, Pat spent nine months at the New Camaldoli Hermitage in Big Sur, a gestation period he said changed his life. Later, he completed a doctorate in literature at Stanford. But it was Big Sur that inculcated his more delicate nuances. Despite failing English, I came to love Robinson Jeffers as much as Pat did. Pat referred to him as "Robin," as if they were boyhood friends, but they weren't contemporaries.

Robin was born in the late nineteenth century and died in 1962. Pat said it snowed that day in Carmel-by-the-Sea (January 20), when he died. For Pat, Robin was part of the canon, a literary titan. Pat approached him with reverence, the same way he did Chaucer, Dante, Shakespeare, and Whitman. He proclaimed Robin America's greatest poet. When I went to college, there was no mention of Robinson Jeffers. On occasion, an obscure reference, but he was never discussed in the classroom. At St. Alban's though, under Pat's tutelage, Robin became an imaginary friend, an intimate. It's striking how the lilt of his words, sounds, and melodies immersed me and consumed my attention. Reading his work put a wall between me and everything else. I could hear, taste, feel, touch, and smell the Big Sur coast. Relentless violent waves clawed an untamed, remote, and distant shore. Robin wrote about hawks, stallions, incest, rape, and the decline of humanity. He rejected human beings as the center of the universe. Irreverent. He called Jesus a megalomaniac. He compared Roosevelt to Hitler. At the height of World War II and American patriotism, he renounced the war.

Robin's language indulged my deepest longings. I imagined the ocean, sky, mountains, clutching the heavens. At night, a spectacular sky blanketed by stars. Big Sur was the transition zone between land and water. Towering redwoods, yucca, chaparral, wet ravines, turbulent streams, all coexisting in violence and beauty. Wildlife on land and sea varied widely. Mountain lions, bobcats, coyotes, deer, squirrels, a realm of fire and regeneration. Otters, harbor seals, sea lions, porpoises, gray whales, abalone, and sea urchins. Deepwater nutrients upwelled to the pungent smell of kelp and sea vines. Big Sur, a province of splendor, fear, and dread. Robin's cadence ripped me open and spoke to an inner self I'd yet to experience.

Nonetheless, I got kicked out of St. Alban's in the middle of my sophomore year. I flunked four subjects, including English, and bid Brother Patrick farewell. The dismissal meant banishment from the Catholic community. It was catastrophic—my first death—and my parents were furious. I sulked and slid further back into myself, confused and bewildered. I retreated to the middle-class churchgoing family home in North Buffalo. My mother, teetering on a nervous breakdown, continued to drink and get sexual with me at night. My father distanced himself and tightened the screws. His personal life remained chaotic. He continued to binge drink and erupt into violence.

Throughout my life, more rejections would follow, but one can't help but magnify the first. It was acute. I'm still terrible with transitions. My ouster from St. Alban's followed me for years. It still smarts.

Back then, I couldn't articulate my disgust for hypocrisy and hubris. I overheard one of the Brothers talking about me before the axe fell. "This kid has a lot of problems. I wish we could address them or begin to address them." I knew what was coming. I feigned illness and didn't attend the dismissal meeting. I couldn't face it when Brother Anselm presented my parents with my walking papers.

My mother cried and my father fumed. She protested, "They don't see his character." He replied, "What the hell is he going to do now?" My mother masked my exit from Alby's in denial.

I made up a story that I'd broken into the library and switched out books. I couldn't bear to tell anyone I'd flunked out. St. Alban's was the bastion of clubiness and soulless white ethos. I knew I didn't belong there and getting expelled was my only way out. I went to public school, where I excelled on the swim team. By then, things were so cold between my father and me that I told him not to come to swim meets. He snuck in and sat in the back row and watched me win the all-high competition. My studies improved, although I still bombed algebra. And through all this, Robin stuck with me.

Pat inspired a need in me to know more about Robinson Jeffers, and this pursuit became an ardent quest. I learned the poet was an iconoclast, a rebel. He fled society for a remote, broken coastline of Big Sur. He wrote in the morning and moved large granite boulders and planted trees in the afternoon. His accomplishments as a stone maker are as wondrous as his poetry. He completed an ever-expanding stone house and three-story Hawk

Tower overlooking the Pacific. In my quest, I related to Robin. He hailed from a bleak, dreary place where winds cut deep, and snow falls some years into May. He was born in Allegheny City, later incorporated into Pittsburgh, and the Jeffers family went west when he was sixteen. Robin shares a birthday with my brother born three-quarters of a century before. This is where the similarities end.

Robin's father was a well-off biblical scholar and clergyman known as "The Doctor." The Doctor was moody and studious, twenty-two years older than his wife. He took a keen interest in his first son's studies. Robin's early education was in Germany and Switzerland. By twelve, he could speak and read three modern languages with knowledge of Latin and Greek. Robin said his father slapped the ancient languages into him. My father was much the same with me with swimming.

Brother Pat had said, "Jeffers had the education Ezra Pound wished he'd had."

Robinson Jeffers graduated from Occidental College in Los Angeles when he was eighteen. During the next stage of his academic career, graduate studies at the University of Southern California, his life took a critical turn. At USC, he met Una Call Kuster, a married woman three years his senior, in an advanced German class, and enlivening conversations aroused more than a passion for Goethe's *Faust*. Scandal followed. For the next seven years, anguish, confusion, longing, and uncertainty consumed both their lives. Robin floundered, tried medical school, and dropped out after three years, although at the top of his class. Later, he sought a geographical cure and relocated to Seattle, enrolled in forestry school, and never completed his studies. He couldn't get Una off his mind and began to drink. Una went to Europe for seven months to forget him on the recommendation of her husband, Teddie Kuster, a successful Los Angeles attorney. Finally, Kuster realized he could not get over the lengthy betrayal and initiated a divorce. Robin and Una married in 1913, the day after her marriage to Kuster was dissolved. Tragically, the following year they lost their first child, a daughter, the day after her birth.

Looking for a place where Robin could establish a writing life, they settled in a remote and unpopulous scenic hamlet, Carmel-by-the-Sea. He had a small annuity, removing the need to work if the couple lived frugally. They had twin sons, Donnan and Garth, in 1916. Kuster also settled in Carmel, remarried, and built a stone house a city block away. He became a significant figure in the early days of the village and founded the Golden Bough Theater. The principals, by all accounts, remained congenial neighbors the rest of their lives. Donnan and Garth called Kuster "Uncle Teddie."

In Carmel, Robin went about beating stone into submission and composing his verses. Then suddenly, in 1918, at age thirty-one, while working stone, he had an epiphany, a sharpening of vision, and his incomparable prophetic narrative poetry began to flow. He credited Una for creating the conditions that allowed his imagination to soar with the hawks he was so fond of portraying in his poems. He said, "My nature is cold and undiscriminating. She excited and focused it, gave it eyes and nerves and sympathies." Yet in temperament, the two couldn't have been more different. Robin was dour, brooding, distant, and Una a communicator, outgoing, and quick to temper. When rage and jealously prevailed, they came to blows. Their union proved enduring but could erupt like a volcano and turn destructive, like a violent storm. A terrifying episode took place in Taos in 1938 when Una attempted to kill herself with a revolver.

The height of Robin's celebrity reached its zenith in the 1930s. He appeared on the cover of *Time Magazine* in April 1932, and Edward Weston, his friend and a neighbor, took the portrait. Simultaneously, Carmel was undergoing a population explosion, no longer an offbeat artist colony but a sought-after tourist destination and highly desirable place to live. Robin's poems were a sensation, and now Big Sur could be accessed by the new scenic Highway 1. The closeness to nature in its rawest form, peace, and anonymity Robin and Una cherished disintegrated. He was discouraged and depressed. And, if that wasn't enough, in stepped the one and only, outlandish, and irrepressible Mabel Dodge Luhan.

Born Mabel Ganson on Buffalo's millionaire row in 1879, Mabel created trouble, both good and bad, wherever she went. To say that she was born with a silver spoon in her mouth is an understatement. She spent lavishly in pursuits to fill her frenetic restlessness. And her resources, like her insatiable drives, were limitless. She had her finger in everything and knew everyone, first in Florence, Italy, where she was associated with Gertrude Stein and her brother, Leo, and André Gide. With her second husband, Edwin Dodge, an architect, Mabel restored a fourteenth-century Medici palace to its Renaissance grandeur and dressed in medieval gowns and turbans. Fascinated by Mabel's eccentric personality, Stein wrote *Portrait of Mabel Dodge at the Villa Curonia*, published in 1912. Mabel, tired of Florence, divorced Dodge and moved to New York, where she became an extraordinary *salonnière* and cultivated the most influential artists, writers, and radicals of her day. By the time Robin was in Mabel's sights, she'd built a retreat for creative renewal, Los Gallos, in Taos, New Mexico. There, Mabel divorced a third husband and married a Native American, Tony Lujan. Together they built a seventeen-room house, five guesthouses, barns, and a stable. A constant influx of compelling and influential guests found their door. She envisioned herself the bridge between the native people and European colonizers, and Taos as the birthplace of a new American civilization based on redistribution of wealth. Most notably, she lured D.H. Lawrence to the Southwest. Others, like Georgia O'Keeffe, Willa Cather,

Martha Graham, Thornton Wilder, Greta Garbo, Ansel Adams, and, regrettably, Robinson Jeffers followed.

Mabel was complex, persuasive, and yet endearing. She fostered a friendship with Una in the 1930s while staying in Carmel, and the twins loved the ranch life, horseback riding, fiestas, native dances, and trips to the Taos Pueblo. Five summers, the Jeffers family took part in extended stays of four to six weeks at her southwestern retreat. In addition to Mabel's affinity for psychoanalysis and modern art, she was a prolific confessional writer. Some texts were so explicit, they were held back from publication. Mabel's devotion to writing as a therapeutic tool was noteworthy. She said, "I must write or die," and, "...put down your own truths, nothing else." Despite all her prolific activities, she wrote five volumes of memoirs, over sixteen hundred pages, and was never far from her day's artistic and political developments. Unhappily for Robin, Mabel was a busybody who manipulated and controlled people's lives. During Robin's ill-fated family vacation in 1938, she introduced him to Hildegarde Donaldson, an appealing, romantically unhappy concert violinist in her forties. He was dealing with writer's block, and Mabel encouraged an affair. There is no evidence except for Mabel's report that they consummated the relationship.

Still, no doubt there was an attraction, and Mabel distracted Una so Robin and Hildegarde could spend time alone together. There is evidence of an intimate walk they had in the early morning hours. Una felt betrayed and deceived, which on the night of July 9, 1938, touched off a maelstrom after hours. After an extended and bitter argument, Una swallowed a bottle of sleeping pills, took Robin's .32 gauge pistol out of a drawer, and discharged the weapon at point-blank range beneath her sternum. The bullet ricocheted, fractured a rib, darted, followed the bone, and exited her back. Robin called for help. "Mabel! Mabel! Una's shot herself! Come...come."

The physician found Hildegard at the foot of the stairs, out cold. She'd hit her head on a low beam when rushing to their aid. After a brief assessment, the doctor left Hildegarde and found Una in the bathtub, senseless and bleeding profusely from her wound. Surgery sterilized the bullet's path, and her stomach was pumped. In a few days, she was back at "Mabeltown," where she convalesced for two weeks before returning to Carmel. This all happened weeks before Robin and Una's twenty-fifth wedding anniversary on August 2.

I often wonder how their sons got beyond the trauma and how Robin and Una went about mending their marriage. They'd entered the deep and somehow found a way to come out on the other side. Although, like all stories if followed to the end, this doesn't end well. Ten years after a mastectomy at sixty-five, cancer metastasized to Una's bones and racked her with pain for eight months. Robin remained attendant at her side. As he said in his poem, "Hungerfield," she learned the mercy of morphine. She died in his arms in 1950. Robinson Jeffers died eleven years later. Over time he recovered enough to write poignant and heartbreaking lines to Una confirming their enduring and everlasting bond. There are far too many choices to include here, but these few simple lines come to mind: "This is my wound. / This is what never time nor change nor whiskey will heal…"

Mark Twain lived in my hometown for two years between 1869 and 1871. He owned a stake in the Buffalo Express, where he worked as an editor and a reporter. He was newly married to his beloved Livy Langford, and his revered father-in-law, Jervis Langford, bought them a stately house in Buffalo with servants. Everything seemed rosy. Then, Jervis died in 1870. The couple's first child, Langford, was born, but the child was sickly. He died nineteen months later of diphtheria. Twain blamed himself for allowing the child to catch a cold. He said, "[It] was a sorrowful and pathetic brief sojourn in Buffalo." And I sense that Robin and Una felt the same about the Southwest.

My response to Robin and his poetry was visceral. Big Sur left me gasping. I wanted to breathe the air, devour it like a cheeseburger, and smoke it like hashish. Robin made his stand on this farthest reach of the continent. He called Big Sur "the noblest thing I've ever seen." For me, though, it would be decades before I'd settle nearby.

How I remember the first time I heard those two terse words, Big Sur. It was in high school from Knuckles, Brother Patrick O'Donoghue.

In Spanish, *el país grande del sur* means "the big country of the south." Ceded by Mexico to the United States in 1848, English-speaking settlers half-anglicized the name and chopped it into two bite-sized bits. In the nineteenth century, Big Sur country was the last American frontier. An impassable mountain range, the Santa Lucia, isolates seventy-six miles of the coast. Jagged cliffs rise straight from the ocean and rise to five thousand feet farther inland, an extent of twenty miles, an insurmountable barrier. In those days, Big Sur was only accessible by horse path. Traveling the coastal trail was slow and tedious. It required sure-footed horses and mules. The sparse population consisted of the last pioneers: homesteaders, farmers who scratched a living from the land. They subsisted through barter and trade. In 1937, all that changed. California Highway 1 connected San Simeon and Carmel. The remote backcountry became accessible but remained untamed. In came artists, dropouts, dissidents, and runaways. The oft-closed two-lane highway remains the only entry point to this day. It snakes and twists along the steep mountainside. The surf pounds a few hundred feet below. Big Sur's primitive territory endures because it's hostile. It's an ever-changing environment suffused with mud slides and wildfires that don't operate on predictable terms. It maintains its mystique. Its residents are rebels, radicals, cynics, skeptics, non-conformists, and Bohemians, un-compromising and self-reliant. There are no formal boundaries. No incorporated towns or villages. No sense of urban sprawl. No malls. More often than not, no cell service.

In the 1970s, Ansel Adams tried to make Big Sur a national seashore to put it under the umbrella of the National Park Service. The surly residents put up a hell of a fight. They wanted to keep it like it was—uncivilized, uncouth, unbroken, off the beaten path.

From the other side, John Steinbeck viewed Big Sur from his childhood bedroom in Salinas. He saw the dark side, the foreboding shadowy heights. Big Sur threatened and disturbed him.

Big Sur, a short, bastardized phrase that means something different to everyone. To me, it's where the proximity of land, ocean, and sky beckon—a call to accept rather than cast out shadows. I came to the left coast seeking freedom and nonconformity. Big Sur is as far left as you can go without drowning (and some do). The whole ragged edge of California represents liberation, something I've always wanted to embrace. But have I ever given myself to it until now? Calypso is its heartbeat.

# 11 JANUARY, MIDDLE OF THE NIGHT

## (CALYPSO INSTITUTE, BIG SUR, CA)

*"She teaches without teaching."*
Lao-Tzu
(likely 6th or 4th century BC)

'M SITTING IN THE LODGE. Wide awake. It's the middle of the night. No caffeine necessary. Two sessions with Zephyra yesterday, and the room felt like a balloon about to pop. Tears, gut-wrenching outcries, teeth-gnashing, anger, frustration, and imprecise angst. It could have been the day room in a mental institution. Like unclogging a drain, obstructions cleared, water flowed again. Sad, impossible situations melted away into smiles and laughter. To observe is harrowing and spine-chilling. As advertised, it's about opening your heart. Standing, sitting, holding hands, listening to music, swaying in time. It stirs and stimulates—what a strange, peculiar family of misfits I've found. And I'm confident that I belong here. There's a genuine *esprit de corps*, a glue that binds us. Always lots of encouragement, hugs, and well wishes. It's an emotional rollercoaster—a marathon, a madhouse, the nineteenth-century vision of a humane asylum.

Gestalt. I took a course in college. It was the 1970s, long hair, dirty feet, bell bottoms. Humid South Florida, unpredictable rain squalls. A free concert at Peacock Park. Dwayne Allman and Eric Clapton jamming in the Grove. Gestalt. Theatrical, confrontational. Free-flowing. People angry and shouting. Sexual desires unleashed. The lid of the id screwed off—the dismissal of propriety, politeness, properness. "Tell me what you really feel, man. Otherwise, it's bullshit." Each of us in our animal bodies knowing full well that we will die. Why do we put this veil between us? A poster on the wall said, "I do my thing, and you do your thing. If by chance we find each other, it's beautiful." Fritz Perls.

I was angry and scared. Vietnam. Draft lottery #44. Kent State. On edge, a catharsis about to happen. The fourth wall in these sessions, paper-thin. The subject sat in the "hot seat." The professor, a twenty-something bearded protege of Perls, sat alongside the client. The rest of us, scattered on the floor in a semicircle, were summoned to play roles—an evolving psychodrama. The beard's job was to probe, barking questions like, "What are you feeling?" "Where in your body are you feeling it?" "If you could talk to your body, what would it say?" And in the hot seat, if you were unlucky like I was, "Do you want to ball her?" An unfortunate nod from me provoked, "Tell her that you want to ball her." And into the circle stepped Lucy Peterson, a seductive blonde from my American history class. We sat crossed-legged, touching knees. I still feel the sweat. And the shame. It was boot camp. The beard was the sergeant. I never went back and took an incomplete.

In Zephyra's hands, Gestalt's different. Six individual sessions yesterday, each about half an hour long. Her method was simple and straightforward, with limitless permutations. She calls it "open seat" rather than "hot seat." And everyone's eager to participate. Group members were waving their hands and standing in line to sit beside her. She's never confrontational, always gentle but firm. She cuts to the chase, never wastes a millisecond, or lets someone off the hook. All eyes locked on and followed her every gesture, although her every utterance was imperceptible except to the trained ear. I'm convinced she has X-ray vision. She listens with superhuman acuity and, somehow, she engages everyone in the room, even those hidden from view. It's alchemy. She sprinkles magic.

She asks each person the same question, "What's important?" And within minutes, they open up and dig deep. They unleash something uncensored from the underground caverns of their unconscious. They launch into something. She invites them to construct a scene and act it out. Each segment ends with music to seal in the heartfelt content. She draws on a confluence of methods and experiences. She's a sorcerer, and we are under her spell. There's no recipe or protocol. I imagine that sitting in the "open seat" is like looking into a whale's eye. The witness cannot lie. She directs the session like a maestro conducts a symphony—the people in the room, her instruments. Even the most secretive and shy get involved. She's an artist choosing precise color and brush stroke.

And Ned, always at her shoulder, interprets everything she says and performs the physical tasks she cannot. She stages scenes, reenactments of participants' traumas. She calls them "exact moments of healing." There's no obligation to partake. She uses no algorithm. Her direction is never forced. It comes from the gut. Like Fellini, she relies on intuition. Even for those observing, time whizzes by, like reading a novel or watching a film. She's inexhaustible. I never saw her gassed, frustrated, or perplexed. No matter how challenging the material, she maintained a steady keel. She's a savant, a channel, a greater force funneling through her and out to us.

There was never a moment I didn't want more. And it's enough to be here. I don't need to sit in the open seat. Ned wrote on the whiteboard: fear, sadness, anger, disgust, happiness, and surprise. And I'm spiraling through all of them. Astonished at what people share and reveal, my predicament doesn't seem so bad. She listens and reflects on early traumas, personal hurts, betrayals, and humiliations. People trust her and feel safe. They're willing to push far beyond their comfort level. It seems so simple in Zephyra's capable hands. Hands ravaged by Lou Gehrig's disease. Hands that can't grasp a fork.

PJ did her work during the afternoon session. More about that later.

First though, yesterday the damnedest thing happened at the baths. The tide in tight, muscular breakers, smashed like broken eggs on the rocks. Ahead was the new innovative, futuristic bathhouse. Memories flooded in. I remembered the old tubs where Victoria and I first soaked twenty years ago. It was a crude cinderblock building that slid into the ocean during the El Nino winter storms of 1998. I visualized its battered and decaying walls. I could smell that marvelous scent, as pungent and pleasing as sex. Fragrances of the body mixed with steam from the center of the earth and massage oil, an aroma that calls me back like chocolate cake and fresh ground coffee. And there were the sounds. Haunting *kerplunks* and splashes that reverberated and echoed off crude concrete walls. A steadfast *plip-plip-plip-plop-plip-plip-plip-plop* from leaky faucets. The hallucinatory visual, an ever-changing light pattern, scalloped rays of sunshine and moon glow reflecting and shifting. Every time of day was complex, distinctive, and ever-changing. The interior sent off a green hue that flickered like a candle. The floor was wet, slick, and always puddled. Random massage tables nuzzled next to hot tubs. Bodyworkers and clients, both naked, engaged in their craft. The structure was a beast, well past its prime. Old and tawdry, but like a well-worn leather wallet, irreplaceable. Some say it's a blessing that it's gone. But for me, it was a holy place, a hermitage, an asylum, a refuge.

What I remember best are the ceiling and walls. Water-stained, soaked, and streaked. It felt like a biblical cave or cavern, an ancient grotto formed by time, lost in time. Victoria and I observed these blemishes with care. We saw stars and galaxies, dragons, Jesus dancing with Kali, and the love positions of the Kama Sutra. And we came up with a different perception every time. Like Calypso, it was an inkblot test. We saw something distinctive, always contradictory to one another. The Rorschach test-like watermarks were always open to interpretation.

And there is one unforgettable memory that remains above the rest. Two decades ago, on that first visit, Victoria and I observed an act of supreme tenderness. An older man with a graying ponytail waited for a woman his age to enter the next tub. She was draped in a sheet with a towel on her head. She dropped the sheet, exposing a fresh scar, an absent right breast. When she removed the head covering, there wasn't a hair on her head. She lay on her back and surrendered her body to the water. With the intention of lovemaking, his soft hands cradled her head. He hummed, rocking her weightless body, and pulled her through the warm soak. I can't enter the new Calypso bathhouse without seeing those ink blots on the walls and remembering that couple.

The last time Vic and I were here, seven years ago, the old bathhouse was rubble washed into the sea. The hot springs had been relocated to temporary redwood vats on the mesa. It's a narrow flat field situated beneath the mountains. Gone were the magnificent views, but the healing geothermal waters remained. We spent hours and hours soaking. Victoria submerged herself completely. She dunked her head, closed her eyes, took deep breaths, and floated. Full frontal, her breasts and pubis exposed to the sky. The hair on her scalp looked like seaweed wafting in the green water behind her ears. She marinated. Her skin was prune-like, but she refused to withdraw until parboiled. She threatened strangulation to anyone who disturbed her.

For Vic, Calypso is a hideaway, a place to go inward and forgo contact with others. And that's our fundamental difference. I'm outgoing and social. During that visit, I met all comers and greeted Calypso seminarians with a smile, often getting into far-ranging discussions. It irritated her, and I couldn't help myself.

When Conrad first read our natal charts, I asked him if we were compatible.

He replied, "Privacy issues, that's the only obstacle I see."

I said, "I'd kill to be with this woman, but I don't want another divorce."

"Your charts match friendship, love, touch, intimacy, and sex. You're both pagans. You're lucky. You're madly in love, but Victoria doesn't respond to strangers and acquaintances like you do. She lacks your curiosity, and you lack her good judgment. You'll find out. She's fiercely loyal to the people she loves. You shine it on for everyone. She never gets that."

I said, "I want to spend the rest of my life with her. Do we have a chance? How do we make it work?"

He said, "Only if you make the difference conscious and are always aware of it."

"What you're saying is Vic's more highly evolved than me."

"Precisely, and if I were you, I'd get used to it. Tone it down, Neal. You don't need everybody to love you when you've got a woman like Vic."

After that visit to Calypso, I worked on it. Yet how Vic and I balance the disparity remains a mystery. She's very tolerant. Before entering the baths yesterday, I made a pact that I'm going to behave like Vic this time.

As I walked down the hill, my jaw dropped when I saw the new bathhouse. Construction hadn't started seven years ago. It took years of research. After the mudslide, the precarious bluff was too hazardous to support a structure. I cheered a little bit inside as I approached. The Calypso community had fulfilled its ambition to keep the baths at the original site. A sleek, Japanese-influenced, three-story concrete complex rose from the mist. It hugged the cliff where the old bathhouse had slid into the ocean. It was a simple, bare-bones design by local architect Mickey Muennig—organic, sustainable, and built to suit the land. The fragile cliff was fastened to bedrock by a metal net secured by five hundred steel rods. Like Venice's Santa Maria della Salute, where there's a will, there's a way. Native plants, flowers, and shrubs make the topsoil resistant to erosion. It maintains the womb-like feeling like the old sanctuary, unpolished and unadorned.

It has seven group cement tubs. The building is split in two, like before, one side private for silence and meditation. And to my liking, there are individual, porcelain clawfoot bathtubs, like the original. Fiber-optic lighting recreates some of the magical visual effects. Throughout, there's a blending of old and new, combining beauty with function. It's long and sleek like a starship. And like the former, I know it will beckon the sad, discouraged, broken-hearted, and inconsolable to the western edge of the continent. It's fitting that such a unique building encompasses these waters. Waters that will bid the most bashful and displaced to offload their garments. How can anyone resist slipping into these resplendent ablutions unadorned? And yet we know this is the California coast. And this is Big Sur, and no one can predict how long it will last. Wildfires are a permanent fixture. Erosion, mudslides, and soaking rains wash acres of mountainside into the Pacific every year. This coastline is ever-changing, fragile, ever volatile. Big Sur itself is a wave of mud, rocks, stones, and boulders rolling toward the sea.

When I got to the baths, to my delight, the place was empty. I scrubbed and scoured a clawfooted tub, filled it to the brim, and slipped in. Then, out of the corner of my eye, I noticed someone enter the showers. I recognized the walk, how he swung his right leg in a circle and hopped a little with each step. After a few minutes, I placed him. It was the guy at the desk in Palm Springs.

I ignored him and eased into the luscious hot water up to my chin. I closed my eyes and breathed in the pungent sulfur smell. Without hesitation, he approached, leaned over, and said, "I know you."

I said, "Palm Springs."

"You stayed at my ex's place. How's it going?"

"I wish I would've taken that Jack Kerouac peacoat. Froze my ass up there."

He nodded. "Oh yeah, I know what you're talking about." He stood over me, his thin, trim body wrinkled and tan.

I looked up at his yellowed scrotum that hung and sagged very low. Around it sprouted a clump of white and gray hair. His penis was long and limp, pencil-thin, and swung like a pendulum. The circumcised tip touched the farthest wrinkle of his saggy ball sack. Between his skinny legs, I looked beyond to the vast expanse of the Pacific Ocean.

He said, "Have you seen any whales?"

"No, they're out too far today."

He turned, and his schlong slapped his thigh. "The grays are out there. I see a spout right now. Look closer, and you'll see it."

He was right. A couple hundred yards offshore, there was a faint, puffy mist, a fountain on the horizon.

"They're running. Those grays are on their way to warmer waters in the Mexican Baja to birth their young. The grays have those long snouts, you know, a slit for a mouth. They don't have a face. Mind if I jump into this tub next to you?"

He reached his hand into the hot water trough without any response from me and pulled the wooden spool. His tub started to fill. Steam rose from the basin.

He said, "I get down to the baths a couple times a day."

"Wow. You're lucky."

He said, "You'll find there's no such thing as luck. I put myself in this position. I got what I wanted."

I said, "What I meant was, what a lovely ritual."

He ignored me and kept talking. "This is the best time of day. Few people around. Also, it's good first thing in the morning before the sun comes up. People are asleep. They don't know what they're missing. I forgot your name."

"Cornelius, or Neal."

"Now I remember. You checked out early, left in a hurry. Your brother died back east. You're in the medical field, aren't you?"

I nodded.

"I'm Earl, Earl Scarborough. My family's from Maine. We come from a town with the same name, Scarborough, south of Portland. That's how you can remember. Ever hear of it?"

I shook my head.

He slipped into the tub.

I said, "Isn't that too hot? Aren't you going to add some cold water?"

"No, never do. Sometimes I bathe in the trough. Mother nature intended it this way. These thermal waters emerge straight out of the earth. They have healing properties."

I said, "You could boil an egg…"

"You could if it hadn't been sitting in the trough all night getting cold. Right now, it's no more than a hundred and four degrees. Ideal. You should try it. Now, where was I?"

"Scarborough."

"Oh, yes. It was first settled in 1635. I graduated from Scarborough High, joined the army, and never looked back. I've burned some rubber on these tires." He raised both feet out of the tub, balancing on his butt, and pointed at his feet. Other than a few ropy varicose veins, they looked healthy, supple, and bronze. No ankle edema.

He said, "They're almost bald, but I'm making the best of it every day. Nothing else you can do. I could tell you some stories about this place."

I said, "I've heard a few."

He hesitated, sat forward in the tub. A smoky mist settled along the cliff. "Has anyone told you about Lew Diamond?"

"Isn't he one of the founders?"

"There's a lot more to know about Lew than that."

"I read about him in the catalog."

"First thing you need to know, you wouldn't be sitting here if it weren't for Lew. And second, the catalog's a sales pitch, a contradiction to Lew's work. He was a non-commercial operator, wild and free. Not a tame bone in his body." He shifted and leaned toward me. "It's not all the Board's fault. They're trying to make a go of this place. Lew still resides in the land. Most of the people who live and work here don't know the extent of Lew's influence."

"Did you know him?"

"We weren't pals, but I was living here when he died."

"What happened?"

"Nobody knows for sure. A boulder struck him in the head. He was alone." Earl turned away from the ocean and pointed to the cliffs behind us. "He was hiking up there. We recovered his body at the Source."

"The Source?"

"The reservoir where Calypso gets its water. It's a mile up the canyon. Most likely, Lew was up there checking it out."

"How long ago?"

"The Tuesday before Thanksgiving. November 25, 1985."

"That's almost twenty-five years ago."

Earl reflected, picked up a can of shaving cream, lathered his face, and swiped a decisive track across his right cheek. He used an old-fashioned, double-edged razor like a surgical instrument, then worked his chin in the other direction with short strokes.

I said, "You don't use a mirror?"

"Don't need one. Gets in the way. Why complicate things? Is there anything more luxurious than sitting in a hot thermal bath, shaving?"

I said, "I don't think so. It's pretty awesome. I haven't seen a double-edged safety razor since I was a kid. My father used one. I nicked myself every time."

"Takes practice. Lew said good therapy is like a mirror, a reflection. He didn't give advice or counseling. Said it didn't work. Somebody else can't force you to grow up. It's something you've got to do yourself. This week, they're celebrating Calypso's fiftieth anniversary, and I'm going to the reception tonight. All the big wigs will be there. It's by invitation only. I don't shave every day. When you get to my age, it doesn't matter. Nobody notices. He stroked his face upward with his palms. "Thought I'd make an attempt. You going to breakfast?"

"I'm in no hurry."

Earl kept shaving. Every stroke was clean and unambiguous. He had a steady hand that never wavered.

I added more hot water and settled back. The sunrise illuminated the horizon in soft, pearly light. The steel-blue sea looked icy, and a stiff, cold breeze raised goosebumps on my arms. Whitecaps battered the rocks.

He said, "I was one of the guys who carried Lew down the mountain." Then he stood, added more water, sat back, and put a white washcloth over his eyes. His cheeks reddened, and steam rose from his forehead. "I forget so much these days, but I remember that day better than what I had for lunch. It was drizzling, and there was dense fog in the morning that cleared in the afternoon. The sky was full of big, puffy clouds. You know the kind I mean that look like dragons and angels? You can't tell which. Lew took off up the canyon, some say, but I'm not sure, to check the waterlines at the Source. He loved to hike. He missed a meeting that afternoon. It wasn't unusual for him to disappear for hours or even overnight. He knew what he was doing. Nobody worried about him. He'd bushwhacked most of the trails around here. He was always dirty and dusty with a big smile, covered in sweat. That summer, the Rat Creek Fire damn near burned Calypso down. Lew won the battle to save Calypso, but it devastated the mountain.

"All the ground cover and underbrush were charred and blistered, the bare earth baked like wax. Only the redwood trees remained. Those redwoods are the heartiest thing on earth. Scorched and burned, they come back. When the rains came, there were debris flows. Boulders the size of buses got loose. The mud was so slippery you couldn't get anchored and take a step. That's what got Lew. Some say he was meditating up there. I don't know what happened. In that environment, anything's possible. When it got dark, a couple guys went up the canyon to look for him. They found him at the Source, half-sitting, slumped in the water. His muscles were stiff. What do you call that?"

"Rigor mortis."

"Well, he'd been dead a long time. That takes a couple hours, doesn't it?"

I said, "Three or four hours."

"There was no rescue attempt. There was nothing anybody could do. Lew was dead. They came down the mountain and told his wife, Valerie. She rounded up a group to recover him. The moon was pink, and the creek was running full. It was treacherous, wet, and slippery. Cobble and unstable rocks made it very slow. We followed the creek bed, and the barbequed spiky redwoods looked spooky. You could still smell the ash and charcoal. When we got there, Lew had a bloody gash across his face and skull. There were cuts and bruises on the backs of his hands. We wrapped him in a blanket. It was tough going carrying him down the ravine. By the time we got to his house, it was three o'clock in the morning. Valerie and the women were waiting. They stripped, washed, and anointed his body, and the next day, the entire community mourned. Everybody packed into his little house. His body was on the bed, covered by a beautiful alpaca blanket."

Earl halted, and we both sat back. A cold wind whipped across my shoulders. The water in my tub was getting cold. I opened the valve and let more hot water in, and mixed it with my hands.

I asked, "How old was Lew?"

"Fifty-five. Still very fit, robust, and wiry. He'd been a wrestler in high school. Lew was still building stone walls and clearing brush. The land was vital to him, and he was developing his Gestalt work. He studied here with Fritz Perls. Lew had the vision. Calypso's big business now. It's lost something. But he's still alive in little ways around here and in the land. I hope Calypso never loses that."

I asked, "Is that why there's that sign at the creek?"

"Yeah, it's fenced off, so seminarians won't go up there."

"Can I hike up there?"

"Not anymore, although Lew encouraged it. Where else you gonna experience the silence of those tall coastal redwoods? The administration got paranoid after he died."

"I'd like to go up there."

He said, "It's not hard to get around the fence. Nobody will stop you."

"I thought you said it's dangerous."

"That's the point. Lew died up there."

"But that was after a wildfire."

"I guess you'll be fine. It's up to you. The sign is there. Calypso's covered if you get hurt."

"Yeah, the sign says, 'Do not go beyond this point.' "

"That's the only restricted area on the property. Otherwise, there are no limitations." His eyes twinkled.

I said, "It doesn't look too dangerous."

"Everybody used to hike up there when Lew was alive."

"But it's a little dangerous?"

He nodded.

I asked, "Do you still go up there?"

"Not anymore. Not anymore." He shook his head and shimmied. "I'll be honest with you. My balance isn't reliable. Fallen trees, narrow passes, and steep drops three or four hundred feet to the creek are unimaginable for me to navigate. Also, there's a ladder near the top I can't climb anymore. But if I could, I would. That's part of the whole Calypso experience Lew envisioned, like these baths. I've been up there many times. It takes a good part of the afternoon to go up and back. After my knee replacement, it wasn't a good idea anymore. I've learned to accept my limitations. How about you? You think you'll venture up there?"

"I'd like to do it."

"Take someone with you."

"Don't you think it's better if I do it like Lew, solo?"

"It's up to you. Lew is still here. He's alive in the land. That'd be as good a place as any to find him."

More frigid air from the ocean shifted into the baths. A smoky fog curled its fingertips and mingled out to sea. The bathhouse was empty.

He said, "Lew didn't do things by the book."

I said, "Did he write a book?"

"No. Said he never would. Calypso's Lew's book. You're reading it now."

When the bathhouse began to fill with people, I bid Earl adieu, showered, dressed, and hiked up the hill to the lodge. Breakfast was over, so I spread almond butter and honey on brown bread, went outside, and sat by the fire pit.

An energetic couple in their sixties were playing covers on a guitar and accordion. A small group gathered and sang along. It felt like summer camp with songs by Joni Mitchell, Neil Young, the Beatles, and the Rolling Stones. The couple knew every request.

A weather-beaten hipster with a crate drum sat in and slapped out the rhythm. The couple acknowledged him with a playful nod. Her accordion and his guitar got juicier. The guitar man stood and sang, turning up his volume to a leathery shout. The drummer called out, "Squeeze Box," and The Who's 1975 classic came to life, including Pete Townshend's deft fingerpicking. Although not Roger Daltry, the guitarist's raspy cat call rang true. She crushed the chords with chubby fingers. Everyone was on their feet, clapping and laughing. The morning glow of the fire licked our faces. It was fun thinking about them making love, and this was the closest thing. Years peeled away. Ocean swells heaved in the background. She adored him with her eyes, and he strummed the rhythm with an electric vigor. Her sexy, square hips swayed like an enchantress.

Then it was on to Zephyra's morning session, where the energy was low. The tribe had sunk into a sluggish, distracted, and inattentive mood. Ned cued a song, and we stood, circled, and held hands. It started quiet and slow—a haunting melody, catchy guitar lick, and lyric. I'd never heard the tune before but recognized David Crosby's angelic tenor. A wrenching, sad song about family angst.

Zephyra entered, Gloria and Sally trailing like bridesmaids. Her hair was pulled away from her face and rested on her shoulders. She rocked a bright yellow silk blouse and gold dangle earrings. Her ever-active green eyes shifted from face to face.

Zephyra was beaming.

Jerry shouted from across the room, "Turn it up," at which point the vocal, on its own, gathered momentum. A noisier, whining electric guitar joined in. The volume increased from a whisper to ear-shattering rock and roll. Jerry adjusted his hearing aid and said, "OK, OK, that's enough." Crosby's voice leaned hard into the lyric. People knew the song and started gesturing and dancing in lockstep. The piece was invoking a riot to rebuke the heartbreak inflicted by family. The bass, drums, electric guitar, and piano cranked up to full volume, and my ears were aching. It was like we were drunk. Everybody stomped their feet and joined into what became an impulsive hoedown. Everyone sang along, gesturing in playful and defiant ways. On request, Ned played it again. Everybody was on their feet dancing and skipping. Sweat, enthusiasm, and laughter filled the room. What started with a faint ticking exploded like a bomb.

Zephyra grinned. Her white upper teeth exposed her pink gum line, and she raised her chin like a mother bear sniffing. She circled the room with her eyes, determining the emotional temperature of the room. She leaned back and dropped awkwardly like a rag doll into Ned's chest and open arms with his biceps placed in her armpits so he could support and direct her weight like a forklift. With some effort, he guided her into the chair. She sat with a thud, and he arranged her limbs and frame. She nodded when she was comfortable. He placed a Lavalier microphone that extended from her right ear across her face. Zephyra winced, and Sally rushed forward. Her pendulous right earring tugged at her earlobe. Sally repositioned it, brushed Zephyra's hair back with her hand, and primed and straightened Zephyra's clothes. Ned checked the sound system.

Then the scene froze.

Zephyra turned and looked at Ned and, in her slurred brogue, growled something about rock and roll.

Ned said with a smile, "Zephyra said, 'He's the rock. I'm the roll.'"

The group roared.

She added another garbled sentence, "I give new meaning to the term, 'high maintenance woman.'"

The atmosphere was now supercharged, giddy, playful, and receptive, and PJ leaped with a single bound into the open seat.

Zephyra welcomed PJ with a nod and a smile, her right eyebrow raised. The two stared at one another for a few uncomfortable breaths. PJ shivered, like she was sitting on a cold rock on the windswept beach below. Until then, I hadn't assessed PJ's brevity of stature. She always seemed larger than life. I knew she was five foot four and weighed a hundred and fourteen pounds. I'd prescribed subcutaneous injections based on her body weight. But at this juncture, she shrank and curled into herself. She seemed tiny, like a child. Her long, auburn hair wrapped around her shoulders. Her slim, athletic body was trembling like a chihuahua.

The back of my neck tingled. I leaned forward and noticed others do the same. The surf hammered the cliff below, crows and seagulls squawked above. Everything slowed down, becoming close and still.

"What's important?"

PJ attempted a painful grin and, in a faint, child-like voice, said, "That's my song. I knew I had to come up here."

Zephyra said, "Your hands, they're frozen."

PJ looked down at her clenched fists.

Zephyra turned to Ned, who lifted her forearms and placed her feeble hands on PJ's.

PJ opened her palms and began to cry.

Zephyra looked into PJ's eyes. Her own eyes welling with tears, she slumped forward and said, "I want to be right in step with you. Me, understanding what you need. You know more than anyone what you need."

PJ said, "I hate my body."

"What do you need to further move through this?"

PJ hesitated. "I trusted someone. I'm not sure I want to talk about it. It's over. It's behind me. Nobody really cares."

Zephyra said, "Look around the room. What do you see?"

PJ raised her head and looked around.

People nodded with approval.

Dan shouted, "We love you, PJ. We care."

A soothing, calming hum passed around the circle. People leaned forward with interest. It felt like the scene from *The Wizard of Oz* when Dorothy wakes from her dream.

PJ laughed, broke into a smile, and said, "People care. I'm still not sure I want to talk about it. What am I doing up here?"

Zephyra said, "Do you want to fill us in on what's going on?"

PJ started to shake again. Her face was blotched and reddening. When she tried to speak, she was mute. Her nose ran, and she blotted it with a Kleenex.

Zephyra waited.

PJ said in a very soft voice, "I'm not sure." Her belly and chest pumped like a sprinter crossing the finish line. She exploded, raised her arms. The bangles on her wrist clattered and rattled like wind chimes in a tornado. She screeched, "I was violated, humiliated by two men! Just because I have this body, does that mean I'm not smart? Does that mean I don't get the same chances? Does that mean I can't compete? I don't want to have babies. At least not now. I don't want to stand behind some man and be a good wife. I want my own life, my career for me."

Zephyra raised her chin and glanced at Ned. He placed Zephyra's hands back on PJ's. Zephyra said, "Do you want to tell us what happened?"

"Isn't that what I just did? Aren't I finished? I've only told one other person. Not my therapist, my parents, my girlfriends."

Zephyra lifted her head, squared her shoulders. "This should never have happened. Tell us whatever details you like."

PJ said, "I'm a student at MIT. At least I was until I got sick. I got a blood clot in my lung when I flew home in December. I'm here now at Calypso, doing work-study. Well, that's all well and fine, not important. Last year was my first year in New England.

My parents live in Santa Barbara. I liked everything about Boston, even the shitty weather."

People chuckled.

"There was a professor, Jim, I liked, and this is probably all my fault. I talked to him after class and sat in the front row. I wore tight dresses, didn't wear a bra. Did my hair up. I know I looked good. It was a comparative literature class. I'm a scientist. I'd never read Walt Whitman, Emily Dickinson, Pablo Neruda, and I didn't see what it had to do with me until I got to MIT. I adored the class, loved his voice and his enthusiasm for the subject. He's Poldark handsome, an up-and-comer in his mid-thirties with a wife and two small children. I don't know what I was thinking. I felt sexy when I was around him. I didn't know if he would do anything, or I would. I had a couple dreams about him. And fantasies. We flirted. I had a steady boyfriend from high school. We were exclusive, still dating."

There wasn't so much as a flicker of movement in the room. Everything had stopped, everyone holding their breath. I heard an old clock ticking on the wall.

"It all went down the week before Thanksgiving. My parents were in Europe. My boyfriend was coming to Boston to spend a few days. Midterms were over, and the professor asked if I wanted to stop by his office and celebrate. Nobody was in the building. You could hear your feet clomp on the shiny marble floor. He pulled out a bottle of bourbon from behind one of his bookshelves. We did shots and got pretty drunk. Then he kissed me. I kissed him back. We made out for a while, and I said, 'What about your wife and kids?' He said, 'Don't worry about them.' I knew it was escalating and tried to leave. I pushed him away, but he was too strong. I said, 'Enough, enough. I have to go.' He pushed me on my back onto his desk. I was wearing a knee-length wool skirt. He shoved it up to my waist and pulled my thong to the side, and thrust himself inside of me. He was too determined.

Too strong. There was nothing I could do. He came fast. I hit him in the chest and pushed him off. Then I slapped him as hard as I could across the face. He grimaced and smiled, and said, 'Tell your boyfriend I was the first one to fuck you this holiday season.' I grabbed my things and left his office. I felt defiled. But I was there by my own volition. I accepted the invitation and the drinks. I flirted with him. He made me hot. It was my fault."

She stopped and looked out the window and made her mouth small. "But this isn't the worst of it."

Tears streamed down Zephyra's cheeks.

"My boyfriend showed up as planned. I picked him up at Logan. I told him what happened, and he flipped out. Said he wanted to kick the shit out of Jim. Also, he was angry at me. Called me a slut. I wouldn't give him any more details like the professor's name. When we went to bed, he insisted that I blow him and swallow his cum. I never liked oral sex. Maybe I never will. It's always been an issue for us. Turns out, it was much worse than anticipated, a big mouthful of vile jizz. I brushed my teeth for weeks. I can still taste it. When I complied, he treated me more like a whore. Like he'd lost all respect for me. There was nothing sweet or loving. He bossed me around. He couldn't get over what had happened between the professor and me. He pouted. It was more like it had happened to him. He approached me like I was just a thing, a body, a piece of property, nothing more. I was only there for his use. There was no compassion. No friendship. No love. He was hateful and cruel. At the same time, he wanted to assault the professor, not to protect me but to save face for himself. To take revenge on another caveman who had violated his property. We broke up. I shipped him out as soon as I could. We haven't talked since. I don't think he knows I'm here or that I've been sick. I finished my classes, including the lit class, and put it behind me. I balkanized my feelings and started cutting myself. That's when they put me on an antidepressant. Then I got a blood clot."

The room grew very still and silent. People in the circle sat closer and some hugged, others held hands. Zephyra motioned to PJ and whispered something in her ear. PJ nodded.

Zephyra announced, "This should never have happened." She had a repugnant look on her face. She said, "PJ's willing to work with it."

The room heaved like the ocean outside and swelled. Coal-black wings flashed by the window, and the relentless crows shrieked. A cormorant plunged deep into the brine.

Zephyra said, "I'm looking for someone to be the professor. Do I have another volunteer to be PJ's ex?"

Hands went up slowly, including mine. I was reluctant to get into the fray. I felt numb, anesthetized, dumbfounded. The other seven men in the group enthusiastically raised their hands. I raised my right palm from my hip, hoping to go unnoticed.

PJ pointed and said, "Neal, you be Jim."

I looked at her with confusion.

She said, "The professor."

It was a punch to the gut, and my heart sank as a chill went up my spine. I stood, then felt faint, like all the blood had rushed to my feet.

She chose a young man across the room named Ernesto to be her ex.

Everything sped up, a whirlwind of commotion as if people and things were flying around the room. Zephyra barked instructions. Ned and Sally lifted her chair to the side. Jerry and Dan scurried across the room. They pulled several gray, plastic-coated mattresses off the stack and summoned others to help. The cushions were turned sideways to create a chest-high barrier. Four men held it in place. Jerry and Dan demonstrated how to use a wide stance, like a boxer, to brace it. PJ stood on the other side. Zephyra signaled for Ernesto and me to come forward on the other side. I felt like a Christian martyr stepping into the Roman Colosseum. People jeered at us, "You dirty bastards. Rapists. You suck. You assholes. Sons of bitches. Blow yourself. You liars. Perps." It was a tribunal. Disparaging epithets were flung from every corner of the room. Ernesto, a slight, short, thirty-two-year-old Filipino, stood next to me. I towered over him. My breaths came fast and shallow. He had done work earlier in the day about whether he should continue with his career in pharmacy or go back to school. He wanted to be a doctor.

Zephyra looked at PJ and said, "Is there anything you need to say to them?"

PJ wrinkled her brow and looked at her feet. "I'm not sure."

Ned shouted, "Make sounds."

PJ grunted, snorted, and let out a whimpering wail.

Dan yelled, "You can do better than that."

Her cheeks and temples flushed, and she let out a blood-curdling scream. "Fuck you! God damn bastards. Mother fuckers. You took something. I trusted you."

The crowd joined in.

Zephyra and Ned egged her on. "That's it. That's it. Let it out. Make noise."

PJ's rage concentrated like fluid out of the head of a hypodermic needle. It was like watching a locomotive gathering speed in slow motion. Her voice went raspy, then hoarse.

Zephyra repeated, "Make noise."

Ned said, "Let us hear you."

The crowd joined in.

A bellow rolled out of her belly. Indignation upwelled through her hips and boomed into her chest. She howled. It was primal, buried deep in her body. She punched the cushion, stormed against it with her shoulder, kicking it with her feet. The men on the other side offered firm resistance. She delivered steady and repeated blows until she fell to her knees in exhaustion. Then she got up and made a run at it from six feet, pointing her shoulder as if knocking down a door. The mattress buckled and pushed the men back.

Zephyra, Ned, and the group implored her to do it again. This time, from ten feet away.

The group continued a constant verbal attack on Ernesto and me, "Bastards. Go suck yourself off. How dare you. Pigs. Narcissists. Men!"

The feisty, little eighty-year-old I met the first night, Lucille from Grover Beach, yelled from the back of the room, "Feckle those feckless fuckers. De-man them. Cut off their balls."

The mattress and men were the only boundaries between Ernesto and me. And it wasn't the physical assault but PJ's outrage that terrified me. It felt like the fury of all women was unleashed in a tidal wave of repugnance, loathing, and disgust. An entire gender locked and loaded.

PJ pushed harder, and the mattress got closer. It was a reckoning. Her outrage drove us back.

Neither Ernesto nor I spoke a word. I waited for a signal, but none was forthcoming.

PJ and the crowd were in a lather. Zephyra was locked into PJ's every blow, as if she were beating the mattress herself. Her head bobbed and weaved like I've seen trainers do when they scrutinize a boxer in the ring. She wasn't paying any attention to us. For Zephyra, the only person in the room was PJ.

The mob continued to jeer, "Assholes. Pigs. Fuckers. How dare you? You'll pay for this."

PJ's elbows and arms flailed at the cushion. She was getting stronger, her blows and kicks gaining strength and accuracy.

Everybody knew it was a setup, but the emotions were real, and my body reacted. I felt panic, made fists, and tightened my abdominal muscles. My shoulders hunched and stiffened. It felt like I was wearing a suit of armor. Then PJ's eyes, white with rage, met mine. I became her oppressor, my body under siege, attacked. No blows were exchanged, but I was ready. PJ kept coming, more determined, more strong-willed. Her face was wet with sweat and tears of rage. And her energy was relentless. I had no idea where this was going and my sense was, Zephyra didn't either. It was improvisational, a moment-to-moment decision. Part play-acting, part real. It felt like we were climbing a tree, and the branches were getting smaller and smaller the farther we got out. Eventually, one would break.

Then Ned cocked his head and whispered in Jerry's ear. And Jerry sent the message down the line. In unison, the men offered less resistance, not all at once but in small increments. PJ gathered momentum, encouraged by the crowd. She pushed harder. Then, I heard a piercing scream. It was tiny Lucille, waving her arms, who shrieked, "No mercy. Kill the bastards." The barricade moved forward in a herky-jerky manner and drove all of us back. PJ shoved with all her might. The mattress was now on Ernesto's chest, and I was holding it with both hands.

The guys were gone, dispossessed. We were an army of two in full retreat. It felt like we were on an ice floe about to go over Niagara Falls. PJ shoved harder. I stumbled as I stepped back but didn't fall. The mob shouted, and she pushed us twenty feet toward the back door. Lucille opened and slammed the door behind us.

A roar went up, then a cascade of applause. I lost my balance on the top step and started falling backward. Ernesto caught me, preventing me from tumbling down the uneven stone steps. He looked at me and said, "What do we do now, Professor?" We chuckled and put our noses to the window. Lucille waved us away. Shunned from the room of pillows and Kleenex boxes, we sat on the steps with our backs to the door. The babbling rush from the nearby waterfall echoed in our ears. Ernesto squatted beside me with his elbows on his knees. A few minutes later (that felt like an eternity), Lucille opened the door and said, "It's time to de-role."

Ernesto and I walked back in. It was a beehive, and the class was whirling around, chatting, exchanging hugs, and high-fives. Nobody noticed our presence. In a loud voice, Ned called for everyone's attention. He looked into PJ's eyes, then mine, and said, "PJ, this is Neal. Neal is no longer playing a role." He did the same for Jason. And then he thanked us. Zephyra growled, "This is a gift. Thank you for providing this for PJ." More applause, and PJ grinned and looked down at her feet, sweating, exhausted, embarrassed, but lighter, less burdened, a glow around her face. The group gathered around her. Ned motioned for everyone to come in closer until we formed a snug cocoon. No one remained outside the circle. I lost sight of PJ, smothered by two dozen bodies.

The entire assemblage commenced swaying from side to side, then forward and back, like a kelp forest rocking in seawater. It was gentle and soothing. I let go of my feet. All shapes and sizes, ages, religions, and races moved like a wave in the shallows, a massive group embrace with PJ buried at its center.

A slow, steady tune came across the sound system. I recognized it, the post-sixties folk ballad, "You Take My Breath Away."

Lucille shouted out, "Lift."

Like an ant colony forming a chain, we located on each side of PJ. Jerry showed PJ how to cross her arms, holding her shoulders. Lucille positioned herself behind PJ's head. Dan reached out and grabbed my wrists, and motioned for me to do the same. We formed a sturdy net. PJ leaned back. Others supported the rest of PJ's body down to her feet. Lifting her to waist level was easy. She floated before us like a magician's trick.

Zephyra barked, "Float her." And this time, I understood her without interpretation.

We lifted PJ above our heads.

She purred and giggled and said, "I like it. I could get used to this."

Ned said, "Take this in, PJ. Don't talk. Feel it."

PJ started to whimper.

I wondered what it was like up there. Her eyes were so close to the ceiling. She hung like a hot air balloon over us, feather-light, supported by dozens of fingertips and hands. And while she floated, the song hit home, the voice so delicate and fragile, and at the same time, so strong. It wasn't the words but the expression. The vocalist reached the top notes with no effort—a bright and ringing tone like a songbird with throaty clarity and precision. Under different circumstances, the tune might have seemed sentimental and maudlin. Or if it came on the radio, I wouldn't have heard it at all. But here and now, I was utterly overwhelmed. So many different emotions flooded in. I glanced at Zephyra, and she greeted me and lowered her forehead. There were puddles in her eyes. She mouthed and emoted each word.

PJ's session floored me, and that was only the beginning of the afternoon. Zephyra transitioned to the next person without a break. Five more people sat in the open seat. Five more gazed into Zephyra's eyes. Songs played, tears were shed, rage and anger were discharged. Laughs and hugs were exchanged.

It reminded me of a story I'd heard about a Tibetan woman, a healer, who stood on a mountaintop. People with all forms of illness, disease, and infirmity came from hundreds of miles around. They formed a procession and waited in long lines. I can only imagine this is what it's like to be Zephyra. Herself infirm, she takes on others' complicated, confusing, and unarticulated feelings. Like a midwife, she delivers people back to themselves. We all carry so much. No one is immune. I felt like I knew PJ. I'd seen her in the clinic. We'd talked on the phone. But I had no idea what she was going through. Her pulmonary embolus was a small part of it. How little I offered or addressed as a medical professional. I've never seen anything like it—the ineffable Zephyra in her prime. No wonder I couldn't sleep. I felt an opening for PJ and also a fresh start for me.

# 12 JANUARY, PREDAWN
## (CALYPSO INSTITUTE, BIG SUR, CA)

*"Don't hide the madness."*
Allen Ginsberg (1926-1997)

WOKE UP SOBBING IN THE darkness, shaking with a chill. I looked out the window, still black as coal. I flailed and pulled my blanket up. My T-shirt was cold and sticky. Disoriented, I vocalized in a husky whisper, "Mick is dead. Mick is dead." A frosty reverie consumed me, and my spine turned to ice. I couldn't untangle myself. "Mick is dead. Mick is dead." I spiraled into madness. How many years? When did it start? He snorted cocaine in high school. When did he lose his job? When did he stop cheffing? When did he stop functioning? Both my parents drank and put up a good front. They fooled people until the end.

What about those frantic phone calls day and night? Conflict with Victoria? He'd attended AA meetings and said he quit drinking. I'd numbered the days and congratulated him on earning a sobriety chip. I went to Al-Anon. He'd start drinking again. Then last year, everything was suspended. There were seven months when he disappeared into a coma, supported by machines, awaiting a liver transplant, the only time he was free from alcohol. I didn't give up. I consulted his nurses, interns, residents, and doctors, and no heroics could save him. All said the same thing, "He'll die if he doesn't stop drinking."

And while Mick drank his therapy, how many seasons did I spend on a shrink's couch? I thought about him all the time. How many friends did I burden? And strangers? Like the "Ancient Mariner," I cornered anyone who'd listen. My anxiety was palpable, seeping into every aspect of my life.

Mick is dead. Mick is dead.

It was the graveyard of night when I slid down from my bunk, changed T-shirts, and pulled on some sweats. I tripped over Ed's boots. No one woke, the monotonous drone of snores steadfast like a chorus of cicadas. Outside, it was drizzling, and a fine mist covered my glasses. I scrambled down the hill to the baths.

Relentless black waves cracked the shore like a whip. A faint, pungent odor charged the air. I drew it in, even welcomed it, and found it pleasant at first, like wet ferns and dank earth. When I recognized it was a skunk, I picked up my step. The bathhouse was empty, and a trickle of water plunked like a metronome. The frosty air made me shiver. I stripped and hopped into the shower. The hot water ran down my back, and steam rose from my shoulders. I leaned forward with both palms on the wall and soaked my hair. My skin, covered with goosebumps, became smooth and flattened.

I wept like a child with convulsive sobs. My belly heaved with each ocean swell. A voice in me said, "Why are you bawling? Get over it. What if someone hears you?" As if I could get outside my body and control its actions. Then it felt like I was watching someone else. I let myself blubber. I cried for my brother. For his affliction. For his loneliness. Why did he have to suffer so? Why couldn't I protect him? My baby brother with long, golden curls and a magic smile. I cried for PJ, for Zephyra, for all the heartache in the workshop. For the river of wretchedness that flows through all of us. I wept for myself. I cried for the whole goddamned world.

And in walked Earl. Startled, I turned to greet him. He dipped in and out of a shower and slid away like a vapor without acknowledging me. As if to say, *Whatever you're doing, keep doing it. Pay me no mind. I appreciate and respect your privacy.*

I felt embarrassed and ashamed. Did anybody else hear me? Public bathing is over at 3 a.m., and Earl had arrived for his ablutions. I presumed it was close to five. The sun comes up late over the mountains. I felt disoriented and moved through the baths with caution. The stone surface was wet and slippery. Most of the tubs were empty, and Earl lounged in the thermal trough behind the single porcelain tubs. He had a washcloth over his forehead and eyes. I advanced to the northernmost end of the bathhouse, naked except for a towel over my right shoulder. "The Point," an enormous, elliptical-shaped stone vat, was full to the brim. It shimmered in the predawn darkness. A warm, foggy cloud rose from its surface. A lone, dark figure, her back to me, was perched on the other side, staring out at the ocean. The Point hangs precariously from the jagged cliff and seats ten, but I've seen as many as twenty people frolicking in it. I slid in.

The warm, piquant smell entered my nostrils and calmed me like a drug. I leaned back and soaked, closed my eyes, and dunked my head. When I sat up, I noticed the swells were smaller. The ocean was flat, and the sky was beginning to clear. Mars appeared first, then Venus. The outline of the kelp forest emerged. Otters paddled on their backs as others slept. I heard a lone seal bark. A colony of seagulls squawked along the cliff. One flew so close I felt the draft of its wings. The air was salty and damp. I started to make out the features of the person across from me. Her body was twisted at the waist. She rested her arms and head on the stone ledge and remained motionless as if she were asleep. We didn't speak. Gentle waves lapped the shore. Ten minutes into my soak, still with her back to me, a voice emerged.

"Can you believe that ninety percent of these gulls have guts full of plastic?"

It was PJ.

Both of us stark naked, I felt like Adam after God threw him out of Paradise. My first instinct was to cover myself. It was dark, and the sun was coming up. What to do? I'd experienced the Calypso tubs many times with women—some I knew, others strangers. There's apathy to gender and nudity here, something I treasure, and it gets your head on straight about sex and the autonomy of what it is to be a human being. But this was a little much. PJ was my patient, and after the downpour of her emotions in the session, I wanted to run. And where my reaction came from, I don't know. And I'm grateful. In a calm tone, I answered, "Ninety percent? I wasn't aware it was that high."

PJ startled, gulped. "Neal? I thought you were Earl."

I said, "No, Earl's over there," and pointed to the thermal trough where he reclined.

With an embarrassed lilt in her voice, she said, "You're up early."

I said, "You too."

"I like to hang out here after the townies leave. What's your excuse?"

"Couldn't sleep. Aren't gulls omnivores? They eat everything and can even drink salt water."

"They can't digest plastic. Their bellies become full of it, and they die. Earl and I were talking about it yesterday. There's a hundred million tons of plastic in the ocean. Between here and Hawaii, there's a swirling dump twice the size of Texas. Seabirds are going extinct."

"I've heard about it."

"The gulls eat plastic because it smells like food. Like the dimethyl sulfide released by algae." She continued to look out to the sea. The edge of the moon was peeking through a smoky black cloud. After ten or fifteen minutes, she stood, then sat on the stone ledge and said, "It's getting pretty hot."

I said, "Earl hasn't budged."

We glanced in that direction.

She said, "He's got skin like leather."

I said, "And a ball sack like a buffalo."

She snorted.

We both laughed.

She eased back into the tub and said, "I heard yesterday that you're going to work with Zephyra."

"Yeah, Ned said they could open up a spot for me."

"You gonna do it?"

"Not sure."

She shifted and pulled her hair into a ponytail. Her wrist bangles jangled, and she said, "You think I should have said that stuff about my ex? About oral sex?"

I said, "What you did was amazing. It sucks that happened."

She frowned and looked back out into the ocean.

I said, "That's not what I meant. I'm sorry. It's awful and terrible."

She said, "Weird. I'm thinking about it. A little embarrassed but feeling better, less burdened. Did I divulge too much?"

"You dared to get up there. I'm not sure I can do that. It helped everybody. What's it like up there?"

"Floating?"

I nodded and said, "OK, start there. What's it like?"

"At first, I couldn't let go. My shirt was riding up my back, and I was sweating like a pig. I felt fat. Then Ned said, 'Breathe your deepest breath.' Something in me halted. I let go, like during a massage or yoga class. It ended much too soon once I got into it."

"Did you ever feel like we'd drop you?"

"No. But first, my feelings were all over the place, and they still are. Getting into the seat was hard. I went on my gut. The song and the mood of the room were right."

"What was it like to sit there with everyone watching you?"

She said, "I was self-conscious at first. Then I forgot about everyone. I trusted Zephyra and let go."

"What about that amazing song at the end?"

"I couldn't believe it. My mother sang that to me when I was a kid."

I said, "That's too much of a coincidence. How did Zephyra know?"

"She didn't. Random, I guess. She reads minds."

I stretched out and leaned back and said, "I've heard the song before but can't place it. But never like that. An English folk singer named Claire something wrote it."

She said, "Claire Hamill."

"Yes, that's it. How did you know?"

"I grew up on this stuff."

I said, "I heard Claire Hamill sing it. There were about fifty people at a place called The Flick, a coffee house in Coral Gables. All the greats played there—Joni Mitchell, Jimmy Buffett, Jerry Jeff Walker. John Sebastian, David Crosby, and Tim Buckley. I heard Dion, Peter, Paul and Mary, and John Denver at The Flick. A bunch of acts you've never heard of."

She said, "I know them all. How about Donovan? Did you see Donovan?"

I laughed. "Donovan Leitch?" I always liked to say his full name. It was a running joke in my college dorm. "I did. Not at The Flick, but at an outdoor concert on campus."

"My mom had the *Sunshine Superman* LP and all Donovan's albums. I sang 'Sunshine Superman' when I was a toddler. I can play it on the guitar."

"That's a pretty intricate guitar riff at the beginning."

"It's fun. I can fingerpick. My parents almost named me Saffron."

"Like in 'Mellow Yellow?' "

I tapped out the beat, and she joined in. "I'm just mad about Saffron / Saffron's mad about me / I'm just mad about Saffron / She's just mad about me."

She said, "That's the one. They decided instead to name me after my grandmother."

I hummed and started to sing, "Superman or Green Lantern baby ain't got a-nothin' on me…"

She responded, "I can make like a turtle and dive for your pearls in the sea, yeah…"

We sang together, "A you-you-you can just sit there a-thinking on your velvet throne. / 'Bout all the rainbows a-you can a-have for your own / When you've made your mind up forever to be mine / I'll pick up your hand and slowly blow your little mind / When you've made your mind up forever to be mine."

PJ said, "I love it. I sang that with my father at bedtime."

I said, "Kind of like your version of Dr. Seuss."

"That's it."

"What about the song when we floated you?"

" 'You Take My Breath Away.' That's Eva Cassidy."

I said, "I've never heard of her. I can't get her voice out of my head. It's so raw and emotional."

"She only performed material that meant something to her. It's a crazy story. A couple years after she died, a BBC disc jockey started playing her songs and she became a superstar in England. She never signed a record contract while she was alive. Nobody'd heard of her outside the club circuit in DC. She worked a day job at a nursery, hauling trees."

"How long ago was this?"

"I was a little girl, so the mid-nineties. Eva had a mole on her back, malignant melanoma. Three years later, it roared back in her hips, bones, and lungs and killed her. She was petite, very casual, never dressed up, wore a baseball cap. Not into hair and makeup. The photos I've seen, she looks like she's going out for a hike. She was only thirty-three."

"How did I miss all this?"

"You were doing other things."

Light rose along the edges of the horizon. I thought about the 1990s, married to Scarlett, full-blown in my career at Duke—lost to myself.

She said, "It's not too late to catch up."

"Catch up?"

"I heard a story about a guy in England who pulled over his car the first time he heard Eva Cassidy's voice on the radio. She was singing 'Over the Rainbow.' And you know how many vocalists have sung that. He stopped the car and wept."

I said, "Her voice gets under your skin."

"And into your heart. When Eva sings, all your secrets tumble out."

"Songs that make you cry. No wonder Zephyra chose her."

PJ said, "The reason Eva didn't get signed is that she was very particular about which songs she sang. Record execs couldn't pin her down. She was shy and self-critical. She didn't like attention." Then PJ stood up and said, "Gotta go. I'm on the gate. Are you still up for the hike tomorrow?"

I nodded. "At three?"

She said, "Meet you at the creek."

Then she stopped, leaned over the iron railing and looked down into the kelp forest, and with the curiosity of a child said, "Did you see the otters?"

I said, "Yeah, they're everywhere."

She lingered and counted the bobbing heads, "I see eight, now nine, and there's ten. It's an entire raft." She pointed at an otter on its back, smashing a crustacean with a rock, and said, "Check it out." She leaned forward on her elbows and seemed to forget about the gate and gazed at the water.

I said, "What about the gate?"

In an instant, as if it flipped off her tongue, she replied, "Carnivores."

"Curious creatures." I said, "They're so playful."

She said, "Don't let that fool you. They eat a lot and kill wantonly. Don't get too close. As a species, they've made a huge comeback and are thriving in Big Sur. In the 1930s they were thought extinct. Maybe there's hope for the rest of us."

PJ's mood was buoyant, her movements effortless, like a Hindu goddess, her wrists bangles clattering. Lean and muscular, her youthful body was silhouetted against the rising sun. I made an effort to avert my eyes and kept looking, exploring her features, wet auburn hair pulled away from her broad forehead falling down her back. Her delicate shoulders were sturdy, supporting long, slender arms and graceful fingers. She widened at the hips, her buttocks and thighs fleshy, narrowing to angular knees. Her ankles were submerged in the hot spring water.

She turned and said, "All these magnificent creatures are full of plastic. And it's in our bloodstreams." Then she stepped out of the tub and walked to the showers.

A pelican splashed in the kelp and three cormorants' long necks trolled the thicket. I sat and observed the gray fingers of light push back the blackness. Along the horizon, a silvery veil lifted. The shoreline calm, waves lapped at the shore, whitecaps relegated far out to sea.

Yesterday, I saw a school of dolphins with their young, otters fed in the surf.

Yesterday, clouds filled the stratosphere, and it got dark, the sun came out. It happened again, and again.

Yesterday, surf riled and becalmed (no pattern).

Yesterday, sunrise, moonrise, millions of stars flooded the heavens. Redwoods rustled in the wind.

Yesterday, routine, repetitious, absorbing. All chronology lost.

Yesterday, I went to the art barn and painted a portrait of the house where my brother and I grew up.

Yesterday, my insatiable appetite for self-expression matched.

Yesterday, my family story, exposed, excavated.

Yesterday, my parents, long deceased, joined me—all their faults, foibles, pettiness, cowardice, along with their desire to love and be loved.

Yesterday, my gaping wound, a chasm. Hemorrhaging, no longer packed with cement.

Yesterday, Zephyra.

Yesterday, a "Walk and Talk." I spoke. Someone listened. And I listened when they spoke.

Yesterday, the baths.

Yesterday, strangers smiled at me along the paths.

Yesterday, an astonishing conversation.

Yesterday, hours and hours talking with new friends, Lucille and Aggie.

Yesterday, now stuck like scraps of leather under my tongue. Fragments jammed in my pen. Can I articulate, assimilate, write it down?

A cocky, balding forty-year-old IT professor from Fresno spoke up yesterday at the end of the session. "How can I bring this inquisitiveness and response to others into my life when I go home? When I got here, I was ready to explode. What do I do with all that anger, rage, and hate? Ask anybody, I was a real asshole. Now, I'm drunk on love."

Dan yelled from the other side of the room, "You're still an asshole."

Zephyra ignored him and said, "Be like you are here at home."

People chuckled.

She continued, "That's the point. The most important relationship is with yourself. Be who you are. If you like who you are here, be who you are there."

As much as the guy annoys me, we're all asking the same question. Is this a temporary respite or something we can do at home? Is it geography? Sixty-five million years ago, two tectonic plates collided. The Santa Lucia peaks pushed up out of the sea. Big Sur's an isolated stretch even today, only accessible by a fragile, winding, two-lane highway. There's nowhere like it. I've thrown out my sense of time. My cell phone doesn't work here, and I've lost contact with the outside world. Who can argue the dramatic skyscape and climactic spectacle force introspection? One can ignore the rest of the world. Whatever or whoever is calling can wait.

Zephyra's exercises are so simple. All they take is time, a particular kind of time. Let's start with the Walk and Talk. Would I engage in such activity back home? What chance of strolling with a stranger for an hour? When one speaks, and the other listens without interruption? Is such an enterprise only possible here?

There were six months after our divorces when Vic and I jumped out of the rat race. We took leaves of absence, bought around the world plane tickets, and traveled. We walked and talked every day—miles of walking in Tahiti, Hong Kong, Kos, and Thailand. There were no gyms or swimming pools. In Greece, I swam in the Mediterranean. But our day-to-day activity was to walk, hours of walking and talking. A relationship needs nourishment. Otherwise, it goes fallow. Zephyra is showing us. These are practice sessions with strangers meant to be applied at home.

What are the essential elements of Zephyra's practice? Yesterday, I read a pamphlet called, "Bitterness is Not an Option." It's a question and answer session, where she lays out her approach. Once started, I couldn't put it down. She said clients drop their defenses when they see her handicap. But it's more than that. She wrote, "ALS is the most inconvenient way to live," which gets closer to what makes her so unique. It's how she approaches living that's heroic and disarming. What she creates in a group looks and feels like alchemy, like nobody else could do it. In a sense, she's indispensable. But the synergy she creates is not supernatural. It's possible. She's working with the same raw material as everyone else. At times, it feels like she's an extraterrestrial recently arrived from another dimension. Or a creature harvested from the deepest trenches of the bluest seas. What's clear to everyone is that she's enlightened. And in that way, she's superseded most members of our species.

Yet, like all of us, she's living on this planet constrained by gravity. She has a ruthless disease. And in this context, disease is a misnomer. Lou Gehrig's disease is a death sentence. Amyotrophic lateral sclerosis is a progressive, ever-worsening scenario with no cure. Debilitating and insufferable, an affliction that reprimands the victim's every waking moment. Only in sleep or death can she find release. In laymen's terms, it means "no muscle nourishment." Simple commands from the brain to voluntary muscles fail. Nerves no longer function. Muscles waste away. For example, it takes a coordinated effort from two hundred muscles to walk. Most ALS sufferers succumb to their fate in a few years. It's better to die, termination a better choice than to continue with this assault on their human dignity.

But Zephyra remains so full of passion, desire, ambition, and hope. If she doesn't feel sorry for herself, how can I? She's licking the most profound odds, and it's reshaping her sensitivities, heightening her intuition, and sharpening its practical application. She chooses to help rather than get stuck on herself. She never revels in her misery, resentment, and bitterness. She's evolved far beyond the average human being. In this sense, her disability is her superpower.

But what's it like to be Zephyra? To wake up in a body that's unable to sit or stand without help? Incompetent to feed herself, to enjoy the privacy of a shower? To toilet herself, to wipe her own ass? She retains an equanimity that outshines the rest of us. Living with ALS breaks the most indomitable spirit. How does she stand up to it?

At the end of the morning session, we paired for the Walk and Talk. Each of us made a date with someone we didn't know to walk for an hour. One person talks for thirty minutes, the other listens. Then roles reverse—the quintessential Zephyra practice.

The group circled and held hands. Again, and now I knew the tune, Bruce Springsteen's "If I Should Fall Behind" is played. But this time it's a stripped-down version, a moving tribute to Clarence Clemons, the long-time band member and tenor saxophonist known as the "Big Man" who died after a stroke in June 2011. Clemons was distinguished for his charismatic personality. He engendered the camaraderie, the glue that held the E Street Band together for forty years. His last performance was in Buffalo, on the day the world commemorates the assassination of John F. Kennedy, November 22, 2009.

Zephyra was into it, standing and swaying, gripping her walker. Her slim alabaster body elastic, she moved in rhythm with each beat. Her lips wrapped around each word. We gazed around the circle contacting each other's eyes. There were no boundaries, only a sense of intimacy, a feeling that we are in this together.

The tune, a rich, layered peripatetic dirge, builds with each verse. It welcomes call and response. Each band member steps to the mic. Everyone sang along, and the words resonated as if we shared a single heartbeat. "Please wait for me. Please wait for me." Zephyra nodded and motioned with her lips. The haunting sax solo, played by Clarence Clemon's nephew, Jake Clemons, had most in tears.

At the conclusion, Lucille raced across the room. She intertwined her right arm with mine. Mutt and Jeff. She looked up and winked. "Walk and Talk?"

I nodded.

She said, "You're from Buffalo, aren't you? Were you at that concert? I would've loved to have been there. It was four hours long. Can you imagine?"

"I grew up in Buffalo. I live in California. You a Springsteen fan?"

"Who isn't? Let's meet after lunch. In fact, let's have lunch, then walk."

The assembly slipped on their footwear at the door and funneled out. Lucille clung to my arm. We were like children bursting out of a classroom at the end of the school day. Enthusiasm unbridled, shouting and laughing, everybody horsing around. The air bright, fresh, and calm, the high sun bounced off the flat mirror-like ocean.

When we reached the bridge, thousands of reddish-orange wings swarmed the sky. Some were low enough to touch, slow-moving, and translucent in the sunshine. The enormous eucalyptus tree next to the bridge pulsated orange and black and white polka dots—monarch butterflies, decorous as stained-glass windows with ornate repeating patterns, like the Taj Mahal.

I said, "I've never seen anything like this."

Lucille said, "This is a winter roost, like in Mexico. They migrate thousands of miles and come back to these same trees. They pack in clusters to generate heat. They die in a freeze."

"How long do they live?"

She replied, "A few weeks, but it's more complicated than that. Over-wintering monarchs live for eight or nine months."

"Over-wintering?"

"There's a Methuselah generation, born in late summer. They migrate back here from the Midwest and Canada, traveling a hundred miles a day. And they come back here—"

I said, "But they've never been here before?"

"Not this generation."

A butterfly landed on my shoulder. I wanted to reach out and touch it. Like a child, absorbed, I forgot about everything else and forced myself to stand still. It flew away.

Lucille said, "That's good luck."

I watched it twitch and glide into the vastness until I could no longer discern the direction of its wings.

She said, "In Mexico, the arrival of the butterflies coincides with the Day of the Dead. People embrace them as the spirits of their dead ancestors."

As we walked the hill, the sky cleared. The cluster of butterflies was only in that spot near the creek.

Lucille picked up her step. "They're serving roasted chicken at lunch. Let's get up there. There won't be any seats left."

About halfway up the hill she bent over, her hands on her knees, and said, "I used to walk this without any problem. Do you mind waiting while I catch my breath?"

I said, "Not at all. How do you know so much about butterflies?"

"I'm a biologist. They're dying off. I've always had an interest in lepidopterology."

"Like Nabokov?"

"Not entirely on that level, but I know what's happening in the field. It's not good."

We strolled the rest of the way up the incline and settled on a bench in the garden before reaching the lodge.

She said, "I heard you got the green light from Ned."

"Not so sure I want to get up there. I'm getting so much out of watching other people..."

She put both hands to her throat. "Don't choke. It might be your last chance."

"I'm chicken shit."

She beamed and patted my knee. "Speaking of chicken, let's go get lunch."

And Lucille was right. The cafeteria was packed. Long lines and congestion.

She said, "No worries. Let's get some tea and wait it out. There's plenty."

I pushed my way toward the salad bar encircled with foragers. After canvassing the offerings, I spotted an abundant cornucopia of fresh fruit and snapped up a plump Satsuma mandarin. Perfection. Big, bold, bright, not too juicy, delicate and light, loose skin, easy to peel, sweet, no seeds. My favorite. We sat down. No sooner had I started to peel it when Jerry walked up and said, "There's a message for you on the board. You better check it out."

Despite the influx of the digital age, Calypso remains fundamental and archaic. It could be the 1930s when the highway first connected Big Sur to the outside world. As mentioned, most of the time cell phones don't work. Also, there are no phones in the rooms—the front desk posts messages on a bulletin board outside the lodge. Seminarians share a payphone next to the parking lot.

I stood up, left the sumptuous Satsuma partially unpeeled, and walked outside. I was thinking about it. How delicious it would taste. It's a short season for Satsumas. Like monarch butterflies, they don't last long.

On the bulletin board was a three-by-five card with my name on it marked "URGENT." On the back it said, "Call immediately," and under it was a 716 area code phone number I didn't recognize. I thought, *So much for Big Sur as a state of mind.*

A young woman was using the outdoor phone booth, so I sat and waited. Her conversation was about her ailments. She complained about insomnia and constipation, said that her eyes were dry despite eye drops. She hated the food. She said, "Enough already. Salad, quinoa, kale soup." She gave me a dirty look, probably knowing I was eavesdropping. She finished her conversation and slammed the phone. As she passed me, she said, "What's your problem?"

Years since I used a payphone, I reached for my wallet that wasn't there and then placed the call collect.

Pixie's voice sounded distressed when she accepted the charges.

I said, "I didn't recognize the number."

She came out swinging. "What the fuck happened to my car?"

"What's going on?"

"Shit! I come outside and my car's gone. I parked next to a snowbank. Like an idiot, I walk around the block. Maybe I forgot, put it somewhere else. Then some guy sees me and says, 'Sister, you looking for the Chevy? It got towed. I saw the repo man here twenty minutes ago.' When he said that, I lost it. I called the loan company, and they said it's part of the estate."

"Was it in Mick's name?"

"Yeah, but there was only one more payment."

"All the more reason it's valuable. Cassie wants to cash in. Why didn't you get Mick to sign it over?"

"Never thought Mick was going to die. He always pulled through. Mick liked to be the man in charge—his name on the water bill, electricity bill, gas bill, and registration. I couldn't take that away from him, especially when he was so sick."

"So, where's your car now?"

"Impounded. It's going to auction. I don't have ten grand. That's what it would take. The man said it belongs to the estate. Do you know anything about this? Are you in cahoots with Cassie? Nobody said anything. They just took it. Mick's chef's hat was in the back seat." She started to cry. "I never had anything like this happen to me in my life. I always pay my bills."

I said, "Horrible. I'm sorry. I'm so sorry."

She said, "It's freezing. Close to zero. Everything's iced over. More snow on the way."

"What's up with the new phone number?"

"I'm staying with my grandmother. My stuff's in her garage."

"What happened?"

"Your sisters sold my bed and kept a bunch of my sweaters and other stuff. That was my bed. Even my grandmother's recipes are gone."

"Why aren't you at the house?"

She replied, "Cassie told me I had to leave, said it's under probate. She said they're appraising everything. I had to leave. I couldn't take anything even if it were mine. She promised me fifteen hundred dollars a month when everything clears."

"You'll never see it."

"I know. That's what my mother said. She said Cassie would get hers. I hope she rots in hell. And she will. Both your sisters will. My mom said not to be bitter. People like your sisters always get theirs."

"Time wounds all heels," I quipped.

We giggled.

I said, "They're awful."

She said, "You sure you didn't have anything to do with this?"

"No fucking way. My sisters are horrible. I'm so sorry."

"And that Saundra, she's even worse. When she's around, Cassie is vile. She put her up to this."

I said, "What're you going to do now?"

"Get a job. I heard Burger King in Lackawanna is hiring. My brother said he'd help me get a car. I'll be all right. I wanted to shop today. I have all my coupons cut out of the paper. It's too cold to take the bus."

I said, "How did you find me here?"

"Victoria gave me the number. Said you'd call me back. Glad

you're not part of this. I'll call you in a couple days. When do you go home?"

"Day after tomorrow."

She hung up.

Back at the table, Lucille was gabbing and gesturing wildly, but her best efforts were drowned out by her companions. All were chomping down on drumsticks, chicken breasts, yams, kale, baby greens, and yapping. My Satsuma lay untouched.

She said, "Grab a plate and then we'll walk and talk."

I said, "The line looks pretty long." I sat down and cracked open the Satsuma.

"Everything OK?" she asked.

"That was a call from home."

She grinned. "I know how that goes. Sure you don't want chicken? Best meal of the week. Don't let it go to waste. You'll feel better if you eat something."

"I'm not hungry."

A woman Lucille's age approached and said, "Hey, Ginger, wanna soak?"

Lucille looked up. "I've got a Walk and Talk. This is Neal."

With a sarcastic smile, the woman extended her hand. "Neal Cassady?"

I looked into her sharp blue eyes and said, "The only people that interest me are the mad ones—"

"Burn, burn, burn like roman candles across the night," she said.

With a tone of jealousy, Lucille said, "What the hell are you two talking about?"

The woman looked at her. "You're ridiculous."

Lucille said, "Is that Ginsberg?"

The woman shook her head. "No, Kerouac, *On the Road*. You're hopeless."

As she shook my hand, the woman said, "Hello, Neal Cassady. I'm Aggie." She refastened her curly silver hair back in a maroon paisley bandana. "Haven't we met before?"

"I'm not sure."

"Did you ever do Robert and Rita Portello's tantra workshop?"

"The one where Rita didn't show up and Robert spent the week trying to convince us they were still together?"

She said, "That was years ago. They're divorced now. Yes, Robert did lay it on thick. I remember you and your wife. What's her name?"

"Victoria. And you attended with a friend."

"Jonathan. He's deceased."

"I'm sorry to hear that."

"He's been gone a while now. He loved to come to the workshops here. It was nothing more than that between us. How's Victoria? Should I ask? Are you two still together?"

"Yes. Although it hasn't been easy."

"Never is," she replied. "You live in the South and work at a big medical center."

"Duke."

"I can never keep them straight. Is that in South Carolina or Virginia?"

"North Carolina. We're in California now," I replied.

"I remember you two were at odds about that. How did you work it out?"

"It took a couple years. An executive decision."

She raised an eyebrow.

I said, "I took a tip from Gladys Knight and the Pips. I decided to live in her world rather than without her in mine. I pretty much do whatever she says."

"Good move. That's what makes a marriage work."

Lucille said, "You should know better, Neal. You can't take a Californian out of California." She guffawed. "They don't cross state lines."

Aggie added, "I know for me there's an absolute connection, a compelling one between California and my interior landscape."

I said, "There is for Victoria too, and it took me years to grasp it. I was angry, and I thought I was a man and it was my job. She should go with me. Live where I wanted to live. It didn't help that we were in the South where everybody, both men and women, agreed with me. I had to stretch, swallow my pride, and that wasn't easy."

Lucille wiped her greasy fingers with a napkin and with a mouthful of chicken, asked, "How many generations has her family been here?"

"Four."

Aggie cracked up. "Neal, what were you thinking? That's biblical, King David stuff, 'Ruth, when sick for home, / She stood in tears amid the alien corn…' That's not how it works anymore."

I said, "John Keats, 'Ode to a Nightingale.' "

"Yeah, I went to Columbia, studied with Mark Van Dorn, among others."

I said, "How long have you known Lucille?"

"Since God made us." They giggled like adolescents viewing Michelangelo's *David*.

"You must have known Lew Diamond."

Aggie quipped, "Of course. Ginger slept with both. We won't mention all the others."

Lucille said, "And you didn't?"

I assumed she meant the founders, Lew Diamond and Mort McGee.

"Why did you call her Ginger?"

Both tittered.

Aggie said, "Have you seen her at the baths?"

Lucille blushed and splashed down a cup of tea. "I don't have that much hair anymore. I don't think anybody could even tell."

They both howled.

I said, "I'm going to get some chicken."

Lucille shouted, shaking a drumstick, "Breasts or thighs?"

Jerry, sitting at the other end of the table, sprayed a mouthful of water all over his plate. Ann Claire rushed to get a towel. The table jiggled with laughter.

I crashed my right knee into the table leg when I stood, smiled, and limped to the food line.

The lodge reminds me of a grand medieval hall. It's a collection of hand-hewn natural beams and dark walls the texture of brown leather. Mounted animal heads are all that's missing. Conversations emerge from every corner. People in outlandish costume, androgynous, striding around in long robes. Women with bare midriffs. Men wearing sarongs. Some barefoot, bejeweled with bangles, nose rings, accented with colorful scarves. A long, rectangular room soaked in unintelligible voices and earthy smells. A chamber sprinkled with shouts, laughter, and ribaldry. Someone was playing the guitar, another plinking the piano—someone else scratched in a notebook at a feverish pace with a fountain pen. And to think this all started as a sanctuary, a healing refuge for the native Esselen people. Slate's Hot Springs came next with colonial expansion. The Native Americans went extinct in the 1880s. Thomas Slate, a pioneer aching with arthritis, discovered the curative thermal waters. He homesteaded and built a private bathhouse. Slate's Hot Springs became Big Sur's first tourist destination.

Very few visited the baths before the highway in 1937. Slate sold it to Mort McGee's grandfather, a physician from Salinas, in 1910. The doctor intended to turn it into a European-style health spa. As time went on, they built motel rooms and the lodge. Henry Miller and his sidekick, Emil White, cavorted here in the 1940s and '50s. Miller in *Big Sur and the Oranges of Hieronymus Bosch* refers to it as Slates Hot Springs. In the '60s, Joan Baez came with her guitar, and Gonzo, Hunter Thompson, with his guns, managed the place. Holy Rollers from Fresno ran the restaurant and lodge, their clientele, gay men, in the baths. It was an incendiary situation, but it's the contemporary iteration that gives me goosebumps. Lew Diamond and Mort McGee brought in the luminaries. In the 1960s, Joseph Campbell regaled spellbound audiences in this very room, as did Aldous Huxley, Carl Rogers, Alan Watts, Fritz Perls, and Abraham Maslow, to name a few. And here I am sitting with two septuagenarians who slept with them. What about the women prophets like Ida Rolf, who played such a significant role? It was a different age. Innocent. Primitive. Patriarchal. And who slept with Ida Rolf?

When I got back to the table, everyone had settled down. At least nobody had the giggles. My plate was stacked with beets, leeks, sweet potatoes, and a hot, steaming chicken breast. I'd piled a serving much higher than my stomach could endure.

Aggie asked, "What do you want to know about Lew?"

I said, "I was in a clawfoot tub the other morning and talked to Earl."

They both roared and started yipping like wolves. Aggie raised her chin and throated a clear wail. Lucille joined in.

I asked, "You know Earl?"

Aggie said, "That Wheedler."

Lucille gestured with her hands. "What did that old fart tell you?"

"About Lew's death."

Aggie said, "That was sad." She took Lucille's hand and added, "Earl was here at the time."

I said, "Earl said he carried Lew down the mountain."

"Did he tell you about Lew? Where he was from, what he was about, how he got here?"

"He told me some."

Aggie said, "How much time do you have?"

Shoveling a bite of sweet potato into my mouth, I said, "I'm free. No more sessions today."

Lucille looked at her. "I thought you were going to the baths?"

"I've got time."

Lucille nodded, shook her head, and looked at me. "Forget the Walk and Talk. Did you see the brownies on the table next to that big kettle of soup? I'll get more tea."

Aggie said, "I'll find us a table outside."

I located the brownies and stacked five high on a plate.

The man behind the counter gave me a dirty look, raised his index finger, and said, "One per person."

I replied, "These aren't all *for* me. I'm with a group."

He shook his head, and I bustled away. When I opened the door to the sundeck, Aggie waved. She was standing under a big Monterey cypress tree, and we sat in its shade at a round table. Lunch was over. Even the stragglers were gone. Plastic cups, porcelain plates, and coffee mugs littered large flat surfaces and counters. A tepid breeze wafted in our faces. I sat looking south at long, undulant ridges banked with wispy clouds. Dappled sunlight peeked through twisted branches, and waves broke hard on obstinate rocks. It smelled fresh. A damp mist of salt spray charged the air. Lucille joined us with her tea. The two now became pensive and withdrawn. The dynamic conversation in the lodge stalled. We sat in silence as if in a meditation circle.

I examined the thick wood surface of the table. Gouged, chiseled, and weatherworn, like the walls of the old bathhouse, a Rorschach test. It, too, had a story to tell. I scratched the surface with my fingernail and traced the outline of what looked like a coyote's head.

The sun, still high, was beginning its long descent. The ocean and sky pooled against each other. I stopped and studied the two women. They continued to look out to sea and either didn't notice or ignored my gaze. Twins. Time had delivered two different packages. Aggie was slender, a worrywart, bright, a logical thinker. Internal. Although the same height, she looked taller. Great ropy veins lined her forearms. If her veins were rivers, they'd be powerhouses like the Nile and Amazon. Her skinny legs were muscular and robust. She works out. She analyses every bite she puts in her mouth. Lucille, in opposition, runs hot, emotional. She's curvy, sturdy, with oceans of flesh overflowing beneath her flowing robes. Always hungry, battling insatiable cravings. She's itching for a fight. How the two shared the same womb is a trick of fate.

I coughed and looked with anticipation first at Aggie, then Lucille. Neither responded. A soft wind came in short, sweet, breathy puffs. It felt like someone was running their fingers through my hair.

I asked, "What is this, a Mexican standoff?"

Lucille shouted, "He never got over it."

I said, "If you don't want to talk about it, we can do this another time."

Aggie shook her head. "Incarcerated. Lew's parents locked him up for a year at a fancy mental institution on the east coast."

Lucille slumped. "He never got over it." Her pretty, round face contorted lengthwise, like a drying fig in the sun.

Aggie's temples bulged, and a spotty, crimson glow crept up her neck and cheeks. "Restrained, restricted, overmedicated, insulin and electroshocked against his will."

Lucille twisted on the bench. "Tortured, it's a violation of his human rights."

"He had fifty-nine insulin shocks and ten electrotherapy treatments," Aggie said.

"They broke him," Lucille said.

Aggie nodded. "They broke him."

Lucille shouted like a protester at a rally, "Without Lew, this place wouldn't be here."

Aggie kicked her feet out and said, "Now there are TED talks and Burning Man. Anyone can get a chair massage at the mall, learn meditation and yoga at the YMCA."

Lucille injected, "And buy organic vegetables at Safeway."

Aggie said, "None of that would have happened without Lew. It all starts with Lew."

Lucille looked hard at Aggie. "Do you remember how fit Lew was? That fucking asylum had him on so much Thorazine, he didn't know whether he was coming or going. I can never forgive them for abusing Lew with insulin shock. The food was crap. He gained seventy pounds." She looked at me, "That's why fresh, whole food is so much a part of this place."

Aggie said, "As it should be. It starts with what we eat."

I said, "They don't do that anymore…"

Lucille replied, "Do what? Lock people up? They sure d—"

"No, insulin shock."

"Like all psychiatric treatment, it's bullshit. And it's unnecessary," Lucille shouted. "Lew was a living example. People with mental illness do worse with so-called treatment. It's invasive, aggressive, and causes severe physical or mental suffering."

Aggie said, "And if they recover, PTSD."

Lucille curled her neck and shook her hair. "Psychotherapy, I'm OK with that, but none of this drug and shock stuff. Mental illness needs nurture. The person needs to figure out what's going on for them. Psychosis is an expression of the soul, and it has to come out. You can't mask it with drugs and electroshock. Lew's psychosis, those voices he heard, that was his vision. 'Don't hide the madness.' "

Aggie laughed. "Good, Ginger. Ginsberg did say that." She sat back, folded her slender hands on the table, and looked up. "Insulin shock was a treatment for schizophrenia."

Lucille said, "Which Lew *didn't* have."

Aggie said, "If you're not familiar, Neal, the doctors and

nurses inject insulin until the patient slips into a coma. It's supposed to jar the brain. Reset it. There was never any proof it worked."

"He was a guinea pig!" Lucille bellowed.

"Insulin overdose," I said. "That was my favorite call when I was a paramedic. You give IV glucose. The patient wakes up. They don't go to the hospital. Cured. An ugly stupor follows. A guy told me once he was sorry we woke him. Unlike all the other calls related to drugs and alcohol, it made me feel like we were doing something."

Lucille said, "If that's a cure, I want none of it. It left permanent damage. There were scars on Lew's brain at autopsy."

"That was from the electroshocks," Aggie said.

"Who knows for sure?" Lucille retorted. She plucked a chunk of brownie, rolled it with her fingertips, and popped it into her mouth.

Aggie said, "Lucille, insulin shock went out in the '60s."

"They still do electroshock. It's a violation. Imagine that done to you without consent?"

Aggie's brow furrowed. She loosened the scarf and fluffed her coiffed, feathery hair with the tips of her long fingers. Her face darkened. "The thing that breaks my heart is that Lew's parents annulled his marriage when he was in there."

Lucille cried out, "They paid his wife to disappear."

"And she did," Aggie said.

I said, "This sounds like Jack Nicholson's character in *One Flew Over the Cuckoo's Nest*."

"McMurphy! Lew got the same," Lucille said.

I said, "Except for the lobotomy."

Lucille stood and stretched. She reached her hands high into the sky in a sun salutation and bent straight at the waist.

We both watched her.

Aggie said, "When Lew got out, he went back to his family in

Chicago and worked for his uncle selling beer signs. It took him three years to recover."

"He was a mess." Lucille sat on the wood deck, extending her legs, and did a forward bend.

I marveled at her flexibility.

"Aggie said, "He saved the money that allowed him to stake this place. He also had some stock."

"It wasn't much, but it was enough," Lucille said. "And to think..." She looked around her. "This all started because Lew flipped out in a bar in North Beach."

We talked for hours. Before I knew it, people were lining up for dinner, and the sun was going down. Long, black shadows engulfed the towering mountains, and the air chilled. I didn't want the conversation to end. Like Jungians, they analyzed Lew's family and divulged his misfortunes. He had a twin brother who died when he was three that his family never fully processed. They gauged his triumphs and explained what transpired during Calypso's formative years.

Aggie said, "Lew kept the lid on this place, allowed it to grow and become what it is today."

Lucille added, "He's our George Washington."

Both agreed that he was flawed and tortured but the rock and the foundation of Calypso. They spoke with reverence and no regret. And it was clear they had devoted their lives to advancing the same ideas.

Lucille said, "You have no idea what it was like—"

"Women like us had little say," Aggie said. "Beat women, writers like Joyce Johnson, stayed at home while their guys went on the road."

Lucille said, "We didn't have options."

"We were so stupid then," Aggie said. "It took a long time before I decided to live flat out. No regrets."

"Girls lived with their legs crossed or spread," Lucille sneered. "There was no middle ground."

"If bimbos are good for the gander, gigolos are no worse for the goose," Aggie interjected.

"In North Beach, we were part of something. The hip poets, artists, and musicians flocked there," Lucille said.

"And visionaries like Lew. Most of America was pretty square. There was nowhere to express your discontent," Aggie said. "We dabbled in Zen, Eastern gurus, and meditation."

Lucille jumped up and exclaimed, "And sex. And don't forget the kooks, hustlers, and drug addicts." She bundled up her things. "I've got a dinner date. I'll see you tomorrow." She turned in my direction. "Neal, let's do our Walk and Talk after Zephyra's session."

"Are you sure? We spent the whole afternoon together talking."

She replied, "But we didn't walk. Lew walked and talked up and down these mountain trails. There's still plenty of ground to cover. I don't know what you do for a living, and I want to hear more about Victoria. I adore Santa Barbara. Also, I'm sure there are many more fascinating things about me you'd like to know."

I smiled, and she whisked away with the eagerness of a teenager.

Aggie said, "Well, this is it, Neal Cassady. Let's make it brief. I'm not fond of goodbyes." She sorted through her backpack, pulled out a musty paperback, and handed it to me.

I stroked its weathered cover with my palm. "This must be a collector's item?"

"Joyce Johnson, Kerouac's girlfriend. Her first book, and she's a better writer. Read it. It'll tell you our story, what my sister and I went through."

"Are you sure? This looks valuable."

"That's why I'm giving it to you." She looked me in the eye, the sun fading behind her. "As I said, let's make this brief."

I stood and met her embrace.

She hugged me with her tiny body and then headed to the baths, her paisley babushka fading like a bird into twilight.

I sat alone under the cypress tree, the sun slid into the ocean, and a blood-orange penumbra lit the horizon. As I opened the novel, it became clear to me: Calypso is the great-grandchild of the Beat Generation. Nowhere on earth is the Beat vision more alive than here. It's easy to proclaim Calypso, the bastion of the Beats. The Sur stimulates free-thinking and makes one feel small yet an intimate part of the cosmos. Everyone is accepted. I'm to add Joyce Johnson to my cosmology of jazz, poetry, art, and the good life. And how we, as sentient beings, must rebel and defy the machine that crushes our humanity. Like the otters in the kelp forests below, never forget the willingness to play. Here at the edge, one can't help but take a radical left turn toward vitality and personal freedom.

# 13 JANUARY, DAWN
## (CALYPSO INSTITUTE, BIG SUR, CA)

*Are you willing to be sponged out, erased,*
*canceled, made nothing?*
*If not, you will never really change.*
D.H. Lawrence (1885-1930)

T ODAY I ROSE FROM ASHES, exhausted, spent. In a few
short hours, I'll be heading home. Back to the clinic. The
Love Shack. The implacable red tile roofs. The moderate
clime where we feast on fire rather than frost. And Victoria.

Yesterday, I gazed at the ceiling from my bunk and imagined
the journey. It's wet. There'll be rocks, slippery mud, and gravel
on the road, and potential slides and closures. But it's Big Sur...
always breathtaking and unpredictable. High cliffs above churn-
ing surf. Salt spewing into the air. A wild country overrun with
tourists that remains primitive, untamed, and dangerous.

I'll roar past Rat Creek. That's where the wildfire started that
caused the slide that killed Lew Diamond. Then I'll wend my way
south down the Coastal Highway like a sinuous river. I'll stop
at Devil's Canyon and look back at this land that grows out of
rock and sea. There's a high perch past the bridge at Big Creek.

It's a majestic vista, two graceful spandrel arches, cantilevered to canyon walls. The renowned, single-arched Rainbow Bridge at Bixby Canyon is thirty miles north. The two are often mistaken, the untrained eye thinks one is the other. At Big Creek, one can observe the ribbon of road blasted and gouged out of these hillsides. It's unstable, precarious, and menaced by slides year after year. Thousands of years before the motorway, the Esselen tribe prospered here and spoke a language all their own. Isolated for two hundred generations, they foraged between the mountains and the sea. They were easy prey to outside infringement and thus wiped out by the mid-1850s. Some say they're still here and that crepuscular spirits, the "Dark Watchers," still lurk in shadows.

One thing is for sure, Big Sur, then and now, breeds a peculiar society.

After the lookout and another series of wiggly passes, I'll be in Lucia, an early south coast settlement with a café and store. There's no gas station. Lucia offers spectacular cliff-side cabins that hang above the surf. A fifth generation of the original pioneers, the Harlan family, still run the place. It took its name at the turn of the twentieth century from its first postmaster, Lucia Dani.

Above Lucia is a steep, two-mile climb, the New Camaldoli Hermitage. Getting there is half the fun. I fell in love with Victoria at Camaldoli. Every time we go, something unforgettable happens. Once when we entered the chapel, a piano concerto charged every molecule in the room. We thought it was a recording and sought out the source. Around the corner, in a hidden, rustic chamber, a monk in brown robes hammered out Gershwin's "Rhapsody in Blue" on a grand piano. He didn't notice us (or appear to) as we stood agape outside the door. Another unforgettable moment was when we sat spellbound while friars in long, white robes chanted. There's a distinctive smell. It's dry and dusty, like old books, with a hint of cedar and salt spray. The gift shop sells books, sacred knickknacks, granola (holy granola), and fruit cake.

And how can I leave out Lucia Joyce? Her mad genius and this place converge. I digress and recollect the tragedy of James Joyce's batty and brilliant daughter. She was the muse of the incomprehensible *Finnegan's Wake*. The Dionysian maenad whom Jung failed to cure. A fantastical child, troubled and lost, abandoned to asylums most of her life. Joyce said she had a fire in her brain. She was born while he conceived *Ulysses* and recovered from his first of a dozen eye surgeries. In the end, these surgeries would leave him blind, like Homer and Milton. Lucia means "light." St. Lucy is the patron saint of the blind. In Lucia, one sees with different eyes.

After Lucia, I'll motor past the lime kilns, a ghost town, now a state park-lined gorge with sky-soaring redwoods. In the 1800s, it was a thriving terminus, a hamlet accessed by bobbing schooners—a pickup point for tanbark, lumber, and lime. Down the road, after a series of switchbacks, Sand Dollar Beach and Jade Cove emerge. Cozy, lost, concealed, wind-rocked stretches of sand, turbulent, turquoise, and cold, and it's here that Highway 1 begins its denouement.

A bit farther south, there's a jumble of commercial buildings, an oddity called Gorda. One of three gas stations in Big Sur, Gorda boasts the most expensive gasoline in the United States. It's next to the lane closure and flagmen I encountered on the way up. Moving south, the land flattens. Ragged Point is next, where I'll fill my tank and get a milkshake. Ragged Point leaves me in rags, full of sadness, because it's here one looks back rather than forward. The vistas are riveting.

That's why it's so hard for me not to pull over on Highway 1, long before I ever reach Ragged Point. I'm never disappointed. Last trip, Victoria and I parked at random and wandered into a steep ravine. To our amazement, we sauntered into a swampy waterway carpeted with trumpet lilies. Bees were pollinating every golden stamen. It was an orgy of efflorescence. The marshy brook steeled in black earth led us farther up the hill. Bright green, youthful shoots stood erect in the bubbly current—a down-rush of fresh rainwater to an effervescent sea.

Back on the road, before I finish the milkshake, I'll pass the elephant seals at Piedras Blancas. How can I resist this stop? The Sur stops seven miles south in San Simeon. These big, blubbering beasts grunt, whine, and sob. The males are macabre, with long, sagging, often-bloodied proboscises they blow up like balloons. They dwarf the females, sometimes ten times as big, and they can weigh over two tons. Elephant seals spend most of their lives in the deep. They're awkward on land and move with graceless slides and shifts, like a fat man flopping on his belly. They haul out at these beaches to mate and molt. It's a rare opportunity to view them *en masse*. They're solitary at sea and spend only a few months here every year. Unlike the Esselen tribe, these antediluvians survived the last century's ecological breach. It's a victory for this delicate coast. Today, these ocean-goers prosper. Although hunted near extinction, their population is now increasing. While dry docked, they take no nutrition and don't urinate or defecate, and they hold their breath at will. It's irregular, even while beached. That's their superpower—they can exploit at will the oxygen stored in their red blood cells and muscles.

For the bulls, life on the shore is combative. They're relegated to the role of contestant, victor, and vanquished. They challenge each other for reproductive rights. With a loud, thunder-like bellowing, they threaten—huge sumo-like wrestlers slamming into one other using girth and teeth. Steam pours out of their massive jaws. The contest is dramatic but not fatal, although blood is spilled. The winner, called the "beach master," impregnates a harem of forty or fifty females. The loser slinks off to another beach where he awaits another duel or surrenders to a celibate season. Three-quarters of the bulls won't mate at all, while almost all the cows conceive.

The genders go their separate ways in open waters. Females swim west toward Japan. The bulls scavenge the shallows along the continental shelf north to Alaska. Carnivores, elephant seals can dive a mile deep and hold their breath for two hours. They spend little time on the surface. What goes on in the deep trenches of the western Pacific remains a profound mystery.

At San Carpoforo Creek, the Sur ends as does the original Carmel-San Simeon Highway. It's near Hearst Castle, the half-way point between Los Angeles and San Francisco. Morro Rock is next, a beacon of volcanic stone once called "the Gibraltar of the Pacific." It sits strong and supreme on the water like the Pyramid of the Sun. I always feel stunned and surprised by it. It points its snout high above the horizon, getting bigger and bigger upon approach. The sun plays with its weathered geometry. And although still imposing, it's a shell, only half the size of what it used to be. The locals quarried it until 1969. Explosions rocked the town for eighty years. A million and a half tons of boulders, gravel, and stone were removed. Now, lazy otters sunbathe in the bay. Morro Rock is one of seven fiery sister volcanoes, plugged and conveyed by the Pacific Plate. It's a five-hour drive to Palm Springs, yet that's where these geological wonders were born. It took twenty-five million years, and they're still moving at the speed of a fingernail's growth, about an inch a year. No longer blasted and pillaged, the Rock is now a refuge for endangered peregrine falcons.

It's here I'll leave the wonderland and after a dry, brown, lonely stretch pick up the freeway in San Luis Obispo and join other frantic vehicles, like beetles on a branch clattering toward uncertain destinations. Closer and closer to home, where a revised life awaits me.

Can I divorce my family?

Yesterday, it was the edge of night, and I couldn't sleep. I ran into Attila (I'm not sure that's his real name) at the lodge. He looks like one of the barbarians who annihilated civilization and it's easy to picture him ransacking Rome. Steely, dark eyes and long, dirty, brown locks past his shoulders. Dressed in rags, wearing fingerless gloves, he puffed like a horse in a cold stable. Thick, steamy breaths flared from his nostrils and, like a smoke-stack, out his mouth. He was burning papers in an open fire pit. The flame glowed an electric blue. The acrid, white smoke made me cough. He muttered to himself, "Fuck, fuck. I'm sorry. I'm sorry." His wail was unrelenting. He paid no attention to me. He heaped a wet log on the fire. It was chilling. I mused on my ancestry. I'm sure my mother's people were Huns. It was cold. My fingers were numb. My heart fluttered.

Before that moment, dwelling here at Calypso in perpetuity had crossed my mind—Big Sur, where America's muscular mountains leap out of the sea. The same thing happened to me as a young man in New Zealand. Despite the energy I'd put into getting there, I knew I didn't belong. And it didn't belong to me. My status was guest, wanderer, dilettante, houseguest. The Band's "Last Waltz" alerted me it was time to go home.

Big Sur speaks to me with big-throated kisses, a wet tongue wrapped inside my mouth. It assaults me, a night sky bursting with stars, planets, comets, and bolides. (I believe the Milky Way originates here.) I feel like I can lick the night sky with the back of my tongue. However, in my heart of hearts, I know this isn't where I belong. I come here when I need it. I'm not a resident.

Attila, and mentally unhealthy vagabonds like him, are not the only reason I'm not staying. In a few short hours after the goodbyes, hugs, and kisses, I'll be heading down that highway, anticlimactic, and alone, the sun hard clasped to the ocean, top down, salt spewing in my face.

Here, I rent. I own nothing and therefore leave nothing behind.

And how I needed it this time. Years go by, and I forget Calypso and Big Sur exists. This time I was mad, a lunatic. And who's to say I'm over it? My world mixed up, sad, spiraling out of bounds, so much confusion–who's to say that Lew Diamond wasn't right? Each of us needs to fall apart without interference. It's the only way one can put oneself back together again. It's so difficult for those around us to watch us flip out, and so challenging for me not to try to save another person from their crazy. But what better place to do it than here? I'll save Big Sur for that. Calypso's not a vacation but a pilgrimage, a refuge, an asylum. I've heard it said that neurotics are a menace to themselves, and psychotics a danger to others. I'll ride the high side of neurosis, as most do. And make my adjustments along the way.

Am I cured? Hell no!

Will I ever be? Hell no!

But once home, I can be less a burden to anyone else.

On Fridays, they serve pancakes at Calypso. They call them "Dexter's Sponges of Love." Frisbee-size, slaphappy, chubby discs hot off the grill. Warm maple syrup soakers that make me salivate, drunk on pancakes. Always, I want more. What I found out this trip is that it's not what happens at Calypso during the day that matters. One must also pay deep heed to the night. My affliction with insomnia was my savior.

There I was, writing in my notebook in the lodge after midnight. It took a few moments before I realized PJ was sitting across from me on the wooden bench. I felt her presence, detected her breath. Sweet, a scent at first I couldn't place. Maple syrup.

She said, "What are you writing? Do you find it helpful?"

At that moment, I was writing about Aggie and Lucille. They'd talked about wars, how they change people and the course of events. After the First World War, the lost generation ran away from America. They found themselves in bedbug-ridden hotel rooms in Paris, or sleeping in a loft of Shakespeare & Company.

Hemingway, Fitzgerald, Gertrude Stein, E.E. Cummings, Malcolm Cowley, T.S. Eliot, all went AWOL.

After the Second World War, Aggie, Lucille, and their contemporaries stayed. Ginsberg, Kerouac, and the Beats went out in search of America. Aggie called them "Whitman's children." As a group, they celebrated the body and forged the Beat Generation. Then Vietnam overheated in the 60s. I'd never put it together before. Calypso is "Beat," and I repeat, a consequence of the "Beat Generation." What about PJ and youngsters her age? What do they want? Is there syzygy between us? I sense we are more alike than different.

I said, "What do you mean, help me?"

"You know, like therapy. Every time I see you, you're writing."

"I need it. I'm talking to myself on paper. I like the way the ink spits out the tip of the pen. I don't know any other way to combat my sadness."

"Is it a book?"

"No plans. It unburdens my soul..." When I said that, I felt ridiculous, then admitted, "I have no idea why I write."

"Then why do it?"

"There are lots of good arguments. It's supposed to reduce stress, improve the immune system...." Again, I felt pathetic and said, "All the arguments don't matter. I just do it."

She said, "I write for a few days and give up. It makes me feel bad."

I said, "I've had that happen."

"When I quit, it makes me feel sad, like I failed."

"I did the same thing until it got a hold of me. The hardest part, even now, is getting started. What did Hemingway say? 'One true sentence?'"

She said, "I wish I could do it. It seems like the only way.

You can write stuff down you can't tell anybody else." Her eyes twinkled. "Wanna make pancakes?"

I said, "I thought that was tomorrow."

"Why wait? The batter's ready, and there are blueberries."

"What about the house rules?"

She laughed and opened her mouth so wide I could see her molars, a couple in the back with gold fillings. She said, "It's fine."

Conrad told me, do something dangerous. I thought, *Here's my chance*. Entering the Calypso kitchen in the middle of the night, now that's dangerous.

There was no barrier. The kitchen had no door. What hit me in an instant was this is the heart, the spiritual core of Calypso. On entering the cookery, I felt exalted, happy, with a sense of anticipation. The sheer size of the operation bewildered me. The commercial chrome range and its big, black rubber knobs dwarfed anything I'd ever seen. Like a Lilliputian entering Brobdingnag, I couldn't get my head around how we were going to whip up hot cakes for two. The setup was designed for two hundred.

Heavy pots and pans suspended from hooks on metal rods formed a closed space like Newgrange. Tall, shiny refrigerators lined the walls. The cutlery and utensils were gargantuan. I thought of my brother and how this was his haven. How he always referred to himself as "Chef," as one might address a medical doctor as "Doctor," or a court arbiter as "Judge." The glazed ceramic tile walls reflected the fluorescent lights like glass. The floor had been scrubbed and scoured clean like a fire engine. The prep table, a thick, wooden slab supported by steel legs, had the appearance of an altar. It was a place of ceremony. I'd never stood behind a range of this magnitude.

PJ handed me a heavy steel, professional pancake batter dispenser and said, "Fill it. The batter's in the fridge."

"How much?"

"How hungry are you?" She raised an eyebrow.

It required both hands to dump the batter from the vast, cold, stainless steel bowl into the dispenser. I picked up a large spatula and thrust it in PJ's direction like a sword.

She said, "Stop fooling around. Fire up the grill."

The taboo I felt on entering the kitchen slipped away. Then came an unexpected shift, a faint rustling like fresh rain. Flat out on a countertop behind us, a fat man asleep in a white tunic shifted and snored. His bushy, yellow mustache fluttered with each breath. His sloppy, pink belly hung over his uniform, cinched by a black belt.

I said, "Shit, who's that? Are we supposed to be in here?"

"That's the chef. He doesn't care. He's a happy drunk."

The figure didn't move except to blow out a single slow hiss, like a leaking balloon. Then he flipped over in a single motion and faced the wall. His pants slid down below his belt, exposing his butt crack.

PJ busied herself with preparations. "Hungry? Want some music?"

She pointed to the corner. There was an old-fashioned turntable with stereo speakers (I hadn't seen one like it since college). Beside it stood stacks of damp, dog-eared LPs. I examined the cover art with wonder. Marvin Gaye, *Let's Get in On*, the Eagles, *Their Greatest Hits 1971-1975*, and Derek and the Dominos, *Layla*, to name a few. There were dozens.

I said, "Does this work?"

"Give it a try."

I flipped the switch. The turntable spun, followed by an explosive pop and loud crackles.

She said, "We're in business."

I said, "Too many choices."

"Play what you like. Crank it up. You won't wake anybody. I've done it before."

I dropped the needle. It bounced and found the Eagles. Not my first choice, but I didn't dare mess with it.

PJ shouted, "Old School."

She knew all the words, and unlike me, sang on key. I liked her singing voice—strong, determined yet vulnerable. She sang in a much lower register than she spoke. She invited me to sing along. During the extended instrumental, she washed the blueberries.

She said, "These are organic from Chile."

Without missing a beat, she picked up the vocal again.

I joined her on the chorus and flubbed, " 'Easy, friendly feeling.' "

Then came a rumbling, ass-ripping fart reverberating from the chef.

PJ, ever-gracious, ignored it and said, "Let's do another."

"What about the hotcakes?"

"Pick another song. I'll heat the maple syrup."

I shuffled through the album covers like a deck of cards, stacking them in piles—a disc jockey's dream. *We could be here all night,* I thought. How could I put on only one? Then I came to *Layla* and held it up for PJ to see.

She called across the kitchen, "That's a painting."

"Beautiful."

She said, "Play it!"

I said, "It's a double album."

"Play 'Layla.' It's the second to last song on the second LP."

How could I sort out the memories? There was Miami, the hot puddles on bare feet in bell bottoms after a dousing rain. "Layla" blaring out the screened dorm window from six-foot speakers. The girls near and far, now old like me. My friends with boggy prostates in blue jeans. Back then, we were gods.

Another singular memory. I was forty-four. I was driving a convertible through the Castro with a friend. Still married to Scarlett, overwhelmed and in love with Victoria, I told him, "I'm in love with another woman." The anguish, the pain, the hurt. The heart is crashing. "Layla," an incredible song to scream to in a romantic crisis, the wind whipping through my hair. Inner demons unleashed, savage, and primitive. How can I settle the score? To kill or to die, to fuck or be fucked, to breed, to survive, to rise from the mud. The flowering lotus. I looked at the cover, glowering in surrealism. A girl's hair whipped into a cloud, covering her left eye, filtering out in yellow like daisies into the sun. The mystery of women to men. Our complete surrender to their will. *Layla, you've got me on my knees.* The magnetism of women—more than cunt, the slit between their legs through which all pass. The terror of their thighs, the shape more beautiful in all its wonder than any other of God's creation. Captivating, terrorizing, suffering, cruel, the source of all manifestation.

PJ said, "Check out the signature at the bottom."

I read out loud, "Frandsen."

"Frandsen de Schomberg," she said. "It's called *La Jeune Fille au Bouquet.*"

"How do you know? You weren't even alive. You should be a contestant on *Jeopardy.*"

She said, "Clapton was in love with Patty Boyd, George Harrison's wife."

"You're showing off."

She said, "Watch and learn. Here's my secret."

She took a slab of butter and cut it into chunks, placed it at low heat in a heavy pan, and skimmed off the milk solids with a spoon, then poured it through cheesecloth. She spread the silky, yellow contents on the grill.

She said, "See, this won't brown or burn."

She plopped batter on the hot grill and poured six huge, moon-shaped pancakes.

I said, "Let me do the blueberries."

She handed me the stainless steel bowl. The berries were plump, glistening with drops of water, some the size of marbles.

I placed them one by one with my fingers. I asked, "Are these really from South America? I thought everything was local…"

She said, "Take your finger and push each one in."

And she was right. The berries were floating on the thick surface like corks, so I followed her directions.

When she flipped the cakes, it surprised me how splendid each one turned out, a toasty brown. It wouldn't be long before we ate.

"Layla" blared in the background.

PJ said, "It sounds better on vinyl. Slow hand dueling overdubs with Duane Allman's screeching slide guitar. You don't hear that on the CD. You miss the rhythmic genius of Skydog."

We screamed the chorus at the top of our lungs.

"LAYLA."

The chef didn't budge.

She said, "He sleeps better with background music."

I said, "I want to write like Eric Clapton plays guitar."

She smiled and rolled her eyes. "You've got a long, long way to go."

We slopped hot maple syrup at our pleasure. The sweet, sticky smell rose with the steam and made me pucker.

The music kept coming.

Bewildered, I couldn't grasp how PJ could know all those songs.

Although, what led me into the wee hours wasn't all batter, pancakes, and maple syrup.

That morning I woke up disoriented and disillusioned. I'd soured on the process. It felt cultish. What do I have in common with these lost souls? Tormented, agitated, uneasy, irritable, anxious, worried, afraid. I wanted to leave. I'd had enough. I was freaking out. I masturbated—what a strange trick in a bunk room where four other men could interrupt at any time. Jerking off didn't help. I started packing, thinking up excuses. I'd tell Ned that Victoria was sick and I had to leave. My mind was running wild. It's coming to an end. It slams a door, cuts like a knife. Tomorrow our little group will disband, never to see one another again. So much has happened. I can't slow it down to explain it all. It's rapid-fire. I felt like it would never end—the see-saw, the love and hate, the exuberance, the anticipation, and boredom. Even the baths seemed ridiculous. Why sit in hot tubs naked with people you'll never see again? Any confidence I had in the process, shaken, was now an illusion. Everything felt like a waste of time, a disappointment. Workshops, self-growth, self-love, helping others—done with it.

Fuck this shit! Why bother?

Instead, I stuck around and showed up for Zephyra's session. My heart flipped and flopped, and pounded like a jackhammer. I tried to clear my throat. "Ahem." Whatever was there, I couldn't release it. My stomach was queasy, and my windpipe tightened. Involuntary short, dry coughs pushed out. Then I belched.

When I entered the room, the chair was open. Like PJ, I leaped and sat down in it. When I looked up, people were clowning around, chatting, making small talk. Was my move premature? Zephyra hadn't entered the room yet. A cold sweat broke out on my brow. It reminded me of swim meets in high school. When I couldn't sleep, riddled with anxiety, I'd agonize over every stroke, flip turn, push off, and when to take a breath. There was no relief until I hit the water.

Everyone was still milling around in the room. Was this a false start?

Within minutes, Zephyra entered, caretakers trailing in pageantry. Her hair was done up and glowing like a sunrise. Her gold hoop earrings dangled. She wore flawless makeup—a hint of rouge, a pinch of orange-tinged lipstick. A white satin collar flared from her neck. She stood erect, both hands on her walker, her eyes wet, like puddles reflecting clouds after a rain. Everyone in the room rose, silent. Lucille reached for me and, at first, I was reluctant to grasp her hand. I was embarrassed because my palms were sweating. Her fingers were like ice. She hadn't removed her alpaca sweater. She carried the morning chill in her palms. Ned reached and placed my right hand on the back of Zephyra's hand that rested on the walker. Her skin was white as cream. I felt the bony structure of her knuckles, the soft body of flesh beneath it. I noticed a few lines, but no liver spots. Her hand was youthful, other than its impairment. A hand possessed with determination and strength, but at the same time, not fully at her command.

Ned squinted his brow and fiddled with the sound system. Zephyra looked over her shoulder, caught his sight line, and nodded. Eerie electronic sounds sprang from the speakers. A raspy female voice emerged, and people in the room started singing along. "Guilt, guilt." A persistent thumping heartbeat emerged like a drum on an ancient battlefield. The word "guilt," a chorus, chanted over and over. I welled up. The group sang along and responded like children in the spirit of play. They moved from holding hands to placing their arms around each other's back. They formed a kick line, like the Rockettes. The experience was less pleasant for me. Terror settling in, I asked myself why I was sitting in the hot seat.

Later, I found out that the world-weary voice belonged to Marianne Faithful. Many of the participants knew her. She'd spent time at Calypso and Big Sur. She was Mick Jagger's waif-like girlfriend, leading lady of the swinging London scene of the 1960s. A seventeen-year-old British pop idol who sang, "As Tears Go By," in 1964. It was Jagger and Richard's first composition, and this tune was nothing like it. It was a hardened cry—a howl from hell. Her deep voice was no longer wispy, melodic, but ragged and cracked, a whiskey and smoke-throated wail casting a long dark shadow. It curled the hairs on the back of my neck.

Is my work about guilt?

When the song concluded, Ned unceremoniously plopped Zephyra with a thud into her chair.

She said, "Let's roll."

I looked around. People were sitting close together in a semi-circle on giant, corduroy floor pillows. Some drank coffee. Others fidgeted, bending forward in yoga positions and sliding cushions for comfort. A few were flat on their back. The sun streamed in. The Pacific reflected a white, mirror-like glow that left me squinting. Waves crashed. The swirling, white water looked like whipped cream, a thick, agitated foam.

Without hesitation, Zephyra said, "Neal, what's important?"

I blurted, "My brother's dead. There was nothing I could do."

What happened next is hard to describe. I started jabbering. All the people in the room faded out. Zephyra's pupils dilated, reducing her irises to an emerald-green rim. Her face softened. I noticed how paper thin and delicate her skin was, the contour of alabaster. Anything and everything that came to my mind, I blurted out as if loaded on cocaine. I lost control, like Dennis Hopper in *Apocalypse Now*. I kept saying, "Fuck man, you know, man—my brother's dead. I'm sorry. Man, I'm sorry. There was nothing I could do. Nobody gives a shit. I'm sorry."

She said, "Look around the room."

I glanced at first, hardly raising my head. It was painful, like readjusting my eyes from a dark room into bright sunlight.

Zephyra reinforced her statement. "I want you to look into each person's eyes."

Ned said, "Breathe, Neal. Take it all in."

I slowed down and said, "It'll take too much time. I can't get it all out."

Ned said, "Take as long as you want."

Zephyra looked around the room and said, "Does anybody give a shit?"

People nodded, even strangers I hadn't spoken to yet. Many called out, "Neal, we care." There were tears in their eyes.

Zephyra said, "Say, 'I'm drowning in guilt.' "

It jolted me. "Guilt?" I said in a whisper, as if my tongue couldn't utter such a word.

Ned prodded me. "Say it louder."

I spoke in a normal voice. "I'm drowning in guilt." It was so hard to get it out, and my heart raced. There was a lump in my throat. The room smelled sweaty, like a closed basketball court in winter.

The group chanted, "Say it, Neal, say it."

I bellowed like an elephant seal, "I'm drowning in guilt. I'm drowning in guilt."

"Louder!"

At the top of my lungs, I shouted, "I'm drowning in guilt!" The voice that came out surprised me. I strained my larynx in a roar. My throat was raspy and sore, world-wearied, like Marianne Faithfull's.

Zephyra said, "Again." She motioned to Ned.

Everybody stood.

She said, "Go around the room and say it to each person."

I felt ashamed and ridiculous. "I'm drowning in guilt."

Each face opened.

And for that moment, time stopped. Everything slowed down—the ache and despair. Time stood still. The natural swings of time itself were irrelevant. What day it was didn't matter. My tears flowed heavy, like drenching rain. I was surprised so much fluid resided in my body, a prodigious wet orgasm of salty tears. Wet, soaking tears. No holding back. I didn't shake. Tears just flowed.

Zephyra said, "What are you feeling?"

"My brother's dead." I felt an inkling of joy.

"Don't go killing people off because they're dead," she said.

I chuckled and wept at the same time, like a madman. It was a mixed bag of emotions. I thought, *My time's up. I did it. It's over.* Sad and spent, I was ready to walk away. Also, I was feeling a sense of self-satisfaction, a spark of relief. I thought, *Now Zephyra will signal Ned to play a song and we'll move to the next person.*

To my amazement, Zephyra said, "Would you like to do some role-playing?"

I understood her garbled speech without interpretation. A chill went up my spine. *Do I have anything left?* I replied, "Sure, but aren't I taking up too much time?"

She raised her chin and sniffed, then said, "Look around the room."

Two dozen shining faces nodded.

She said, "Is Neal taking up too much time?"

Someone shouted, "Do it. We love you, Neal." It was Lucille.

Zephyra locked her eyes with mine and repeated, "Look around the room."

People waved and cheered.

Zephyra said, "Who do you want to bring into the room?"

I gulped and said, "Mom."

She looked to the group. "Let's have his mother. This is where it all began."

Every woman in the room raised her hand, even youngsters like PJ. Lucille beamed and smiled, willing and waiting. It felt right that I chose Lucille to role play my mother.

Zephyra looked at me and said, "Where are you?"

"In my bedroom."

She motions Lucille to come forward and shifts her eyes toward Ned. He starts to unstack mattresses and summons others to assist.

"How old?"

"Thirteen."

"Where are you?"

"In bed."

"Lie down."

I reclined on the mattress. Somebody handed me two pillows. An imaginary bedroom with walls and a door were created around me.

"Where's Mom?"

"At the door. She wants to come in."

"What happens?"

"She slides the accordion door open and says she wants to kiss me goodnight."

"What's she wearing?"

"A very flimsy, see-through nighty above her knees. She's naked underneath."

"What do you feel in your body?"

"Confusion. Aroused and ashamed. I know this is wrong."

"Do you have an erection?"

"Yes."

"Where's your father?"

"Away on a business trip. He travels several days a week."

"What happens next?"

"My mother comes to the side of the bed and leans over. I see the outline of her breasts and nipples. One pops out of her night-gown. I reach for her and pull her down. We wrestle, and I play with her breasts. I suck her nipple. She lies beside me, then pulls away as I reach between her legs. After she leaves, I masturbate. I'm so hard, I can't stop myself. I know she's listening."

Zephyra said, "Look around the room."

Some people were crying, others speechless, horrified, angry. All were open with expressions of acceptance and love.

She said to them, "What do you feel?"

Ned shouted, "Child molester!"

Others joined in. "Disgusting! Pervert! Perpetrator! Monster! Arrest her. She can't get away with this."

Zephyra said, "Mothers bear such great responsibility. Such capacity to love and to hurt. They carry the weight of the child's ability to give and receive love. Without love, the child won't be truly nourished. The mother creates the child's world. A confused, misguided, and abusive mother deeply damaged the feminine inside of you. Let's fix this."

I started to cry like a baby, shaking out of control. The weeping earlier was much more comfortable when I cried like a man. Now my belly and sides ached. My mucus membranes were gushing like a waterfall, snot pouring out of my nose. Someone handed me a towel. I dried my face, pulled out a handkerchief, and blew my nose.

Zephyra said, "Fritz used to say, 'To die to be reborn isn't easy.' "

I nodded.

She motioned to Lucille to enter the room and, taking her cue from Zephyra, Lucille sat on the bed.

Zephyra said to the group, "We have to change this mom." Then to Lucille, "Show him how a mother treats her thirteen-year-old son."

Lucille stroked my forehead and said, "How was your day, Neal? Everything going OK at school?"

I nodded.

"Is there anything you want to talk about?"

I said, "I'm scared."

"About what?"

"What's next? High school."

"It's a big transition, but your father and I are here to help you. It's not easy. It wasn't easy for him, and it wasn't for me." She held my hand. "This weekend, your father's taking you to a

Buffalo Bills game. That'll be fun. You two will have some time to talk."

I said, "That's cool."

"Goodnight, Neal." She kissed me on the forehead, stood, and walked out of the room.

Everybody applauded.

Ned motioned the group to come closer.

Someone shouted, "Puppy pile!" and people stacked on me like pancakes. Engulfed in belly laughs and the weight of cuddles, I offered no resistance. It felt good. A woman on each side grabbed a foot and pressed knuckles into my soles. Ed scratched my scalp and pushed my shoulders down. Skilled hands worked the defenseless shores of my body.

"Close your eyes, Neal. Take it in. Take deep breaths and feel it, take it all in," Ned urged.

One by one, people dismounted and burrowed like pups beside me. Ed held my head between his palms like a basketball and said, "Let go and allow me to hold all the weight. Relax." He moved my skull from side to side, adjusted my neck, and tugged it. The women at my feet grabbed my ankles and stretched my body in the other direction. It was a coordinated effort.

"Be grounded, Neal. Find your center," Ned said.

The music started, first with the church-like chimes of an electric guitar. Eric Clapton, conflicted and vulnerable, cried out, "Holy Mother, where are you?" Pavarotti's booming tenor joined in, matching his intensity. People snuggled closer to me. A young woman near my head bawled like a baby. Others sweated and sobbed. Clapton's whining guitar blending with Pavarotti's tenor drove the lyric to the heart. Ned turned up the volume. Finally, an African American church choir locked in and filled all the space. I cried until I was dry. Looking back, it was embarrassing and awkward. We all mourn. We all need to weep. Some of us do it, but most hold it in. Tears never released are self-inflicted bullets

to the heart. We all know that, but it's so confusing, uncomfortable, and raw to let it out.

Where else could something like this happen? Victoria had
been right. I needed Calypso.

Victoria and I had done this work together in Durham when
we returned from our world travels. Once, in a weekend marathon
with a psychologist, six men had held me down while a female
therapist taunted me, "I'll do whatever I want. I'm your mother.
Kiss me." I raged, screamed, and flailed. I damaged my vocal
cords and couldn't speak beyond a whisper for several days. Victoria's capacity for the truth was never more appreciated than at
that moment. I knew then, despite my divorces, I'd married well.
I'd never admitted what happened with my mother to myself or
anyone else.

When the music stopped, a few perspiring bodies still blanketed me. A dozen more crowded my shoulders and legs—a roiling river of body parts. Like a pile of humanity in a biscuit, wet
armpits, chests, bellies, arms, buttocks, and thighs enveloped me.

Zephyra barked, "Let's roll."

Ned motioned for us to break.

A petite, young Asian woman scampered like a crab to the
open seat. The heap on top of me emancipated itself, like sweat-
soaked basketball players after a scrum.

I stood and touched my lips to Zephyra's forehead. It was cold
and clammy, like a corpse, which jarred me.

Her eyes, lidded with tears, rose to meet me like moonbeams.
She turned in the direction of Ned and repeated, "Let's roll." She
added, "He's the rock. I'm the roll."

Same joke, but people laughed.

All for me, bittersweet. Empty and spent, I visioned a painting, rose petals strewn on knee-high, muddy alleys in London
during the Hundred Years' War.

Zephyra signaled, and the room went silent.

I reclaimed my yellow corduroy pillow by the wall. Lucille nestled beside me, held my hand, and said, "Not bad. Although, you've still got work to do."

The young woman in the chair began to relate her story fraught with heartbreak. Her name was U, and there was no hesitation. She talked about her calamity without tears.

Zephyra said, "With trauma, the most important thing is to find a way to express where it resides in the body."

And I knew then that's what I'd been trying to do with my mother's sexual improprieties my entire life.

U screamed, "I can't talk about anything with my parents."

Zephyra said, "Why not talk about it now?"

U's bright face darkened. Her abundant, jet-black hair was pulled back into a ponytail, exposing her broad forehead. Large veins pulsated at her temples. She was angry and confused, but too polite through training to protest. She wore an oversized Chicago Bears football jersey that extended to her knees. Barefoot, she'd left her brown, lace-up leather boots at the door. She crossed and re-crossed her legs, exposing her muscular thighs. She tugged at her hair and started to cry.

She said, "I never cry. What a surprise."

She spoke with a whine that masked a choppy Korean accent. Her language was very precise, interspersed with frequent "fucks" and "fuck yous." She said that neither of her parents spoke English. The family immigrated from Pyongyang to Chicago when she was a baby. She hated her parents and wanted to run away. She said they were frugal to a fault and embarrassed her. Although they could afford to buy clothes, her mother insisted on making everything she wore. And it pissed her off. She recounted her brother's death, hit by a car on a freeway. It threw him ninety feet, killing him on impact.

She repeated, "How can he be gone? He was just here. What

was he thinking while flying through the air? What was he thinking?"

He was a freshman at the University of Miami, an engineering student on a scholarship. While driving the causeway to Miami Beach with a group of friends at night, he got a flat tire. When he got out to fix it, his life ended, splattered across I-95.

Zephyra moved to the role play, and U asked me to play her brother. We couldn't look into each other's eyes, and both of us started to cry.

Zephyra said, "What do you want to say to your brother?"

U said, "What the fuck you doing? You stupid asshole. I love you." Then she looked me in the eyes and said, "I love you." Her body heaved.

Zephyra played, "Just Breathe," sung by Jennifer Warnes.

The group circumambulated, all of us swaying with the music. All week, U had been wearing a stovepipe hat, like Abe Lincoln. Someone handed it to her, and she secured it on her head.

The session ended at 12:30. After lunch, I hustled across campus to meet PJ for the walk to the Source. From a distance, I caught sight of a young woman near the garden swinging a hula hoop around her waist. Her hips shifted with ease. From a distance, she looked like a gyroscope. Her head was close shaven, her shoulders relaxed and still, eyes focused on the ocean. A huge rock close to shore shattered every breaking wave and sent it down the other side like a waterfall. Like the planet itself, she seemed to rotate and spin with minimal effort. She wore a form-fitting, black yoga halter that exposed her six-pack abs. Lycra tights accented her sturdy rump and legs. I tried not to stare. I sensed she was watching me.

When I reached her, she halted and said, "That was good work."

"Thanks."

"I'm London." She reached out a slender, wet hand and shook mine.

I said, "You were near my head when I was on the floor."

"Yeah, that was me bawling my eyes out. So sad about your brother and U's brother. Weird you guys went back to back. It's too much."

"Do you have a brother?"

"Two younger, two older. They're all alive and well." She grimaced. "Sorry about your brother."

I nodded. "You work here with PJ?"

"She's kinda new. I've been here for a while. I'm a patriot, not a mercenary. I live here."

"What do you do?"

"You're looking at it." She extended her right palm and traced a semicircle."

I said, "The farm and garden?"

She nodded, bent down, broke off a leaf, rubbed it between her fingers, and said, "You know what this is?"

I sniffed. "Lavender?"

"Good. How about this one?"

"It smells lemony. I don't know what it's called."

"Lemon verbena."

"How about these others?" She pointed and named, "Fennel, parsley, chives, rosemary, sage, mint, cilantro, dill, tarragon…"

"OK, OK, I've got it. You're into herbs."

Then she pointed toward the farm. The air was crisp with a salty spray. "Do you know what vegetables we're harvesting?"

She walked me down row after row and denoted kale, carrots, turnips, fava beans, broccoli, cucumbers, leeks, and bok choy. I felt the life force of each plant pushing its way to the surface.

"It's beautiful. This job must be in high demand," I said.

"I started cleaning rooms, then moved into the kitchen. I wanted the garden from the start. I grow things."

As we spoke, I remembered her work with Zephyra and the story she'd told. Her father's business partner and best friend came on to her. She was twelve, and he slipped into her bed, drunk, while his wife and London's parents partied downstairs. He felt her up. She'd never told anybody.

I said, "You did good work too."

She scowled and looked much older, her face no longer the equal of her well-muscled, youthful body. Wrinkles and even a few gray specks surfaced in her short crop of dark hair. The brilliant sunlight wasn't kind. Her anger toward men and her sense of betrayal were palpable.

I took a deep breath.

She said, "You look like you're in a hurry. Where're you going?"

"To meet PJ. We're walking to the Source."

She said, "Don't roil the water where you may have to drink."

"What do you mean?"

"My mother used to say it. You shouldn't stir things up."

I said, "Did you ever walk up there?"

She said, "It's a long way, and it's steep…"

I persisted, "Do you go up there?"

"Of course, but I wouldn't expect my parents to do it. It's a long way and a crazy vertical. There are points where you need to climb a ladder. Maybe you should take a walking stick."

"I can do it."

She said, "Suit yourself. By the way, you did good as U's brother. I could feel it. You weren't acting."

"I felt her love for her brother and let it in."

She said, "You really got into it. My parents split, and my mom's an alcoholic."

"I'm sorry."

"What are you sorry for? It's not your fault."

I said, "Do you want to walk with us?"

"Yeah, I got time. Think PJ will mind? You two are pretty tight."

"I knew her before. It's strange we ran into each other again up here."

As we sauntered, London identified more vegetables—rainbow chard, green onions, and beets.

I asked, "How did you learn all this?"

"I work here. This is my garden."

We waited for PJ beneath the eucalyptus trees near the bridge. A few monarch butterflies flapped around above us. Ten minutes later, she bounded down the hill. She greeted London with a hug and said, "You coming?"

London gave me a once over and said to PJ, "Think he can make it?"

PJ said, "I'll vouch for him."

"I told him to get a walking stick. It's gnarly and vertical."

PJ said, "He'll be OK."

London said, "We'll carry the old man if he collapses."

They cackled like crows.

We approached the pipe-braced fence. Tall, old-growth pines behind us near the ocean lent dappled shade.

I said, "What a weird, wonderful gate. My grandfather did stuff like this. He crafted a door latch in the shape of a whale."

PJ said, "That's so cool. It's whimsical."

"Looks like junk art to me," London said.

I said, "Who's the artist?"

"I don't know, but somebody really put some time into it. It's been here a long time," London said.

Six vertical bars hung on a heavy, rusty steel frame. As I rubbed my hand along the sandy, oxidized slats, I felt the artist's intent. Each bar was hand-hewn and bent into a serpentine pattern. It emitted a dingy yellow glow—the weight of its heavy casting counterbalanced by a tin can of hardened concrete hanging on a chain.

PJ said, "It looks like rivers."

London said, "Flowing waters. Why am I afraid?"

"Solitude. You're not used to it," PJ said.

"It's more than that. What if something happens…"

I said, "What's the big deal? I've climbed mountains before."

A weatherworn, wood-burned sign cautioned, "ENTER AT YOUR OWN RISK. PLEASE USE CAUTION. PLEASE TREAT THIS AREA LIKE A TEMPLE."

PJ unlatched and pushed the gate open. It made a harsh, grating sound, and the tin can rose. It descended as she closed it.

London said, "Do you really think this is a good idea?"

Carved in the concrete, right-side-up from inside at our feet, were the words, "BE FREE."

The dirt path was tight, cramped, and dusty with close undergrowth. Ahead, water spurted down the mountainside like a fire hydrant, happy and unhindered. The creek emitted a howl, exhilarating as a rock concert. I felt an invisible hand beckon me.

London pointed and said, "That's poison oak."

I was wearing shorts and the thicket brushed against my legs.

She scolded me, "Do you really think wool socks and hiking boots are enough? What a tenderfoot."

She extended her right and left index fingers like pistols, and exclaimed, "It's over here and over there. Look at that vine…"

A snaky, creeping plant crawled forty feet up the side of a tree.

She crouched down and observed, "If you run through this stuff, it'll ruin your day."

The plants she identified presented a mystery. They all looked the same to me. Some were big, some small. One branch had bright, brownish-red leaves, another green. Some leaves were slim, others stout. Some were spiny, others soft and innocuous.

I said, "Should I go back and put on long pants? I'm reactive and hypersensitive to everything. A few years back, I was in an allergy clinic. An injection sent me into anaphylaxis. I passed out. The nurse called a doctor who administered epinephrine that brought me back. After that, they kicked me out of the clinic."

PJ said, "Show him how to tell the difference."

London squatted and examined the foliage. After contemplation, she said, "Leaves of three, don't touch me."

I said, "But almost everything has three leaves."

"Yeah, so don't touch it."

PJ said sarcastically, "So glad you came along."

I wasn't sure if she meant London or me.

We started the climb and, like opening a book, we entered a new world. The terrain changed, everything dominated by thick, red shafts of skyward-seeking trees. Each step was cushioned by centuries of redwood duff, and the soil grew dark and moist. I felt like I was wearing slippers on a plush carpet, and I'd accidently put my shoes on the wrong feet. For a moment, I was part of it— the rushing water, thick coyote brush, glistening rhododendron, sword ferns, and towering trees. Then I tripped on a protruding rock.

London's face stiffened. "Watch your step, Tenderfoot."

I snarled.

The path, strewn with roots, stumps, and fallen branches, made for rough going. It was unpredictable and precarious. Light streamed through, like in a cathedral, in spotty patches. As the forest enveloped us, we became insignificant specks in a heap of organic debris. Straining my neck to the heavens, I couldn't see the treetops. The needle crowns rose to unrivaled heights a football field above us.

We halted on the first ridge and studied the creek as it rushed to the ocean a few hundred yards away. Whitewater spurted like a fountain from the ascendant mountain. The stream jumped with enthusiasm, and the air smelled clean. And like some people, some of the water lingered. Upstream, rivulets formed tiny waterfalls. Silver sheets shimmered, water dribbled over pale gray rocks and broken trees.

None of us spoke, captivated by the intricacies of the flow, like watching a fire on a cold winter night. Our retinas were assaulted by a riot of green along the banks.

"*Sequoia sempervirens*," London whispered. She drew a tiny, green pinecone out of her pocket and picked up a colossal, brown, bushy pinecone off the ground. The edges extended beyond her fingertips. Looking up, she said, "Which one?" She nodded in PJ's direction. "If you know, don't say anything."

I said, "Trick question?"

She grimaced. "OK, OK, you already know the answer. Big tree, little pinecone," and she launched into a monologue. "People compare these forests to those old, dark cathedrals in Europe. I've been to Chartres, Notre-Dame, and Hagia Sophia, and none compare to this wilderness. These forests are a sanctuary, solemn in a different way. The silence you feel here is to be alive among living and sentient beings. Each time you exhale carbon, these trees give back oxygen. And they've been here since the time of the dinosaurs. We're living and breathing with them now. It makes me quiet. Forces anyone who's sensitive to it to whisper and better yet hold your tongue. A thin layer of cells called the cambium pumps nutrients. It's like our heart. *Sempervirens* means 'always alive,' 'evergreen.' A lifespan measured in centuries."

I said, "What kills them?"

"Lightning, fire, insects, and we've cut ninety-five percent of these forests down. Like people, ageism gets them. When you live a long time, bad things happen. The foundation fails. They fall and break. The roots are shallow. There's no taproot. Long tendrils extend under the ground that intertwine and support each other. That's what gives them their strength. When a tree topples, a new tree can sprout from the carnage. Look around. There's no perfect symmetry. It's not like the Parthenon. There's randomness, yet each whorl reveals the Fibonacci sequence in every pinecone." She held both pinecones up for us to observe. "There's no Michelangelo or da Vinci in this wilderness. It all happened long before the Greeks, Romans, and medieval cathedrals. It drives me nuts when people compare the redwoods to human-built things."

PJ said, "Let's keep moving."

We crossed a bridge constructed of a fallen redwood tree ten feet in diameter with furrowed bark a foot thick. Only with the help of a metal stirrup-step were we able to mount it. It was still a balancing act, requiring skill and dexterity to navigate a hundred feet to the other side.

I thought, *Glad I don't have the burden of a walking stick.*

On the other side, the big trees started to show noticeable scars from the wildfire the summer before. I'd heard about it but didn't realize how close it had come to Calypso, the campus a stone's throw away. Some of the trees had burned to stumps. Others had been cored out, gouged by flames. There was a dirty charcoal smell. A pungent chimney of vapor came out of one of the cave-like openings. Three kitchen employees were smoking a joint inside. We passed them as if they weren't there. They were laughing and joking and paid no attention to us.

London identified tan oaks, Douglas firs, madrone, and Sitka spruce. She was looking for a Santa Lucia fir, a rarity that only grows here.

PJ said, "Let's tell some secrets." I noticed her wrists were bare. She wasn't wearing bangles. Her inner wrists were scared with tiny cuts, crusted, and healing.

I felt a knot in my stomach.

London said, "Isn't that what we've been doing all week?"

"And that's why we're here," PJ said. "The truth will set you free."

"Yeah, yeah, yeah," London said. "You can't have the future

you want without cleaning up your past. I've read *A Course in Miracles* too. I think it's overrated."

PJ turned to London and said, "Tell me something you've never told anyone."

London shrugged. "I told that story about my father's friend."

PJ raised an eyebrow. "There's more…"

"Well, I've had to deal with that bastard my whole life. He was at my wedding," London said.

"You're married?" PJ said.

"It didn't last very long."

PJ said, "I thought you were gay."

"It took me a while to figure it out."

I said, "What happened?"

"It didn't get better. It got much worse. I had an affair with my piano teacher."

PJ said, "See, that wasn't too hard. What about you, Neal?"

"Three marriages."

"That's no big deal," PJ said. "You're old enough to have had four or even five. My therapist, who's your age, has had five. And I'm sure you told somebody that before. At least your current wife. I want to hear the good stuff. Stuff you've never told anybody."

"What about you? What are your secrets?" I asked.

"My birth mother isn't my mother. My father conceived me with a nun, and my mother adopted me."

London said, "A nun?"

"Yes, my father did some law work for the Carmelites."

I said, "That's a cloistered order. They don't get outside the walls."

"She handled the outside business. They fell in love, and it's quite romantic. I'm a love child," PJ said.

London said, "Where is she now?"

"She stayed in the order. Catholics confess, then all's forgiven. My mother decided to live with it. Here I am."

I said, "You're the daughter of a nun?"

"Sister Payton Jean, please. What about you, Neal? It's time to come clean. You have all this guilt. Let's put it this way, what's the guiltiest thing you've ever done? It will do you good to talk about it."

I paused and thought about it. *I'll never see these young women again, and if I do, it'll be in a different context. Who cares?* Although, once I started talking, I didn't know where it would lead.

We continued to climb, and the path narrowed.

I said, "We'll be bushwhacking before you know it."

"No," London said. "It's tight but well-marked. Like the stirrups in the redwood tree bridge, somebody thought this out."

I said, "I lied to my wife."

"Which one?" they both asked.

"Well, all of them. But this was a big lie. The second one, I kept it to myself for eight years and never told anybody. Don't you have stuff like that too? Where it's too shameful to reveal, even to yourself?"

"Go on, spill it," PJ said.

I said, "Do you want to hear the whole story?"

London said, "Enough already, just tell it."

"It started over a salad in the days when airplanes served food. I heard a flirtatious laugh. When I turned, I saw a woman in a lively conversation with a man a few rows back. She shook her hair. I wasn't the only one looking. Little did I know anything would come of it. I smiled back, and later she told me it's OK to lie naked with a man as a friend. But I'm getting ahead of the story."

PJ, London, and I continued the long slog up the mountain. I heard the cadence of our boots punching the hollow ground. The slope was getting steeper. When I looked down through the chaparral, the creek bubbled three hundred feet below.

I said, "It was the American Heart Association National conference in Milwaukee. I was on my way from North Carolina. The plane stopped in Chicago, and on stepped Marla Most. She was hard to miss, not a beauty but a woman who knew how to use what she had. When we got to the baggage claim, we realized we were going to the same meeting. On the street, she asked if I wanted to share a cab. I said sure, and we began a conversation that lasted four days. When we got to the hotel, our room assignments were next to each other, assigned by last name. I helped her with her bags. It was a huge place, a convention center with maze-like hallways. People were running in every direction, arriving in crowds from everywhere. She said, 'Let's meet for dinner.' "

London ran ahead and shouted, "That's it!"

She pointed skyward, at a thick, straight Christmas tree jutting out of the mountainside.

It was greener than the rest, like in the hills in western Ireland. The tree held the elegance of something rare, a one of a kind, a shooting star, a hapless moment.

London said, "I've never seen this one before."

I said, "A Santa Lucia fir?"

"Yep."

"Keep the story going," PJ said.

We trekked on.

I said, "Marla told me about her life as a nurse and exercise physiologist in a small hospital in Evansville, Indiana. She was furious with her husband. She said he was fat, a psychologist, and getting pushed around by the DRGs. Funny how I remember the expression, 'pushed around.' "

"What are DRGs?" PJ said.

"I think it stands for diagnosis-related group. It's a way to categorize costs. At the time, it was new. She felt he wasn't getting reimbursed and making enough money. They had a five-month-old baby. I told her about my aspiration to become program director at Duke and my ambition to build something that never existed before there or anywhere else. I blabbered on about the Rice Diet and Dr. Walter Kempner. He was in his late eighties and had been at it for fifty years. He was the pioneer, the one who set the stage for treating heart disease without drugs or surgery. She looked at me as if we were making love. I forgot about the food. The moment went still, like a photograph. Her eyes wet, her attention gripped, and I locked into her. The meeting I'd fought so hard with my boss to pay for became irrelevant. Marla said, 'It's not the meetings that are important. It's the people you meet.' And I've practiced that rule ever since."

A little bark interspersed with squeaks and chirps came from the underbrush.

"That's a ground squirrel," PJ said.

"Listen again," London said. "Become an ear. Ninety percent of perception is listening."

We stood still as a rivulet oozed across the black, wet earth. A slimy, slow-moving, eel-like creature slithered from under a log. Brown and spotted, the size of a small trout with hands and bulging eyes, it slipped back into the darkness.

PJ said, "Looks like a mini dinosaur."

"They haven't changed much since then," London said.

I said, "How long ago is that?"

"Two hundred and forty-five million years, give or take."

"Is it a lizard?"

"No, it's amphibious, a Pacific giant salamander. It has no scales. Didn't you notice its moist skin? I've seen them up in Santa Cruz but never here. Most salamanders are mute, but this one growls and clicks. They're not dangerous. You can pick it up if you can catch it."

I said, "I don't want to pick it up."

PJ hopped a little in delight. "Yippee! A Santa Lucia fir and a funky, foot-long salamander on the same day. Wow. Now let's hear the rest of the story, Neal."

I said, "It seemed like a setup. Why was Marla's room next to mine? Why were we having dinner together? I tried to brush off the intimate and penetrating looks. Both of us locked in, not letting go. How could this happen? How could this be possible? All my boyhood dreams of meeting a total stranger and making love to her all night were within reach.

"We lingered over drinks and bread. The night of long shadows under fluorescent light at the convention center felt like a café on the Seine. In search of each other in every corner, we couldn't escape each other's stares. Neither of us wanted the evening to end, and it slowed to a passion of wonder. Both hesitated, uncertain, excited, and visceral. The restaurant closed around us. But I thought, *What about my wife? I'm chairman of the Bahá'í Assembly. I work at Duke.* Then there was the constant pang of not being good enough, of having a pot belly, pimples, and glasses. We kept talking. She was tall and lean. What about her new baby at home with her husband? What was going to happen when we got back to our adjacent rooms? There was a locked door between the rooms, sometimes used to connect them as a suite. I could taste my blood boiling. Neither one of us wanted to separate. Sleep was out of the question.

"Ice cubes melted in cold, dripping glasses. The restaurant closed. I'd come to Milwaukee to attend lectures in dark rooms with sunburned slides. She said, 'You go to everything, don't you?' I said, 'I went to the mat with my boss to come here. He objected, but he wasn't willing to take on the war.' She said, 'I don't think that's what you get out of coming to something like this.'

"Then I got paranoid. Had I been set up? First, her flipping her hair on the plane and that flirtatious laugh. Then, sharing a cab and finding out we had adjacent rooms. The pheromones were popping between us like soap bubbles. I knew if I succumbed, my marriage was over. I could never tell my wife with any hope of forgiveness. So, the first night, facing massive resistance, I said goodnight without contact. With a profound ache of disappointment, I said, 'Thanks for the evening.' She looked at me and said, 'What?' I closed my door and entered my room aroused, knowing she was next door. I knew I couldn't go there. I called Scarlett and told her I'd gotten to Milwaukee and was getting settled for the meeting tomorrow. I said, 'I met someone on the plane. We had dinner together.' I left out that she was an attractive woman and in the room next door. And she was calling me into her arms. It was a hopeless situation. Tomorrow ensued, the light we'd lit now an inferno. I wasn't able to white knuckle it or douse my desire with willpower."

"That's it?" said London. "What's this, the G-rated version? We want details."

PJ said, "This didn't end well."

I said, "No, in fact, it haunts me. What do you want to know?"

London said, "Well, you had sex?"

"I haven't told you the worst part. The next day, we skipped all the meetings, rented a car, and went to the Bahá'í House of Worship in Willamette. My enthusiasm bubbled over. I wanted Marla to know everything about me. I held nothing back."

"What's Bahá'í?" PJ said.

"It's a world religion."

London said, "You took her to a church?"

"That's romantic," PJ said.

"It's a huge, domed temple surrounded by fountains and gardens," I said. "There's only one on each continent."

"Very romantic," London said.

PJ said, "I've never heard of it."

"Seals and Crofts?"

Both of them looked at me, quizzically.

"Summer Breeze?"

PJ said, "Oh yeah, soft rock. They also did, 'We May Never Pass This Way Again.' "

I said, "And 'Diamond Girl,' 'Get Closer,' 'Hummingbird,' and lots of others. Seals and Crofts got me through PA school. Jim Seals and Dash Crofts did concerts all over the world promoting the Bahá'í faith."

PJ said, "I'd forgotten the name of the group."

London said, "That was a long time ago."

"Being a Bahá'í was a big part of my life and the foundation of my marriage."

"You really fucked up," said London.

I said, "All kidding aside…"

"I wasn't kidding." London said.

They both laughed.

London said, "How the hell did you get involved with the Bahals?"

I corrected, "Bahá'ís."

"OK. Bahá'ís."

"After Aleida left me, I met Scarlett, and she took me to a meeting, called a Fireside."

"You joined?" they both asked in unison.

"I was a mess, having panic attacks, almost burned down my apartment in Ft. Lauderdale while making rice. I was desperate, looking for something, and it made a lot of sense."

"Sense?" London said.

"That all religions are one religion, and every human being is a citizen of the earth."

"Sounds good," said PJ.

"Also, they believe in the equality of men and women. That there should be a single currency and intermarriage between the races. They repudiate gossip and backbiting. And sexual intercourse is only permitted between husband and wife—"

"That's where you really fucked up." London giggled.

I continued, "I remember the ride from Milwaukee to Chicago, full of flashing lights and road work. Why didn't I get the message and turn around?"

"Don't be too hard on yourself, Neal. We all do stupid things we regret," PJ said.

"I wish I hadn't talked about this. The sex was crazy. Marla was talking to her husband in the next room while I talked to Scarlett in mine. It was complete deceit, and I wasn't the victim but the perpetrator."

"Let's hear about the sex, and don't leave anything out," London said.

"The Bahá'í temple is surreal…"

"When are you getting to the sex?" London pressed.

"Soon, but this seems like an important part of the story. It was a dark, dirty, dreary day, and it took a couple hours to get there."

London said, "I know the area. It's a straight shot on 94 South along the shores of Lake Michigan."

"You know Willamette?"

"I've never been there, but it's north of Chicago, right?" London said.

"You know better than I do."

PJ said, "This place sounds amazing."

"The temple rises above trees. It's overwhelming. You feel like a dwarf and not only because it's enormous. It exudes spiritual energy. Every surface is hand-carved and ornate, like the Taj Mahal. It looks like a wedding cake, super-white, like fallen snow. They mixed concrete and quartz to get the effect. Marla and I were having 'This isn't Kansas anymore' moments. We walked around the gardens and she motioned for me to hold her hand. The backs of our hands touched. The staff was so gracious and hospitable, people of all ethnicities work there. They rolled out the red carpet and couldn't do enough for us. We felt it. Inside the circular dome, there are comfortable padded chairs—nothing in a straight line like pews in churches. Huge vases overflowed with flowers. The dome is ten stories high, modern and classical at the same time. Marla looked up in wonder and said, 'I've never seen anything like this.'

"We stayed for three and a half hours, and it was hard to leave. We drove back to Milwaukee in silence and awe. That's when she said, 'It's OK for a man and woman who are friends to lie naked together.'

"I thought I'd heard her wrong, but that's what she said. We parked, took the elevator, and walked down the long, florescent hallway to our rooms. She went to her room, and I went to mine. Ten minutes later, I heard a knock on the door. When I opened it, she stood there in a white, knee-length trench coat. She unbuttoned it burlesque-style and flashed her pink flesh."

London said, "Now, we're getting somewhere. Go on."

PJ said, "First, we've gotta get up this."

She pointed toward a straight up labyrinth of chaparral and tangled madrone trees a few feet ahead. The footpath became tortuous and sharp. We rambled deeper into the wilderness.

London said, "Did you notice the peeling red bark? No two are the same."

I said, "Are you sure this is the right way?"

"Keep going. It's well marked," London said.

Each twist and turn seemed more slippery than the last. I wondered how we'd find our way back. I used my hands to climb. Black, grainy, sandy soil slipped between my fingers and cut my palms.

When we got to the top, London said, "What happened next? You left us in suspense."

I was breathing hard but said, "How many more..."

"Another ten minutes, maybe fifteen. There's a ladder not too far from here."

"Where was I?"

"Marla's bare ass naked at the door," PJ said.

I noticed a raised mole on her upper lip I hadn't seen before. I said, "Have you ever been to one of these places?"

"A hotel?" London laughed.

"No, a large convention center. This place had a thousand rooms with a skyway between the buildings."

"So, what's your point?"

"It was huge. Every room smelled like new carpet."

"Toxic, volatile, organic compounds," PJ said.

"A foul mix of carpet chemicals. I forgot all about that until now. It made me hoarse, short of breath, and my sinuses clogged up. All that didn't matter. Marla and I wrestled and kissed and fell onto the rough, worn, polyester bedspread. She helped me slip off my clothes. We touched each other, timidly at first. She said, 'I'm very fertile. I didn't want the last one.' My pecker was about to explode. She said, 'You can come in my mouth,' and she sucked me."

As we walked, the trees twisted around us like red spikes. Bulging burls appeared at the base. Ferns grew taller, and we were no longer looking down at the creek in the ravine. We'd come parallel and closer to its source.

PJ said, "We're almost there."

London said, "What happened next?"

"The usual stuff."

"Like what?

"You've seen pornography."

"Don't leave us hanging," PJ said.

"The arousal was phenomenal. I felt like I was outside my body. Marla's temples flushed and reddened. To the touch, it felt like a bad sunburn. Hot blood, like a rash, crept up the sides of her face. I wondered if it had something to do with being recently pregnant. It was new to me. Her skin boiled. My cock seeped seminal fluid, and I was so hard I couldn't let down. It hurt. Too aroused to turn back, I rolled on top of her. When I put my cock inside her, she said, 'Is it in yet?' So stretched out from the baby, her crease was beyond anything I could fill, but the passion never ceased. I plowed every furrow, jackhammering at times. I, too, didn't want to come, afraid of the consequences."

"So, what happened?" London asked with half-open dowager's eyes.

"All three nights, she wouldn't sleep with me in the same bed. I never entered her room. She'd knock on the door, and we'd fuck. She'd take a short nap after intercourse, we'd do it again, and then she'd leave to call her husband and inquire about her child. After that level of intimacy, soaking in her body fluids, it was odd to be alone at the meeting. My body longed for her. She was in my body, and I was in hers. I knew people from all over the country. I thought they sensed what was going on but were playing dumb. One morning, I walked through the exhibits by myself. A treadmill salesman in a polyester suit smirked and said, 'You look like you had a really good night.' Sure he knew, I went crimson and didn't attend any meetings. Marla and I went to restaurants, and on the last day, we rented a Harley."

"A Harley?" London said.

"She was into bikes. She drove, and I sat on the back. We went to Kenosha."

"Yeah, there's a beautiful waterfront," London said.

"That's it. That's where we went. Once, while we were in the act, Marla said, 'If we lived in the same place, I could fall in love with you.' "

"Is there more?"

"She'd suck me before and after intercourse. She couldn't get enough of me in her mouth. It felt a little creepy, like she tasted herself. And I thought about the baby, the amniotic fluid, the waters breaking like Niagara Falls. Worn raw, she wanted more. Her gap was huge, but with eager anticipation, I obliged. She said in the peak of passion, 'You can never tell anyone. And if you do, I'll deny everything.' "

I paused as we climbed, then asked, "Is that enough? Did I come clean?"

"Only you know that, Neal. Is there more?" said PJ.

London asked, "Did you ever see her again?"

"We never saw each other again. A month later, Marla wrote me a letter on her hospital stationary asking for more information about the Rice Diet. I never answered. I never told anyone and lived in denial for eight years. Even my therapist told me not to tell Scarlett. Sometimes I wish I hadn't."

"You told Scarlett?" PJ said.

"Only under duress. Victoria and I connected while Scarlett and I were still together. It was an unstoppable force. Scarlett was convinced she could salvage the marriage and wouldn't let go. She released me and found her rage only after I told her about Marla. Before that, Scarlett was a doormat, clinging to whatever scraps remained. Once she knew about Marla, she took pleasure in punishing me and seized our assets. She called me a murderer. Overwrought with guilt, I complied."

"Was it worth telling her?"

"It's always better. Lies to protect people don't work. There's always a reckoning. A year later, she remarried another Bahá'í. We're both better off now."

PJ said, "I guess you're not a Bahá'í anymore."

"*Persona non grata*," I said. "It was bad, and I resigned. Scarlett's family rejected me. My brother-in-law, who was my best friend, wrote me a letter. It was too painful to read. He said I was a covenant breaker, and he couldn't have anything more to do with me. I wish I'd kept the letter. So painful at the time, I destroyed it."

"Why do you wish you kept it?" London said.

"Maybe in hindsight I'd understand what it was all about. I've tried over the years to make contact, and they reject me as if I'm dead."

"That's the thing about religion. You're either in or you're out," said London.

"Would you do it again?" asked PJ.

I said, "Talking about this makes me think about that period of my life, and all of it was a lie. Scarlett wasn't honest, and I was a fake. I hated who I was and what I was becoming—an overstuffed shirt and a tie. A garden salad had more feeling."

PJ flashed an empathetic glance. "I mean if I you could go back."

London said, "Yes, would you have white-knuckled it with Marla?"

"No, I was desperate, and Marla broke the curse. I wouldn't have lied. That was the mistake. It ate me up inside. Now I know better."

"How did Victoria come into your life?" PJ said.

London added, "Was it passion?"

I said, "How much farther to the top? When are you going to tell me your stories?"

"Don't you think it's cool that we're interested?" London said.

PJ added, "It's like Zephyra's Walk and Talk. Go with it."

I said, "The X-rated version. We fell in love while married to other people."

London exclaimed, "I knew this was going to be good."

"And yes, it was passion. I would've killed to be with Victoria. It felt like destiny, but we hurt a lot of people. And yes, I would do it again. You can't go back and change things. And you can't regret what you did for the rest of your life."

We came to a twelve-foot ladder leaning against a steep drop-off.

"This is it," said PJ.

Looking at both of them, I said, "You didn't need to carry me."

The western wall of mountains blocked the sun. The dark, somber dignity of the redwoods blanketed us like a shawl. There was profound silence, only the sound of the water percolating through earth and stone. We had come to an end of this little canyon that opens into the sea. We'd tracked the waterway to its source.

"Is this it?" I asked.

Water bubbled beneath a shoal of gray rocks.

London said, "Did anybody bring snacks?"

PJ pulled out a greasy plastic bag of trail mix and said, "I made it myself."

An unsavory blend of sweaty cashews, granola, and melted chocolate chips streaked the sack.

London turned up her nose. "When? During the Mesozoic Era? That's all you brought?"

"It's all I've got. Don't take too much."

I grabbed a handful and said, "Delicious."

London said, "I'm going to pee." She walked a hundred feet into the woods and squatted.

PJ and I sat on a fallen log.

Fifteen minutes later, we commenced our descent. My knees were stiff, the air cold and moist, and twilight threatened. A salty fog tightened its grip like a lasso around the needle tops. Long, opaque shadows followed us down.

When we reached the gate, I assessed my body. My legs were bruised and battered. I'd scraped both knees and a line of clotted blood had hardened on my shins. My palms were scratched and browned with mud. But worse, I didn't feel the sense of satisfaction I thought I would. There was no cause for celebration. PJ and London went to dinner. I told them I was going to wash up and meet them later. That's all I remember. I crawled into my bunk and fell asleep. When I woke, it was dark, my bunkmates were snoring, and stale breath and perspiration permeated the room. My mouth was dry, like I'd taken a drug. I scrambled out of bed like a crab. Once my feet hit the cold floor, I shivered. It was an agony to stand or bend. My throat was sore. I waddled like a penguin, pulled on a sweatshirt, and hobbled down the hill.

When I got to the baths, there was a mob. What time was it? There were dozens of people I'd never seen before. They wore cut-offs, makeshift bathing gear, and abstained from nudity. The dressing room looked like Walmart on Black Friday. A few tired shreds of humanity bustled in every direction—T-shirts, jackets, and socks were strewn across the puddled floor. There was a sense of urgency and anxiety out of sync with my expectations. I had trouble locating a hook to hang my clothes. Once stripped, I felt self-conscious. I turned my ankle on someone's muddy work boots. But in the shower, I felt at home, as if I belonged, a loner to this moment and time. No one could take this experience away from me. A full moon beamed a highway of light across the ocean. The agitated brine beat like a washing machine.

All the tubs were full. I squeezed in with a half dozen others— two young women in lime bikinis soaked with four men in cut off denim—all with worn, pickled faces. Though comfortable and warm, it felt glacial. No one spoke. I extended my tired legs and looked at the moon. Within five minutes, they fled. For a few delicious minutes, I was alone.

Then I heard voices, an Irish brogue from two men standing by the iron railing. One was tall and lean, the other short and stocky. They stretched their necks out over the ocean.

The tall one said, "You're shitting me. Noel and Mike got fifteen grand for that?"

The short one replied, "Sure enough, and we can make a stack like that too, Johnny."

"They did hardly nothing."

"That's what I'm telling you, and they'll pay us mightily in LA."

I thought for a moment, wondering if they were talking about the Cranberries. The tall one was lean and rangy. The moon glow backlit his long, thick, black hair. The short one's skull reflected the lunar radiance like a mirror. Bare-chested, wearing cutoffs, they carried on the debate. Muffled by the waves, I could hear only fragments. I perked my ears. The subject shifted.

The tall one said, "Leaving a woman for another woman is no way to find yourself." Then he plunged into the water like a pelican and dunked his head. His locks spread out like Medusa, and he remained face down for several minutes.

I looked at his friend.

He said, "He does this all the time. Likes to play dead. Gives him a sense of immortality." The short one strolled down the steps, into the tub.

After an uncomfortable pause, the tall fellow sat up with a jolt. He coughed and gasped for air like he was drowning. His hair draped like seaweed on his slender pale shoulders. He said, "What are you in fer?"

I looked at the stocky one.

He said, "He's talking to you."

"My brother died," I said.

"So that's what people come here fer, reflection and redemption?"

"I've never heard anybody put it that way. In my case, it's more like resuscitation."

"I wish we had something like this back home, don't you, Dave? For the love of God, look at that moon."

The short one said, "Oh shite and onions! I don't want to eat your head off, just look around ye. They look like a bunch of headers to me. All these bloody gowls running around bullock naked. I have to say, it's not for me. I'll play the feckin' hand I'm dealt."

"Not necessarily. We all need a wee bit of a vacation from ourselves. Isn't that what this place provides?"

I nodded.

The tall one reached out his hand. "Johnny Rayge."

His friend buried his shoulders in the water. "Dave."

I said, "Neal."

"That's no way to introduce yourself, Big Wave Dave," Johnny said.

I smiled. "Big Dave Wave?"

"No, Big Wave Dave, and if you ever see him swim, you'll see it for yourself. Hands, arms, legs all moving like a windmill. He's a feckin' turbine. Show him what you can do, Dave. Turn this cistern into a washing machine."

Dave rolled his eyes. "Stop acting the maggot, Johnny."

I said, "Where you from?"

"Well, I'd be shitting you if I said Ar-kan-saw. He's from Limerick, and I'm a culchie from Roscommon. We live in Dublin."

Dave said, "We're in a band."

"Like U2?"

"I reckon," Johnny said.

Dave said, "Johnny sings. I play drums."

"Lead guitar," Johnny said.

"Feck off. You wanker like Mick Jagger."

I said, "I love Ireland."

"We do too, but you gotta come to the big land to cash in your chips."

I said, "You staying here?"

Johnny said, "No, drove up from LA for the night, or the morning, or whatever you want to call it. Wanted to see the place where Henry Miller spent his prime."

I said, "This wasn't his prime. He was fifty-three years old. He'd already written *The Tropics* and *Black Spring*."

"Ah, so you know a little something about literature?" Johnny said.

"I like it."

"You say you like Ireland. Isn't that what he said, Dave?"

"He said he *loves* Ireland."

"What about June 16, 1904?"

"Bloomsday, James Joyce, *Ulysses*, the whole book happens on that single day."

"We've got a scholar here, Dave. But do you know why James Joyce chose that day?"

I said, "Something to do with the Irish Revolution?"

"Wrong, you're a decade late. Got any other ideas?"

"There was a war going on between Russia and Japan. Wasn't a ship sunk?"

Johnny's eyes flashed in the moonlight.

Big Wave Dave sat up straight.

"He's also a historian," Johnny said. "Done guessing? Want me to tell you?"

It felt like he had me in a choke hold, and it was time to tap out.

Johnny said, "Because that particular day far exceeded Mr. Joyce's expectations."

Dave chuckled.

Johnny said, "And these are the man's own words: 'You slid your hand down inside my trousers and pulled my shirt softly aside and touched my prick with your long tickling fingers and gradually took it all, fat and stiff as it was, into your hand and frigged me slowly until I came off through your fingers, all the time bending over me and gazing at me out of your quiet saintlike eyes.'"

Dave said, "Beautiful, Johnny. 'Twas 'The Prick with the Stick's' first lick with Nora Barnacle."

I looked at both with suspicion.

Dave said, "The man wrote the words himself. Addressed his lass as 'my dirty little fuck bird.' "

"Have you read the letters?" Johnny said.

I shook my head.

"So, your brother died," Dave said. "I'm sorry. My mother died giving birth to my sister."

"That's a long time ago," said Johnny. "Let's not talk about that."

Dave said, "And that's what brought you here?"

"I'm in a Gestalt group led by a woman with ALS, Zephyra? Have you heard of her?"

"Can't say I have." Johnny said.

Dave shook his head.

I said, "At LAX I ran in front of bus, wanted to die. Did you ever want to kill yourself?"

Johnny said, "All the time. Sometimes me life just sickens me. I question if I want to live at all. Why was we born?"

"You're getting morbid," Dave said.

"Rebellion's the only thing that keeps us alive," Johnny said.

"It doesn't get any darker than not wanting to live," Dave said. "That's as dark as it can go, I suppose. Be smart. Let's talk about something else."

I said, "What kind of music do you play?"

"What do you think? We're the niggers of Europe."

"Don't say that too loud," I said.

Dave said, "We're proud of it."

"Yeah, but it's not cool to use the N-word in the States."

Johnny said, "The N-word, is it? Nigger, nigger, nigger. I'm black, and I'm proud."

I sat back and looked at the moon. The Milky Way salted the entire maritime sky.

Johnny hummed and sang softly at first. Dave joined in, "And we're all off to Dublin in the green, in the green. Where the helmets glisten in the sun. Where the bayonets flash and the rifles crash to the rattle of a Thompson gun."

He sang each verse in a loud, confident Irish tenor. Dave joined in on the chorus, and I sang along.

"So, what goes on with this lady?" Dave asked.

"People talk about themselves and reenact painful episodes in their life. She uses music to help them get clearer, closer to the emotion."

Johnny said, "What did you talk about?"

"I'd rather not say. I've been talking ever since I got here. I write too."

Johnny said, "I knew you were a writer."

I looked at him.

He said, "Because you've got a pencil for a dick."

They both chuckled.

Dave said, "But really, what happened in this group of yers?"

Johnny said, "Did it help?"

"Yes, it helped. It's not what I talked about. It's what I acted out, what took place in my body. I have a lot of guilt."

Johnny said, "Never let your mind get in the way of a good fuck."

Dave stood up and said, "Johnny, we need to get back to LA."

"A few more minutes. The craic's 90." Johnny said.

Dave twisted his face and got serious. "We got a meeting in the morning."

Johnny replied, "Where?"

"Century City."

"Ah, we'll make it fine. Five more minutes," Johnny said.

Dave looked at me. "Sounds like you had an epiphany?"

Johnny said, "Don't let the words get in the way of what you're trying to say."

I said, "The most important relationship you have is with yourself."

"Well, doesn't that tie a pretty bow around it," Johnny said. "I'm sure it was glorious, but it doesn't give you everything. Nothing gives everything. Isn't that right, Dave?"

I said, "I didn't say it did."

"Don't get defensive. I didn't mean it that way. Just don't hang all your hopes on one thing," Johnny said.

Dave got out and said, "I'll take a quick plunge in the cold."

Johnny arched his neck and looked around. "Spectacular. Brilliant. Why would anybody ever leave here?"

I said, "I'm ashamed to say I never got through *Ulysses*. I've tried. It's always ranked as the best novel ever written."

Johnny said, "You're trying to understand too much, man. Nobody can read *You-Lysses* thoroughly and deeply. You can't scale a mountain in a single leap. It's just another book. A *good* book. Lots of wordplays, puns, anagrams, allusions, double entendres..."

From a distance, Dave shouted, "The man spoke seventeen languages."

I asked, "What's he doing over there?"

Johnny said, "Sitting in the cold bath. It pinches the capillaries."

"It doesn't make any sense," I said.

"Comfort and convenience make you weak?" Johnny said.

"Why freeze your ass off when you could be sitting here?" I said.

Dave shouted, "You oughta try it."

I called back, "No thanks." And addressed Johnny, still luxuriating across from me in the warm water, "I love *Dubliners*, especially "The Dead," and *Portrait of an Artist*, but *Ulysses* and *Finnegan's Wake* leave me listless. And I've tried."

He nodded with a smile. "You're not alone, and it's not so tough if you suspend your expectations. There's no tight plot or compelling narrative. Accept chaos. You won't get it all in one reading. Approach it sideways. It'll open you up. It'll change your life."

I inquired, "Why didn't you want Dave to talk about his mother?"

"You don't need to ride back to LA with him."

"That's why I'm here, so I'm forced to talk about it."

"Good on you. It's Neal, isn't it?

I nodded, and he continued, "As I said, don't take it personally. Dave's not ready. The inner world is different from the outer. You have to respect it in the same way. Don't complain about a problem from the outside. Go inside. Most people don't know this. They try to solve the problem with a solution that always causes new problems. Mr. Joyce thought grammatical sentences betrayed the chaos in which we live." He rose from the tub and walked away.

I sat in solitude, looking up at the sky. There were so many stories I wanted to tell. The ones I thought lost were still part of me. And I wanted to hear other people's stories.

Dressed, the Irishmen came back.

Dave said, "Neal, I can tell it's going to be a good year for you."

"You know Joyce was almost blind when he wrote *Ulysses*," Johnny said.

"He had syphilis," Dave added.

Johnny said, "It will make it easier. Read the book."

"And don't forget, Joyce was an arrogant prick."

Both reached out. I stood, and we shook hands.

Johnny said, "Come see us in Ireland."

"I thought you were sticking around LA for big money."

"We'll be back," Johnny said.

"Remember you love Ireland," Dave said.

"Erin go Bragh," I said.

Johnny said, "The boy speaks Irish."

Dave said, "Remember, Neal, time heals all wounds."

They walked away. The bright moon gave the baths a silver candescent glow, like a black and white photograph.

After they left, I was alone. And it came out of me like an awkward belch. "Time wounds all heels." I sat upright and repeated it. And then said every word with intention, "Time wounds all heels." I convulsed with laughter and closed my eyes. I heard Pixie's voice, *"They'll get theirs."*

Steam rose from the surface, smooth as a teacup, warm and delicious. I inhaled the acrid smell. A cold, stiff breeze brushed my cheeks, and I submerged. In a single motion, I opened my arms, spread eagle, and floated. I extended my fingertips and looked up at the vast spectacle of the Milky Way. The red flashing light of an airplane drifted through the powdered sky of stars.

So many hours spent suspended and weightless in the Buffalo Athletic Club pool when I was a kid. My father would drop me off and go upstairs to drink at the bar. I'd find ways to amuse myself. I became amphibious, never a creature of either realm. Both my parents are dead, and now my brother, my sisters left behind to torment me.

"Time wounds all heels."

In the distance, I heard a ruckus...quarreling voices. Dave and Johnny were bickering in the dressing room.

"We've got time. I tell ya, we'll go direct," Johnny said.

Dave barked, "You eejit! You're putting us on the long finger. What about the other blokes?"

When I arrived, I thought they might come to blows.

Johnny said, "Come here to me," and strapped his right arm

around Dave's shoulder. "What are you foostering about? Let's do this. Show me for once you've got some avocados."

Dave's face turned crimson. "It's fecking six hours, and God knows if we'll get past the slide."

"Don't bodge this, Dave." Then Johnny broke into a brogue, gesturing in an old woman's voice, and said, "Do ya know who's dead now? You do know him, ah, you do. You know him to see. He got a great sendoff anyway." Then he reverted to his normal speaking voice. "That's what they'll say, Dave, when you're gone. Do you want that? Let's burn and go down giving it the socks."

A familiar presence was lurking in the shadows. I couldn't place him at first, but when he spoke, it hit me with a jolt. It was the locavore, the guy who had kicked me out of the seat in the cafeteria.

He said, "You'll be out of here by the time the sun rises. Plenty of time to get to LA. You won't have to drive in the dark."

Dave pleaded, "We're already up to ninety." He looked at Johnny. "You always do everything arseways. Scarlet for your ma for having ya." He paused for a moment and looked up with a crooked smile. "Where we swimming, anyway?"

"You're massive," Johnny said. "Grand."

"Just over the hill on the other side of campus," the locavore said.

Dave said, "We're here for the hot water, thirty-five bucks. We're not registered."

"No problem. They'll be a group. Nobody will notice," the locavore said.

Johnny looked at me. "We're taking a dip. Want to join us?"

"Where?"

"In the feckin' ocean. Where else?"

I said, "It's fifty degrees. People drown here. The currents are hellacious. Nobody swims here."

"I beg to differ," the locavore said. "It can be dangerous, but that doesn't mean you shouldn't do it. Each of us needs a healthy degree of danger to thrive. Wouldn't you agree?"

"I've never heard of anybody swimming here before," I said.

The well-muscled locavore stood and said, "Which is good, because it's secret. You can't tell anyone. You're lucky. Your friend extended an invitation. And we will hold you to the same. You can't tell a soul."

"Do you wear a wet suit?"

"No."

"It's ice water."

Johnny said, "That's why we do it."

"What about the great whites?"

"Face your fear," Dave said.

I said, "This isn't Ireland or some country lake in summer."

Dave said, "Ever skinny-dipped the Forty Foot at Sandycove?"

Johnny said, "A gray, sweet mother? The snotgreen sea. The scrotum-tightening sea. *Epi oinopa ponton.*"

"What the hell does that mean?"

"You really haven't read your *Ulysses*, boy. You'll find that in the first few pages."

I pulled on sweatpants and a thick cotton hoodie. The fog rolled in. It was still and dark, not yet dawn. The cold penetrated. The locavore was barefoot, shirtless, wearing a pair of baggy cargo shorts. All of us puffed white clouds of mist.

The locavore looked at me and said, "Don't forget a towel." His big right bicep flashed his colorful tattoo. "*Dulce periculum.*"

I said, "You don't have one."

"I'm acclimatized. You'll want to bundle up and get dry when you get out."

Dave said, "Afterdrop. You know that feeling when you come in from the cold and your hands start warming up and it's good but also crazy painful and you're convinced that you're suffering permanent nerve damage that will impede your fine motor skills for life? Then, after a few minutes, the pain goes away and you feel nothing but good?"

"Hypothermia," Johnny said. "Dave can speak on a wide range of topics with impeccable precision."

Dave said, "Mars, how long will this take?"

I said, "You know each other?"

"Yeah, we go way back. I met this wanker a couple years ago in Poland. He's of an ill mindset. He climbed Mount Snezka in the nip," Johnny said.

They snickered.

Mars was older and shorter than I remembered, stocky and weathered like a construction worker. Bare-chested and stout-legged, a wrecking ball of a man, not fat but a bulky bundle of muscle. My first impression was, he looked like a bare-knuckle street fighter. In ancient times, he'd stand resolute among the three hundred Spartans at Thermopylae. In his present get up, all he needed was a spear and a shield.

Johnny said, "Do what he says, or you'll be lyin' in 2 North with a bowl of grapes and a bottle of Lucozade."

I grabbed a ragged beach towel and followed the three ren-egades up the hill. And with each step, it got closer—a deep, drumming sound, like an irregular heart beating beneath our feet.

Mars flipped on his flashlight, illuminated an insect ten times the size of an ant, and said, "Jerusalem!"

"For the love of God," Johnny said.

"No, Jerusalem. Jerusalem crickets."

"Savage. Quare. Are they from Jerusalem?" Johnny said.

"And look at that tiny head. It's humanoid," Dave said.

Mars said, "They're not from Jerusalem. Not even close. And they've got lots of other names too: child's face, skunk bug, skull insect, old bald man, devil's spawn, monkey face, earth baby. The pioneers, those pious bastards, used 'Jerusalem' like a swear word, the way we use 'holy shit' now."

The marbled little monster, a nasty, bald, rust-colored head plodding on six thick legs and sticky frog feet, looked fierce, ready for a fight, like an awkward alien war machine stalking its prey. Long, probing, hair-like antenna protruded from its beady eyes.

Mars said, "Pick it up. Generally, they don't bite."

None of us took him up on it. He shined his flashlight along the surface. There were a dozen probing and protruding heads rummaging around the damp earth. Some were frantic, flipping around on one another. Mars's stern blue eyes flashed. He squatted and directed one of the tiny humpbacks into his open hand. Slow-moving at first, the creature played dead, then proceeded with caution. It investigated the creases of his palm. It looked amphibious but too well armored, clearly an arthropod. The air around us felt solid, a wall of thumping wanton heartbeats.

Dave said, "Enough acting the maggot. Let's get on with it."

Johnny said, "Is it some kind of grasshopper? What's that yoke there?"

Dave said, "Johnny, we don't have time. What are you smokin'? There'll be wigs on the green."

"Stop being a ball bag," Johnny said.

"They don't jump, and they don't have wings? Some call 'em potato bugs, something you Micks could understand," Mars said.

"Never seen 'em over there or anywhere else," Johnny said.

"That's 'cause they're here and in Mexico. In Spanish, it's *Niño de la Tierra*."

Dave said, "Child of the earth."

"I didn't know you spoke the language," Johnny said.

"Don't need to. That's the ugliest, most grotesque and repulsive living thing I've ever seen. Only the earth could love it like a mum. Look at that bum."

"Put a Santa hat on it and call it Randall," Johnny said.

Mars let the little beast loiter on his hand as if he were playing with a pet. He stroked it with his index finger. Its long, formidable, black and white-striped rump bulged and emitted a foul smell.

Dave said, "Stink McCrink."

"Why they making such a racket?" Johnny said.

"Take a guess."

"On the prowl?"

"Brilliant conclusion. They're all sex fiends," Dave said.

Mars said, "That's it. They live underground, come out only at night, and they're half-blind. They thump their bellies on the ground calling their mates. Most of the time, the female eats the male after they connect."

"That's why they're runnin' around," Johnny said.

"I knew it had to be one of the four Fs," Dave said.

"And what would that be?" Johnny said.

"Freeze, fight, flight, or feck."

"All you potato heads need to know is that they're having a hell of a night with lots of blood and carnage," Mars said. He crouched and, with gentle hand, returned the critter to the ground.

We resumed our trek beneath the shadows of pine trees.

As we crossed the campus, I said, "Mars, what's the deal with swimming in the friggin' ocean? It's dangerous, and it's ice-cold."

Dave glared at me and flashed a hostile stare.

"Don't get him started. He's obsessed," Johnny said.

Dave gave Mars a once over, dropped his shoulders, and said, "Shite, hope you're up for the full tour."

Johnny said, "He's mad. The maniac's on a crusade."

In that instant, I witnessed a metamorphosis. Mars puffed out his chest like a silverback mountain gorilla. He exploded into a fountain of words, his torrent breathless, so as not to permit interruption. He made it clear. He was taking no questions. He flapped his arms in excitement, like a man waving off a swarm of bees. It was only then that I noticed he was wearing a long, white scarf wrapped a couple times around his neck. It fluttered in the wind and, on occasion, rested on his muscular pecs. His skin glistened with a fine sweat. In contrast, the Irishmen were silent and glazed over with each step. All I heard were their leather boot soles *clacking* and *clomping* on the asphalt path.

The upshot of Mars's credo was that Homo sapiens had gotten soft. He extolled, with lugubrious glee, the benefits of cold exposure. How it tweaks insulin production, tightens the circulatory system, and heightens mental awareness. He said, "We seek comfort to our detriment. Dependence on technology makes us weak. Your ancestors knew what it was like to be hungry and cold. Easy calories and artificial environments cause obesity, and it's an epidemic. Humans and their house pets are the only animals with diabetes, high blood pressure, heart disease, and kidney disease. Nowhere else in nature. We've lost our resilience. We've become willing hosts to dozens of other chronic illnesses. We must reclaim our animal nature."

Johnny said, "And that's why we were taking a swim in the feckin' frigid ocean before dawn…"

Mars continued, "We live in thermogenic cocoons. Never touched by cold or harsh elements, we're out of sync with the natural environment. We fall short of our destiny and our true potential. There's a psychological aspect too. We need the fix, the edge, the near-death experience to remind us that we're alive."

I said, "Danger?"

He traced human history back a hundred and thirty thousand years, saying Neanderthals crossed frozen Eurasia with very little food, shelter, or clothing. He contended that we possessed the same genes and used the word thermogenesis over and over, stressing that mammals *make* heat. And Mars was a living example, without a shirt, sweating in the morning, chill-drenched fog. He said anyone could reclaim the power to resist the cold. He said the secret is to relax and settle into it, not resist or fight it.

As he rambled, I thought, *As long as I can remember, I could swim.* Long strokes, breaths from side to side, blow bubbles out underwater, hand over hand, and glide. I was slippery when wet. It was something I could always do and do well. There are family stories about my father putting me in the pool at six months and me taking to it like a tadpole. At the same time, I've always sought comfort. When not comfortable, I've complained, got depressed, angry, and resentful—most of my swimming had been in heated lap pools. As a child, I'd wondered how Native Americans survived winters without central heating. In grade school, I'd learned they huddled all winter in longhouses. But winter in places like Buffalo is too damn long, often extending into May. Even as a kid, I'd never bought that explanation.

Mars gave the example of Samoset, the Native American who greeted the pilgrims in 1621. Samoset showed up wearing a loincloth that first bone-chilling winter at Plymouth Colony. And what he was wearing was common throughout the region. Massachusetts's state coat of arms displays a bare-chested Native American. Mars explained that indigenous people put their babies in the snow for a few minutes each day, and their nervous systems accommodated. Mars's approach intrigued me.

I still couldn't imagine subjecting myself to a frigid ocean swim before sunrise, so I said, "I'm gonna watch this time."

He reached over and pinched a roll of fat hanging over my belt line. "Wouldn't you like to get rid of some of that baby fat?"

I pushed his hand away but knew he was right.

The Irishmen picked up the pace.

Mars said, "Sugar cancer. Overfat and over forty—it's only a matter of time. And you know it as well as I do. Have you had your A1C checked lately? You can reduce calories. That doesn't last long. Exercise. But what about the cold? All the big-time professional athletes do cryotherapy. Don't leave your health to doctors. All they can give you are pills. Get in the water. A cold swim builds brown fat that burns white fat." He looked around, first to the ocean, then the mountains. "Overconsumption. Waste. Obesity leads to diabetes and ends in blindness, hardening of the arteries around the heart, brain, and kidneys. Look around you. We're choking the whole goddamn planet. Too much garbage, like too much sugar in the bloodstream riddles every organ. A slow, insidious death. Why would anybody choose that?"

Dave broke in. "Van Wick was right."

I said, "Who's Van Wick?"

Dave said, "One of the blokes from Poland."

"He cured himself of diabetes. Lost seven stone," Johnny said.

I looked at Mars quizzically and said, "What's seven stone?"

"Ninety-eight pounds." Mars said.

Johnny said, "Hey, Mars, what do you hear from Van Wick?"

Mars leaned his neck from side to side and pulled back. "You don't know? He…"

Dave said, "What?"

"Killed himself," Mars said.

"Cat. When was that?" Johnny said.

"A couple months ago, back home in Holland. Hung himself in a closet."

All I could hear was the scuffing of the Irishmen's shoes.

Johnny said, "My old man used to say offing yourself is a permanent solution to a temporary problem."

"That's cold," Dave said.

I was shivering and wrapped the towel around my shoulders. A gray flint of light salted the horizon. I said, "I want to die quickly. An arrhythmia, ventricular tachycardia. I hope it kicks me in the chest like a mule. Suddenly I'm down, gone."

Dave said, "I hope death isn't a place where I have maggots or those little Jerusalem beasties crawling all over me, biting me, and I can't defend myself. Where I'm limp and have to stand by and watch. Nobody wants to linger, but it isn't our choice."

"What you saying, Dave? Van Wick did the right thing?" Johnny said.

"There's some credence to it. Too bad people left behind have to suffer."

"He had a daughter, didn't he? I saw some pictures," Johnny said.

"Yes, and a son too. She's thirteen. The boy's older, in his twenties," Mars said.

"What gobshite. Mayhem, pandemonium…they must be in shambles," Dave said.

Johnny said, "He seemed like he was having fun in Poland. All those Beatle songs…"

"He played pretty well, and all that fingerpicking of the Donovan stuff. 'Wear Your Love Like Heaven,' " Dave said.

Johnny sang, "Wear your love like heaven," and Dave echoed.

Dave said, "Ah, that's an oldie. I still don't know how the cocksucker did it. I've felt inadequate, down and out, depressed, so desperate I couldn't move, but that's fecked up. I don't have the guts."

Johnny said, "Sounds like a curse. What's the problem?"

"Wife left him. Couldn't cope," Mars said. "He was desperate. It doesn't get any darker than not wanting to live. That's as dark as it can go, I suppose."

"He was drinking?" Dave asked.

"Maybe he got what he wanted," Johnny said. "A permanent solution to a temporary problem."

Mars led us down a rusty metal stairway. Narrow, more like a ladder, it rattled and swayed with our weight. I can best describe it as a fire escape, and it led to a hidden cove near the creek runoff. An annoying racket reverberated off the cliff—*clack, clack, clack*—and it got louder as we approached the beach. Still dark, it was hard to identify where we were headed.

Once we were flat on the sand, Dave pointed. "She's busting his dial."

London was fifty yards away, pummeling Attila's long, unkempt locks with a rock against a sea stack.

"Savage," Johnny said. "She's gone Kmamchee."

Dave flipped his head. "And he's got a face like a bulldog chewing a wasp."

Johnny said, "She's a stunner."

"I'd eat chips from her knickers," Dave said.

Mars said, "But this one's a couple fries short of a happy meal."

"Say no more," Dave said.

When we reached London, she said, "Attila asked me to trim a few split ends."

Johnny said, "Caveman style." He turned to me. "You're next."

Attila stood and shook his head, then fluffed his long locks with both hands. "You think this marvelous deportment comes without a price?"

Under his breath, Johnny said, "Even the tide won't take this brute out."

Quarter-size pebbles clattered with every wave, and the full moon beamed across the edge. We spread our towels on the sandy spit beneath the cliff. It looked like a yoga class.

Mars signaled for us to lie down. In a gruff voice, he said, "Deep breaths into the belly. Fill it up. Blow it out through the mouth. Breathing activates the brain stem. Breathe like a woman giving birth. We'll do thirty reps and then hold your breath."

Noisy intakes and expulsions of breath, raucous "hoos" and "haas" echoing, encompassed me. I joined in the communal huffing and puffing at first with trepidation. By the end of the first round, I was howling with the best.

Mars said, "Hold."

I held as long as I could, a minute or so. He counted half minutes using a stopwatch. Most of my compatriots stayed much longer. But with each set, my time increased. After the third, Mars had us tighten and relax each part of our body, starting with our toes and moving to our heads.

The cold, wet air didn't seem to penetrate my jacket with the same urgency. When I opened my eyes, I noticed it was getting light. I felt pleased, pleased with everything.

Then London took over. In contrast to Mars, her voice was sweet and harmonious. Like a she-god, her subtle inflections floated under the ocean waves. Her timbre somehow integrated and became part of it.

"Find your center," she said in a whisper. Whatever she vocalized penetrated my brain. She repeated what Mars had said, "Breathe in through your nose and out through your mouth," but it was different. Light-footed, she stepped through our supine corpses and stretched limbs, adjusting our bodies. On occasion, she squatted and placed her open palm on someone's belly. "Good, good, deep breath. Breathe, deep breath, blow your belly up like a balloon. Follow your breath out, slow. That's it, that's it. It's a good body."

Standing in the center, she bowed her head and invoked a prayer.

"Mother Earth, your breasts feed the world. Thank you for grounding us. Father sky, thank you for shedding radiant healing light."

Extending her hands above her head, she turned. "Great sea serpent of the south, thank you for wrapping your coils around us. You shed your skin and teach us to shed the past."

Pivoting toward the ocean. "Great white shark, child of the west, thank you for the burden of hunger. You are never satisfied. Never let us become complacent, smug, or act superior."

Turning north. "Hummingbird, thank you for bringing joy. Your high vibrations charge this space. Thank you for giving us the courage to make the epic journey so we may nourish ourselves from the nectar of our own lives."

And finally, rotating her body, palms open beneath the cliff. "Magnificent condor and eagle, long wings of the east. Thank you for teaching us to see with our hearts. You who touch your feathers with the Great Spirit, allow us to open our lives to what is fresh and new. Never stagnant, let the river always flow."

Then it was quiet, except for the rumble of the restless and relentless waves.

With no further words or invocations, we began to shift and shuffle. Like sleeping pilgrims, we rose from the ground, shedding tops, bottoms, undergarments, and footwear without declination. Like freshly hatched sea turtles, Johnny, Dave, Mars, and London scurried toward the sea, naked bodies, ball sacks, boobs, gravity challenged extensions, in migration.

In route, Johnny tossed me a swim cap and goggles and said, "This will keep your head and eyeballs warm. Can't vouch for the rest of ya."

Despite this dazzling display of bravura, something held me back. The icy Pacific from my earliest days in California had been my nemesis. I knew its teeth, and a primal fear paralyzed me.

*What am I doing here?* I observed the others and savored their sense of vitality and playfulness.

Back east, I'd be the one leading the charge to the water. In North Carolina, I sought out lakes and quarries, rivers, and mountain streams. My career started as an ocean lifeguard in Ft. Lauderdale, where I swam all winter in the Atlantic. I played in massive, death-defying waves before and after hurricanes. In Buffalo, I swam across the Niagara River. All these experiences I'd taken on with delight and a spirit of adventure. But when I'd landed on the west coast, the vastness of the Pacific had suffocated my zeal.

Once, in my forties, at Aquatic Park in San Francisco, I wanted to die. My chest collapsed as the cold bit and raged through my body. My core temperature plummeted. So deep was the chill, I shook for hours after a thirty-minute swim. Defeated, benumbed, and bedraggled, ever since then I've limited myself to pools on the west coast. The Pacific never soothed me. It only drove me away. These thoughts flashed through my mind like a lit match.

London approached. "Aren't you going in?" She scoffed at my hesitancy. "It'll be fun. Who are those guys with Mars? Are they Australian? Are you going to introduce me?"

"They're musicians from Ireland."

"Let's go."

I left my clothes on the beach, put on the cap, and spit in the goggles.

The boys were screaming and splashing, Johnny in for a quick dip with no intention to swim the distance. Best he could do was get his head wet and vault to the shore.

He shook like a cocker spaniel near the shore, shuddering, sputtering, and trembling, draped in a towel. His body was mottled and crimson with sodden hair. It was all in good fun. But the pain on his face sent a chill up my spine.

I said, "Maybe I'll pick this up next time."

London grabbed my hand and dragged me.

I protested, "I'm a flabby old man. You could grate cheese off my belly." I started to shiver, and my teeth chattered.

London said, "You can control it. Like a sneeze, you can hack the autonomous nervous system. Take a breath, concentrate, stop. Try it."

Following her instructions, the panic ceased. The shivering and chattering slowed. I was still cold and almost welcomed the blanket of frigid water.

She said, "It's better to dive in rather than ease into it. Remember, once you're in, breathe, keep moving. It's mind over matter. Show me something." She dropped my hand and plunged into the icy mass headfirst. When she surfaced, she free-styled toward a buoy offshore.

Big Wave Dave had already launched. He thrashed the water in deference, like Keith Moon playing the drums. His body twisted like an eel at his hips. His arms and legs were flailing. Whatever he lacked in technique, he made up for with sheer will and determination. His knife-like hands cut the surf. Dave and Mars stroked toward the buoy with London in pursuit.

I wanted to ease into it—or skip it altogether—but leaped headfirst following London's lead.

Wham. What I'd expected—bone-rattling numbness. The freeze was so intense I felt heat and tingling in my tongue, like it was stuck to a frozen steel pole. My lips swelled with the electricity of salt. Prickles on my face. A steel band around my forehead. An iron vice constricting my chest. I was unable to breathe. My ribs were being crushed by invisible jaws. I floated, treaded water, sculled with my hands, bobbing in a barrel of ice, trying to catch a breath. It hurt, and I knew if I quit and swam for shore, it would feel worse.

I remembered London saying, *"Don't fight it. Can you be*

*aware of the inflow and outflow of your breath without changing it in any way?"* No air was moving at all. In my panic, I'd forgotten how to breathe. I pulled a blast of salty spume through my nose as deep as it would go. I noticed only an inch or two below my neck at first. I squeezed my toes and feet and worked my way up through the tingling muscles throughout my body. I breaststroked and, to my surprise, broke into a Trudgen crawl. My body still deadened, I remembered how to glide, pull, take a breath, and recover.

I decided to swim out to the buoy. A door opened to another world. I looked back at the land like it was a different province—my brother and his death were behind me, part of that world. I knew I needed to come back to shore. I was a land creature first bound by gravity, not weightless and buoyant. Halfway out, I saw Mars, Dave, and London returning. They paddled long, gliding strokes around me.

Dave waved and called, "We're doing it again. See you on the rebound."

The goggles helped. I watched my fingertips and pulled hard with my shoulders and pecs. Fifty muscle groups worked in unison as I kept a steady beat with my feet. The salt made me buoyant, and my chest and shoulders rode high. I still had a terror about sharks or bumping into an otter or seal. A greasy, thick blade of kelp brushed my side and startled me. Pelicans flew in a formation above, and cormorants fished the shallows. I wasn't worried so much about endurance but succumbing to the cold. It seemed imperative to keep moving.

When I reached the destination, Big Wave Dave joined me. His mirror goggles flashed like a fish lure, and I felt his presence.

He said, "Think you can keep up with me?"

I said, "I'll try."

It says a lot about a person…how they walk, how they write,

and how they swim. Dave's stroke was violent and created turbulence. He wasted energy with every stroke. And this was his second trip to the buoy. Was he tired? I couldn't gauge how fast he was, or if I could keep up with him. But I decided to try, and this wasn't a competition. Mars and London joined us and like a pod of dolphins we swam to shore.

# WEEKS LATER, DAWN

## (SANTA BARBARA, CA)

*We teach history, but history is not determinism.*
*We don't have to just relive our history over and*
*over again. It's possible to move beyond it.*
Eric Foner (1943- )

ODAY FEELS LIKE SUMMER IN Buffalo, the air clean, sun streaming through a window. It's February, and pink hibiscus buds open into jagged-lipped flowers. Seeds scatter through long tongues into the light. All my life, I've felt threatened and lived in fear of something terrible happening. One of my first memories, when I was five, was when my father stood drunk in a narrow vestibule. I can still smell his profuse sweat and the saliva-soaked vodka on his breath. The sheer hulk of the man filled the hallway. Like an intoxicated bear entering his lair, he escaped the subzero temperatures outside. His heavy wool overcoat hanging to his ankles, he was unsteady, a titan ready to topple. Dizzy, confused, dumb, one hand on the wall for balance. My fear, even then, had been that he'd lose his job and leave us destitute. How could I support my mother? I was a kid. She denied he drank. The cycle never snuffed out, always maintained. And this feeling of impending doom, the bottom about to fall out ever-present. Even now.

I'm back in the clinic, and thank goodness Victoria welcomed me home. Open arms, soft breasts, forgiveness. The most crucial element in marriage is a short memory—Zephyra's magic days at Big Sur are behind me. Victoria could tell from my attitude that I'd done the work. I haven't stayed in touch with anyone from Calypso, not even PJ. But music now plays everywhere, in the cottage, in the car—our ears absorb new rhythms. Victoria loves Eva Cassidy.

The other night, I cooked Italian—Mick's chickie parm. We lit candles and ate al fresco beneath a flaming red bougainvillea. We played Eva's "Fields of Gold." The stars were out, not like at Big Sur, but the night dazzled. Vic put up tiny Christmas lights along the fence while I was gone, and they gave a steady watery glow. She praised my cookery and savored each bite, nothing dainty about her appetite. At each stage of preparation, I'd put something into it. Even the parm, which I'd grated into curly shards. She's so appreciative, to cook for her is like making love.

Pixie's called a couple times. She's found work at Burger King, and her brother got her into a pre-owned Ford Escort. She'll be leaving her grandmother's soon and moving into a small apartment. I've ignored phone calls from Cassie and blocked Saundra. It's better that way—too many lies, more than I can digest. It's not a war. It's apathy—no more entrenchment. Mick's gone, and my obligation's over. When Cassie repossessed Pixie's car, I saw the light.

Impermanence. The Japanese say, "*Mono no aware.*" As one sheds their beauty and scatters their youth, everyone disappears.

This morning, I found myself praying. It seemed too early to rise. Before sunrise, the proximity of death prevails. Since then, I've been cold and scared, troubled with the certainty that each of us must die.

When PJ asked me why I write, I'd had no answer. It's an exercise in truth-telling. I learned to fork my tongue at an early age. When I write, I have no debt, burden, or obligation, and no one to please. It's the only place I can tell the truth with impunity. Today, my pen is fluid. I could keep going, write down every thought and memory in my head. Resurrect the past, see the dead faces, those who have altered the trajectory of my life.

There's an old lady with a large, gold cross around her neck that I pass on the street. She dresses like a schoolmarm, buttons to her neck, and high-top, laced-up leather boots. She stopped me and said, "A number of miracles are going to happen over the next few years, and you're going to be part of it." It was like she was a robot, the words pre-recorded. She had no notion that she'd stopped me the day before and announced the same proclamation. She's a prophet, like John the Baptist, with a distant glint in her eye. I said, "Thank you," like I did before, smiled, and walked on.

The day before yesterday, while browsing the sale rack at the library, I struck gold. It's a terrific book, weird title, and hard to pronounce and remember the author's last name. Philip Gourevitch, *We Wish to Inform You That Tomorrow We Will Be Killed With Our Families.* Why the author didn't call it *Rwanda* or *Genocide*, is beyond me. Yet his writing's so rich and vivid he can do anything he wants. In the title alone, he uses the past tense, throws in a squinting modifier, and gets away with it. The man's a virtuoso—brilliant, compelling, kick-ass, to-die-for prose throughout. What lured me was eight hundred thousand dead in 1994 by machete in a hundred days. Gourevitch's analysis bends the mind, and the slaughter supersedes the efficiency of Hitler and Pol Pot. I can't get my arms around why Homo sapiens behave this way. And the author promises to explain it if I read on. An aside, the other world expert on Rwanda, Alison Des Forges, lived in Buffalo. She died in that fatal Continental crash on February 12, 1999.

Gourevitch, at heart, is a fiction writer. He employs a vast array of dramatic techniques to flesh out his story—the African tribal perspective connected to what's happening all around me now. There isn't that much time left for our species, ten to twenty years. Hate to see the whole species crash and burn in my lifetime. Who knows what to believe anymore? And it's never black or white. It's nuanced. If one is right, the other is wrong won't play anymore. It's this kind of thinking that has to go. We're in a race to evolution, a reach that if we don't succeed, the human species will go extinct.

What stunned me about Gourevitch's sobering book is the dedication. "For my parents." I envy those who love their parents and sing their praises, but don't they doubt them as I do? Didn't things happen, traumatic and truth-telling, that revealed Ma and Pa as wrongdoers, lawbreakers, and offenders? And isn't that why marriage, living with someone in such an intimate way, is such a risk? All those traumas have the opportunity to trigger and be replayed. And nobody can hurt us like our family. Nothing is neutral. We all bring thousands of memories to every situation. It's easier to sew it up and put a bandage on it than open it and drain the pus.

I went to Calypso and learned to open up, accept my crazy—enjoy, feed, and comfort it. Only someone in desperate need of a revelation goes there. The message: if you want to find yourself, look to your past. The only way out is to create, and my life to be internal, quiet, reflective, rather than external. My time has come to go inside. Zephyra administered her healing like in one of Sophocles's plays. She wanted my mother to find help, to apologize, to admit what she'd done. She said, "You haven't diagnosed your story," which gives me hope. At Calypso, I peeled away another layer. I hate my mother for what she's done but still cut my sandwich in three pieces as she did. The heart knows no darkness better than its own.

Does it matter if our species survives? We don't even like each other. What's the loss? The planet is better off without us. At least the butterflies might survive. Yet the driving force remains, how do we connect hearts? Each of us will leave this planet—actually, we don't depart but become part of it. There are fantasies of heaven, but what makes us any different than a dead bird under the fishing pier? Our carcass rots, putrefies, and we, as we were, become extinct. The end comes for all living things bound to the flesh. We all die. That's all any of us know for sure. I've given up on any other certainty.

Yesterday, though, I woke up feeling close to fantastic. It'd been a long time since it wasn't a chore, and I didn't hate myself or my life. The heaviness was gone, negativity had lifted. I was free, and my mind was full of new ideas and optimism. When you're feeling good, it's hard to remember why you were feeling bad. Everybody struggles. Too often, the fabric of life gets worn and thin.

Looking back at my life, I'd have to agree that a man is the victim of his cock. Why didn't my father tell me that? A simple phrase, "Your prick will control you," would have saved a lot of pretense and grief. I dream of cunt, the raw force of it. The sagging lips, like a sea creature, the hard nub of the clitoris that hardens like a shaft with stimulation. The reaction of my own body, the stiffness, the want, the aching. All humans enter life through a serpiginous channel full of tubes and strictures. How can I stop my obsession? Each female, unique yet uniform, pudendum, the source of arousal, orgasm, and micturition. A stiff cock knows no conscience. A woman's drive to procreate bears the same recklessness. The best sex, hot, reckless, dangerous, only cares for completion, the fulfillment of itself. The consequences don't matter, and there's no face to it. And this is from whence I came, lucky, fatal combustion.

Can I forgive myself? Three wives? Each a romance, a joy,

and an inspiration. And for a time, with every intention of completion, to death do us part. Now, for the first time with Victoria, I'm devoted to another person and not to my prick. I wasn't fit for marriage because I was living a lie.

We walked to the mission yesterday afternoon. The sky was high and bright. We lay back, the crowns of our heads on the sandstone steps, and spied a red hawk as it circled higher and higher, riding a thermal updraft, never bending a wing. The backdrop was spectacular, a puff of white cloud, the soaring creature deftly negotiating hidden spiral rungs. We got quiet and relaxed, spellbound. What would happen next? Higher and higher. In a flash, the predator tucked its wings and plunged to earth like a missile. Expansive space closed in tight.

And for that moment, we felt the freedom of flight.

And I heard the Mother, all women, soft breasts, wide hips, thighs of abuse—too many men. Too much wanting and taking, holding, having, gorging without content. Nothing pleases those who are full and glutted. We streamed like ice cubes through the water, melting, melting, melting. How short our little lives. What do we leave behind?

Good earth, forgive the smokestacks. We didn't mean to choke you. Forgive our wanton desire to live inside and avoid your harsh weather. Everybody wants comfort. Can't you understand? Erosion, deforestation, and toxic air are part of the deal. Loss of insects, wildlife, and acidification of oceans are part and parcel of the trade. What's standing in you now? A cesspool of piss, shit, and vomit.

Go with me to the river. Please, dear earth, wash my aching body clean. Forgive the piles of junk mail that passed hand to hand to garbage. Forgive the violation of your trees. The plastic… how can we keep your dead dinosaurs in the ground? I plead with you, give me a clue. I wander the banks of the river littered with dead fish and old shoes. Please, in my years left, let me provide rather than take.

But I need to eat.

I need shelter.

I need to be warm.

I need to wash and clean myself.

I need to scrub my sullied clothes.

I need space to consume my waste.

I need, I need, I need.

Each of these multitudes of insects also needs to feed.

Mother, you do it so amicably. You give. We take and cannot grasp your gift. If we want more, you give it. Will you be exhausted? What straw will break the camel's back? I see you move naked in the pits of the ocean—a humpback whale with her young. The big tail flaps and you're gone, no care for conservation, no love of holding back, you spend. Healing comes with time, with sleep, with desire pushed aside. How nasty life can be to us who don't know this. To rest when weary and power forward with everything we have when not.

Dear earth, I am smothered in your fragrance. I've known you every moment I've lived. You have never failed me. Always you emerge with wonder—the sunrise, the darkness, the fog.

Is it only me who won't survive?

# A PARABLE OF LIES SOUNDTRACK (PLAYLIST)

Florence and the Machine "Cosmic Love"
https://www.youtube.com/watch?v=S-Lo1wxuB7s

Otis Day and the Knights "Shama Lama Ding Dong"
https://www.youtube.com/watch?v=9rfnwsb-dg0

Chicago "Colour My World"
https://www.youtube.com/watch?v=cWkXmx-0phc

Fleetwood Mac "Rhiannon"
https://www.youtube.com/watch?v=wgmRb3MlpHQ

Marvin Gaye and Diana Ross "Stop,
Look, Listen (To Your Heart)"
https://www.youtube.com/watch?v=4nweodsX9HQ

Creedence Clearwater Revival "Lodi"
https://www.youtube.com/watch?v=yA7iGxV6rt4

Sinéad O'Connor "No Man's Woman"
https://www.youtube.com/watch?v=09Bm9g6ceKE

Curtis Mayfield "We the People Who Are Darker Than Blue"
https://www.youtube.com/watch?v=W37A-pwHi2c

Neil Young "Heart of Gold"
https://www.youtube.com/watch?v=X3IA6pIVank

Crosby, Stills, Nash & Young "Find the Cost of Freedom"
https://www.youtube.com/watch?v=3YUkiAU7aRM

Rolling Stones "Gimme Shelter"
https://www.youtube.com/watch?v=QeglgSWKSIY

Jimmy Buffett "Son of a Son of a Sailor"
https://www.youtube.com/watch?v=tO8K9b5iOfA

James Taylor "Carolina in My Mind"
https://www.youtube.com/watch?v=Yx_LHSrjsCg

The Band "It Makes No Difference"
https://www.youtube.com/watch?v=ZfBqWNFOVo8

Patty Griffin "Be Careful"
https://www.youtube.com/watch?v=2XMD9_uiToU

Donovan "Mellow Yellow"
https://www.youtube.com/watch?v=GBXbiIi1IRA

Donovan "Sunshine Superman"
https://www.youtube.com/watch?v=hTuPbJLqFKI

David Crosby "That House"
https://www.youtube.com/watch?v=XGMnP0qkhtQ

Eva Cassidy "You Take My Breath Away"
https://www.youtube.com/watch?v=QHfxMGEb9iE

Bruce Springsteen "If I Should Fall Behind"
https://www.youtube.com/watch?v=RmUG1ffgKFw

The Eagles "Peaceful Easy Feeling"
https://www.youtube.com/watch?v=NjofshOBV5s

Marianne Faithfull "Guilt"
https://www.youtube.com/watch?v=eW6XPpYjn-o

Eric Clapton, Pavarotti "Holy Mother"
https://www.youtube.com/watch?app=desktop&v=x9uYu4R2nk8

# ABOUT THE AUTHOR

The essence of Lawrence Spann's work is to make the unconscious conscious through writing. He's led over a thousand therapeutic writing groups and maintains a daily journal. He graduated as an English major from the University of Miami and worked various jobs before completing physician assistant training at Duke University. After earning a PhD in creative writing, Spann compiled *Poet Healer* and *Blood on the Page*. *A Parable of Lies* is his first full-length piece of healing fiction. He lives in Santa Barbara, California.

CPSIA information can be obtained
at www.ICGtesting.com
Printed in the USA
LVHW010826200821
695555LV00011B/993